stone heart

Born in Derry, Northern Ireland, Peter J Merrigan was first published at the age of 17 in the Simon & Schuster anthology *Children of the Troubles*, edited by Laurel Holliday. His first novel was *The Camel Trail*.

Following a Bachelor of Arts in Writing and English from London, Peter spent nineteen years in England as a marketing and advertising professional before returning to his native town. He lives with his husband in Co. Tyrone.

Find Peter online at peterjmerrigan.com

BY PETER J MERRIGAN

THE AILIGH WARS SAGA
Stone Heart
Stone Forged
Stone Soul
Stone Fall

THE RIDER SERIES
Rider
Lynch

STANDALONE NOVELS
The Camel Trail

STONE HEART

PETER J MERRIGAN

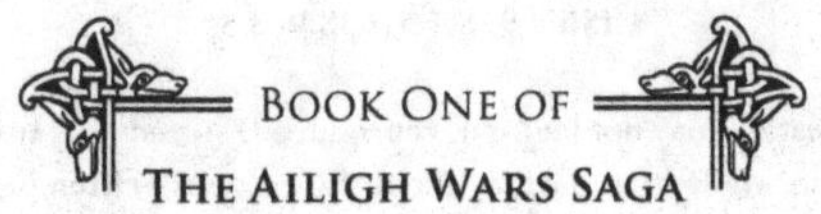

Nightsgale Books

3 5 7 9 10 8 6 4 2

First published in 2018 by
Nightsgale Books, Co. Tyrone, Northern Ireland
This paperback edition published 2020

ISBN 978 1 9163838 3 8

Cover by Nightsgale Books

A CIP catalogue record of this book
is available from the British Library and the
Library of Trinity College Dublin

Typeset in Perpetua by Nightsgale Books

For Declan

*Tiomnaithe do
mo bhuachaill, le grá.*

Author's Note

While the places, locations, attitudes and some of the recognisable names of the people in this novel are based on accurate historical data, with a healthy sprinkling of the Celtic myths and legends that permeate Ireland's history, I have taken the liberty of being rather loose with the time period and some of its rituals, for which I hope you'll forgive my indulgence. The Ó Mordha tribes-people within these pages are an invention of the author that I have constructed to predate the Uí Néill, a tribe known to have flourished in the same area some 1,500 years ago, and who are widely reported to have built the current iteration of Greenan of Aileach (or in its native Irish: Grianán Ailigh) which still stands to this very day in what is now Co. Donegal. The site is believed to have been in use long before the Uí Néill—for many centuries, in fact—and this is how I, with all my artistic license, envision it to have been in the region of 2,300 years ago, complete with outer palisade walls and a wealth of thatched homes.

According to Irish mythology, the Fir Bolg were defeated by the Tuatha Dé Dannan and were either offered Connacht as their province, or made to flee Ireland altogether, depending on which version of the myth you believe.

Áed, his family and his companions are entirely fictional. But as Oisín is reported to have said, 'All legends are true and false all at once.'

My deepest gratitude to the curators of the JSTOR library for their invaluable research papers.

P.J.M.
June 2018

N
Thúr Rí
Northern Druids
(Doagh)
Grianán Ailigh
Knockdhu
¥ Uí Ultan Stronghold
Giant's Ring
Carrowmore
Emain Macha
Tomb of Maeve
Mac Dalaigh
Stronghold §
Ó Nallon
Stronghold
Cruachan
Castlestrange
Stone
Teamhair
(Hill of Tara)
Clonycavan
Poulnabrone
Baurnadomeeny
Ó Hargon
Stronghold
Ardgroom
Drombeg
¥ Áed's birthplace
§ Rónán's birthplace
ÉIRINN
50 miles

Pronunciation Guide

As you are no doubt already familiar, the Irish language has a host of spellings that stump even the most educated man. What follows are some basics on pronouncing the names of people or places within these pages. The pronunciations are as close an approximation as can be given in the written form.

Áed	*aid*
Rónán	*row-nan*
Grainne	*grawn-ya*
Maebh	*maive*
Odhran	*or-an*
Oisín	*osh-een*
Déaglán	*deg-lan*
Orlaith	*orla*
Achall	*a-kal*
Cáer	*care*
Faolán	*fay-lan*
Ailigh	*a-lik*, with an elongated *a* as in *say*
Knockdhu	*nok-ghoo* (dh has a 'ch' sound in Irish, but with a 'g' basis)
Eochaid	*awk-aid* (all foreigners' names are pronounced very much as they are spelled. Where a 'c' is present, it is always hard (as in *cat*)

Chapter 1

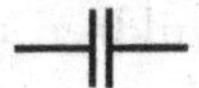

The old druid coughed and the coarse sound of it rattled across the grasses and the herbs outside his home. His tribe, led by their chieftain, came one by one to his bed, whereupon they would touch his hand and he would tell them their truths. For Áed, eight winters old, he assumed he had no hidden truths to tell.

The men of the clan had been off at war since before Beltaine, the fire celebration that marked the beginning of summer, fighting a foreign force that had brought massive warships to their shores. The wives and children that had been left behind had heard nothing of the fighting in the east since it had begun.

Áed stamped his feet on the cold ground. It was almost Yule and the sun was weak. A black storm fogged the southern horizon and it was coming in fast.

The line of tribeswomen and children before him stretched beyond the old druid's garden patch and across the central field in which Ultán would normally perform his ceremonies. But he had been bedridden since Samhain, the festival that celebrated the end of harvest.

He shuffled forward as the line moved, an older woman

coming out of the druid's roundhouse, her face contorted in tears. Áed wondered what her truth had been.

'What kind of truth makes a woman cry?' he asked. He clung tightly to the deer-fur cloak that was pinned around his shoulders. He could see his breath on the air before his face.

'Hush, child,' his mother said. 'Show some respect.'

Doirean had kept her children close to her since her husband left for war last year. Áed had been too young for war, but that did not stop his mother from entrusting him to his father's smithy. Before he went to battle, his father, Airic, had gone to his knee in front of his only son and said, 'Continue to learn the metals, and look after your sisters. You are the head of my house while I am gone.'

They shuffled forward again.

'If Ultán knew he was dying,' Áed whispered, 'couldn't he have done it in the summer?'

Grainne, his sister, lowered her head and chuckled into her fist.

Doirean smacked them both on the back of the head, and then she adjusted young Bec in her arms. Her youngest daughter, whose real name was Maebh, was known among the settlement as Bec, meaning small, since the moment that her tiny legs could carry her around and she was capable of crawling through the narrowest gap in a fence or barred doorway.

They could hear Ultán's cough again as the line of people moved forward another step. Áed was convinced the old man would die before they made it to his doorway. He strayed aside from the queue and kicked a stone, but his mother pulled him back.

When the skies opened and the rain lashed them, nobody

moved, respecting the will of the gods. Ultán had served the tribe for more than fifty years and speaking to each of them from his deathbed was an honour that no one would fail to fulfil.

Áed groaned and now even Grainne, a year younger than him, nudged him to silence with her elbow. She was shy and homely for the most part, preferring to learn the arts of weaving from her mother, or picking flowers from the gardens to string into a crown for her mother's head. Áed, on the other hand, would much rather tumble in the fields, chasing the sheep as though he was a mighty warrior destined for greatness.

All boys had the same dream: to fight in a great war and return home the victor, rich in property and land. Since Áed was old enough to walk, he would brandish a wooden sword and shield and he would fight against his friends, each desperate to outmatch the other.

The grasses, browned from the winter, flattened against the wind and the line moved again.

When they had reached the old druid's door, they waited to be called inside. A much younger druid, who had come to the tribe's sept at the request of Ultán to act as his aid in his failing health, opened the door and asked that they enter.

Doirean pushed her children ahead of her, like herding drunken dogs.

From the darkness within, Áed's eyes took a moment to adjust. A single candle lit the old man's face as he lay on his pallet bed, covered by thick furs. The roundhouse's central hearth burned red embers.

Ultán raised his hand and beckoned them forward.

Áed tried to breathe through his mouth; the smell of the

druid's herbs and potions accosted him, a pungent odour that permeated his very flesh. It was a stench that he would remember for the rest of his life.

Doirean knelt at the druid's side and Ultán reached to take her hand. She lowered her forehead to his fingers. 'The gods see you well,' she said.

Ultán's laugh became a cough and he could not speak for some time. The younger druid, Odhran, came to his side with a cup of water and the old man sipped from it, wetting his thin lips and his chin. Odhran mopped his face.

'Your husband,' Ultán said, and Doirean leaned closer to hear him. Áed stood at the foot of the bed to listen. 'The war has been brutal in the east, but our men fight hard and brave.'

Doirean nodded. 'We have had no word, Ultán. Does Airic live?'

Ultán closed his eyes for a moment, and then he looked at her. 'I am sure that he lives.'

Doirean cried.

'Hush, now,' the old man said. 'The men will be home soon, and the war will be over for a time.'

'You are a mouth for the gods,' Doirean said.

The old man reached out and touched young Bec's cheek. 'A happy child will be marred,' he said, but he did not explain his words.

Doirean kissed his hand and then stood, nudging Grainne to kneel before the druid.

Grainne's eyes were wide. She was reluctant to touch the druid, and the old man could sense it. 'Water,' he said, and when Odhran came to offer him a drink, he waved the young man away. He looked at Grainne. 'Water,' he said.

Grainne took the cup from Odhran and, with a hesitancy she was trying to hide, she held the cup to the old man's lips, catching the spills with a fabric cloth under his chin.

Ultán leaned back on his straw mattress. 'You are the earth,' he said, and Áed had to lean closer at the foot of the bed to hear him. Grainne lowered her eyes to the painted floor that had been mostly softened with fur rugs that helped keep the chill of winter at bay. 'You have the earth in you,' Ultán said now. He took her hand as if to inspect her fingers, and he turned it so that her palm faced upward towards him.

Doirean, sensing her daughter's unease, placed a hand on her shoulder to calm her.

Ultán said, 'As a druid, you could do great work, little one.'

Grainne pulled back from him, just a little.

Ultán took Odhran's hand and made him clasp the girl's fingers. He coughed again before speaking. 'Bring her to the arch-druid. He will know how to help her.'

Doirean tightened her grip on her daughter's shoulder. 'She is just a girl.'

Áed could tell his mother had not wanted to speak out against the ancient druid but could not hold her tongue.

Ultán nodded. 'As was I when I was called forth. Even before your father's birth, when I was little more than Bec's age, I showed the signs of earth and sky in me and was chosen. I have not the will to enforce it,' he said, and coughed, his fit lasting an eternity before he was composed enough to continue. 'But she has the gift. I can sense it in her.'

Grainne looked up at her mother, tears unbidden on her thick lashes.

Odhran squeezed the girl's hand and said, 'Do not fear. To

become a druid, is to be at peace.'

Ultán released them and beckoned to Áed to approach him.

Kneeling before the old man, Áed could see the thin line of spittle at the corner of his mouth. 'I am not to be a druid, too,' he said.

The old man laughed and the candle beside him flickered, throwing dark shadows into a dancing whirl. 'Your fate, I cannot see.' He cleared his throat from the fog of death that had taken hold of him. 'You must be strong—not just for your father, but strong for others. You can lead, but only if you can see it within yourself to do so.'

Áed was disappointed. He had expected a tale of great fortune.

When Ultán closed his eyes again, Odhran said, 'Ultán Ó Urlah thanks you for your respects.'

They turned to leave but stopped when the old man spoke again. 'The war may soon be over, but more will come. We will all face our enemies, each in his own way.' He looked at Grainne. 'Listen to the gods,' he said, 'and you will hear them calling to you.'

When they left his home, the rains had stopped. He would not be alive by the Yule celebrations, Áed was sure.

'You cannot send her off to be a druid,' he said.

Doirean said, 'It is not for me to decide. Grainne must make her own decision. But the druid sees something in you, my little one.'

Grainne kept her head low, kicking the grasses as she walked. 'Let him find someone else to look at.'

'If you do become a druid,' Áed said, 'you can offer me a better fortune than telling me to be strong.'

Doirean smacked the back of his head again.

When the old man died two days later, his body was laid out for visitation before burial, and when he was interred in the ground, Grainne agreed to travel north with Odhran to meet with the archdruid. The settlement was left to its quiet longings.

By Yule, there was still no word from the war in the east. Áed, who spent his days between the fields and his father's workshop, collecting wood for the frozen months, and beating metals into delicate items, had been tasked with three other boys to chop and carry the logs to the field for the Yule fire that was burned for twelve days when the sun stood still. His hands, toughened from his metalworking labours, bore calluses from the axe when they had finished chopping the trees and stripping the logs of stray branches. The logs were brought to the central field and applauded, until the last—the largest—was dragged to the staged area. Áed jumped on top of it when it was in place and bowed low to the uproarious amusement of the gathered women and elderly. 'May the Yule be short and quick to spring,' he shouted.

'Spring from the Yule,' they replied with vigour, and he jumped into the arms of the women who caught him with a grunt. 'You're getting bigger every day,' his mother said.

On the evening of the darkest midnight, six days into the fire celebration, when the day was at its shortest and the night felt eternal, the four boys who were honoured with the cutting of the logs were awarded food and gifts for their efforts. Standing on a raised platform in their red deer furs, they sang songs and acted the heroic deeds of their ancestors. They were given pride of place on chairs in front of the burning log and the women bowed to them each in turn. In the absence of a druid, for Odhran had not yet returned, the chieftain was called upon to lead the sun praises and the festivities carried on until near dawn. The four boys were the last to retire, long after the elderly and the women, and as they tended the fire to keep it stoked, warmed with pride, Áed said, 'Our fathers will be home soon.'

'How can you know?' the others asked him. 'It has been over a year without sign of them.'

He shrugged. 'I feel it.'

'You're not a druid,' one said. 'That's your sister's job.'

'Maybe she bit him as a child,' one of the others said, 'and gave him some of her ways.' They laughed and although he joined in, Áed's words were said with hope rather than certainty. He had spent the day trying to recollect the face of his father but could summon to mind no more than a red moustache and the single braid that fell to the left of his eyes, eyes that were either blue or grey or green; Áed could not remember.

As the sky brightened with a sluggish approach in the east and the moon's bright face was still visible in the darker regions, a cloud descended from the north and brought with it the men of the settlement, returned from battle, sore and exhausted from so long away. They approached the field where the fire burned and stood before the four boys. Litters were carried behind them with men covered by sheets, and Áed looked from one face to another in search of his father. He recognised most of the men, but some were strange to him. As he walked among them, calling his father's name, Airic stepped before him and said, 'Son.' He had grown a beard, like most of the men, but Áed saw now that his eyes were unmistakable. They could never have been forgotten, or at the least he recalled them when he looked at them.

'Green,' he said. And as his father came to his knees, Áed wrapped his arms around his strong neck and smelled his thick hair and choked to stop from laughing.

When the women were brought out and the men each found their wives and mothers, Airic swept Doirean into his arms and kissed her. 'We need to go to the chieftain,' he said. 'This war is over, but others will follow. Where is Grainne?'

Airic was a respected man among the tribe. Those men and women in positions of skilled work formed the basis of the chieftain's counsel. Ruari, son of Dalaigh, ruled the tribe with a strong heart and the ear of the people. He had been elected into power over thirty years ago when his predecessor had lacked the confidence of his tribe. There was no battle, no contest; Ruari was the stronger man and everyone knew it. He would have gone into battle with his tribesmen in the north, but he was in the winter of life and walked with a slight limp, though he was no lesser man because of it. 'What news?' he asked of the men.

Airic spoke. 'Invasion wasn't their goal. They raided, pilfered and retreated, forcing their way west. They were testing our strengths. When the Ó Mordha reinforced their side, the foreigners came in stronger and harder than before. We brought the war to them, for no man takes our shores and leaves uncontested, and we lost many good fighting men in the process.'

'Hostages?' Ruari asked.

'One,' Airic said. 'But he dishonoured himself by attempting to flee and he was killed. At first, we thought they were

Albannaich or the people of Ellan Vannin, but we have trade agreements with them. These men, they fought like hardened northerners and died like bitter southerners. The Ó Mordha is calling for an army, to train them. It's unprecedented at this level, we train our boys and we fight when we must, but with a unity across all the northern tribes, the time is right. Our boys are to go north to the Ó Mordha for formal instruction.'

Ruari considered this before saying, 'Let us grieve the loss of our men. This is not a time for discussions of war but a time of respect for the dead. Until the feast of Imbolc, this will be a mourning period. You, the returning men, are the strength of our tribe and there will be a feast tonight in your honour. After that, the mourning will begin. When Imbolc is over, all boys past the age of eight and below the age of marriage will travel to Grianán Ailigh for training under the Ó Mordha.'

Chapter 2

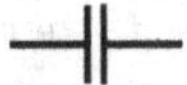

Seven days after their return from war, when the yule fires had been put out, the dead were buried. The naked heather bushes, whose petals were out of season, ringed the settlement's burial ground and a light mist hazed the morning fields. In the warmer months, the petals were used to fill pillows so that living heads would touch the same flowers as the spirits of the dead who rose to journey to the Otherworld.

The crunch of grass underfoot broke the icy dawn as Áed fell in line behind his father for the procession to the burial site. Thirteen graves had been dug in the days before, one for each of the brave, fallen warriors whose honourable deaths on the battlefield would cause worthy reincarnation in the afterlife. The men's bodies had been cleansed and were wrapped in linens decorated in the patterns of their tribe. Then they were burned and their ashes were buried with their swords and shields and with enough food to see them into their next life. Áed helped with the placement of the tumulus stones over each of the graves and when the last stone was put in place he stood back and observed their work. Stamping his feet on the frozen grass——they were cold while the rest of his body sweated from their labours——he asked, 'Where exactly is Tír na nÓg, father?'

The Land of the Young, where warriors went when they died, was the subject of many tales.

'West,' was all that his father said.

The mourners walked sun-wise three times around each mound and the keening of the women was strong. Odhran, no longer a druid's acolyte, had returned three days before and whispered directions to the Otherworld into the ears of the dead. It pained Áed to know that secret, even though all the tales informed him that anybody who went there living never returned, or did not return in his own lifetime.

When Odhran walked barefoot into the settlement in his grey cloak, his first deed was to seek out Doirean and Airic and advise them on Grainne's progress with the archdruid. She had passed his tests and was to be further instructed into the Order. 'She sends her love,' he told Doirean, 'and she misses you dearly, but she is happy. She is working for the earth now.'

'My fruit is the earth's fruit,' Doirean said, and she left to weep on her own.

After the burial rites for the thirteen heroic warriors, Airic went to his smithy to absorb his mind in his work. There had been unfinished projects when the call to arms had come and, to forget the long months at war and the passing of his friends, he sought solace in the repetitive beat of his hammer. Áed presented his father with the shield he had made the year before.

'I made this,' Áed said, adding at a whisper, 'for you.' He realised soon after finishing the shield how little he knew of forging and how unskilled his childish carvings were. For the intensive labouring he had spent on it, he looked on it now with an abhorrent disgust. 'I'll make another,' he said, an apology. 'I get better at carving in bronze every day.'

Airic took the shield from his son and looked at it for a long time. He hefted it in his hands, levelled the brace of it with his eye, and slid his forearm through the straps at its back. 'It's a fine thing,' he said at last. 'A fine thing.'

'It's Néit,' Áed said of the face on the shield's front. 'To help win the wars. But it's poorly made. I can make a newer one. I am older and better now.'

'There is no finer shield in the land,' Airic told his son. 'And I will proudly wear it into battle.'

Áed sat on the wooden stool opposite the iron forge at which Airic had been working, and he smiled, lowered his gaze, and scuffed the dirt at his feet. 'Tell me about the war,' he asked.

With the shield still attached to his left arm, he came and knelt in front of Áed, digging the point of the shield into the floor. 'At this rate it won't be long before you find out for yourself. After Imbolc, you'll travel to the Ó Mordha for training.' He looked at his son's innocent face, at the shaggy hair that fell about his cheeks. 'War is a foul business. It is as much a part of life as it is of death. You don't need to hear my stories, you'll make your own. The only advice I can offer you is this: when you strike, strike hard. When a man comes before you on the battlefield, he is not your friend. He is the embodiment of every enemy you've ever faced before and every one you'll face thereafter. He is not to be feared; he is to fear you. Every warrior you face independently is the only war you will know. There will be no end to it until he has fallen at your feet without a head. Show me your hands.'

Áed held his hands out for his father's inspection. Airic took them and turned them over, touching the calluses he had earned from his smith work and tracing the cracks in his palms.

'You are ready,' he said. 'Strengthen your body like you've strengthened your hands, and in time, no man will hear your name without looking over his shoulder in terror.'

When the Imbolc festival period arrived, a celebration of the goddess Bríg's return to youth, it began and ended with a sunset feast. At dawn, homes were swept clean and tallow candles were lit and burned until nightfall. The beginning of spring and the lengthening of the days marked the start of a new harvest year and the hopes for sustainable crops. Lambs would soon be born and heavier cloaks could be shed in favour of lighter wear.

For Áed and the other boys of the tribe, it marked not only the beginning of spring, but their entry into adulthood—in two days, they would travel north to commence their training as warriors in preparation for battles yet to be conceived. Although spring work began in earnest, the sept was a sombre place for those final days before the boys left. The chieftain met with each of them and gave him a gift. 'Without you, we would have no tribe in the days to come. You boys are the future of our kind,' he said. 'Take this stone of our earth as a reminder of where you came from and where you shall return.' Standing alone in the chieftain's hall with the old man, Áed studied the surface of the black basalt stone he had been handed. It was smoothed on one side, into which the swirled pattern of their tribe had been carved, and a hole had been punched into it so that it could be worn around the neck. Since the day of his birth, Áed still wore the rune of strength that the druid had tied to him. This new stone would have to be worn elsewhere.

'Be proud of who you are,' the chieftain continued, 'and of what you will become. Fight for your people and you will be honoured on your return.'

Áed put the tribe stone into his travel sack and on the morning that their journey began, all the people of the tribe came out to see them off. Little Bec clung to his waist until her mother pulled her away, and then Doirean held him tighter than he had ever been held before. The Ó Mordha's forward thinking, initiating a training programme that took boys from their mothers at such an early age, had never been done before. A permanent standing army was unheard of. To Doirean, it signified a shift in culture. That the Ó Mordha would consider such a programme necessary, they were preparing for a war of such magnitude as had not been seen since the Tuatha Dé Danann fought the Fomorians. Doirean held her boy's face in her hands and committing to memory every contour, every line and hair.

Airic took his son's forearm in solidarity. 'Do not dishonour your people,' he said.

Led by Cormac, one of the older boys, their four-night journey north was met with a constant salvo of rain. They huddled together under fearnóg trees when it was torrential, and dug pits to sleep in, covered with a sackcloth that had been weighted down with stones to stop from blowing away in the early spring winds that drove in from the southwest. On the third day, during a lull in the rain, they came to a pair of standing stones as tall as men. One was rounded on top and the other was square and fatter. 'Walk between them, hand in hand with a woman,' Cormac said, 'and she'll bear you many children.'

'What if you walk through with another boy?' someone asked.

'His dick will fall off,' Cormac said. 'He'll become a woman and she'll bear you many children.' He pranced between the stones on his own and said, 'Who wants to be my woman?'

None of the boys dared to cross between them. 'Anyway,' Cormac continued, 'we're a day away from Ailigh. This is the border of the Ó Mordha stronghold. There's a burn about twenty fertach that way, I think. We'll camp there for the night and present ourselves to the overking tomorrow evening.'

As they lit a fire and drew water from the stream for drinking and washing, Áed opened his travel sack and found the last of the breads his mother had made for the journey. He had no honey left and he had finished the cured meats earlier that day. The other boys were in the same situation. Each had eaten more of his rations than he should have in the first few days of the journey. It was good that they would arrive at Ailigh tomorrow. One of the boys took out his cruit to play. His father was a woodworker who carved the instruments for the bards and, in return, the travelling men taught him and his son to play. It was one of the common three-string versions and the boy's bow- and finger-work were amateur but pleasant to listen to.

In the morning, as a dark grey sky roused them with its first fat drops of rain, they set out hungry but in high spirits. The Ó Mordha people were renowned for their superior abilities in combat. They had taken over much of the Uladh and Cruthin provinces in the north of Éirinn a hundred years ago and had since formed treaties with their neighbours. There were always border disputes, but nothing the Ó Mordha could not temper. They were a proud and fierce tribe, descended from Mordha the Terrible, called so for the terrors he bestowed upon his enemies in battle. It is said in song that he was over eight feet tall and as broad as a tree at the shoulders. If you could believe it, they say he fought alongside the Dagda and made Morrígan weep for her love of him.

The boys were met at the outer rampart of Ailigh, an impressive fort at the top of a hill, and were told to wait in vigilance, awake and watchful, until called. The gate was barred and they were left unattended. Other groups of boys had already arrived and remained on the grasses along the outer palisade, and more boys were coming up the hill behind them. Two days they waited in the harsh wind and rain, huddled under deer pelts, with what little food remained from their journey. When Áed's group of boys had emptied their sacks, they begged for some food from the other tribes, whose stalwart refusal soured the air around them. One group of boys, who all had the same wheat-coloured hair that was lashed to their faces from the rain, offered them a round of bread that wouldn't stretch far but gave Áed's group a morsel each.

By the second night outside the wall, when the rain had stopped and many of the boys were asleep or weak with hunger, the gate was opened and a man, tall enough to have to lower his head, came out and addressed them. He gave them each a small stone—some white, some black—and ushered them in and up the hill to the fort proper. As they gathered at the entrance to Grianán Ailigh, inside the third rampart, seat of the overking of the Ó Mordha, they were warmed by the heat of the fire from within and the relief was visible on their faces.

'Once inside, you will be given food,' the man said. The black sheepskin *cocholl* cape that covered his shoulders was matted with the rain and his braided moustache was dripping on his leather boots. 'Anyone who received a black stone outside may return home in the morning. You are not fit for service here.'

'Why?' a voice rose from the back of the assembly of boys. 'It took us five nights to reach Ailigh.'

'And a five-night journey home,' the man said. 'When you arrived you were told to wait in vigilance. You weren't told to fall asleep. Two days without food and look at the shape you're in. When you're on the battlefield, you could go longer without. You are weak of spirit and have not the stamina for war.'

'You can't make me go home,' the boy shouted.

The man nodded. 'I can't make you a fighter, either. This day is the beginning of your adult lives. Those who survive will return home as heroes. I don't want my men dying on the battlefield, much less during the early days of training. The weak have no place here. Blackstones can eat tonight and leave at dawn. Whitestones, welcome to Grianán Ailigh. This is your home until it is deemed otherwise.'

Áed's first thought was that the blackstone boys could swap or steal from the whitestone recipients, but the idea was put from his mind. Whitestone boys clung to their own so tightly that no one could wrest it from them. It was ingenious, he thought, and as he ate at one of the long tables that ran the length of the thatched building they had entered, his flat white stone never left his hand. Straw-filled pallets had been laid for them in an adjoining room but there were not enough to compensate for every boy and some had to share. The boys collected together in their own septs and tribes, preferring to be surrounded—particularly when sleeping—by their own people rather than integrate with the other tribes, and one boy from each sept was elected to take first watch in case stone-theft would occur in the night.

With morning and at last some rainless sunshine, two third of the boys left for their shameful journey home and the others gathered in a field just outside the fort's outer wall. The man who spoke to them the previous night introduced himself as Oisín, 'Like the legend,' he said. 'And like the legend, I am just as fierce. Do not cross me or I will clout you with the back of my sword. You are all Ó Mordha men now. You will be taught to act as an Ó Mordha and you will be taught to fight as one. When you have mastered the dagger, you will be taught the arrow, then the sword. When you have mastered the sword, you will be taught it again with your weaker hand. In time, you will lift men and snap them as you would a twig.

'There will be no scrapping among you,' he continued. 'There will be no tribal disputes—why? Because you are Ó Mordha men now. Your chieftains and your fathers have pledged you to us. You are mine to train and you belong to the overking. In reparation for your servitude, you will return to your people as men. But you will always be Ó Mordha. And when you are called, you will come. If you do not die honourably on the battlefield, you will die honourably of age. And you will be mourned by many and remembered by all. This is your life: the life of an Ó Mordha. You are not friends, you are not neighbours. You are brothers. And if you will not fight for your king, you will fight for your brothers.'

Oisín walked the length of the boys, looking each in the eyes, and returned to his elevated mound in front of them. 'You will be grouped according to your current strengths and you will train together until your hands bleed and heal and bleed again. And by the time of the Tailteann games, you will know to a man the name and voice and strength of everyone gathered here today.' At that, he pointed at each boy in turn and separated them into groups based on apparent strength or on height and weight.

Of the seven other boys in Áed's collection, he recognised one as the wheaten-haired boy who offered his sept some bread outside the walls. 'I didn't get to thank you for the bread,' he said.

The boy shrugged. 'You were hungry; we had plenty.' He offered his hand. 'I'm Rónán Ó Coileán.'

'Ó Mordha,' Áed corrected him, and they laughed.

'These groups,' Oisín said, 'are designed to improve your strengths while leaving no man behind. If one of your group members is weaker than the others, you train him in your own time to bring him in line. You will eat together, train together, and bunk together. And regardless how tired you are at night, you will make certain you have enough energy for training the next day.' He positioned the boys of each group to form a perimeter around a patch of grass six steps wide by six deep. 'We will start with fists. Pair off and let's see what you're made of.'

Áed turned to Rónán and said, 'Are you a good fighter?'

'I guess you will find out soon,' Rónán winked. 'Are you?'

Áed shrugged. 'I'm the son of a smith. My hands are the hardest part about me.'

'I can only apologise,' Rónán said with a smirk.

'For what?' And Rónán punched him square on the nose. As he went down, Áed's only wish was that this didn't mean he would be issued with a black stone.

Rónán helped him back to his feet, laughing at the blood that gushed from Áed's nose, and with his new adversary off guard, Áed gripped the back of his head and punched him twice in the face. As Rónán held his blushing cheek, he said, 'That's two. I owe you one.'

Oisín tapped both boys on the top of the head. 'Blood,' he

said. 'That's what I like to see.' To the others, he said, 'If the smell of fresh blood doesn't make me sick before the day is out, you can all go home in shame.'

Later that evening, as the orange sun rode westward along the ridge of the distant mountain range, when they were weak, tired and bruised, Áed found Rónán in the hall, waiting in line for a bowl of stewed mutton. They had bathed with cold water from the nearby well and were given nettle water to drink for their aches and balms for their bruises. There was not a boy among them who got through the day without a battle mark on his face. One child, not much older than Áed, had to be carried off from the field on a litter, his arm twisted and his ear torn. They had not seen him since.

'What was your father's occupation?' Rónán asked him as they took a seat together. 'A smith?' When Áed nodded, Rónán said, 'They'll put you to work with a forge before long. They'll have us working as well as training.'

'What about your father?' Áed asked him.

'Fletcher,' Rónán said. 'There's not a man in all of Éirinn that can shoot an arrow as well as my father. Men come from all over to pay for his fletching skills.'

'Have you seen the overking yet?' Áed asked.

'No one has. I don't think he's even here. They say he goes on hunting parties for weeks at a time.'

'I hear he's taller than Oisín.'

'No one is taller than Oisín, unless you count Mordha the Terrible, and he's dead,' Rónán said. 'One thing I know is he's hard as iron; you don't get to be overking without slaughtering your way there. And he has the respect of every tribe in the north.'

In bed, Áed considered the lot of his short life so far. He hoped that at his death he would ride alongside Mordha and the Dagda in the Otherworld. He touched the emblem of strength at his neck and wished for the power to become the greatest warrior since Mordha himself.

And when he dreamed that night, he stood side by side with Rónán on a bloodied battlefield, facing off against a horde of beasts that may have been wolves if they had stood on all fours.

Or they may have been gods.

Chapter 3

As Rónán predicted, the boys were put to work in the professions of their fathers. Those with occupations that weren't necessary to the daily running of Ailigh were sent to the fields as farm hands or shepherds, ploughing, sowing, and protecting livestock. They worked in the mornings and trained in the afternoons when the sun was at its highest, and soon the spring weather took hold, the bleating of the lambs flavoured the incessant buzz of the bees, and the training fields were soaked with sweat and blood every day. Áed was put to work in the smithy under the tutelage of a sullen man called Néall who corrected mistakes with a clip to the ear and rarely gave praise where it was earned. He was first tasked with proving how much he already knew of bronze forging before Néall allowed him to start smelting iron. The smith started him with inconsequential trinkets that held little value, things that could be recast later—a simple arm torc, or a cloak pin that lacked any form of decoration. By the time of the midsummer feast, he had amassed an impressive collection of belt buckles and cat statues.

Rónán, on the other hand, took to fletching as though he was born for it. His father had been a good teacher and there was always a need for well-fletched arrows either in war or in hunting. He plucked tail-feathers from chickens and shaped them as delicately as he could. The arrow shafts were pre-slit and metal heads had already been fastened to their tips before he affixed the fletched feathers and ensured their weighting was balanced and true. He released the arrows at a fixed target on the field to test their accuracy and the other boys talked about his skills and how he would be leading the archers into battle when the time came. He would win the event at the games without doubt.

Rather than travel south for the official Tailteann games and interrupt their training, Oisín decided that they would host their own games. The boys and men of Ailigh gathered on the fields for the sports—unarmed combat, archery, spear-throwing and swordsmanship—as well as the board games of fidhcheall and bran dubh. In the bay, they hosted rowing and swimming contests. Not adept at the board games, Áed registered his intent to compete in all the other sports. His fists were quick in fighting and his arm was strong with the sword. He had taken some lessons in archery from Rónán but he knew he would not beat him in the tournament.

With a blunted sword and bronze breastplate for point-marking, Áed took to the field and beat down his first three opponents in swordsmanship with ease, using a combination of short jabs and broad strokes, careful to recall Oisín's words of feigning predictability while pulling hits from his challenger's blindside. His stance was strong, weighting himself on the flats of his feet with a slight forward posture and maintaining his balance against all forms of frontal attack. Every tap to the breastplate was awarded a point and every time the contest bell signalled a new round, Áed went in with a smile. In time, his opponents became stronger, older, more experienced. He had outclassed his own squad and rousted each of his competitors out of the field, but with each successive contest he felt his arm weakening and his balance softening. He was beat down by Dillon, a boy almost twice his age who, when he turned and bowed to his audience, did not witness Áed returning quickly to his feet, his cheeks burning, and barrelling into the boy's back with his shoulder. As Dillon fell and rolled onto his back, Áed stood over him and thwacked the blunt end of his sword against his breastplate.

'Unfair,' Dillon called.

Áed looked at the contest judge who shook his head. 'He got in before the bell rang. It was your own fault for taking your eyes off him.'

Áed held a hand out for the older boy who refused to take it. He got to his feet and gripped the hilt of his sword in both hands.

'That's enough,' the judge said. 'Simmer down before I take a buckle to you.'

With narrowed eyes, Dillon turned and walked away.

'Maybe you should ring the bell now,' Áed said.

Despite the unfortunate melee with Dillon, Áed fought on against his ensuing competitors and ended the contest in third place among all the boys at Ailigh. With the awarding of placements in two days, and spear-throwing and swimming tomorrow, he took to his pallet at dusk while the rest of the boys celebrated on the fields. In the insipid darkness that stirred into the room, he stared up at the thatching and recalled every stroke of the sword he had made that day. With an analytical self-awareness, he knew where he could have performed better, especially against Dillon, a boy who could not lie on the battlefield, who looked at the side he was going to attack to despite feigning otherwise with his body language. When Áed held his sword in his hand, the blade became a blur while the person before him became a study. He had mastered the art of searching his opponent's eyes for attack manoeuvres while being able to synchronously block, parry and jab. Oisín called it sword-smart.

Áed had not expected anybody to return to the room so early, so when the door opened it startled him, and as he rose to his feet, he was pushed back down onto the bed. Dillon gripped his throat with strong hands.

'Why don't you fight me with fists and see who wins?'

Áed clung to Dillon's forearm, holding back the pressure, and said, 'I won squarely.' He could feel his cheeks burning.

When Dillon wound back to punch his pinned quarry in the face, he stopped and looked over his shoulder.

Rónán held his bow aloft, an arrow nocked and drawn, its sharp tip held just by the soft skin of his neck. 'He's half your size, big man,' he said. 'Doesn't seem like a fair fight to me, especially when you have him pinned.'

'Point that thing somewhere else, cur,' Dillon said.

'Take your hand off his throat,' Rónán insisted. 'We're not supposed to be squabbling. We're all Ó Mordha and he beat you fair on the field. Oisín said—'

'Oisín can taste my fist as well. This little bastard deserves a beating for what he did. You have no right to interfere.'

Rónán smiled. 'Fine,' he said. 'Punch him in the face. But I should tell you that my fingers are getting slippery. Have you seen the damage an arrow can do at such close range? I'm getting tired.' He yawned wide and long. 'Not sure I can hold this much longer.'

Dillon let go of Áed's throat and Rónán lowered his bow just enough so that he could draw it again if he needed to.

'Neither of you boys should go to sleep tonight,' Dillon said. 'If you do, you might wake up to find one of golden boy's arrows wedged in your arse.'

When he had left, Rónán sat on the edge of Áed's bed. 'I'll hide the barbed arrow heads just in case.' He laughed.

'Why aren't you out celebrating your archery wins by the fire?' Áed asked. He had no desire to say thanks for the rescue and none was expected.

'I came looking for you,' Rónán said. 'Let's get out of here.'

Áed shook his head and lay back down. 'I'm tired.'

Rónán stood. He pointed towards the window and the horizon beyond it. 'Too tired for the lough?'

Áed rose to his elbows. 'Outside the walls? We'd never make it over the first without being caught and flogged. I'd rather have Dillon's fat fist pummelling my freckled face for an hour instead of receiving one lash from Oisín for disobeying an order.'

'We won't get caught,' Rónán said. 'Besides, old man Tadhg is drunk and'—he reached inside his quiver and felt around between the arrows—'I have his keys.'

They crept between the huts to the palisade gate, crouching low. They could hear the revelries from behind. Outside the walls, they kept an eye on the position of the moon and circled around to the rear of the outer rampart. In the valley far below, where the waters met the shore in a small lough, tomorrow's swimming contest would be hosted. Tonight, the bay was quiet save for the sounds of the water and the sweep of blackened seaweed along the small sandy ridge. A marker had already been set in place as the competition's starting point, kicking off from the northernmost dunes of the small beach, and they would be required to swim around a floating station out in the bay and then back to shore in a team relay.

'Do you live near the shore?' Rónán asked.

Áed sat on the damp sand. 'My sept lives inland, but with a well. There's a river where we swam, but it wasn't very big.'

'And what is your chieftain like? Is he good?'

Áed shrugged. 'He's been chieftain for all my life and before. He gave me a stone with our tribe-mark on it.'

Rónán skimmed a flat stone along the water that disappeared in the murky darkness after only two hops, and then he came back to Áed. 'That's not the stone at your neck.'

'No.'

'Then if you are proud to be of your tribe, you should set the stone in the pommel of your sword. You're a smith, after all.'

'What about your chieftain?'

Rónán sat down beside him and bore his fingers into the sand. 'If he isn't shouting angry insults at the farmers, he's usually asleep. Or at any rate, he's in bed with one of his wives.'

'Won't the men take the seat from him? If he's not good—'

'They wouldn't dare,' Rónán said. 'He has many sons, all with strong arms. One of them may take the seat from him, but until then, he fights with the farmers, takes his wives, makes more sons, and we've yet to be invaded. I guess he's doing something right.'

'You should take a bow to his head the way you did with Dillon,' Áed said. 'You're good enough.'

'I'd get more than an arrow in my arse if I tried,' Rónán laughed. 'He'd probably cut me to pieces before feeding me to the farmers' pigs.'

'If he has so many sons, why have none of them joined us at Ailigh?'

'He exercised his right to retain any boy he saw fit, to help protect his borders. And the only boys he saw fit were his own.'

They walked along the shoreline as far as they could, and as the evening darkened, they stripped off their short *léine* tunics and swam out to the floating station. It had been weighted with a sack of rocks to the bed of the lough so that it would maintain its position, and it was broad enough to carry them both and stay afloat.

'You miss your sept, then?' Rónán asked.

'Yes,' Áed said with an unreserved candour. 'I like it here, but I miss my family—even my sisters. One is to become a druid. My mother did not like that, but she came around to it long before my father came back from the war.'

Rónán turned aside and lowered his feet into the cold water. 'I want to miss my people. I suppose I miss my father. I think. But I belong here. We'll grow up, fight wars, be heroes—legends, even. Here, I am Ó Mordha; there, I am just the fletcher's son.'

Áed stood up on the platform and allowed the rocking motion of the wood to settle. 'Fletchers are respected. Does your father not have the ear of your chieftain?'

'No one has his ear but his first wife. Muirgel is the real leader. Nothing happens without her say so, not even harvest. I'm fairly sure the sun only returns every morning because she wills it.' Rónán touched his thumb to his forehead. 'She has the chieftain beaten down and everyone knows it. But as his wife, she's above law unless he is relieved of his role—and the one son they have together would never allow it. They say Muirgel slept with the god Ogma and told our chieftain that the child was his. But I don't believe that. He's strong, I grant it, but nothing an arrow or two wouldn't take down.'

'I thought you said you wouldn't dare try to take them down,' Áed said, his arms out for balance as the water swelled the raft beneath him.

'Not yet,' Rónán said. 'But one day, I'll take them all down.' He glanced over his shoulder at Áed's feet. 'And I'll start,' he said, 'by taking you down.' He swung his legs round and took Áed off balance, sending him backwards, his arms spinning in a failed attempt at staying topside. As he tumbled back, he twisted, fell, and hit his face on the wooden platform before disappearing into the dark water.

Rónán's laugh soured in his throat and he knelt on the edge of the platform, staring down into the murk below. 'Áed?' When Áed failed to return to the surface, Rónán stood, filled his lungs with air, and dived into the lough. In the darkness, it was hard to see. He groped left and right as he used his feet for direction, pulling back up for air before touching what he thought was a hand or a foot, gripping it and swimming upwards. He put his arm around Áed's neck and dragged him back to the raft, hauling him back onto the wood. He laid him out on his back, knelt over him, and shook him by the shoulders.

Áed's body shuddered and he coughed up water and phlegm. He sat up, wiping blood from his face. 'That's twice you've bloodied my nose,' he said. 'Are you trying to kill me?'

Rónán smiled. 'I just saved you. Anyway, stop making it so

easy for me.'

And they laughed.

Áed stood and shook the fugue from his head. 'The moon is getting low. We should head back and get some sleep before I beat you at swimming tomorrow.'

'If you beat me, it's because I let you win,' Rónán said, 'because I feel sorry for almost killing you.'

In the morning, not long after they had crept back to bed, Rónán returned the gate keys to old man Tadhg, claiming he had found them on the field by the fire where the gate warden must have dropped them in his drunken revelling the night before. After a breakfast of oats, Áed met Rónán on the shore, pointed to his nose, and said, 'Try not to kill me today.'

As they prepared for their relay tournament, Rónán said, 'I can't make any promises.'

As they were on the same team with two other competitors, swimming one after the other only when the previous boy had returned to shore, they agreed that they would count numbers without cheating to see who the stronger swimmer was. Whoever was the fastest would be king among them for a day.

At the horn, Áed was the first to go, followed by a teammate, then by Rónán and the final member of their group. Rónán had counted to one hundred and thirty-seven by the time Áed made it back to shore, and on his turn, Áed counted one hundred and thirty-four. It was a fair loss, one he accepted with grace, but said, 'I'm still better at everything else.'

'Except archery,' Rónán said.

'Except that,' he conceded.

The afternoon contest in spear-throwing rounded out the last of Áed's tournaments. His aim may have been off, but his

arm was strong. His spear whittled through the air with a wob-
ble in the breeze, but he had thrown a good distance, enough
to put him in the final three in his age class. His second throw
was better, but it was not enough to claim first position and he
made do with second in spear-throwing and third overall in
swordsmanship. At the awarding of placements, Oisín called
him out in front of all assembled and gave special mention to his
swordsmanship. 'Never before has a boy fought so adamantly
that at his first games he has made it so far with the sword. This
one is after my job, for sure.' From his position in the centre of
the collected boys, Áed could see Dillon's icy stare.

At the feast that followed, Rónán sought out Áed by the fire
and nudged him in the ribs. 'Dillon has been staring at you all
night,' he said, 'but don't worry, he won't try anything. I put an
arrow head in his bed; he'll know what it means.'

'I wasn't worried,' Áed said. 'But thanks.'

'Now, then.' Rónán rubbed his hands together. 'Fetch me
some meat and a drink. I'm famished.'

'Get your own,' Áed said, punching him on the shoulder.

'Your king commands it.'

Áed rolled his eyes. 'Fine. But when this day is over, we'll
have to have words about what a king can and cannot do.'

'Let me enjoy it while I can,' Rónán said.

Chapter 4

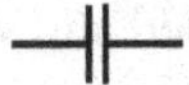

The following Imbolc, Áed stood on the guard platform that commanded a view over the entire hillside, and he watched as almost seventy boys gathered outside the walls to receive instruction from the great king of the Ó Mordha. He could not hear the words that Oisín spoke to them but he knew their intent—stay vigilant, do not sleep. Those who did would be sent home.

Rónán, his hair still damp from bathing, came to his side. 'There were hundreds of us when we first arrived.'

'We were every boy over the age of eight. These are the ones who were too young to come last year.' He pointed. 'I recognise those two from my tribe.'

'They'll have news of your family, then,' Rónán said.

Áed nodded and turned away. 'I can't even remember my family, these days. All I know is sword fighting and spear throwing.' He climbed down the wooden steps. The boys would be camped on the grass for two days before Oisín let them in, and during that time, Ailigh's existing trainee army would not be allowed outside the walls. They were to run laps around the outer rampart and practice their war crafts behind huts. Already, not long after breakfast, the sound of clashing swords rang out across the compound.

'Will you run arrows for me?' Rónán asked.

They went to a section of the outer rampart that had been prepared for them, a stationary target at the end of a walkway one hundred paces long. Rónán cocked an arrow as Áed crouched beside the target, hidden behind a double-strength shield. He kept his eyes closed and waited for the whistle of the air and the thump that followed, indicating the target had been pierced. Rónán would send down five arrows before Áed could retrieve them and run them back to him.

After the fourth punch of the target, Áed shouted encouragement. 'Hit him in the balls. You can do it.'

He felt a crack as the arrow smacked into his shield and the thud of it rang through his arms. He stood and saw Rónán rolling on the ground in laughter.

'Watch it!'

'Did I get you in the balls?'

He pulled the arrows free and walked the distance to Rónán. 'I should stake you to the ground with them and leave you for the crows. You could have killed me. Again.'

'But it was funny,' Rónán laughed.

Áed turned and walked away.

'Hey,' Rónán called. 'It was a joke.'

Áed returned to him, punched him in the arm, and grinned. 'You think I huff like a girl.'

'Next market day, I'll buy you a dress,' Rónán said, rubbing his shoulder.

'If you want me in a dress, I can borrow one of yours,' Áed said. He punched him again and he ran. Rónán chased him.

Later, when the new boys had been let in and fewer than

thirty of them had survived the two-day hardship outside the walls, training resumed as normal in the fields. Áed had long since mastered the sword with his dominant hand and was learning manoeuvres with his weaker arm. At first, he continued to bring his leading arm forward to correct his sword's position and stroke, but Oisín strapped the arm to his side and forced him to concentrate with just the weaker hand. For five days he was made to train and eat and sleep as though he had only one arm, and when the strap was removed, he no longer sought to bring it up as an aid. He could slice a plum with the sword in his left hand just as easily as he could with his right.

As the summer sun warmed the grasses and the boys took to wearing shorter tunics, Áed studied the newer boys to check their progress. He could scarcely believe that in just over a year, he, Rónán and the others, had developed their fighting techniques with a ferocious tenacity befitting any warrior. Seeing the younger boys fumble on the field, he was convinced that he had never been so clumsy.

On a late afternoon, when a summer storm was threatening from the west, one of the young boys pointed towards the distant south and shouted, 'The hills are on fire.'

When they looked, they saw three columns of black smoke rising towards the clouds.

In the morning, all the boys and men of Ailigh were assembled on the training field with their fighting equipment. The overking, King Déaglán, took to a platform to address them. He stood before them in his finest tunic and cloak, the gold discs of his status visible at his breast. When they had first met him, several weeks after their arrival, they were each made to kiss those discs to swear their loyalty to him as their chieftain and leader. He held their shoulder and thanked them all.

Now, with the smoke still rising in the distance, he called for hush. 'You know why you are here, boys. I won't give you a rousing speech. You are training for war and, now, war has come.'

A ripple of whispers tore through the collected boys.

Déaglán raised his hands for quiet. 'This is a minor infraction of our borders from an overzealous chieftain in the south. Knowing that we are busy creating true warriors, he thought to encroach on our territory when our backs were turned. But the signal fires behind me alert us to all threats. He is a foolish man and we will force him back.'

The boys raised a cheer.

'Oisín will hand-select a delegate of young warriors from among you to accompany my men south. You have been training long enough to fight with the Ó Mordha spirit. We will leave at once. When your name is called, step forward. Let's show these southern bastards what we're made of.'

On their march south, selected among one hundred other boys, Áed and Rónán wondered at their first battle. They spoke of heroic fights that lasted days, bodies littering under their feet, blood running like a river around them. When Oisín overheard them, he clipped them both on the ear.

'Those are men, just as you are,' he said. 'They may currently be the enemy, but yesterday they were neighbours and tomorrow, those who are left, will return as such. Have respect for their lives. Haven't I taught you anything? The only man worth nothing is he who journeys his life believing he is worth something. When you get close enough to make your first kill, every one of his pains will be delivered to you in your dreams.

Make the kill swift and do not gloat, or you will suffer for it later.'

When they reached the battlefield, they squared off against the neighbouring tribe who had impinged upon Ó Mordha's borderlands. Their leader, Oisín pointed out, was Gerrit Mac Tomáis, ruler of the coastal tribes of the west. He was a brutal man covered in battle scars, one side of his head shaved to reveal the tattoo of a horse, signifying the swiftness with which he could charge into battle. Although a treaty existed between Gerrit and Déaglán, formal border lines established, he often ventured beyond his bounds to pilfer game or capture minor territories. He had not done so in years, Oisín said, and they had hoped he had learned his lesson.

The two opposing leaders faced each other on the field. 'You have overstepped your lines,' Déaglán called to Gerrit. They remained too far from each other for quiet discussions. 'Retreat to your own territories and I will let you go.'

'Your lands get fat like your men,' Gerrit shouted. 'I will mark a new border with the bones of your kin.'

Negotiations were complete. Gerrit barked an order and his men ran onto the field.

Oisín gave a call. 'Men first; boys to follow behind. I'm not losing any of you before you've forgotten the taste of your mother's milk.' He drew his sword and charged.

Behind the line of men, Áed and the other boys hesitated for a moment before drawing their swords or hefting their spears, then they ran onto the field. This was what they had trained for but sparring against their friends was different from facing an enemy. While they had pulled their blows on the training field, their actions now would require a deliberate follow-through.

They were no longer knocking opponents down; they were aiming to kill.

The clash of swords against shields rose before them, the screams of grown men, the battle cries. A wind circled them as though it was containing their essence and swelling the noise.

'Shields!' someone shouted, and Áed raised his own with instinct and crouched low. Shield-wall formations had been practiced on the training field, but he wasn't close enough to anyone to form a wall. When he rose, he raised his sword to swing at whichever enemy was closest, but he was still too far from the front.

Before him, fighters were already falling. Men, even warriors, screamed when a sword penetrated his stomach or severed his arm.

He steadied his resolve and, seeking out Rónán among the taller men, he gripped the hilt of his sword tighter and entered the dispute.

He was surrounded by his own men forcing their way forward, and when he made the front, he raised his shield and hefted his sword. One of the enemy saw him, a child among adults, and laughed before swinging his broad sword.

Áed planted his feet and crouched, raising his shield further. The sword beat against it. By impulse alone, he followed the blow by swinging his own sword in a low arc. It connected with the man's shin and he bellowed. Still shielded, Áed jabbed forward, but his mark was off. The man gripped the blade in his hand and pulled, bringing Áed off balance.

He stumbled and they fell together.

The man's punch clipped his shoulder.

Áed rolled, twisted, and tried to bring his shield up for

protection.

As the man struggled to his feet, blood coursing around his foot from his wounded leg, Áed jostled backwards and punched out with his sword.

The angry man, a massive trunk with long hair and deep creases on his brow, lunged forward and swatted the blade aside.

Áed kicked and screamed. His shield took the worst of the man's fall.

He squirmed aside, got to his knees, and swung the sword. It connected with the man's upper arm and cut into his flesh.

With the blade lodged in his enemy, Áed struggled to his feet, kicked the man in the face, and tore the sword free. He swung again. And again.

And again.

He did not realise he was still shrieking until someone barrelled into him and they rolled together on the slight incline of the hill. A hand clamped over his mouth and a shield covered their bodies.

Áed thrashed against his assailant, but he went limp when Oisín said, 'Still yourself. He is dead.' He helped him to his feet and said, 'You made your kill. Retreat to the rear. It is almost done.' As Áed turned, Oisín added, 'Don't get yourself killed.'

Áed weaved his way back to the hills behind them. Other boys were already there. When he saw Rónán, he ran to him.

'Did you kill one?' Rónán asked.

Áed nodded.

'He nearly got me,' Rónán said. 'I was looking this way and that, but then this enormous bastard was right in front of me, swinging his sword and screaming in my face. I ducked through his legs and stuck him when he turned on me.' Although he was breathing hard, Rónán was smiling.

Already, Áed was feeling the defeat of war. He had killed a warrior, and he had survived, but now a man was dead at his hand. Oisín was right—it would haunt his dreams for months to come.

He refused to watch the rest of the fighting. With his back to the field, he could imagine the carnage unfolding. Before the sun was low in the west, it was over. King Déaglán was the victor, although Áed did not know if Gerrit Mac Tomáis had survived, and he did not wish to ask.

They trudged back towards Ailigh, singing songs of victory.

When Áed walked apart, even from Rónán, Oisín came to his side.

'What pains you more?' he asked. 'Killing the enemy, or killing a man?'

'He was fighting for what his king believed was right,' Áed said. 'I know they were wrong to breach our borders, but what of his family? He must have had a wife and some children.'

'You dwell too much,' Oisín said. 'It is good to consider the opponent's side—when you do, you can understand his reasoning—but you cannot brood over a man's life. He went to battle; he will have made peace with his family. Your actions back there helped us win. But your anger got in the way. You ended him with one blow. The others were borne of aggression and they were unnecessary. Remember always to keep your guard up even when your shield isn't. When a man falls, whisper a god's name and move on. If you do not keep your eyes high, you will end up lying beside him with a blade in your back. You did well. Next time, you will do better.'

When they returned to Ailigh to the cheers of all the gathered boys, Áed bathed and changed his tunic, and then stood up on the platform that overlooked the outer rampart. The signal fires had been put out and several men were dispatched to restock the braziers. Rónán found him as the sun was setting and the evening darkness cloaked the distant mountains.

A runner was drawing up the hill towards the outer gate.

'He's in a hurry,' Rónán said. 'Doesn't he know the battle is won?'

They heard his cries from below, begging to be let in.

'I hated it,' Áed said. 'Killing a man is not an easy pass time.'

Rónán nodded, his eyes shining in the thickening night. 'The day it gets easy is the day you should fall on your own sword. But it is necessary.'

'Yes,' Áed agreed. Below them, the gate was opened and the runner entered. He was taken further into the fort.

'It will get easier,' Rónán said, 'the more we do it.'

'The actions may get easier, but the dreams may never leave us.'

They stared out into the blackness beyond them. As necessary as it might be, killing was ugly. He would fight for his king, but he could not be forced to like it.

When Oisín approached and shouted Rónán's name, they turned and scrambled down the steps from the platform. The runner stood behind him, still panting from his hurried journey.

'You're going home,' Oisín said. 'You'll leave at first light.'

'What's happened?'

'It's your father.'

'Was he involved in the fighting?' Áed asked.

Oisín ignored him. Rónán stepped forward.

'Your chieftain has sent word. Your father is dead.'

Chapter 5

Oisín gave them a carbad to speed their journey, a low-riding open warfare cart pulled by a single horse. Ordinarily, the two-wheeled horse-drawn vehicle was ridden into battle with a driver kneeling at its fore and a warrior throwing spears from its rear as it circled around the enemy. Its base was low enough for the warrior to jump upon his quarry, rushing his sword deep through his chest, and step back on with ease. Today, it bore a driver along with Rónán and Áed.

They had returned to their quarters last night and Rónán sat on the floor, his back against the wall, and he curled his arms around his knees. He did not cry. Áed sat cross-legged in front of him. 'Your father is dead,' Oisín had said, without emotion or sentiment.

Áed had helped Rónán into bed, and then left in search of Oisín. He found him in the smithy, talking quietly with Néall, and before either of the men could enquire as to his presence, Áed said, 'I'm going with him.'

Oisín stood, towering over the boy, and frowned. 'As is only fitting. But do not presume to give me orders. Defiance can be met with severity; there is nothing about you that I cannot replace with another lad.'

Undeterred, Áed said, 'I am a good swordsman. One of your best.'

Oisín said, 'Ask a question, do not command me. Arrogance will get you killed. A true warrior knows when to sheath his tongue as much as his blade. On the field, with neither friend nor master to argue with, you can direct all your ferociousness against your foe. Until then, have the decency to respect me.'

Wilting, his voice low and unsure, Áed said, 'May I go with him?'

Oisín scratched his stubbled cheek, his eyes never wavering, never softening. At last he said, 'It is right to honour the fallen father of a brother. You have my leave for a twelve-day absence. You will take a carbad and return it to me with a promise.'

'What promise?' Áed asked.

'When you both return, you will promise to be my greatest warriors, whatever the cost.'

Áed shrugged. It seemed like such a mindless statement. He made the promise, and as he left the smithy to return to bed, he heard Néall saying, 'He's already one of your best, Oisín, and you know it.'

He had not the energy to listen out for Oisín's reply.

They set off at first light, Rónán keeping his face low against the blinding sunlight. He sat on the floor of the carbad, staring out at the road as it fell away behind them. In such a small vehicle, there was no room for privacy, but oftentimes Áed would disembark and walk alongside or behind it when the terrain was too rocky for speed, allowing Rónán some solitude. Their driver spoke only once each day, announcing time to make camp for the night. In the mornings, he merely packed up his blanket, doused the fire, and climbed into his spot on the carbad, waiting patiently for the boys to follow. They came unhurriedly, sluggish from a lack of sleep on the rocky ground.

As they ambled over a small hill and through the low wall that bordered the outer reaches of the lands of Dáirine on the eastern coast, Rónán stood and gripped the side wall of the carbad to stare at the many faces of the people who peered at them openly from doorways. The driver stopped in front of the chieftain's hall but did not dismount. A red-haired woman, well within her fiftieth year at Áed's reckoning, swallowed in deep red furs despite the summer warmth, came from the hall and stood before them, her arms outstretched in welcome.

'My poor child,' she said, addressing Rónán. 'A terrible misfortune has plunged our tribe into utter darkness. For days you could hear the keening of our womenfolk for leagues around. Embrace me so that I can take your troubles upon myself.'

Rónán stepped from the carbad and the woman enveloped him in her furs, wrapping him as a baby to her breast.

'A most unfortunate accident,' she said, her hair sweeping down to cover Rónán's head. She held him at arm's length then, crouching to see him better. 'You have grown so much these last few years, and yet you are still a poor suffering child, orphaned at such a young age. Come, the chieftain wishes to speak with you.'

She took his hand and led him into the darkness of the hall before them. Áed, for a moment, had thought to follow, but their driver placed a staying hand on his shoulder and shook his head. Áed knew some of what would be said within the great hall between the chieftain and his friend. With Rónán's mother dead in childbirth, and now his father dead, it was the chieftain's responsibility to raise the boy under his own standards.

There would be a blood pact and Rónán—despite his vehement dislike for their sept's leader—would be forced to call the old man Father. The whole sept would rally together to care for and protect the boy, but it was ultimately the chieftain's role to act in guardianship for the sake of the future of his people.

Áed sat under the shadow of a tree across from the chieftain's hall and waited. It wasn't long before Rónán came out of the darkness of the great hall, blinking momentarily in the bright sunlight, and then strode purposefully across the yards. Áed hurried to catch up with him. 'Where are we going?' he asked.

Rónán said nothing, walking fast until he approached a small home. He entered and Áed followed timidly.

Inside, a group of women sat vigil around the body of Rónán's father who had been laid in wake awaiting his funeral rites. The body was covered in furs, only his head and shoulders visible, his skin ashen and mottled, closed eyes almost sunken in their place. His hair had been neatly braided and his moustache trimmed.

'Father,' Rónán said. He went to his side and, from the corner by the door, Áed saw Rónán try to lift the furs but they would not move. Bodies were not usually covered like this, and when they were, the coverings were never tied.

'I want to see,' Rónán said, pulling at a knot that held the furs in place.

'Please,' one of the women said. 'There is no need to see the wounds.'

'I must see,' Rónán demanded. He picked further at the knots, despite the women's protestations, and soon had the covers removed.

Áed tried not to gasp in sickness. The man's body had been

crushed; from below his chest to his groin, it was as if someone had scooped out all the meat and bones from within and left the skin mostly intact. Along his sides, a couple of ribs had fractured through the flesh. There were tears in Rónán's eyes, but he did not sob.

'This cannot be an accident,' he said. 'Who was with him?'

None of the women answered.

Rónán looked at Áed, accusatory lines around his eyes. 'It cannot be an accident,' he repeated.

'Rónán,' Áed said. Rónán fled the home in tears.

When Áed finally caught up with him, at the top of a hill, west of the squat dwellings, Rónán was on his knees, weeping openly, his arms limp at his sides. Áed knelt in front of him and Rónán stared through him. A sob caught in his throat and he wiped tears from his cheeks. Áed put his arms around his friend and held him there for a few minutes, unmoving, barely breathing, until Rónán had quieted himself.

'He was fixing a wagon,' Rónán said to the unasked question. 'Down in the fields; down there,' he nodded in the direction of the accident. He pulled away from Áed, sat down and shouldered his running nose. 'He was crushed. Who does that? Who fixes a wagon by himself? He was already dead when they found him.'

Áed sat next to him, shoulder to shoulder, and said nothing.

They sat that way until a hulking man in his twenties approached, his tunic blood-stained from a day slaughtering sheep. He had the smell of sweat and copper about him. 'Father calls you for supper,' he said, spitting in the grass and sizing the boys up.

At supper in the chieftain's hall, Áed felt smaller than he had in a long time. Next to the muscular frames of the chieftain's boys, even the two boys that were a year or two younger than him, Áed was a grass-blade in comparison. Even Rónán was filling out in the chest faster than he was.

The table was laden with food, a sheep carcass crisp and browned in the middle, breads and eggs and berries, nuts and fruits, delicious amber gooseberries ripened and plucked at just the right time. Áed's chin was already sticky with their juices. Rónán ate little, picking here and there at some meat and bread, sullenly looking at nothing but his plate. Donal, the chieftain, hunched his shoulders towards the table and ate until he belched, then ate some more. No one spoke, the only sounds were those of slurping and chewing and spitting the occasional seed. On Donal's right, his first wife, the red-haired Muirgel who had greeted them as they arrived, picked carefully at some bread, dipping small chunks in meat-fats, and stared unflinchingly at Rónán.

Donal's other bride-wives were not present, for everyone knew Muirgel was the prize for sullen company. The rest of the table was filled with the chieftain's seven children. Faolán, the eldest and his only son with Muirgel, took his father's left-hand side. He looked harder in the face now than he had when he fetched them from the field a short time ago, though his hair was now tied back and the blood had been washed from his hands, his tunic replaced. The youngest boy, seated next to Áed, stole some prime meat from Áed's plate and Áed would have protested if not for the look he received from Faolán.

When Donal resolved that his belly was full, he sat back in his wooden chair and cleared his throat. Supper, apparently, was finished; food that was still in hand was placed back on

plates and chairs were pushed a notch back from the table signifying an end to their feasting.

'Your father,' the imposing man said, 'the finest fletcher in
all our lands, will be buried two nights hence under the light of
the stars so that the Otherworld will reveal itself most bright
for his entry. The Ó Brádaigh tribe's druid has already whispered directions to his soul, for we have no druid of our own
anymore.' He sucked grease from his fingers before continuing.
'The following morning, you will be blood-bound as my kin.'

Áed glanced at Rónán without turning his head. Blood pacts
generally followed seven days after the burial and, despite its
nature, was all but a public display of receipt into the chieftain's
family. There was no need to rush the ritual.

Rónán only nodded acceptance of Donal's words.

'You will return to Ailigh as my eighth son to continue your
training, and on your return, as a fierce warrior that I can be
proud of, you will have the pick of all our women—after my
other sons, of course—whereupon you will follow Faolán into
the life of a farmer and help protect my tribe as any proud father's son should.'

Muirgel leaned in close to her husband and whispered in his
ear. Donal nodded and said to Rónán, 'Your father's home will
be appropriated for fiscal matters and from now until your last
days you will always have a place to rest your warrior's head
under my thatching.'

Again, Rónán only nodded, although Áed could sense the
tensing in his jaw and his eyes.

'Now,' Donal said, turning to his youngest son. 'Let us hear
a song before I kick you all to bed.' Important matters had been
concluded and the chieftain would speak no more of it.

As they lay on the rush-covered floor in the bedroom section with two of the other boys, Áed knew Rónán was awake even as he pretended not to be. When he was convinced the chieftain's sons were asleep, Áed whispered, 'Rónán?' He said it twice before Rónán turned on his side to face him. 'I'm sorry,' Áed said.

Rónán lifted his head from the straw to shake it without making a rustling sound. 'Hush,' he said, his voice a murmur, his eyes darting to the two other sleeping forms in the room. 'There is nothing to say.' He looked into the darkness and, as if in response, they heard the titillated laughter of Muirgel or some other of Donal's wives coming from the far section. They would not be able to talk, Áed realised, until they were alone—perhaps not until they had left Dáirine behind them for good. And it would be for good; this he knew. He could see it in Rónán's face even in the darkness with the lanterns shuttered and the moon on the far side of the hall. Rónán, although he would bow to the chieftain in a couple of days and bind blood with him for all eternity, would never step foot willingly back in his home tribe. Duty-bound to his surrogate father, he could suffer to do his bidding when called upon, but he would never return to these eastern shores to take up the life his chieftain had ordained for him. Rónán was right; there was nothing to say. His face had already spoken it.

They spent the next two days in hushed vigil beside the body of Coileán Ó Conaill, the anchors to his ship before his time to venture boldly towards the Otherworld. The sept's womenfolk came and swept their hair on his face and the men placed coins upon the furs over his body. Once, Muirgel led a procession of the chieftain's wives through the room, each one standing behind Coileán, holding his shoulders and kissing his forehead before leaving again in silence.

As the sun turned the western ridges to gold and the moon was already visible, seven days after Coileán's passing, every member of the sept, as well as those from the tribe's other septs, gathered together and keened for him. He was measured with an aspen rod by the druid and seven men carried him to his resting place between two lines of his tribesmen holding candles and torches. He was laid in a mound with his perfectly crafted bow and his gleaming sword and enough food was left with him to see him through to the Otherworld. Gold was granted to him that he could pay his passage fee and the druid brought in from a neighbouring tribe, since Dáirine was without their own, burned heather in his hands and sang words that only the dead could understand. He knelt, touched his forehead to the ground in front of the mound, and said, 'Step lightly, sail fast, to the houses of the gods.'

The chieftain recited an elegy that touched and warmed the hearts of all present, and then he held Rónán's cheeks and kissed his head. Everyone in attendance lined up and did likewise and when Áed stood before his friend, seeing the emptiness in his eyes, he held his cheeks and kissed his head and then hugged him tight.

The two boys were the last to leave the tumulus, the others returning to the settlement to celebrate Coileán's passing with fire and feasting. They were alone, with or without the soul of Rónán's father, who may have already boarded his spectral ship heading west, and yet still it did not feel like the right time to talk openly.

'Your blood-binding is tomorrow?' Áed asked, though he knew the answer.

Rónán, staring at the mound before him, nodded once. The sun had already set and the soft glow from the moon turned Rónán's blond hair to white. 'The dead never return,' he whispered. Áed had to lean close just to hear him. 'The soul goes—where?—West? Says who? No one has ever been. Or no one has ever come back alive, at least.'

'Some do,' Áed said. 'Never in their own lifetime, but they come. I think a day in the Otherworld is like a hundred years for us.'

'Legends go and come back. And what are legends but old stories told by frail warriors at the ends of their lives? None of it is real.'

'All legends are true and false all at once,' Áed said, quoting Oisín.

'Lies,' Rónán spat. 'All legends are nothing more than half-truths at best. In battle, you could kill ten men and by the time news reaches your people, it'll have been a hundred men, a thousand. There are no such thing as legendary warriors; it is lies, all of it. We are born in this wasteland of grass and hills and we die in it. We tend sheep and we train and we fight fierce battles, and none of it means anything. We die and we are nothing more than rotting flesh in the ground, buried under stones that do not rot. Better to be a stone than a man.'

'The gods won't like what you say,' Áed said, his voice matching the quiet tones of Rónán's, not least because he hoped the gods weren't listening.

'What is a god but another legendary tale? Let the gods come and fight our wars for us if they are so attentive to our needs and our devotions. We make peace with them daily and where are they now?' His eyes shone with tears and anger. 'They are nowhere because they are nothing. No,' he said. 'Men become gods. In the minds of the people left behind, a man becomes a god. No gods exist without us.' He turned his face to the sky and shouted, 'Do you hear me? No god exists without me. We give you life and all you do is take life from us. What good are gods who do nothing but take our fathers?'

He fell to his knees and wept.

Áed crouched before him. 'The gods are real, and no one knows why they take from us what does not belong to them. Maybe they're lonely. Maybe they can't bear to see us happy. But do not say they are not real for I cannot bear to see you struck down and taken from me.'

'I cannot lie,' Rónán said. 'I feel what I feel.'

'Then don't lie,' Áed said, gripping Rónán's shoulders. 'Speak true as you see it. And when the gods come for you I will fight them myself and lose my soul in the wager. Believe what you need to, and my belief will cover us both.'

Rónán laughed. 'You? Fight the gods?' He playfully pushed Áed away from him. 'As thin as a twig and twice as dim; how could you take on the gods?'

'If the gods aren't real, then it's a fight I'm sure to win.'

Rónán stood, wiped his cheeks, and said, 'Come on. They're celebrating my father's life without us.'

The dawn was quick to come, bringing with it a new father. Áed stretched in the rushes on the floor and nudged Rónán with a foot. 'I can hear the druid already chanting outside,' he said.

They washed from the bowl that had been provided for them and dressed. Outside, tables had been erected and laden with food. Every celebration, be it a blood pact or a birth or a death, was an excuse for a feast. It surprised Áed that they were not all fat and slovenly.

The people were already gathering. Many remained from the other septs, most of whom had stayed for today's festivities and the chance at feasting again. Witnessing the burial of a man and the blood-binding of his son within a day of each other was not to be missed. News had travelled fast that Donal was not waiting the customary mourning period before the binding and it was assumed by all that this was due to Rónán's pledge to Ailigh; he was needed there for his training and delaying the new son of a chieftain was surely the easiest way to lose the forthcoming wars that were inevitable. The chieftain, they said, was wise in his haste. Áed, sitting cross-legged in the front row of the gathering crowd, could hear the men whisper that Donal's new son—with a few more years and his Ó Mordha training—could rival even Faolán as successor to the chieftain. But he noticed that they did not say these things anywhere near Donal's eldest son, or the fiery-tempered Muirgel.

While the funeral the night before had been a sombre, peaceful and reflective procession, each man contemplating his own mortality, each one thankful he was not the one being carried to his final resting place, a blood pact was a boisterous and cheerful affair. The druid called for hush among the crowd and announced the Day of Blood-binding of young Rónán, son of Coileán, child of Mordha, to the chieftain, Donal an tSaoir Ó Dáirine.

He placed a crown of gorse, no longer flowering this late in the summer, on Rónán's head. Most of its thorns had been stripped but Rónán scratched at his head all the same. A cheer erupted through the people as he turned to face them, standing at Donal's side outside the great hall.

The chieftain and his surrogate son clasped hands and the druid said, 'From death comes new life. From darkness comes the dawn.' He looked at the boy. 'An orphan through wretched circumstance, you, Rónán Coileán Ó Mordha, after this jubilant day, will henceforth enter into the house of your chieftain as Rónán Coileán Ó Mordha Dáirine, never forgetting the life your father gave to you and always worshipping your new life as the son of your pleasing chief.' The people clapped their hands and the druid turned to Donal. 'As is customary, it is your right and your honour to request of your surrogate son a labour such as you desire so that he may prove his worth as your kin. What is it that you choose for him?'

Áed leaned forward. Blood-binding labours were often-times funny—kiss the bosom of every woman present; steal the hip-dagger of a willing man without getting caught—or small, practical necessities such as chopping a log for the evening's fire or bathing the chieftain's feet in honour of their new pact. Surely Donal, in all his cunning, would have Rónán perform some treacherous thievery that would embarrass his very senses.

Donal nodded slowly, as though he was thinking it over. 'I have a field left unploughed,' he said. 'It is a perfect labour for the son of a chieftain.'

A blood-binding labour was a labour only in name, a small act of obedience by the new son or daughter to prove their willingness to commit to the laws of their surrogate father. What Donal had requested of Rónán was a day's work; it was cruel and unheard of, but no one spoke.

'It is said,' the druid announced. 'Do you accept?' he asked

Rónán.

With a quick glance at the chieftain, Rónán nodded. 'I accept.'

A two-handed ard was tethered to a pair of oxen and the chieftain led the boy and the crowd to the field in question. While it was not the biggest field he owned, it was not the smallest either. A lot of the grass had already been cleared and the soil, in the heat of midsummer and from a lack of rain, would be hard and compacted. Rónán called and cooed the oxen into the field and, without a word, began to plough the ground.

Many of the people sat on the stone wall to watch—a boy, all of eleven, ploughing a field on his own. The chieftain had disappeared shortly after Rónán had started, and the druid tended to the fire in the sept's central enclosure. Áed stood on the wall and called encouraging words to his friend.

The sun baked the top of Rónán's head but at least the thorny gorse kept the hair from his eyes. He hollered and whistled at the oxen to drive them forward, his hands on each arm of the wooden ard, keeping it balanced and straight. Already, to his ankles, he was filthy as he followed behind the first ploughed line. The iron spike that drove through the earth broke and lifted the soil but did not turn it. After a full pass of the field, a farmer would shift and plough widthways to diamond-cut the land. Would Donal expect, Áed wondered, the double plough, or would a single pass suffice?

As if managing the ard as it scarred the soil, keeping it true, forcing it through the tougher patches, wasn't difficult enough, the crowd laughed the first time Rónán had to force the oxen to turn and travel back the way they had come. He left the ard and tugged on their lines, whistling and shouting. When that didn't work, he rushed behind them, thumping their rumps and clapping his hands. Eventually, they started to move again, and Rónán slipped in the cool under-soil before being able to catch the handles and direct his charges.

By the end of his third line, leaning further between the ard's handles, his voice cracking in dryness just as the soil was, his tunic was already splotched with the stickiness of sweat at his back and underarms. He paused only long enough to pull it off over his head and throw it to Áed, replacing the gorse crown and then calling at the oxen again and moving forward, his bare feet sinking further into the broken ground as if the sweat that clung to him had made him heavier. At times, he stopped, inspected his hands, and blew on them to cool their blistering redness.

When only a third of the field had been ploughed, many of the crowd had grown bored and wandered back to the central enclosure. The chieftain had returned with a stool and sat to watch. Áed continued to shout encouraging words.

On another pass near the chieftain, Rónán stumbled in the dirt and fell, punching the ground before him in anger as the oxen continued their way, the plough skittering up and over the soil. He struggled to his feet to catch the ard's handles and muttered quietly. Fat beads of sweat circled under his eyes and dripped from his hair to roll visibly down his back.

At length, there were only a few men watching—the chieftain, a few of his council members, and Áed. Someone within the village had begun to play a cruit, the sounds of vibrating strings coming lonely across the field. The sun had rolled higher in the sky and it was all Rónán could do to keep the sweat from stinging his eyes, wiping his face every few seconds. Even from this distance, Áed could see the raw blisters forming on his hands.

When he fell once more, Áed thought the labour was over. Rónán did not move as he lay on the ground. Áed ran to him.

'Bury me here,' Rónán said. 'The ground is cool underneath.'

'Get up,' Áed said. 'The chieftain doesn't look happy.'

'I will,' Rónán said. 'I'm getting up.' Yet he lay there.

As Áed reached out to help Rónán to his feet, the chieftain called for him to move away. 'The labour is not yours to attend to.'

Rónán raised his head. 'My legs sting and my back is twisted.' He lowered his voice and whispered, 'If he doesn't kill me, one day I will kill him.' And then he fought to raise himself onto his elbows, his knees, and used the plough to right himself. Standing, covered in mud, he took the handles, breathed heavily, and hoarsely called the oxen to work. He moved slower now, each step an effort, each shout and whistle enough to hurt his dried throat. Áed fetched a wineskin from the druid and brought it to Rónán, who drank as Áed held the skin aloft, unwilling or unable to stop moving his legs, one heavy foot after the other. A blister on his left hand had suppurated and leaked across his wrist.

He was gaunt and soaked and sunburnt when he had finished a full pass of the field. It was mid-afternoon, many hours of work had been bled into the soil, and as Rónán struggled to turn the oxen one more time, forcing them widthways across the field, the chieftain rose to his feet. 'Enough,' he said. 'I have deemed your labour complete.'

As the few remaining tribesmen clapped, Rónán fell to the

ground in exhaustion. Áed helped him back to the great hall and he was awarded time to bathe. When he came back out into the sunlight, he was clearly drained of all energy. The crowd regrouped for the final ceremonial act, the blood pact.

Rónán and the chieftain were directed by the druid to wash their hands in a bowl filled with fresh spring water. The druid took his alder-handled dagger and sliced a cut across their right palms. Rónán's gnarled and blistered hand cracked under the blade and his blood soothed and comforted the sores. 'Now bind yourselves as kin,' the druid said. When they locked their hands together, the druid said, 'It is committed.'

'Welcome to the family, my son,' Donal said, and slapped Rónán on the sunburnt back. 'Let us feast.'

Chapter 6

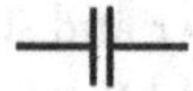

In the six nights it took Grainne, Odhran and the two druid initiates to arrive at the dwelling of the archdruid, Grainne had all but forgotten what her mother had smelled like. It was heather, perhaps, or maybe the musk of taproots. She missed her mother terribly, and her father and little Bec, and even Áed. After brief introductions with the archdruid and a number of his people, Grainne was escorted to a single-room hut made of stone with a log roof. There were no windows and the door sealed so perfectly behind her that it allowed for no light to penetrate its seams. In the room was one small wooden stool that had been pushed to a corner, and nothing else.

In the utter darkness, she had crawled to the corner of the room and pushed the chair into the middle, sitting on it to think. 'The first thing we require of you,' the archdruid had said, 'is that your mind be clean and at peace.' Although only seven years old, she had already understood the concept of serenity, and likened it to the quiet and solitude of the fields, with no one to speak to but the sheep, no thought but the warmth of the sun in her hair. 'When you close your eyes, there is darkness,' the archdruid had told her. 'But the darkness cannot be allowed to penetrate your mind. If you are strong of will, in even the darkest of places you will find light.'

When he had presented her with what he called the sensory confinement hut, she asked, 'How long will I be inside?'

'Until you can see sunlight in dimmest night,' he had answered.

Sitting alone in isolation, with no awareness of the passing of time save for the hunger pangs in her stomach that came in waves, she could feel the heaviness of the air around her, felt the darkness pressing against her skin as warm fingers. Dots of dancing light had crowded her vision for the first few minutes after the door had been closed but now, eyes open or shut, she was blind. After a while, the black didn't even feel like darkness any more so much as it felt like a nothingness, an absence of everything. Even the stool beneath her had begun to feel a part of her so that, if she had allowed herself to believe so, she could have been floating on an invisible cloud. There was no time, she thought, in either this life or the afterlife, where there was nothing; nothing could not exist, because there was always something. She pinched her arm to ground herself, to remember that she was in a windowless hut and not drifting in a dream. She rubbed her stomach and knew that evening meal had already been and gone. Were they going to feed her, or leave her here until she saw sunlight in darkness, unfed and thirsty?

She tried to imagine the sun and could sense its warmth on her face. But this was not what the archdruid had meant. He was an old man, stooped and thin, wearing brown robes that bore no difference from the other druids around him. The only thing that marked him apart from the rest of the men and women she had seen here were the wrinkles on his face. When he smiled—and he seemed to smile often—his eyes disappeared in folds of skin. There was nothing else to reveal the hierarchy of his office save for the silence that swallowed his movements and the low bows from his subjects. At home, the chieftain always wore the finest furs, the biggest torcs on his arms and head. When he passed a stranger they would say, 'This man is clearly the chieftain. He bears himself as a man of station.' But the archdruid had no such outward indication of his stature. In a village such as Grainne now found herself, the chieftain, the leader, was no more distinguished than his followers. How could he lead without separating himself from his people? How could he be above everyone if he looked just like them?

A druid conversed with the gods. How could he possibly present himself before the goddesses Áine or Ériu, or the incredible god Néit, wearing a brown robe with tattered sleeves? Did the gods not demand magnificent sacrifices and preeminent fealty, requiring the blood of new-born lambs and—when truly angered—a human sacrifice? And yet the archdruid, in the few moments she had spent in his company, exuded a quality of character that she had not come across before. Grainne, in truth, had been awed by him despite his humble appearances. The tears she had shed on her journey here, away from home, were unceasing with every step. The pain in her chest had grown more brilliant with each passing night. Odhran had reassured her that her path was a righteous one, held her hand and comforted her where he could, but every moment away from her mother's side drove an unbearable stave through her being. She had not felt at ease until she was presented to the archdruid and he had touched her cheek with a tenderness that made her think, now, in her darkness, that it had not been fingers that stroked her flushed skin but the silent wings of butterflies. And if a man could touch your face and make you think of butterflies, certainly he could kneel before the gods and they would not care what he wore.

Grainne lowered herself to the floor, her hands groping in front of her to make sure nothing was in the way, and knelt, touching her forehead to the cool ground. This was what druids sometimes did, although she had no idea if she was facing west, and she hoped the gods did not mind that she was not yet a mouthpiece for their words. Show me the light, she said to them in her mind. Show me the sunlight in the darkest night and I will do as you please for all eternity. In the silence that followed, she was not sure if she was expecting the sun to appear above her head, or willing it to do so. She sat back on the stool and felt dizzy from the sudden movement; how long she had been locked in isolation now, she did not know. Her stomach churned in want of food that it had not had in a day or a week or a year.

The only way she knew, in this profound darkness, that her eyes were closed, was the feeling of relaxation in her face. How much effort did it take, daily, to keep one's eyes open to see? And even then—the thought came to her—how much was seen and how much imagined? Her mother's hair was brown, her eyes a dusky green; but did she remember that from sight or from imagining? No. You see once, remember forever. Unless you expressly will it, you do not see something twice. You witness it and then you store it in your memory, and the second time it is seen, you barely even look but you know it is there. The same way she knew the ground was beneath her and the wooden roof was above—she saw, and now, in the absence of light, she simply knew. The world had an order to it and things did not change. Your mother's eyes were green and they never became blue or brown. The sky was always up, even if you stood on your hands and were facing down. Nothing changed except for people.

People change. Father, just a few months ago, was an iron-smith. Then he was a warrior, fighting foreigners for a purpose she could not understand. Áed, an equally short time ago, was just her brother. Then he was the provider until Father's return. Little Bec, so early in her life, was unchanged, still the baby sister until father returned and mother bore him another child. And then Bec's life would change also. And Grainne, never far from her mother's side, who wished now to be closer to her than ever, understood that for years, if not for a lifetime, she may never see her family again. She was changing also. Her tears had stopped the moment she stood before the smiling archdruid—although she was certain they had not dried up forever—and she had set foot on her journey to becoming a member of a people she knew little about. And that journey had only just begun, here in this blackened hut. Her travels from her family's sept, north towards the coast and the cool air and the dense forests, had been nothing more than a bridge from the old Grainne to the new. Life is not one journey, but many hundreds that make up the story of a woman's soul. You do not stand before the gods in all your spectral magnificence and recite the deeds of your life in one half-breath. Each decision you make, no matter how agonising, begins another journey that leads to another and another. And the gods, in their infinite wisdom, will listen until you finish recounting each journey of your life before they allow you into the Otherworld or make you wander the wilds until the crows fall from the skies. How cruel the gods are, insisting on hearing your misdeeds; how cruel humans are for performing them.

Grainne opened her eyes against the blackness and turned a quarter-circle in her seat. Perhaps this was west. Would the gods even care?

She did not know if she wanted to become a druid, to serve the gods and the people in matters of devout servitude and law and medicine. But the path had been chosen for her by her sept's druid who even now was on his way to the Otherworld to recite his journeys before the old gods. He had seen something of the earth and sky in her, he had said. It meant nothing to Grainne, only that it took her away from her family, and although she resented him for that course of action, she knew that without his intervention, she would not have met a man who touched her with butterflies. In her own god-story, that act would feature heavily.

She could hear nothing from outside the hut and, as she sat in quiet wait, she hummed a dirge that she had heard the druids chant at funerals. She could not remember the words, nor claim to understand them, but the tune was simple enough. Curling up on the floor for sleep, the vibrations in her throat from the humming soothed her and she rocked her shoulders back and forth, back and forth, until she was dreaming of floating towards the sun.

She woke with a start and rose to her knees. There was darkness still, darker perhaps than before, and if not for the touch of the wooden stool beside her, she could have been forgiven for thinking she was back home, awake in the dead of night, one small cry away from the comfort of her mother's arms. In that brief moment, she thought she could see stars in the black sky above her and hear the yapping of dogs in the yard. But the sight and sound were ripped from her instantly and she clamped her lips shut for fear of screaming. In the emptiness that encroached upon her thoughts, perhaps even her screams would be silent.

The pain in her stomach was a constant reminder that she had not eaten since before arriving at the druids' settlement. She, Odhran, and the young initiates who had travelled with them, had breakfasted on cured meats and hardened bread by a slow-running burn, swatting flies that circled around them. Whether that was this morning or a week ago she could not be certain.

She stood, found a wall by touch alone, and placed her back against it, stretching her arms out and taking small, tentative steps forward until her fingers found the opposite wall. Then she inched towards a corner, faced it and inhaled the thick dampness of the stones. She turned again and walked the length of the wall, her hand never leaving the cold stonework. It was nine steps long. Its adjacent wall was seven steps. If the hut was used for anything beyond punitive isolation, she could not begin to imagine what.

'Until you see sunlight in dimmest night,' she said aloud and her voice startled her with its gravel. 'How am I expected to see anything when I'm blindfolded by the dark?'

She lay down on the ground again and rubbed her stomach. Sleep was long in coming, but when she woke this time, the hunger pains were cruel and unbearable. She retched and nothing came. Her head swam and she clenched her eyes against the ache. She tried to moisten her cracked lips with a desiccated tongue but there was just a stickiness on the inside of her cheeks. Now she was certain she could see swirling wisps of smoke or fog in front of her, following whichever way she turned her head. And there was a noise, behind the fog; something like a voice but not a voice.

She could feel a gummy sweat on her forehead and the back of her neck, knew her cheeks were flushed even as she touched them. Her stomach cramped and she retched again, rocking herself on her knees, her toes digging into the cold dirt.

And then that noise again, and a word this time. 'Chide.'

She squinted in the complete darkness, peering through the fog.

'Chide.' But it wasn't *chide*, she decided. That word had no purpose in this blackened hut.

'Child?' she asked the dark. There was no reply. She lowered her head to the ground, knives in her stomach and her head and her back. Her breath was shallow and fast, puffing her cheeks each time. If she could wring the stones of their dampness, she would drink it.

A scuffling beside her. A voice. 'Child.'

She looked up and could see, clearly, plain as midday, a woman, her long black hair only partially covering her nakedness. The woman—no, not a woman; a goddess—had alabaster skin that glowed blue-white and was devoid of all blemish. Even her toenails, Grainne could see, were pristine and blushing.

A name came to her at once, though it had not been spoken. She recognised the woman as Cáer, goddess-daughter of Ethal Anbuail, dream-walker and wearer of a swan's skin. Cáer smiled at Grainne's unspoken acknowledgement of her.

'Child,' she said again, although she shone too bright to notice if her lips were moving. She stooped and cupped Grainne's chin in her warm fingers, the heat radiating through the girl's body. Her hair crackled at the back of her head.

'You come in dreams,' Grainne said. 'Am I asleep?'

'We are both daughters of life.' Grainne did not understand the statement. Cáer continued, 'You are a child of the soil and the air. Knowledge resides within you.'

'You are naked,' Grainne pointed out.

Cáer's smile was resolute. 'I am only all that I am.'

'Am I to worship you above all others?'

'Worship what you are.'

Grainne wanted to move, to rest her back from the awkward position she found herself in, but she did not want Cáer's fingers to stop touching her chin. 'I am just a girl.'

A laugh, tinkling and quiet.

Grainne looked into Cáer's amber eyes and saw all the stars and all the peoples and every blade of grass within them. She saw mountains form and rivers dry, and could feel the tenderness with which Cáer held dear all that the gods had given to the world. And she saw pain and misery; war was the truth, the ways of an uneasy people. War was an inevitability and her purpose, if she could deem herself worthy of a purpose in the sight of such a woman, was to embrace it as all children will. She could hear angry waves on a cliff-face, though she was in a dense forest in a sealed hut. She could even feel them splash upon her face.

'Daughter,' Cáer said. 'Sister of might.' She gave no further comment.

'Are you the reason I am here?' Grainne asked. 'Are you the sunlight in the dimmest night?'

Cáer laughed again, but not a reproaching laugh. There was

warmth in it. 'No, child. You are.'

She breathed on her and Grainne lay down, closed her eyes, curled herself tight, knees to her chest and heels against her buttocks, arms locked around her legs. 'I am just a girl,' she said again, but Cáer did not answer. The goddess was no longer there.

When the door of the hut finally opened and bright daylight fell upon her like a fishing net, trapping her to the ground, the archdruid came to her, knelt, and said, 'What is the sunlight in the dimmest night?'

Grainne's arid voice was nothing more than a whisper. 'I am,' she said.

Weak and stooped and old as he was, he picked her up in his arms and carried her from the hut. 'Rest now and eat,' he said. 'We have much work to do.'

In the three years since that day, in all her studies with the druids, the image of Cáer never left her, though she had not seen her again. In her first few months with the druids, she would lie on her pallet at night and close her eyes and hope for utter darkness and for the warming touch of radiant fingers. She would beg to all the gods to have one more momentary glimpse of the black-haired, amber-eyed goddess, but they were unhearing or uncaring of her pleas. She could not even find the sensory isolation hut again and she had tried many times. The druids' village was a complex jumble of dwellings and meeting-huts and stores, lacking order, grown organically over the years or centuries since the first druids made camp here. Beyond it, the forest encompassed them on all sides and she dared not venture too far from the village for fear of losing her senses and her mind in the heady green smells of early spring. Perhaps the sensory hut had been demolished. Perhaps its sole purpose had been for her, although she vilified her craving to be so important. She was, after all, just a girl—one of many.

As the months fell away behind her, she at times considered the prospect that her meeting with the goddess Cáer had been imagined, that it had been the grand delusions of delirium. But that could not be the case. When gods or their mothers spoke to you, there was a truth to it that could not be denied. Madmen talk to swine and the swine squeal in response. Druids—even a young girl fresh to the path—spoke to swine and the gods parted their lips with wise discourse. Cáer's brief but powerful apparition had been tangible. Had she not felt the touch of her fingers on her face?

Grainne's thoughts kept returning to Cáer's words, that she was the sunlight in dimmest night. Despite being a remarkable sentiment, that anyone could bring brightness to the dark, how could Grainne begin to do so? She was not the one who walked between worlds, was not the one who touched faces with butterflies. Right now, she could not even identify which leaf before her was comfrey and which was burdock. The druids held the knowledge of all the plants and flowers, and in studying them she was preparing for the life of a healing touch. In time, she would return to her village, or to another, and would administer to the sick with this root or that one, to heal bones or to stop the unwarranted excesses of a woman's flow. She would rule over disputes and oversee ceremonies of joy. She would guide the spirits of the deceased towards the Otherworld and she would preside over handfastings and bring blessings upon the happy couple. Hers was to be a life of servitude—to the gods, yes, but also to man and to nature.

If only she could remember the uses of dandelion beyond making a tasty drink.

Herbalism was her weakest subject. In matters of the gods, she could recite them all—names, tribal associations, the crafts and seasons that each were identified with. Equally, her knowledge of the laws that governed her people was as full as it could be. She knew how much a misdeed would cost the wrongdoer, when it was appropriate for the sacrifice of a man who murdered another without warrant—a practice with which she held reservation despite knowing how much it appeased the gods. And yet, when you remove the flower and the stem of a plant, one taproot looked much like another.

In bed, Grainne lay on her stomach, her face buried in the cloth of her pillow, holding her breath and praying to all the gods and all the ancestors of Éirinn that they would want to reveal to her the ways of the earth—and perhaps, if they so desired, they might show to her the image of Cáer one more time. Once more wasn't being covetous; once more would prove to her that she hadn't been delirious. In her dreams that night she stood above the flames of a tempestuous fire that swept through a nameless village, and she touched the hand of a white-haired boy but was unable to save him before he was engulfed by the fires and died with his strangely-coloured eyes wide open, staring at her in endless plea.

In the morning, she washed the dried sweat from her limbs, scrubbing hard against the depiction of that young boy that charred the darkest depths of her mind, a face she would never forget. She told her instructor of the dream after a breakfast of breads and honey, spoke of every flame as a shard that pinned her heart, of the feel of the boy's fingers in her hand before he slipped from her, of the cold look in his purple eyes that sparkled with accusation. She could count, she remembered, every one of his white eyelashes as though she were still staring at him even now.

At first, the instructor said nothing, turning from Grainne and busying herself with preparations for a class on the seasons of the gods and the turning of the world towards its eventual dusk. Then, her voice soft and hesitant, she asked, 'What was the boy's name?'

Grainne looked away in disgust. 'Was it not enough,' she asked, 'that I should remember every detail of his strange face? You want me to know also his name?'

The instructor, a woman long into her fifties, the slightest silvering at her temples exaggerated by the leather strap that pulled her hair back from her usually gentle face, finished what she was doing, excused herself, and left hurriedly.

And, as Grainne set about her day, those purple eyes looked over everything she did, staring, unblinking, with an abhorrence she could not get away from. She had asked for Cáer and was given a death-stare as her penance for being so forthright.

As was only fitting.

Chapter 7

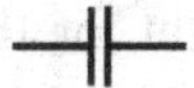

The unbearable heat of the smithy hung around him in a dense smog and he blinked sweat from his eyes. Áed wiped the blackened scale from his hands on the leather apron he wore and ran his upper arm across his forehead, smearing the grime of a day's work into his skin. The bellows had been pumped and the blade he was fashioning from bronze was glowing in the coals. He took it from the hot pit and struck the flat of the blade with a forge hammer, shaping the blade so that the edges were sharp while the run of the blade itself held enough weight to balance with perfection. When the blade was formed, he would shape the cross guard, and score his pattern into the flat of the sword, marking it forever as an Áed Branath weapon. Much like Rónán's fletching, forging was more than a work form, it was an art, and the charm of a sword well-made is in the embellishments of its artist. In the last two years, since returning from Rónán's village when his father was buried, Áed had dedicated his time between practicing with a sword and making them. As his physique matured—his muscles hardening, his features lengthening, the ravages of adolescence thrusting his body into the grotesquery of adulthood—so too did his engraving skills develop. Across the breadth of Ailigh, everyone could recognise an Áed Branath sword by the swirled knot that formed from a stag's antlers, below which was engraved along the length of the blade—always the same—the runes that illustrated his mantra: *Into the West the battle ends*.

Hammering the blade with precise movements, he turned it, beat it, moved it, smacked it, and drove it back into the heat of the pit. With Néall absent for the day and the bellows boy sleeping off a gluttony of wine the night before, Áed pumped the bellows himself until the coals glowed white. A smith could only struggle when working alone, and this blade needed more attention than his others; this one was a gift for the overking. Oisín had tasked him with the forging of a king's sword and he had three days to complete it before its presentation to the man who ruled their every move.

Bellow-work was laborious but necessary. As a child, he would sit for hours beside his father's pit, pumping air into the coals until his arms ached. It was a smith's rite of passage, his initiation into the field. The progression from bellows boy to striker to apprentice smith was an indispensable ethic. One begot the other in knowledge. Being a striker was as close to being a true smith as any child could deem to be. Before his father allowed him to work with bronze, Áed had spent many long months striking metals that had no importance other than to his study. Airic would hold the bronze with one hand and point with the other, and if Áed's strike of the metal with the forge hammer was misplaced, he would get a slap to the arm in reprimand, and each successive miss-strike came with a heavier smack. A striker learned to judge his aim in his early days or he would lose his apprenticeship, even if that apprenticeship was to his own father. Men did not pander to their boys as the women did; you either worked correctly and efficiently, or you were beaten for your failed attempts. Áed himself had many welts on his back and arms in those first days as a striker, and again when he came under the direction of Ailigh's own smith, Néall, who was just as hard on him as his father had been.

Áed pulled the blade from the coals and beat it again, his strikes accurate, his handling precise. Despite working alone, it would be the finest sword he had forged. He had the shape and feel and style of it in his head long before he had lit the coals; a true smith looks at his raw ore and sees the end product before smelting begins. Being a smith was part exertion, part intuition. He was a druid of metals.

As he struck the bronze, twice, three times, then rebounding off the stone anvil to strike again, he heard a shuffling from the doorway and paused in his work. Rónán was watching him, leaning against the doorpost, eating a green apple and grinning.

'What?'

'Nothing.'

Áed returned to his striking. He had often found Rónán watching him, not just in the smithy but on the practice field and at dinner. Since turning fourteen, Rónán had grown taller than most and he towered now half a head more than Áed. His wheat-coloured hair that had not darkened with age curled at its ends and fell around his shoulders and face in a veil that often covered his eyes. Below his tunic, his thighs were thick, the legs of a runner, and his feet—always muddy—were an adult's feet on a body that was struggling to adjust to its height.

He would speak when he was ready and, until then, Áed beat the bronze and kept only in mind the final design of his king's sword. Part exertion, part intuition—and a whole lot of concentration.

He could hear the crunch of Rónán's apple between his strikes, enough that it interrupted his workflow. But in this game of deducing his friend's intentions, Áed was too preoccupied with the prized sword to allow it much consideration.

'Is there something you need?' he asked.

'How long are you going to be?'

'I have three days to make the greatest sword ever imagined. If I don't get this finished in time, Oisín will gouge the insides of my stomach out with his bare hands.'

'So...?'

'So I'll be finished in three days.'

'You'll have to stop at some point; you're beginning to smell foul.'

Áed lifted his hammer arm and sniffed his armpit, then resumed his beating. 'I don't have time to bathe. If Oisín—'

Rónán laughed. 'Sword. Three days. Stomach contents. I understand.' He came further into the room, watching Áed at work.

'Don't get too close,' Áed said. 'Someone told me I smell a bit.'

'What foolish man said such a thing? I'll rip his balls off for you.'

'If you're going to stand there, at least make yourself useful and pump those bellows.'

Rónán squatted on the ground and began to pump air into the coals. 'Like this?'

'Not so fast; you want to fan it, not blow it out. How come you aren't fletching, anyway?'

'The whole of Ailigh has stopped for mealtime. Everyone

except you.'

Áed plunged the flattened bronze into the coals and mimed the spilling of his intestines from his stomach. 'I have no time to eat.'

Rónán nodded, looked back at the coals. 'I can bring you some curds if you want, but I'm not feeding it to you while you work. You won't be on the practice fields this afternoon, then?'

'Oisín has encouraged me to train later than the others so that I can spend my days trapped in the smithy making a sword for a man who has said all of three words to me since we arrived a million years ago.'

'I'm sure he'll say thanks this time. And that'll be four words more than he's said to most of us here.'

'He commended you on your bow work last Beltaine.'

Rónán shrugged. 'He'd have been lying if he didn't.'

Áed pulled the blade from the coals and drew it quickly to the anvil, picking up his forge hammer in the same action. 'Strange that no one has ever commended you for your modesty, though.'

'What is modesty but a man too afraid to tell the world how astonishing he is.'

Beating the metal before him, Áed said, 'I have Oisín breathing down my neck already, I don't need you quoting his words to me, too.'

Rónán left, laughing as he went. Despite the interruption, Áed valued their precious time together. Since returning from Rónán's village and commencing his promise to Oisín to be one of his best warriors, a true elite of the Ó Mordha, Áed and Rónán had only transient moments together at meal times and on the practice fields between bouts with sparring partners and exercise regimes. In the last two years, they had grown closer by being apart for longer periods of time, although never a day went by without their night time ritual of conversation before bed, often keeping them awake for hours after dark to the shushing of the other boys.

Áed returned to his bronze and, pleased with the shape and feel of it, set about sculpting the edges into a gleaming blade that would slice through a human torso as easily as it would a blade of grass. The sharpening process was not to be hurried. With an oilstone, his strokes were slow and calculated. In matters of smithing, he understood the process of blade-care more than he did the notion of feelings. You knew what a blade wanted from you as much as you knew what you wanted from it. A man, on the other hand, could lie as easily as blink, and his intentions were not always as he stated.

He put aside his thoughts and laboured until dark, sharpening the blade and engraving it with his markings. Tomorrow, he would form the hilt and cross guard, and on the last day before presenting it to his king, he would fashion its scabbard. As the sun set and he placed the bronze workmanship on a pair of hooks that held it away from the wall, the metal gleamed with an etherealness that put him in mind of the legends that accompanied his overking. It would be the finest sword in all the lands.

He went straight to the practice field rather than begging food from the cooks who, this late in the evening, were probably drinking wine and discussing the best cuts of a pig, or whatever cooks talked about when they weren't stirring pots and turning spits. The field was empty, but the distinct smell of sweat and blood from years of use hounded his senses. Not a boy in Ailigh had gone more than a few days on the field without sustaining a cut, a bloody nose, or a black eye and broken bone. Áed's own left knee had taken a particularly nasty kick from one of the boys he was training with a week ago and it was only now beginning to feel normal and pain-free again.

He sparred against his lengthening shadow, jumped and rolled and flexed, warming his muscles and preparing his mind before drawing his sword and cutting slices through the air. The first thing he learned about fighting was that you did not simply jab and stab and hope for the best. There should be a dedicated plan to every single movement, each stroke and parry an answer to the last. He cut forward and bounced back. Perhaps he did not look graceful in his actions, but it was certainly elegant in his mind. He twisted, spun the blade, the hilt turning in his hand so that the blade was pointing to the rear, and he pushed back with his shoulder, stabbing at an imaginary foe behind him. There was no pause; he turned, pulled the sword back, swung wide and hard, slashed and stabbed again. He could hear the clash of two swords in his head, could feel the tear of flesh as he lunged and jabbed. He ducked, weaved, rolled on the grass and returned to his feet in one swift move, the sword always moving, always cutting, even as his back was on the ground. He trained that way until the sun had finally dropped behind the mountains, and then he picked up his shield and continued parrying with his imagination, using both the sword and the shield as weapons, pushing forward with the leather-clad shield as much as it was used for protection.

With each jab forward, he moved further across the field until he had reached the hanging bags. They were sacks filled with grain and suspended from tree branches, a series of eleven of them, dotted throughout the small copse of trees on the valley's edge. He had hung them there himself, but others, seeing him practice, now also used the training sacks. When a boy was done, he would fill new sacks and hang them for the next boy, taking the spent and torn sacks with him for mending, an unspoken rule that each boy honoured. You did not walk away from the practice fields without leaving it as you found it.

Áed pushed the first sack away with his shield, swung with his sword as the hanging bag returned to him, and spilled its contents at the tree's roots. He turned, hunkered down, and thrust upwards at the next bag, jumping out of the way as its blood, its grain, leaked from its weight. He rolled, stood, jumped and sliced a third sack while simultaneously knocking the fourth with his shield before spinning and taking it out with his blade. At the eleventh sack, the highest mounted bag among them, he came to a knee, dropped his sword, pulled his dagger from his waist and thrust it forward, springing back to his feet, leaping into the air, grabbing the dagger's hilt and tearing it down with him as he returned to the ground. The grain fell around him as he knelt, panting from his exertion.

He got up and ran, taking his shield and sword with him. A swordsman needed not only to be good with his hands, but he also had to be fast. Unlike a sack of grain, an enemy would not stand still for long, not until you cut him down. He bordered the whole perimeter of the main practice field, running as fast as he could, powering through the burning in his thighs, and when he had run between the hanging bags twice, he stopped, released his weapon and his shield, and fell into a series of push-ups to strengthen his upper body.

He would rise before dawn to repeat the regime, but for now

he took the torn sacks from their trees and carried them back to Ailigh. In the slim chance that another boy had planned to practice during the night, he filled eleven fresh sacks with grain and carried them three at a time back to the trees. Even when exhausted, each boy was expected to do his duty.

The candles had already been extinguished by the time he went back to his shared bedroom and he knitted his way blindly through the beds towards his own.

'About time you gave up for the night,' Rónán said in hushed tones.

Feeling his way in the dark, Áed plunged himself down on the straw mattress beside Rónán. 'Thought you'd be asleep by now.'

'And miss the friendly stench of your sweaty body?'

Áed laughed weakly. 'Do I really smell that bad?'

'Worse. How's the new sword coming along?'

'I'll get it finished in time. Hilt and scabbard, then a month's work of polishing the blade—all within two days.'

Rónán nudged him. 'It'll be fine.'

They lay shoulder to shoulder in silence for a time, until Áed twisted onto his side and said, 'What did you do today?'

'Killed an entire army of foreign invaders while you were locked away in the smithy.'

'Singlehandedly, I'm sure.'

'Naturally.'

They laughed. They hadn't made up battles and destruction since before Rónán's father had passed. It felt like their younger days again, slowly peeling away the layers of young adulthood that was pulling them in opposite directions. While Áed spent his days in the smithy, Rónán was raising his own chickens to use their feathers in his fletch-work. 'The breeding has to be right,' he had said, 'to get the right stock of feathers, light-weight but durable.' Their night time conversations, usually nothing more meaningful than jokes and tall tales, was one of the few times they had together that reminded them of their younger days when they had first arrived at Ailigh.

Even in the darkness, with the soft moonlight casting the faintest glow between them, Áed could see the soft downy hairs at Rónán's upper lip, the only outward appearance of his new manhood save for his recent increase in height. He had retained the youthful exuberance about his face and, where his fingers were long and thin, his nails were always childlike dirty.

'What are you going to say to the overking when you present him with the sword?'

'I have to speak to him?'

'You'll have to say something if he asks you a question. What if he asks you how your days have been?'

'I'll say the last time I saw sunlight was before I started forging that damn sword.'

'I'm fairly sure that will be when he takes up the sword and lops your head off.'

'If that means no more forging metals, I'll let him.' He scratched the back of his head and Rónán forced his arm back down.

'Maybe I should ask him to cut my head off; at least then I won't have to smell you.'

Áed tried to laugh but was too tired. 'I'll bathe in a minute,' he said. 'Just let me rest for a second.'

When he opened his eyes again, the sun was just beginning to brighten the sky outside the window. Rónán's arm was draped over his waist and he could feel a hardness pressing into his lower back. He turned and looked at Rónán's sleeping face, debating whether to wake him and point and laugh. He decided to leave him there asleep—nobody else deserved to be awake this early. Carefully raising Rónán's arm, he slipped off the mattress and went to bathe before heading for the smithy.

When Oisín called for him two nights later, at the beginning of the celebrations of the overking's birthday, just as the sun was dwindling and the fires were being lit, Áed wrapped the sword in a cloth and carried it to the dais that had been prepared for their king.

Déaglán had governed over the north for as far back as Áed could understand. Oisín was Déaglán's cousin and his tanist, his heir-presumptive, but there seemed many years left in the old man before he would die or otherwise relinquish his rights to the title.

A druid was officiating over the giving of wares to the king, a man much younger than any druid Áed had seen before, and it made him think of Grainne, made him wonder how different she was now, growing into a young woman and learning the truths of the dead and of the living. He supposed she already knew the way to Tír na nÓg.

The chieftains of their clans were also present and he recognised his own, though he had no time to speak with him yet. The guard presence around the outer parapet was doubled; with so many important *flaiths*—noble chiefs—in attendance, Déaglán and his people could not be too careful. Because of the security, and with so many strong warriors nearby, nobody felt uneasy.

When it came time for Áed to step forward and make his

presentation to the overking, he found he could not move for fear of what to say. Oisín gave him a forceful nudge and he stumbled forward a step before continuing the rest of the way of his own accord. He knelt at the foot of the dais, before his seated king, and held the wrapped parcel aloft. He dared not open his mouth.

'Speak, boy,' Déaglán said. 'What is it that you present to me?'

At this close range, Áed could see the wrinkles around Déaglán's eyes, the loose jowls and the silvering hair.

'It's a sword, my king.'

Déaglán flicked his fingers, indicating Áed to bring it closer. The king took it from him and unwrapped the cloth covering as Áed returned to kneel before the dais. He inspected the scabbard first, juggling the weight of it, and then drew the sword, stood, and thrust the tip towards Áed's neck.

'Is it sharp, boy?'

Áed tried not to swallow, the point of the blade pressing against but not cutting his skin. 'Very.'

Déaglán laughed. 'Very good.' He brought the sword back to his face, inspected its design, the symbols that marked its length. 'Into the West the battle ends,' he read aloud. 'What is its meaning?'

Áed kept his head lowered. 'All battles end in the West, in death,' he said. 'When you cut a man with this blade, he will make a speedy journey to the land of the dead.'

'It will be his glory to die at my hands,' Déaglán said. He raised the sword aloft. 'It is a fine weapon, worthy to be held in my hand.' The crowd cheered. 'You made this by your own vision?' he asked.

Áed nodded.

'Where's that old fool Néall?' Déaglán shouted, and Néall grunted from the crowd. 'Perhaps it's time you retire and give this boy your smithy.' When the laughter had died down, Déaglán returned his attention to the kneeling boy before him. 'I am not familiar with your name,' he said.

'There are so many of us,' Áed said, 'that I'm not familiar with everyone's names, either.' More laughter, before Áed hurriedly told him his name.

'Áed Branath of clan Ó Mordha, I shall not forget your name again. Now go and drink and feast and I may call on you for some fineries in the future.'

Áed scurried back into the crowd, confused and lost in the moment. Rónán stopped him as he moved through the people, wrapping an arm around his neck. 'Did he just say he'd ask you to make things for him? The overking actually wants your service?'

Áed looked blank. 'I don't know what he said; my heart was beating so fast I couldn't hear anything.'

Rónán laughed. 'Come,' he said. 'You need some wine.'

Later, when he had calmed down and drank some wine and ate his fill of meats, Áed wondered why he had been so distraught by the ordeal. He and his king—a man; just a man— had exchanged some words, he had bestowed upon him a gift of his own making, and he had walked away. His tongue had not been tied by fright when finally he had opened his mouth, and Déaglán had spoken to him as one man to another, not as a king to a dog. He had not been laughed at, except for his foolish comment about names, and no blood had been spilled, despite how close the blade's tip had come to his flesh. Rónán had inspected the area on his neck where Déaglán had pressed the sword and confirmed there was not a scratch to be seen.

'That's true swordsmanship,' he said. 'No one could thrust a sword the way he did and fail to sever a man's head, let alone manage not even to nick the skin.'

'I could,' Áed said.

Rónán laughed. 'You're good, I give you that, but you're not king-good.'

'One day.'

'I have no doubt. Come on, let's steal some wineskins and head to the lough like we used to.'

There were already boys on the shore, groups of youngsters who had grown bored with the festivities and came down to run and jump in the sand and water, or to drink their woes away. Another batch of boys had joined Ailigh last Imbolc.

This evening, Rónán chased a few of them away from the rocks on the shore's edge and he settled down on the largest basalt formation, looking, in the bright moonlight, like a pale spirit against the black rock.

They drank and they chatted, and it occurred to Áed to mention the funny incident in bed the other morning, when they had fallen asleep beside each other and Áed had woken to the press of Rónán's keenness against him. But it was less a funny story than it was an embarrassment for himself. Many of the boys took to each other's beds at night and it was an acceptable part of growing up. Oisín and the other men of Ailigh knew of its occurrence, and approved of it in principle, boys being boys, energy being spent, but as they aged, the taking of another boy should give way to the more mature notions of intercourse and marriage. Áed, for years now, had closed his ears to the sounds of rutting boys in their shared bedroom. He and Rónán had giggled at such things at first, too young to know of its meanings or too innocent to process them. But as they grew and understood more, Áed buried his longings in his workload and his training.

Rónán stood, drew his tunic over his head, and said, 'Race you to the other side.'

Áed looked out across the lough. 'I'll never make it to the other side,' he said. 'I've had too much wine.'

'Fine,' Rónán said, 'but we're still getting in the water.' He took off at a sprint across the sand, his legs flailing in the lough until he got thigh-deep and he dived within the blackness. Áed got to the shoreline before stripping off his tunic and diving into the water.

They stayed in the lough for some time, long after the other boys had left the shore, their wineskins discarded on the sand, their tunics flapping in the wind on the rocks.

'King Déaglán likes you, you know,' Rónán said as he rose to his feet in the lough, chest deep.

'Huh?'

'Everyone does.'

Áed shrugged. 'I'm a likeable person.'

Rónán splashed him. 'I see I'm not the only modest one.'

'You've taught me well.'

'Will you make me a sword?'

'What kind of sword?' Áed turned and swam back to the shoreline, sitting on the sand with the foamy waves touching his ankles, and waited for Rónán to follow.

When he did, Rónán said, 'A shortsword.' He stood on the shore and shook his body and his hair like a wet dog. 'And a dagger,' he added, 'for a belt that I'll never take off. One I can sleep with and swim with.'

'Who do you intend to kill in your sleep?'

Rónán sat beside him, his voice unnaturally quiet. 'We've been training for six years. Who trains for that long? Whatever they expect us to fight, it won't be easy. We need to be ready—always ready. Everyone should sleep with a blade. Just in case.'

'When my father came back from the war, he said the foreigners came from the east.'

'They could have been Fomorian,' Rónán said. 'Or worse.'

'What's worse than a Fomorian?'

'Two Fomorians?' he laughed. He leapt out at Áed and pinned him to the sand, their noses touching. 'Fomorians that come to eat your children and rut with your wife,' he said, his voice turning to the huskiness of a bard mid-tale.

Áed turned his head away, wrapped his arms around Rónán's back, and twisted, his legs whipping out and down, turning over so that Rónán was pinned and he was in charge. 'They can take my wife,' he said. 'And as for the children—I hear they're tasty.' He snapped his teeth playfully at Rónán's exposed neck and Rónán struggled back, writhing underneath Áed, their arms grappling each other. They rolled into the water's edge, laughing and fighting and their grappling hands turned to tickling. When they stopped rolling, Rónán was once again on top, his hands now caught around Áed's wrists, holding them down. Their faces were aligned and Áed could feel Rónán's panting breath on his eyelashes.

He struggled, pulled himself away, and got to his feet. He walked to his tunic and pulled it on, covering himself in decency. 'Anyway,' he said, not looking back, feeling the warmth of the blush that coloured his cheeks. 'Of course I'll make you a sword.'

'And a dagger,' Rónán said, his breath still laboured from their tumble.

'And a dagger,' Áed agreed. He walked back up the hill. 'Are you coming?'

Chapter 8

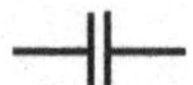

The women came two days after the Beltaine celebrations like an army of flesh descending upon Ailigh. Ranging in age from twelve to twenty, they were a gift from the gods—or from the chieftains—for the relief of their male solitude. They were road-weary and hungry when they rushed through the inner gate and into the hall where the boys had just settled down to eat. The younger ones, shy, reticent, remained by the door, their eyes downcast, wiry hair obscuring their faces, while the older girls hurried towards the stoves and cooking fires, eager for sustenance and oblivious to the stares of the boys around them. They gorged on mutton and breads and drank wine like fighting men before turning to face the boys.

King Déaglán, normally ensconced in his own quarters during mealtimes, entered from the kitchen dugout, greeted the girls warmly, and raised his hands for silence. In a sheath on his back was the sword that Áed had made for him.

'Word arrived to me some nights ago of this gift of happiness,' he said. 'I had hoped the girls would have been here for our celebrations but the wind was not on their side.' One boy in the crowd made a farting sound with the back of his hand against his mouth and there was an eruption of laughter.

'Tonight,' Déaglán continued, 'we reignite our celebrations and worship our magnificent gift from the gods themselves.' He winked at one of the girls. 'Tonight we will lap like dogs at the milk of womanhood.' The girl, a stocky twenty-year-old in a simple dress, bellowed a deep laughter and curtsied to her overking.

There was a wolf cry from one of the boys and Oisín slapped the flat of his sword against a table top. 'You can pant and cry like dogs later. I want fifteen laps of the outer rampart. Go.'

A groan swelled among them.

'Go!' Oisín shouted, and the boys shuffled out into the late afternoon sun.

'Rónán,' Oisín said. He indicated the boy should follow him instead of running laps outside.

Áed and Rónán shared a glance before Áed left with the others.

He had little interest in the arrival of the girls, although he knew it would shift the dynamic of the entire stronghold. Boys would no longer concentrate on their duties and tasks, and the noises and movements from beds at night would change. That Rónán would seek out one of the girls, he had no doubt. Perhaps he should do likewise, although there was nothing about any of these girls that beguiled him. He considered returning to the smithy after their exercise on the field, before the renewed feasting of food and flesh, and entrench himself in his work. He had set about his promise to Rónán to fashion a shortsword and a dagger for him. If King Déaglán's blade was remarkable, this new one would be forged as though by the gods themselves. The sword would be simple enough, practical for its purpose, weighted correctly and understated in its design, still with his mark on the blade. The dagger he could have much more fun with. It would be intricately carved, blending Áed's own mark with the symbol of Rónán's father's name, combining both in a knotted swirl. The blade would be short and thick and serrated. It could double as a hunting knife by day and the sharpest, death-giving dagger by night. Rónán had been right; in time, everybody would see the practicalities of wearing a dagger to sleep. If the battles finally did come—*when* they came—all men will sleep with a blade in his hand and an eye on the shadows.

As he was completing his sixth lap of the outer rampart, Rónán walked towards him, his head low, eyes boring a path into the grass before him. Ten paces behind him, a girl of perhaps twelve or thirteen shuffled in his wake.

'Looks like you've picked up a stray,' Áed smiled. The look that Rónán threw him was a dagger in itself; he had no need of a blade in his hand when he had eyes like that.

'She has been given to me.'

Áed stopped running, turned back to his friend. 'Oisín picked one for you?'

Rónán shook his head, stubbed his toes into the dirt. 'She is the daughter of Donal's sister,' he said. 'We are to be handfasted when she's of age.'

Áed laughed at the joke, but the sound caught in his throat when Rónán looked away in disgust. That Rónán's chieftain could arrange such a thing was in keeping with his duties as surrogate father, but the very idea was preposterous to Áed. Rónán was to be a warrior; he could pick his own bride. But immediately Áed could see Donal's reasoning behind the arrangement—if there was to be a mighty warrior in his family, he would cement his claim by deed or by claw.

'But—'

Áed had no other words. He looked from Rónán to the waif of a girl, and back to Rónán.

She stepped forward and said, in a tiny voice, 'it is my uncle's pleasure that I be the bride of the—'

'Quiet,' Rónán whispered.

The girl nodded.

Áed came closer. 'What is her name?'

Rónán shrugged.

'I am Achall,' she said, raising her chin in greeting as a man would, pinning a shank of thick blonde hair behind one ear.

'Ak-al?' Áed said, sounding the word in his mouth. He had never heard such a name. It sounded vile.

Rónán wiped his nose with his forearm and set off towards the lough in the valley below. Achall began to follow him but he yelled at her, 'Stay where you are. Leave me alone.'

The tone of his voice glued her dirty feet to the grass. She looked at Áed. 'Who are you?'

'I'm his friend,' Áed said. He turned, abandoning his exercise, and started down the hill in the direction Rónán had gone.

'I wouldn't do that,' Achall said. 'He told us to stay here.'

'He told you to stay here. Not me.'

'Nice to meet you,' she called after him. As he glanced over his shoulder, he saw her stooping to pick at the long grass. She would stay exactly where she was, just as Rónán had instructed. He hated her for that.

He caught up with Rónán on the shore. He was sitting on the dark sand, his knees tucked up to his chin like a sad child. He neither looked at Áed nor acknowledged his presence when he sat next to him.

'She's…pretty, I guess. Or she will be after she bathes.' Rónán did not respond. 'Your chieftain—'

'I will gut him from throat to groin,' Rónán said, his voice low both in pitch and in volume.

Áed had no reply to that. They sat together until the lough's cold waves touched their toes, and then they rose.

'I have a right to choose who I want to bed,' Rónán said. 'It is not for my fat, lazy chieftain to decide. I'm already his son; there is no need for this.'

'I'm sure they won't be here for long. Once the girls are gone, it won't matter.'

'Of course it matters,' Rónán said. 'Wherever she goes, whether she stays or leaves, she is betrothed to me against my will. What kind of benefit does Donal get from this? She can't bring wealth to the family if she is already a part of it.'

'I don't think that's his plan,' Áed said. 'If you're to become the great warrior I know you will be, your chieftain won't want your wealth leaving the family.'

Rónán turned from him, staring across the lough. 'Do you think my father was killed?'

'Murdered?'

'By Donal. Or Faolán. Or any other of his family.' He turned back to Áed. 'What riches will I have as a warrior—even a great one—that could warrant Donal's destruction of my family and the murder of my father? What just cause would he have?'

Áed shrugged. 'Warriors are worshipped. You will have prominence, an estate of your own. If what you say is true, with you as his son, would Donal have a right to your property? A right over your children?'

'I don't know.'

'I wish we had a permanent druid at Ailigh,' Áed said. 'He'd know the answers.'

'I'll quiz the girl,' Rónán said. 'What did she say her name was?'

'Something weird,' Áed said. They walked back up the hill.

Áed returned to his work, wondering how long the girls intended to stay. With Rónán's mind in turmoil, he would appreciate his new sword and dagger even more. He stoked the fires and set the billows. He was grateful for the family that he had. His own father would never have arranged such a farce. A marriage was usually for the good of a family or its sept, but the two parties involved were equally invested. Their handfasting was a period of adjustment and trial. If, at the end of the term, they were not agreeable, they could walk away without fault. What Donal appeared to be proposing was a forced handfasting and a regulated marriage. If it had not been the way of things, he might even have tried to skip the handfasting term altogether.

He turned his attention to Rónán's new sword. Already, its striking form was taking shape in his mind. A sleek and powerful weapon rivalled by none. He tied his leather apron on and set to work.

It was the sounds of revelry from the inner rampart that made him stop and look up. The sun had set and the smithy was lit only by the glowing embers of the fire in its pit. He doused his body in cool water to cleanse himself and remove the grit of a day's labour, changed his tunic and, somewhat reluctantly, he joined the other boys and men who were openly venerating the new arrivals. The girls were lapping at their unbridled attentions and in darkened corners of the roundhouse, shadows rutted together in beast-like arrangements. The faces of boys as young as ten glowed red not just from the light of the fires but from the attentions of these assembled courtesans. He knew he should feel the same wanton lust that he could see clearly, even in this half-light, in the other boys' eyes, but he did not. He dipped a cup in a vat of wine and drank greedily; if he had not the courage to speak to a girl, at least the wine may numb him to the ordeal.

He sought out Rónán and discovered him sitting at a table with his bride-to-be, her slight frame looking all too childlike next to his strengthening body. Achall whipped her head back in some odd semblance of laughter and her hair lifted, revealing a slender, soft neck. It was thin enough that one hand might be all that was required to extinguish her sorrowful life.

As Áed stepped his way over giggling and sweaty bodies to reach Rónán, the unmistakable face of King Déaglán came up from among the half-nakedness of three young women on the floor. 'You, boy. My cup is empty. I need wine.'

Áed fetched a cup for him and when he returned, Déaglán was sitting up, the girls intent on his words. 'This lad, he is a fine Ó Mordha boy,' he told them. 'If he can get as hard as the metals he so skilfully fashions, you'll be walking sideways from Beltaine to Samhain.' He licked the neck of a girl and pushed her towards Áed.

She giggled, touched Áed's strong chest. 'You can't be very old,' she said.

Áed turned. 'I need a drink.'

The girl followed him. She wasn't much taller than him, but her legs were long, her breasts under the fabric of her dress were large and round. He guessed her to be seventeen or eighteen years old. He found a seat and she draped herself against

his side, sharing his wine cup, holding it to his lips like a grand-
mother nursing a child. He took it from her, drank it all, considered how many more he needed to drink before the sickening heat of the room would leave him. She pulled him back onto
the seat when he rose to get another cupful.

'Don't you want to know my name?' she asked.

Áed shook his head and she giggled.

'You probably wouldn't remember my name, anyway. Once
we're gone, you'll all forget about us.'

'When?' he asked. 'When do you leave?'

'When we're told to.'

Déaglán was clearly enjoying himself; he would have no reason to send them away any time soon. And Oisín was nowhere
to be seen—perhaps buried under a mound of feminine flesh
in a corner, or preferring the intimacy of his own quarters with
one or more of the girls. In truth, it felt to Áed that he was the
only one present who had no desire for their company.

The girl put a hand high up on his thigh, buried her face in
his neck. Over her head, he caught the eye of Rónán. He tried
to wave, but the girl took his hand and slipped a finger into her
mouth. He could feel her teeth on the edges of his knuckle.

He pulled his hand away. 'Look,' he said. 'You seem nice.
But we don't have to do this.'

'Orlaith,' she said.

'What?'

'My name is Orlaith.'

'It's hot in here,' he said. 'I'm going to get some air.'

Orlaith giggled and trailed after him.

He walked faster, hoping her drunkenness would slow her
down, but it did not. Even as she stumbled in the grasses outside

Ailigh, she was surefooted enough to remain close. 'It's okay,' Áed called over his shoulder. 'You don't have to follow.'

'If my king tells me to do something, I must do it,' she said. 'Where are we going?'

She followed him down to the shore of the lough where he sat on the damp sand. The chirp of insects irritated his senses.

'Did your chieftain promise you as a bride to someone, too?' Áed asked her.

She stood ankle-deep in the water, the hem of her dress darkening. 'They gave us some herb,' she said, 'as the sun set. They gave us some herb to eat and—gods, do you ever feel so alive you might burst?' She began to sway, her hands touching herself.

'Rónán has been given a wife. Were you given to someone, too?'

'I can see every colour in the blackness. It makes me feel... alive.'

'Why would his chieftain do that? There's no reason for it.'

Orlaith untied the string at her neck and her dress fell around her, floating in the water at her ankles. 'Do you like what I have to offer?' she asked.

Áed looked at her. The whiteness of her skin in the moonlight only darkened the staining of her nipples, the shallow recess of her navel a shadowed hollow above a darker, more mysterious aerie. He turned his head. 'They're to be married once she's of age,' he said.

Orlaith stepped out over her dress and allowed the soft, undulating waves to carry it away. She came and stood before him. 'Am I not desirable?'

'I'm sorry,' he said.

'Stand up.'

He stood. When she reached for his tunic, he allowed her to lift it over his head. He could feel the cool evening wind against his naked body. He turned his head, his eyes scanning the dark horizon, unwilling to meet her gaze.

She was disappointed by her inspection. 'Why do I not arouse you? Are you damaged?' When he did not respond, she said, 'You have a man's body but the mind of a child.' She spat in his face and he did not wipe it away.

Orlaith turned to fetch her dress but it had been taken away into the darkness. She covered herself with her arms.

Áed stooped, picked up his tunic, and handed it to her.

'It's the wine,' she said, slapping his face. 'No man can perform after too much wine.'

'Yes,' he readily agreed. 'Too much wine. I'm sorry.'

'Too much wine,' she repeated, 'and a boy named Rónán.' She took the tunic and pulled it on.

He did not deny it.

Orlaith sat on the sand and pulled him down beside her. 'If I lie for you, what will you give me?'

'Lie for me?'

'"Oh, you should have seen how big he is,"' she crooned. '"It hurt to have so much inside me."'

Áed lowered his head in shame. This is what she had expected; this is what he should have been able to provide to her. 'Why would you do that?' he asked.

'Boys are all the same,' she said. 'They all want a quick shuffle in the dark—a moment, maybe two—and then they will brag about it to any other man stupid enough to listen. When you marry, you do it for how many cattle her father owns, not because you like the smell of her hair. You do it so that she can give you a son who will grow up to rut with one girl and wed another because her father has one more cow than my father. But you,' she said, 'there's something different about you.'

He looked at her, his legs crossed in the sand, his hands cupped over his groin.

'You'll marry one day,' she said. 'Because you'll have to. Because you'll be expected to. All boys must become a man eventually. But you know love, don't you? You already know what it feels like to offer your heart to someone.'

'I don't——'

She slapped his face, but not with malice. 'Hush. Don't offend me by speaking false. I may be drunk, but I'm not stupid.' She stood, pulled him to his feet. 'What will you offer me to tell every boy and every girl here that you're the dirtiest dog I've ever laid with?'

'You already have my clothes,' he said. 'What more can I give?'

'This,' she said, touching the stone of strength at his neck.

'No. My father gave it to me the day I was born. I will not take it off.' He remembered the voice of his mother, many lifetimes ago, secretly whispering to him the story of his birth, of how difficult her labour had been for her. Without this rune, perhaps his life would have succumbed. Perhaps it was the only thing that kept him alive.

Orlaith shrugged. 'Well, you could always hit skin with me while you think of Rónán.'

Áed took the runestone from his neck, his fingers struggling with a knot that had been tied fourteen years before so that she had to turn him around and help him. He tied it around her own neck.

She cupped his testicles. 'It does nothing for you?'

'Sorry,' he said.

'I had to try.' She turned and walked back up the hill just as a boy and girl were coming down. She stopped the girl, held her shoulders, and said, 'Don't bother your time with this little disgrace of a boy. That lad down there can make you stare into the faces of all the goddesses who ever walked these hills, just with his fingers.'

Áed cupped himself instinctively. Orlaith waved at him and ran the rest of the way back up to Ailigh.

When he returned to his room, many of the beds were occupied—including his own. Under the deerskins, a boy and girl were dampening his mattress with sweat. Rónán's pallet was empty. He lay on it, breathed in the scent of his friend, and fell asleep.

The dawn light brought the wine-snores of boys, and Áed woke with an erection. He cursed himself that it had not happened the night before. His neck felt naked with the absence of his runestone. When he could, he would string the stone of his tribe around his neck. Not since arriving at Ailigh had he looked at the stone his chieftain had given him. It was under his mattress with some other treasures.

Rónán had not come to bed, with or without Achall, and Áed rose, dressed, and went to bathe before eating. In the kitchens, he took some breads and a jar of honey to a table, sitting apart from the other boys. Rónán was nowhere. Attentive to his morning meal, the first indication that someone had approached was a shadow that fell across his bread. He looked up and Achall sat down. Áed scanned the room behind her, searching for Rónán.

'He's gone to bathe,' she said. 'We slept in the grasses last night.' She took some of his bread, dipped it in the jar of honey, and ate. 'He spoke of you last night.'

'I'm sorry,' he said. That she was only twelve and he, almost fully grown at fourteen, towered a full head above her even as they sat had not escaped his attention. Like he to Orlaith, Achall was a child to him.

'We'll be married when I'm old enough. You can come to the ceremony,' she said. 'You should do; as Ó Mordha, you're brothers, after all.'

'I will be glad to witness it,' he told her. 'I'm sure your uncle will make a fantastic feast. Do you see him often?'

'My uncle is an important man. I see him as much as any relative of a chieftain.'

'He must think you incredibly special to offer you to a man such as Rónán.'

'I am special,' she said.

He offered her some more bread and pushed the jar of honey towards her, leaning close. 'What did he tell you of Rónán before you came here?'

Dipping breads, she said, 'The Ó Mordha are making the greatest warriors of our time. Our future depends on Rónán— and the rest of you. To be his bride will be a great honour.'

Feigning indifference, Áed leaned back on his bench, pushing his meal away like he was full, picking at a battle-wound scab on his knuckles. 'When the war is won and Rónán returns to your sept—with you as his bride, of course—how will you live, with songs being sung about your husband?'

'The bards will sing about him?'

'Your uncle didn't tell you? All great warriors have songs made of their greatest deeds.'

'Then they shall sing about me, too,' she said.

'I have no doubt,' Áed told her. 'The wife of such a great hero will be loved by many. Your uncle will be so proud.'

'I like that.'

Áed nudged another piece of bread into her hands. 'What will your uncle do then? When you return.'

'What do you mean?'

'After the war that is still to come. When we win and Rónán takes you home as his wife. Surely your uncle has a plan for that, no?'

'I don't understand. We will have children and live well.'

'Your uncle didn't tell you what will happen then?'

'What do you mean?'

'Surely you know that warriors don't work the land like ordinary men. As a noble man, you will have to tend for him. If a field needs ploughing, you'll be the one to till it.'

'My uncle will provide for us, as is the law for a noble,' she said, but her eyes were searching his for truth.

'But a noble warrior,' he said, 'is much greater than a chieftain. Where will your uncle house you?'

'I'm not old enough to know everything yet,' she said. 'But my husband will be a great warrior and all the tribe will rally behind him and our chieftain will provide for us. Besides, if he's that good of a warrior, my uncle says, he could even be king one day and I'll rule beside him.'

'King?' Áed scoffed. He did not doubt Rónán's ability to rule, but now he knew his surrogate father's intent.

'And why not?' Achall asked. 'Great warriors are rewarded

with great things. When overking Déaglán is dead, why shouldn't my future husband take his place?'

Áed laughed. 'There is a succession already in place. Oisín is Déaglán's tanist; he will have the right to rule when that time comes.'

'And when Oisín dies?' she asked.

Áed had no answer. It was well known that Oisín had no heir. Without bestowing the role of tanist on another, the seat of overking was a battle for the taking.

Standing, walking away, Áed muttered to himself, 'Despite any plans from an arrogant chieftain, there'd be no better king than Rónán.'

Chapter 9

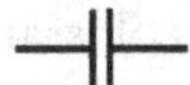

When Áed had left their home to go off to the north, Maebh was bereft. She had already lost her big sister to the druids and now she was alone. At night, between bouts of tears, she could hear the deep, sleep-riddled breathing of her parents and it was only half the sounds she was used to. Back then, she had not the words to express how alone she felt. 'My dear Bec,' her mother would croon, rocking her in her arms each night until she fell asleep. 'You are all I have left. Our family is broken and we are so alone.'

Her father, not long returned from war, was a stranger to his youngest child. He still called her Bec instead of her real name, still referred to how small and nimble she was, still ruffled her hair when she was near him and playfully punched her shoulder as any father might, but he had been gone so long at war that she did not remember him well. She knew of his existence, knew who he was supposed to be, but at such an age, she was developing so fast that he had not left an impression upon her. It took some time for her to become accustomed to his presence within their home. In truth, for a while, she saw him as a grown-up Áed. Áed was gone and this giant of a man stood in his place. When she sought comfort, she would turn to her mother and

Airic would leave them and hide in his smithy. He brought with him, when he first returned from war, new smells that she did not like—smouldering metals and the stench of adult labours. But in time, they became familiar and ordinary.

By midsummer she was no longer afraid of the giant who grumbled in the mornings and evenings and ate more than she could imagine possible. His colossal, ore-blackened hands were no longer a threat to her, and she was quick to squirm out of his way if she had been lying on the ground as he approached; he would not have trod on her deliberately but his feet were bigger than her face so that she did not want to be on the receiving end of an accidental kick.

As she aged, her diminutive stature remained, and so did her nickname. Only when her mother was angry at her did she hear anyone utter the name she had been given at birth. Maebh was, to Bec, another girl who did naughty things, and at times her mother had called her name three or four times before she realised and responded.

With the absence of siblings to play with, and the other children—those who had not followed Áed to the north—busy with their families' businesses, Bec had many long hours in which to endure her solitude. She was not made for the smithy with her father, and her grandfather had employed a new hand to tend his sheep. Bec would stand watch every year at lambing season, squealing with delight as each newborn animal bleated his awakening, but her grandfather was as distant to her as her own father had been. The old man was a quiet sort. When he spoke, it was perfunctory, clipped. He was always busy, no time for pleasantries, and so Bec learned to watch him from the treetops as he worked, but never approach.

Despite her size and slightness, she was quick and agile. Climbing trees was as easy—if not easier—to her than walking. She would sit on a high bough, watching the days slip away below her, until the bark had imprinted itself on the backs of her legs and the stars would wink at her even before the sun had fully fled. Her mother would call to her and she would drop lightly from the cover of thick leaves and startle blackbirds into flight. Bathing each night was a nuisance to be suffered, and when she was clean, she would eat swiftly and then scrabble around in the dirt again until her fingernails were black and her hair was clumped. She would go to sleep listening to the sounds of the sheep in the nearby fields, and the murmuring of young mothers as they sang to their newborn babies.

By the time she was six, she could no longer recall the faces of her siblings, although she asked her mother about them often. 'Grainne,' Doirean would say, 'is studying the earth and the sky so that others won't have to. And your brother Áed will one day lead an army against a fierce foe, and then he will return, victorious, and you can hug him as much as you want— but only when I'm finished hugging him myself.'

Their names were forever in her head, even if their faces were not.

The only relief to her solitude during the days was from the young druid, Odhran. He had been the one to lead Grainne to the archdruid for her training, before he himself had returned to the sept to act as justice, healer and peacekeeper on behalf of the chieftain. His open face always had a ready smile and the blue of his eyes were as the sparkling blue of a clear winter sky. Even as she celebrated Beltaine in her tenth year, she knew that she was in love with him—or at least the sound of his soft voice.

They would sit together often, discussing this herb or that penance, and when she was not dangling upside down from a tree bough, or rolling head over feet down the hills, she would sit in his doorway and watch him work, grinding taproots into powder or shaking the blackened shards of chicken bones into patterns on the floor.

'What do they say today?' she would ask.

'It will be a short winter.'

'What do the bones say this time, Odhran?'

'The sheep are plentiful but the lambs are not.' He was the only one, she could be certain, that had no desire to lie to her. 'Sometimes I don't really know what I'm doing,' he'd say. 'Or at least I doubt myself daily. But let's not tell the chieftain, eh?'

She coughed the truth from her mouth into her hands and slipped it under the sleeve of her dress to show that his secret was safe.

This morning, when she came to him, he was mixing a murky grey paste with an alder branch and spreading it on strips of brightly-dyed cloth. He smiled when she called to him from his open doorway. 'It's a bit pungent in here; you might want to stay outside until I'm finished.'

She draped her arms around a lazy dog's neck and waited patiently until Odhran came from inside, holding his bowl at arm's length. He dropped it on the ground and said, 'I'll clean it later,' and then he sat down on the ground beside her, un-afraid of lowering himself to a child's perspective, unlike most adults.

'Have you thrown the bones yet this morning?'

He nodded. 'The sun will fall from the sky tonight as it always does and, thankfully, it will climb back up again tomorrow.'

She giggled.

She asked him, as she always did, what Grainne would be doing today. Often, his words would float over her head—words like divination and recitation. But when he could see her face scrunch in question, he would explain himself more candidly.

'How do you communicate with the gods?' she once asked.

His smiled was one of amusement. 'With great difficulty.'

'And what do they say to you?'

'When they say anything at all, it usually makes little sense.'

'Why is that?'

'Their language is not like our language. The gods understand more than we do but sometimes forget how juvenile we are in our knowledge. It can take many years to decipher one strand of information from a god-dream or vision.'

As she helped him wash the bowl in which he had mixed his poultice, she asked, 'What is the greatest thing that Grainne will have learned so far?'

'Patience,' he said. 'When your father forges a sword or mends a broken tool, he knows he cannot just hammer at some iron a couple of times and have a finished item in his hands. When your grandfather's sheep mate, he knows a lamb will not be bleating at him in the morning. Everything takes time and being impatient won't speed its arrival. If Grainne is true to her training, she will know by now that patience is her most important ally.'

'No,' Bec said. 'What is the greatest thing she can *do*?'

Odhran laughed. 'That is the greatest thing she can do: remain patient. Without that, she will learn nothing else.'

A sharp cry could be heard from the far side of the sept, a

long, painful howl. They looked at each other and were quick to their feet. One of the old men, who had lost his son in the war six years ago and whose daughter-in-law had never remarried despite his protestations, had been pinned under the stone perimeter wall he had been mending alone. It had been reinforced with iron struts and, as the stones had tumbled, so too did one of the struts, piercing his shoulder and pinioning to the earth.

As the villagers gathered, they quickly palmed off some of the large stones, but his screams intensified and Odhran leaned close to inspect him. 'Every time you lift a stone, the balance of the iron strut is shifted. It sounds as though it's gouging through his skin with every movement.'

'What do we do?' they asked him.

The old man's torso, arms and head were hidden under the rubble, only his twitching legs visible. 'There's a narrow gap here,' Odhran said, 'but my arm is too thick to get through. If we can release the iron and quickly shift the stones, I can tend his wound before too much blood escapes.'

'I'll do it,' Bec said.

'You won't be strong enough.'

'You've seen me swing from trees one-handed. I can do it.'

Odhran nodded.

Doirean objected, trying to hold her only remaining child back from the fray. All the villagers had gathered around and the men were getting in position to lift the stones. 'They could collapse on her arm and trap them both.'

Odhran said, 'Airic, Sean, if you two can hold this stone in place—make sure it doesn't move—then the other rocks will stay where they are until Bec is clear.'

They moved into position and Bec looked at her mother. 'Let me. I can do this.'

Doirean released her grip and nodded.

As she got on her knees and nudged carefully towards the stones, the old man said through gritted teeth, 'It's in my shoulder. Be careful.'

Bec said, 'Just like removing a splinter. A very big splinter, but it's the same principle.' She slid her arm through the gap between the rocks, her fingers feeling forward with caution, touching the rough surface of basalt. When her fingertips felt the slick coolness of the old man's blood, she stopped, paused, took a breath, and moved her hand forward slowly. She touched the iron shaft, nudged it accidentally, and the old man took a sharp intake of air. 'Sorry,' she said. She raised her left arm over what was visible of his face. 'Bite my sleeve. Just don't puncture my skin, okay?'

'Get on with it, girl.'

'When I was six,' she said, 'I hurt my ankle. Do you remember? Of course you don't—what do you care about a little girl falling out of a tree?' She eased her fingers around the iron strut. 'Odhran patched me up with one of his foul-smelling poultices. Have you ever smelled those things? They're disgusting.' She gripped it. 'Couldn't walk for six days, but'— she tightened her hold—'as soon as I was back on my feet, do you know what I did when I could walk again?' She could feel the stickiness of his blood; it was oozing over her fingers. 'I climbed back up that same tree, that's what I did.' She looked up at her father. 'I fell again. I've probably fallen out of every tree in a league's distance.' She faced the old man. Her grip on the rod was tight, secure. 'I love climbing trees. But a little fall doesn't——' She tugged upwards. Her hand moved further than the slick rod, but it moved all the same. The old man sucked in a lungful of air, the rocks on his chest heaving. His eyes rolled in his head. 'Are you listening?' Bec asked.

'Shut the fuck up and get it out of me.'

'But a little fall,' she repeated, tightening her grip again, 'doesn't put me off. I keep climbing trees and I keep falling out of them. But one of these days, I'm going to reach the highest leaf of the highest bough.' She braced herself against the ground, preparing for the final assault. 'And I'm going to look out over the entire world and I'm going to see my brother and my sister——wherever they are——I'm going to see them from the top of that tree.'

She pulled. Under the weight of the rocks and the reluctance of the iron shaft to suck from the old man's shoulder, her hand didn't move far. But it was enough; the strut released itself from him and she could feel his thick, warm blood washing over her fingers. 'Now,' she said to her father. They pulled the rocks from his body as Odhran leaned close with his mystical pack of salts and herbs and brooklime-infused cloths.

Bec touched the old man's clammy face, lifted one of his eyelids and could see only the white of his eye. 'When you wake up,' she said, 'you're going to help me find the perfect tree to conquer.'

'Come away, my love,' Doirean said, taking Bec's shoulders. 'Let the men do what needs to be done.'

As they walked back to their home, Bec said, 'He's going to be okay.' She lifted her bloodied hand to her face, sniffed her wet fingers. 'I can smell it in his blood. Odhran told me when people die there's a reason for it. That man has no reason to die yet, does he, mother?'

'How can he die,' Doirean said, 'when he has to help you climb trees?'

That evening, full of herbs and wine, the old man came to Airic's home and asked to speak with the girl. Bec and her parents came outside where he remained, a slaughtered sheep on a pallet behind him. Bec could see the track marks in the ground where he had dragged it. His left wrist was tied up near his neck with the stem of a dock leaf and his shoulder had been swaddled and patched.

'I would speak with your daughter if you'll allow it,' he said to Airic.

Airic nodded.

'Child,' the old man said. 'You did a brave thing today. Braver than any girl I have ever known. I would offer you this sheep for food, but now that I see you, how small you are, it does not seem enough repayment for your deed. You saved and old man's life and I——two sheep; I should have brought two. Or ten.'

'Hush,' Airic said. 'There is no need.'

The old man shook his head. 'There is every need. My son he——well, you fought alongside him, Airic. You know what happened. My daughter-in-law feeds off my land and refuses to marry another; I do not know what to do with her. But if I had another son, I would offer him to your daughter that he could give her strong babies in time, that my family could become a part of yours and be duty-bound to you as much as I feel I already am.'

Bec stepped forward, touched the old man's hand. 'I am too young to marry and you have no other son. I am sorry about your only son and about your daughter-in-law who is lazy. And one sheep will be more than enough as thanks. I did only what any other person with thin arms and small hands would have done. I am glad you are feeling well.'

The old man came to his knees in front of her and hugged her tight. 'You have given me life,' he said. 'It is my honour and my duty to serve you.' His tears soaked her cheek just as his blood had soaked her fingers earlier. 'I am in your debt until the day I finally die. And at that time, I hope you smile for the life you extended to an old man who did not deserve to have his life extended in such a way.'

They ate meat for the next three days and in bed that night Bec cried herself to sleep. Not for the old man, whose son had perished in war, or whose daughter-in-law refused to marry again and ate the old man's food without care, but for all the hurt and pain in the world, a world undeserving of such cruelty. While her brother was in the north, training to fight to save their way of life, and her sister was deep in the study of the earth and the sky, Bec was a nobody in a nowhere village. She wished that she could pull the iron struts from everybody's shoulder and help, in some small way, to make the world a place worthy of their presence.

As Odhran had told her once: offer to others what you cannot afford and the earth will offer to you more than you need.

Chapter 10

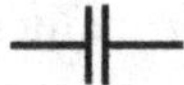

Since Achall's arrival twelve nights ago, she and Rónán had been forced to spend all their free time together to become acquainted. He sat with her at meals, walked with her in the evenings as the clouds came down to shroud them, and swam with her in the mornings before practice. What he did not do, Áed was relieved to know, was sleep with her. Each night, he offered up his bed for her and he slept on the floor between their two mattresses. Áed lay awake in the dark, staring down at the sleeping body, wondering if Rónán was staring back in the blackness, or staring at Achall; or simply asleep, unaware of the turmoil that Achall's presence was causing.

In the morning, as the girls were preparing to return to their septs to continue their normal lives until it was deemed they should return, the boys and men of Ailigh gathered to say their farewells. Work and training was postponed until after meals. King Déaglán was resplendent in his finest garb, his polished sword strapped to his back where, it seemed, it had remained since Áed have given it to him. He bowed low to every girl and gave them each a white stone. The boys laughed. When the girls studied their stones and looked at Déaglán for explana-tion, he winked at them and said, 'My boys understand. And that is enough. Until we see your fair faces again, you will be sorely missed. Especially you,' he said, slapping one of the girls on the rump.

The boys strode forward to the girls they had come to know, and kissed them and made promises of faithfulness until their return—not that any other girl would be present for the duration. Some girls cried at romances that would likely be forgotten by sundown, and some—the guiltless younger ones—stalked by the gate, eager to return to their mothers' arms, or perhaps to other boys they had left behind.

Áed lowered his gaze and accepted a kiss from a couple of girls who had conceivably mistaken him for another boy. Orlaith hugged him warmly, then cupped his genitals through his tunic. 'Still nothing?'

'I wish there was something there, Orlaith. I really do.'

She nodded, took something from her pouch and handed it to him, wrapping his fingers around it. When he opened his hand to look, he said, 'No. I gave you this to honour a promise. You should keep it.'

'It's a rune of strength.' She looked around, back up the hill at the inner rampart, out across the lough at the dewy fields beyond, at the sheep that were badly in need of their furs tending to. 'You need it more than I do.'

She helped him tie it around his neck where it belonged.

'Your friend is missing,' she said.

Áed looked across the sea of boys and girls. 'And so is Achall.'

'You should find him,' she said. 'Be well, Áed. The sun is on your side.'

'The sun is on your side,' he responded. She hugged him

again and slipped into the crowd of girls.

Áed walked around the rampart, moving like he had no-where to go, not willing to call Rónán's name, but searching all the same. He found them sitting together on the grass, halfway down the hill towards the lough. They were sitting close, but they were not touching. He did not want to stay and listen, but he was drawn to their conversation, remaining behind them out of sight. But when Achall broached the subject of their handfasting, Áed turned and left. He could not stand to hear any more.

He returned to the smithy. Néall was polishing a bronze shield in the back, singing a dirge to himself for the loss of the heat of a woman, and so Áed wrapped his apron on and filed the dagger he had fashioned for Rónán. Keeping busy these last days, training hard and working harder, he had managed to as-suage the discomfort he felt in his heart. The girls had become a normality, a constant presence that he had numbed himself to. He no longer flushed when one of them spoke to him, said he was promised to another when they made advances. Orlaith kept her pledge to him and nobody knew of his inability to per-form. In the evenings, for a brief while, she would wrap her body against his and smile and laugh at his words. No other girl would intervene when a boy was otherwise occupied. At length, each night, she would kiss his cheek, touch the warmth of his neck, and then seek comfort in another boy's bed. With their parting, Ailigh would look to its training to fill the void. In time, the girls would be forgotten and boys would again pair themselves off at night in a lapsed ritual of passionless heat, an involuntary action of relief in a malapropos custom. And Áed would lie in bed each evening with his eyes clenched shut and his hands to his ears against the sounds that he longed to understand.

Later, when the girls had gone and the wind no longer smelled of flowers, Áed sought out Rónán on the training field. 'You are going through with it, then?'

Rónán weighted an arrow in his hand, refused to look up. 'It is my father's bidding. I cannot refuse.'

'Surrogate father,' Áed said.

Rónán took another arrow, hefted it in his left hand against the one in his right. 'He is my father and my chieftain. It is my honour to please him.'

'And Achall—she wishes this, too?'

'It is good for the fortune of the tribe.'

Áed dropped a parcel at Rónán's feet; the sword and dagger inside made a dull clank. 'You should listen to yourself, Rónán. Where is the boy I knew?'

He turned and walked away as Rónán shouted after him. 'I haven't been a boy for a long time. None of us have.'

Áed took his sword to the hanging bags in the mouth of the woods and eviscerated them, one after the other. From one, he spilled a chieftain's guts; another, he tore limbs from. Each one, as it lay filleted on the mossy ground, its seeds slopped in all directions, was the cold remains of Donal, his wife Muirgel, and their giant of a son, Faolán.

He dug his sword into the ground, jumped to a low-hanging bough, and pulled himself up and down, strengthening his arms, feeling the burn as he breathed and lifted, lowered and raised. And then he sheathed his sword and ran. He ran to the lough, all of it downhill, before turning and sprinting back up, touching Ailigh's outer wall, and racing back to the shoreline below. He ran along the water's edge, this way and then that, the resistance of the water dragging his feet, exhausted, muscles fiery under his skin, his cheeks flushed and burning, vision blurring with heat. When his knees were as heavy as iron and his runestone itched the hollow of his neck with sweat, he dropped his sword from his back and ran into the chilly water. His tunic billowed around him as he got waist deep, and he dived in, hands outstretched before him, breaking the crash of the surface against his face. In the muddy fog of disturbed waters, he frogged his way across the lough to the distant shore, gripped the marshy rushes on the bank to steady himself, breathing hard, and then pushed himself away, back towards Ailigh.

On the sandy shore, Rónán watched him. In his hand he held the gleaming sword that Áed had made for him. 'You don't understand the ways of my tribe,' he said.

Still in the water, wiping his face, Áed said, 'What tribe? You are Ó Mordha.'

'In name I am Ó Mordha. In deed I must be my chieftain-father's son. She will be a good addition to the family.'

Áed came from the water and scrunched the edges of his tunic to release some waterlogging. 'She is your chieftain's sister's child. She's already a member of the family. You have changed, Rónán. I know you can see that.'

'Fight me.'

'What? No.'

Áed turned to walk away but Rónán pushed him, made him stumble. He raised his sword. 'Let me see what your handiwork is made of. Fight me.'

'I will not.'

Rónán flicked the point of his sword towards Áed's face. 'Fight me, boy.'

'Boy?' Áed was enraged.

'We walked through that gate six years ago as boys,' Rónán said. 'Everyone grows up except you. Know your place, Áed. Fight me.'

Áed leapt, lifted his sword from the sand, drew it from its sheath, and spun on his toes just in time to block an overhead blow. He dropped back on his heels, swung wide with his blade, a slow arc that Rónán was quick to block.

'You're pulling your blows.'

'I don't want to kill you.'

'What makes you think you'll kill me?' Rónán weaved, parried, ducked another swing.

'Why are you doing this?'

A thrust, their blades sliding the length of each other before they pulled apart.

'Because I'm not your little boy. I'm not your wilting bed-mate.'

'I never—'

'Stop pulling your blows like a child and fight me.'

Áed crouched, leaned to the side, swung tight and strong. Rónán leapt aside, double-handed his sword downwards to block the incoming thump. In anger, Áed barrelled forward, shouldered Rónán in the stomach, their swords and their bodies flying earthward. Pinning him to the ground, he tried to grip Rónán's wrists, restrain him. Rónán squirmed, twisted, grunted. He wrapped his hands around the back of Áed's neck, pulled, head-butted his nose.

He managed to coil a foot around Áed's leg and shift his

weight, rolling so that he was on top. He punched Áed's already bloodied face. 'We have to grow up,' he said. 'It's what we do. We grow up and we get married. It's how things are done.'

Áed flipped his arms in between Rónán's, forced them outwards. As Rónán's grip weakened and he slipped, Áed raised himself on one elbow, circled Rónán's neck with his other arm, and yanked hard, enough to cause an involuntary cough. 'You're wedding her because you're afraid.'

'Afraid? I'm the bravest man alive. It's you who are weak and afraid.'

'You wanted to kill him two weeks ago.'

'You're afraid to be a man.'

'You thought he killed your father.'

Rónán whipped an arm back, tugged at Áed's hair until he loosened his grip around his neck. Áed jabbed him in the side with his knuckles.

'A boy can't fight a war.'

'A man would know when to quit.' He managed to raise a knee from the ground, drove it into Rónán's back, gripped his shoulders and pulled.

'You're a scared little child.'

'Shut up. You're my friend.' He punched an elbow into Rónán's neck.

Rónán retorted, fist after fist. 'We're not friends.'

Áed kicked out, pushing Rónán's leg away. Rónán smacked his forehead into Áed's temple.

'You're my brother,' Áed said.

'You are nothing to me. I will never be your friend. We are done.'

Áed went limp against the side of Rónán's body as they lay on the shoreline. Rónán punched him again.

'Fight me.'

Áed buried his face in the sand.

Rónán slapped the back of his head. 'Why won't you fight me?' He twisted Áed's face towards him. 'You want me to kiss you,' he said. 'You want me to touch you.' He leaned his face closer, their noses touching. 'Go on then, kiss me. Kiss me.'

Áed squirmed out from under him and stood, retrieved his sword.

From the ground, Rónán said, 'Fight me, then.'

Áed walked away, his tunic and hair wet and rooted with sand, the point of his sword dragging limply behind him.

'I will never be your friend,' Rónán shouted. 'Do you hear me? Never.'

In bed that night, Áed lay with his hands behind his head, staring up at the candle-cast shadows on the thatching. It was long after dark when Rónán came in. He flopped on his bed, stomach down, then turned his back on Áed and drew his deer furs over his face despite the warmth.

In two weeks, they had not spoken a word to each other. At meals, they sat apart, they trained a field's distance away from one another, and at night they slept in neighbouring beds and feigned ignorance of each other. The pain of loss burned in Áed's chest. One morning he woke to find the sword and dagger he had fashioned for Rónán propped against the wall beside him. He placed them back on Rónán's bed and the following morning they were once again at his feet.

Áed returned them to their rightful owner's place, offering an understanding that, while they may no longer be friends, a gift was not to be returned. As the cock crowed the arrival of

dawn and Áed rose from his sleep, the sword and dagger were
nowhere to be seen.

Chapter 11

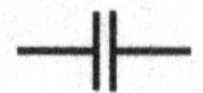

Grainne knew she was dreaming even as the fires fanned towards her. Always, they parted at her bare feet, burning around the rock she stood on, hemming her in at the rear before flaming its way along the hazel-rod trackway between the village's buildings. The young boy, whose white hair gleamed in the sunlight, whose purple eyes stared at her, whose pigment-free skin was ashen and pale and flushed all at once, was engulfed in the flames, his hands stretching out towards her in a silent plea.

And, as always, she reached for him, her fingers brushing his, missing, feeling the wisp of air as he slipped from her. She cried. Screamed. Even through the bright flames she could still see his wide eyes accusing her. He parted his pale lips, said a word that was swallowed by the flames, and he disappeared.

She woke, drenched in sweat, her eyes still searching for a little boy that was not there. She pummelled her straw mattress with balled fists. She knew she was dreaming and yet she could not save him. She had questioned her tutor, Emer, about the purpose of dreams, about their consequences, although she had not the daring to mention the detail. Dreams, Emer had told her, were often as not just a shadow of disturbance within your spirit, but occasionally they were the words of the gods put into pictures for the dreamer to understand.

'But what if they have no meaning?' she asked.

'If they are the words of the gods, they always have a meaning. That you don't at once understand them is your inability to converse with a power beyond your reckoning. It is not a master's duty to bark at a dog so that the dog understands the command, but rather a dog's duty to learn the words of his master and translate them for himself.'

'And how do you learn the language of the gods so that you can arrive at this understanding?'

Emer had laughed. 'With great patience and study.'

She had given her some clues—dreaming of this flower signified an imminent death; smelling rich herbs meant a birth; five-legged cattle implied a fruitful harvest—but none of it was helpful in Grainne's situation.

'What about dreaming of a death?'

'Of someone you know? Someone close to you?'

'No,' Grainne said. 'Someone I do not know.'

'The death of a stranger,' Emer said. 'It depends on how his life was taken. War? A bolt of lightning from the sky? Familial treachery?'

'Fire.'

'Well now,' Emer had said. 'That could mean any number of things. It is you who must carve out an understanding.'

Grainne sought Emer out again this morning and found her at breakfast, stripping a vine of its ripe berries and eating them individually.

'You got my message, then,' Emer said.

'What message?'

Emer shook her head. 'I sent Érimón to fetch you. We are

leaving for a few days. You should pack at once.'

'Where are we going?'

'A little south of here. Not far.'

Emer walked with Grainne back to the girl's room so that she could collect a few things for the journey, and Grainne asked, 'Which studies will we be engaged in?'

'Legal,' Emer said. 'A property dispute.'

'Cattle?' Grainne asked.

Emer nodded. 'As is most always the case.' She was a mature woman, thin but not scrawny, the bronze lock-ring in her hair simple and unadorned, the twisted twine of their order wrapped three times around her left wrist as a reminder that, should she marry, her first priority was always the good of the earth, second her husband, and third her children.

'I have had another message from the gods,' Grainne said as they walked.

'A recurring dream does not always stem from the gods, child. We've discussed this before.'

'But I am convinced of it. This boy who burns, he is trying to tell me something.'

'And are you any closer to understanding its meaning?'

Eyes downcast, following her toes as they protruded from the hem of her robe, Grainne said, 'No. But I will. One day, I will save him before he dies and he will tell me what he needs me to hear.'

'And at that time, the gods can rejoice and my ears can rest.'

'Hey,' Grainne said, but when she looked up, Emer was smiling.

'Come. We must get on the road if we wish to arrive by nightfall.'

Grainne dressed in some travelling clothes and leather footwear, and packed a clean robe for their officiating duties, although she was there solely to observe and study. She could ask questions during the trial, but only to Emer directly, not to the appellant or the respondent. Hers was to listen and observe the ways of the law; the more cases she witnessed, the sooner she would graduate. She was not the youngest acolyte to leave the confines of the druid's village on a legal case, nor the brightest, but this was her first one and she welcomed the opportunity to progress in her studies, work that had felt almost stale of late. The principles of law were her forte and scrutinising a real case would reinforce her position at the forefront of the brehons. She had even learned, by sheer force of will, the roots and herbs that she had once struggled with. Medicines were now a part of her very nature, and the names of the gods and goddesses that looked upon her with little interest were etched in her mind. She could scarcely remember the homely child she had once been, always close to her mother's side, never straying far. Now she had learned everything that she could without advancing into upper classes and this excursion was a welcome interruption to her daily routine.

When they arrived, they were greeted warmly by the chieftain, a heavy-set man with a silvering moustache and his hair braided once at the back. 'We have applied for our own druid countless times this last year since our old man took himself off to the Otherworld—may his spirit wander freely—but it would seem there is a scarcity of learned folk this while.'

'Indeed,' Emer said with a tender smile. 'We are stretched far and thin.'

Laughing, the chieftain said, 'A ruse, I'm sure, to obtain

higher payment.'

The people had gathered to watch their arrival and, to a man, they were all wary of these cloaked travellers. Grainne could remember how her old druid had made her feel in his presence. He was lofty, studious, knowledgeable, and she a simple child of unknowing. That she was to become the very thing she feared as a girl was only now dawning on her. It was a well-known fact among the foolish people that a druid could curse you as quick as look at you. Having studied to become one, Grainne knew that was just not true—it took some herbs and a lock of hair, too.

They were quickly ushered towards the chieftain's hall for food and drink and given a bowl of warmed water to wash with. The chieftain, who introduced himself as Cabhan, son of Eoghan, took the head of the table and his two wives sat either side of him. Emer praised their hospitality, as was right, and thanked the gods for providing them such a magnificent host. Custom dictated that no one should eat before the master of the household had his first bite, and they waited as he regaled them of stories from his youth and of his father's great accomplishments. Grainne's stomach grumbled and she squeezed herself with her hands to dampen the sounds.

At last they ate, and when the meal was finished, the chieftain sang them a warriors' song while one of his wives played along on a cruit. In the morning, the trial would begin but, for now, it was a time to drink wine and sing about brighter days. The whole land had heard about what Ó Mordha was doing in the west, amassing an army of boys and training them as warriors, and speculation was rife as to who they could want to fight. Everyone had heard of the skirmishes some years ago and they were calling it a scouting party, an advance infiltration of their lands from a wicked group of foreigners. But even in her studies, Grainne knew that they had treaties with their neighbours across the water in the east and north-east, trade agreements that would not stand to be cast aside by either party. Some said it was the gods come to enact vengeance on a wayward people, others said it was the Fomorians here to slaughter them all, yet others said it was the people of Ellan Vannin revolting against them despite their accords. Either way, it would be a war of wars, they said; nobody forms a permanent, standing army without just cause.

With the dawn came a chill westerly wind and a heavy rainfall that delayed proceedings for a short while before it abated enough that they could assemble in the central grounds outside the chieftain's hall. Emer was presented with the appellant, a man named Enda, who quickly summed up his case: his neighbour and brother-in-law had stolen one of his bulls and slaughtered it for food. 'A working bull, he was,' Enda said. 'I have not the strength to plough with just one bull.'

'Liar!' a woman shouted, presumably his sister.

'Silence,' Emer said. 'Where is the accused?'

'I am here, and I did not steal his damn cow.' The man stepped forward and bowed to Emer in appeal. 'I know the laws and I don't go around thieving.'

'State your defence,' Emer said.

'I have my own cattle, each one known to me like children. Why would I thieve another man's stock to eat when I have enough of my own?' He stopped. His entire defence rested on the fact of that one statement.

Emer turned to the accuser. 'And your case?'

'My case is this,' Enda said, pointing to his brother-in-law. 'Turlach, here, has hated me and my brethren ever since he wed our sister. Three years they have been married and she has not given him a child even though our old druid gave her foul-smelling concoctions to drink and to rub upon her body in places no brother needs to know about. Turlach blames our family line and refuses to blame his own bad seed for his lack of children. Three years she has come to me saying she cannot get pregnant with his child but our other sister has six youngsters and my own wife has three. There is nothing wrong with my family's line, neither wombs nor seeds.'

'Marital problems aside,' Emer said, 'what grounds have you to claim he stole your cattle?'

'A twelfth-night ago, he came to me, drunk as any man could ever be, accusing my father—may his spirit wander freely—of giving him a broken wife who was barren and worthless. I said to him, "Be on with you, you drunken fool. You've no business darkening my family name." And he says, "Curse the name your father gave you, for he gave me a fruitless woman as a wife."' There was a murmur from the gathered crowd.

'"I've a right to tan you up a hill and back," I say to him,' he continued, 'and he spat at my feet.'

Emer nodded patiently. 'And the cattle?'

'He took a swing at me but missed, the drunkard. So he says, "Watch your back a night or two. You'll suffer a while as I did." And then he stumbled away on all fours like a drunken dog. I thought for sure he was going to do something stupid against my wife or my daughters so I locked them up at home away from any harm. I didn't want something rotten to happen to my family; no man needs his wife or daughters raped for spite. A night goes by and nothing happens. And then another night and my wife and my daughters are safe and I'm keeping an eye on them and nothing happens. And then the sun comes up on the third day and my family are all safe and I go out to the fields to tend my cattle as I always do, and who should I see standing at the edge of my field with a fat belly and a glint in his eye? Turlach is standing there and he smiles and he says, "Your field's looking a little light, is your fence broken?"

'Now I knew I had no broken fence. Those cattle are my livelihood and I for sure would never let one of them loose. But I checked all the same and sure enough one was missing but I had no tear in my fence, like I said.'

'And you confronted your brother-in-law?'

'I confronted him immediately and he said I was wrong. But I knew by the look on his sorry face, just as he has it now, that he done ate my bull and lied about it. He ate that bull and fed it to his wife as sure as I'm standing here in front of you.'

Enda stopped, breathed, waited for Emer's words.

She turned to Turlach and said, 'Do you dispute your brother-in-law's claim about your threat to him?'

'I admit I was drunk a night or two of recent, but I don't recall threatening no man, brother-in-law or not.'

To Enda, Emer asked, 'Do you have a witness to the accusation?'

'I do not,' he said. 'But it's well known that he despises my family's line and would do us harm on a whim.'

Emer looked from one brother-in-law to the other. The weight of one man's fate now rested in her hands. 'I wish to see the field from which your cattle went missing.' When Enda led them to the field, Emer inspected the fencing and saw no sign of damage or recent repair. 'I am satisfied,' she said. 'Now I would speak with the accused's wife.'

They spoke in private, Grainne standing in the corner of the room, observing.

'My husband's no cattle thief,' the woman said.

'What of the accusation that he blames your father's line for your lack of children?'

She hesitated only slightly, but even Grainne could feel it.

'He has a mouth on him when he's had a drink, like most men. But my husband and I are happy.'

Emer reached into the folds of her cloak and withdrew a small pouch. She did not once break her stare with the woman. As she opened the bag and poured the contents onto a table—browned chicken bones—she said, 'I can see the truth. Always.'

She looked at the bones, at their placement on the table, which ones were touching, which ones were not.

The woman was quick to say, 'He'll blame anyone but himself, it's true. But I'm his wife. You must understand. I am his property as much as his cattle are.'

Emer nodded. 'We are done here. Please wait outside until I have come to my decision on the matter.'

When they were alone, Grainne stepped forward, looked at the bones. 'What do they say?'

Emer swept them back into her pouch. 'They say it will rain tomorrow.'

'But—'

'Hush, child,' Emer said. 'I did not tell her the bones were the source of any wisdom. Only that I could see the truth. Always. And did I not get the truth from her? You have a lot to learn still. Being a druid is not the mystical sorcery the common people assume. It is education and guesswork as much as it is prayer and power. Come, I have decided the way of it.'

Back under the dull sky and in front of the whole sept, Emer decreed that Turlach was guilty of the crime with which he was accused. When a druid passes judgement, it is accepted as truth, whether it is welcomed or not. They are a learned people who know things beyond normal man and their word is as the dawn that never ceases to arrive when it should.

'You will repay your brother-in-law two-fold. Two bulls you are fined and then the matter is done.'

'But I do not have two grown bulls. Just a couple of pups.'

'Then you shall give to your brother-in-law the two bull-calves and until they are strong enough to pull an ard, you will work in their place alongside Enda's one remaining bull.'

'I can't pull a plough through a field like a bull, it will kill me.'

'I have spoken,' Emer said. 'Pay the fine.'

Chapter 12

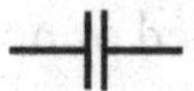

A loud rumble of thunder woke Áed from his sleep. It had rained for four days without finish and the ground had been saturated. Low clouds had descended over Ailigh as a fog and, without Rónán's companionship, he had felt alone and forgotten by the world.

He looked at Rónán's empty bed. For three weeks since they had argued, they had spoken not one word to each other and, often, Rónán had not come to bed. Áed had seen him in the training fields, laughing and playing with some other boys, boys who were known to get themselves into trouble at a whim. He had thought to speak with him occasionally but every time he found Rónán alone, another boy appeared and called him away.

Lightning lit the sky with white fire. In the stillness that followed, Áed heard low voices from outside and the squelch of feet in the mud. When the door opened, three boys staggered in, holding each other up. Rónán was in the middle.

Áed got to his feet. 'Is he drunk?'

All three boys vomited at once.

'Poison,' one boy managed to mumble.

Rónán fell on his bed. His skin was soaked, whether from rain alone or mixed with sweat, Áed could not tell, but his face was flushed and burning. The two other boys stumbled to their own beds, gripping their stomachs.

Áed stood over Rónán. He considered returning to bed, burying his head under his furs and ignoring the quiet moaning from his friend, but Rónán's hand whipped out and gripped Áed's wrist. 'I hear the trees,' he rasped.

'What? Let go.'

'They want me dead. All the trees. So many trees.'

'What did you eat?' Still, Áed was reluctant to show any compassion. For weeks Rónán had ignored him and he was hurt. Whatever mess he was in had nothing to do with him. But looking at Rónán's eyes now, watching the large pupils jiggle in their sockets, he knew this was no small matter. 'What did you eat?' he repeated. He came to his knees, touched Rónán's soaking chest, felt his heart drumming fast. 'What happened to you?'

'All the trees,' Rónán said.

'I don't know what you mean.'

Rónán twisted his head, vomited again, groaned and clutched his stomach. The stench of leaked urine rose from him. Áed stripped him of his wet clothes; his skin was like the glowing underside of a heated cauldron. He fetched some water and tried to make him drink, but as it passed his lips, it came back with a gag. His eyes rolled and twisted in his head and he fouled himself where he lay. Áed gagged, used Rónán's tunic to clean what he could.

'You have to tell me what you ate.'

He had not seen until now, but clutched in Rónán's hand was a small section of a mushroom. He prised Rónán's fingers apart, held the segment up. 'This? Is this what you ate?'

Rónán held his throat, tried to breath but the air was coming in only short, difficult bursts.

Áed ran from the room, out into the torrential rain. He slipped in the mud, stumbled, regained his balance and ran. 'We need a druid,' he shouted. 'A druid!'

Ailigh did not have a permanent druid onsite. He came once a week to tend cuts and bruises received from the training fields, and to lead sacrifices of appeasement.

The smith, Néall, was first to call out to him. 'What are you crowing about, boy?'

'Rónán, the others, they are poisoned.' He held up the piece of mushroom.

'This isn't edible,' Néall said.

They woke Oisín and they assembled at the boys' beds. 'They are burning up,' Oisín said. 'You, boy. Do you know where the druid lives?'

A boy, sitting up in his bed to watch, said, 'It's twenty rods from here.'

'Go,' Oisín said. 'Hurry.' He turned to Rónán, touched his forehead. 'What the bollocks were you thinking?'

'Trees.'

Áed knelt beside his friend. 'Will they be okay?'

With anger, Oisín said, 'We taught you all the difference between good plants and bad.'

'He's going to be okay,' Áed said.

'The gods grew these very mushrooms to punish boys that do not listen.'

'But they're going to be okay.'

'Water. We need water to cool them down and to make them drink.'

Later, when the druid had hurried up the hill, carrying with him a sack full of his herbs and treatments, Rónán and the other boys had seen no change. They slept mostly, or raved in their delusions. Once, Rónán had sat up in his bed, his eyes boring straight through Áed, and he said, 'We are all going to die. The tallest trees have spoken it and we will not make it to the Otherworld. We will be doomed to walk the lands barefoot and naked until the skies are darkness only and the last of the insects have chewed our flesh from our rotten bones.'

He writhed then, and fell asleep.

'How often have they vomited?' the druid asked.

'Enough to make the room smell,' Áed said.

The druid delved into his bag, withdrew a small pouch of dried, blue flowers. He ground them in an earthenware jar and mixed them with a liquid he poured from another jar.

'Make them drink it. All of them.'

'What is it?' Áed asked.

'It will make them vomit. Get the poison out. Make them drink it and then stand back. Trust me.' The druid lifted one boy's head and poured the discoloured liquid into his mouth.

Áed tried likewise with Rónán. 'Come on, drink this.' Rónán gargled and spat the liquid out. 'No,' Áed said. 'Drink it. Come on, Rónán. Drink it.' At last he got some into him. 'How much should he drink?' he asked the druid.

'A little will be enough. It will churn his stomach, make it spasm.'

'Will it get all the poison out?'

'I cannot say at this point. This should have been administered at once when they were found. The poison has been in their bodies for an evening already. There is no way of knowing the damage that has been done.'

At that, Rónán's body contracted and he vomited profusely. Áed had just a retching warning that allowed him long enough to leap out of the way.

The vomiting continued into the evening and, as the rain got heavier, Rónán's body began to cool. His breathing, while still erratic, was returning to normal. The druid gave each of them a second concoction, said it would stop the vomiting now, and set up camp in the corner of the room to sleep. Áed lay on the ground beside Rónán's bed and, before dawn, Rónán was looking down on him, nudging him awake.

'How do you feel?' Áed asked.

'What happened?'

Áed sat up. 'You ate something bad.'

'I feel sick.'

'You can't vomit again—there can't be anything left inside you to come out.'

Rónán retched but did not expel. He lay back down again and shivered.

'You were delusional,' Áed said. 'Ranting in your sleep about trees. Tall trees wanting everyone dead. Do you remember?'

'How can trees kill people?' Rónán asked.

Áed shrugged. 'I guess if you cut them into spears and arrows.'

'Water,' Rónán said.

Áed poured a cup of water and brought it to him. 'The druid gave you some awful drink that made you vomit. Everywhere.'

When he had drunk enough, Rónán put the cup on the ground. 'Did I get any on you?'

'A little.'

'Good. I'm still not happy with you.'

'You're not happy with *me*?'

Rónán turned away from him, said quietly, 'You know she means nothing to me. I must do what my chieftain tells me.'

'I know.'

'I may not like it, but it is the law. He's my surrogate father now, and the head of my heart. Anything I do now is for his name.'

Áed sat on the end of Rónán's pallet. 'Not in Ailigh. While you're here, you are Ó Mordha. Within the confines of these walls, our fathers are not our fathers. Their rules are overridden by the laws of the overking.'

'Déaglán would not disallow a marriage because I ask him nicely.'

'He doesn't need to. We just figure out how to postpone it until we can think of another way. Achall isn't even of age yet, anyway.'

Rónán patted Áed's knee before turning away again. 'You are a good friend.'

'Friend,' Áed said, wistfully.

'Are you not?'

'Of course I am.' He had wanted to say more, but the words would not form in his mouth. 'You are weak,' he said instead. 'Rest.'

Three days later, Áed stood on the top of the inner rampart wall and stared out over the low, grey clouds that concealed the ground and the lough from view. There was a chill wind but it did not bother him. He shielded his eyes from the sun that, above the clouds as he was, dazzled him. It was in its evening swan-dive into the distance, on its way to light the days of the Otherworld. In the stillness of early evening, he hollered into the fog, a long, low, guttural cry that said nothing and everything.

He had not heard the soft, shuffling footsteps approach from behind and was startled when Rónán spoke. 'If the sun hollers back at you, you'll fall over the edge of the palisade.'

He turned. 'If you keep sneaking up on me, I'd just as likely fall over, too.'

Rónán stood next to him and stared out into the distance. He was wrapped in a heavy fur blanket, holding it tight at his neck. For all the adult-like strength in his muscles, he looked like a weak child, ashen-faced and sickly.

'How are you feeling?'

'My stomach heaves but nothing comes, my head aches like a banshee, and my bones are weak. But I am over the worst. I have hardly seen you in three days.'

'Try three weeks,' Áed said.

'I'm sorry.'

'No, I'm sorry. Look, Rónán, I—'

'Don't,' Rónán said. 'You don't have to.' He turned to Áed. 'Truth is I've been a real cur. We were best friends and I was upset; upset at myself, at my situation. I took it out on you.'

'You did.'

'I said things that I shouldn't have.'

'You did.'

Rónán's smile was pitiful. 'I'm trying to apologise here.'

'I know,' Áed said. He held his arm out. 'Friends?'

Ignoring the hand, Rónán pulled him in for a tight hug. Áed could smell the freshness of his skin above the headiness of the furs; he had recently bathed. He breathed him in deeply.

Without breaking the embrace, Rónán said, 'I don't even like Achall. I like you.'

Áed's pulse quickened but he held the embrace a moment longer.

'I like you, too.'

He could feel Rónán's gentle laughter against his ear. 'I know,' he said, and kissed his cheek. Then he pulled away, wrapped the furs tighter around himself. 'Can we go down now? It's freezing up here.'

Their friendship was strong—the proposed marriage of one of them was not going to be enough to eradicate that. And in the months that followed, they quickly resumed their old ways. Their lengthy night-time talks rambled in a sprawling manner, never reaching its point—not having a point to reach. They walked to the lough on their downtime and swam, and lay on the grass as the sun, when it decided to shine, was strong enough to warm them. They trained together when they could, and they ate together. They sat side by side, elbows and knees touching, the heat of their desires burning through their tunics. Neither moved to kiss the other, though Áed was certain they both wanted it. In time, when it felt right, it would happen, and he was content with that.

Oisín, ever-present on the training fields around their base, insisted they push themselves harder, training long into the night, the air ripe with the scent of sweat and drying blood. The four hundred boys of Ailigh soon became six hundred as more became old enough to join them, and other tribes across Éirinn's lands began to follow suit. Soon, there were reports of standing army camps as far south as the Mac an Bhreitheamhnaigh and Ó Cochláin tribespeople.

Ailigh swelled and the boys were put to erecting a fourth rampart wall, extending overking Déaglán's stronghold with further sleeping quarters and store huts. The wall took four weeks to construct, each timber bole placed and tied to the next after their ends were sharpened. The extra wall would slow down an invading army's advance into Ailigh and allow time for the boys to escape through the narrow tunnel under Déaglán's quarters and out to the lough below, where they could turn and assault the enemy from behind.

Talks of skirmishes in the east brought with it a fear that the invaders had returned at last. But any brawl in the distant lands meant little to the boys of Ailigh and there was never talk of a final assault. For now, they trained and they waited.

Shortly before Áed was to celebrate his sixteenth birthday, Oisín assembled all the boys on the field in rows of thirty men, twenty deep. They stood with sword and shield, spear or bow.

'It won't be long, lads,' he said, his voice ringing out in the morning stillness. 'The world is at war and we will soon be faced with the battle you have been preparing for. What are you?'

'Ó Mordha,' they shouted.

A drum beat once.

'Many across Éirinn's fields will lose their lives. I cannot pretend we won't be among them. But we will fight. We will fight without relent. Because you are what?'

'Ó Mordha!'

Again, a solitary drum beat.

'This is our land,' Oisín continued. He did not need to raise his voice; every boy among them was silent as they listened. 'These are our fields and our cattle, and the air we breathe is ours. No one will take it from us, am I right?'

'Ó Mordha, Ó Mordha,' the boys chanted.

Oisín let it continue for a brief time before raising his hands for hush. Even the birds had stopped singing so that they could hear him.

'When the first of you arrived here almost eight years ago, I made you a promise. If you do not die honourably on the battlefield, you will die honourably of age. Your time has almost come, boys of Ó Mordha. Sing each slice of your blade as you cut at the enemy, just as bards and women will sing of you in futures yet to come. Are you ready to be sung about in folklore?' he asked. 'Are you ready to be legends?'

The boys erupted in cheers and the clash of weapon against shield. The drum player beat a swift rhythm to their chanting.

At length, Oisín stilled them and said, 'For three nights you are free to do as you please. Drink, dance, fuck—your favourite womenfolk are on their return; they should be here by sundown. But after that, your training will resume in vigour. You will cry out into the night as wolves that are ready and unafraid. Keep your swords sharp, men, and your wits sharper. When we march out into battle, know the man in front of you and the man behind. They are your brothers. They are Ó Mordha. You are all Ó Mordha.'

The boys cheered again.

Chapter 13

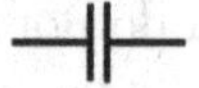

Rónán joined Áed on the wall again. The sun was setting on their left and, before them, figures were emerging from the woods far below. A light rain had dogged the afternoon but had lifted a short time ago, as did the spirits of most of the boys of Ailigh who awaited the arrival of their women. Áed's spirit had slumped and it dragged around his ankles when he walked.

'Just when I was forgetting what she looked like,' he said.

'I could never forget what she looks like,' Rónán said. 'Her image is burned in my eyes. That first night she was here, she stripped herself of her clothes and offered herself to me.' He shuddered for dramatic effect. 'I have never seen something so miserable in all my days; all pink and slender and clean. If girls want boys to like them, they should roll around in the mud and punch each other's faces for bruises.'

'They smell like flowers,' Áed agreed.

They watched as a stream of boys flooded from the open gate and down the hill towards their prizes.

'You aren't going to greet her?' Áed asked.

'She'll find me eventually.'

Áed pointed down into the grey twilight towards the girls. 'Is that her, there? Is she carrying a child? Did you give her a baby?' he laughed.

Rónán elbowed him in the ribs. 'She'd be lucky.' He leaned against the wall, facing away from the approaching throng. 'Do you know she likes to talk?'

'We talk.'

'We talk about important things. She talks about homes and property and the future. She has no idea. I think she expects me to take over as chieftain when Donal passes on. Has she forgotten about Faolán? And Muirgel would never allow it. I don't want to be chieftain, anyway.'

'You just want to fight,' Áed said.

'Exactly.'

With reluctance, they came down off the wall as the girls filed in through the outer gate, lost in a sea of boys who were already groping and kissing them. Áed was greeted with a strong hug from behind and when he turned, he smiled. Orlaith kissed his cheek. 'Did you miss me?'

'With every breath,' he smiled.

'You,' she said, turning to Rónán. 'I trust you've been kind to the greatest warrior in existence. Your future wife is among the girls somewhere. She spoke of you often on the journey here.' She linked her arm around Áed's. 'Come, let's get drunk and make thirty-seven babies.'

'Thirty-seven?' he questioned, suppressing a grin.

'One for every god my tribe worships.'

'Are we going to sacrifice one to each of them?'

When they had walked far enough from Ronan, Orlaith asked, 'Does he know yet?'

'Know what?'

'That you pine for him?'

Áed lowered his head. 'No. I mean, perhaps.'

'Well, "perhaps" is at least better than last time I was here. Perhaps he's stupid, is that it?' She tapped her temple in example. 'Is he lacking a civilised mind that he cannot see what is in front of him?'

'Don't you have men to fondle?' he asked.

She slapped his face. 'I could fondle you, but I know what would happen.'

With his cheek stinging, they entered the hall and he drew two cups of wine from the barrel. He had missed her; he had not realised how much until her return. She was someone to talk to, someone who understood him. He could say things to her that he dared not mention to any other boy.

Behind them, Rónán entered with Achall clinging to his side. The boys exchanged a glance that implied the pain of it all, but they both smiled. Achall could be tomorrow's problem. For now, Áed wanted only to get drunk and talk to Orlaith. She had a way with words, a way of making him think. She was like a drunken, cussing druid without the robes and the wrinkles.

As the evening wore on and Áed's head began to fuzz around the edges, the music and dancing begin in earnest and he moved with a gangly awareness of himself as Orlaith twisted and bowed in front of him. For one particularly lively movement, the girls assembled against one wall and the boys on the other. They wove in and out of each other with as much grace as the alcohol would allow, and when they were at the opposite side from the girls, Áed asked Rónán how his evening had been.

'My dagger is under my léine. Draw it quickly across my throat and let me bleed out on the ground.'

Áed laughed. 'That's one way of avoiding a marriage, I

suppose.'

The girls came forward again, turning around the boys, and their conversation was halted.

Later, as the rains returned and everyone was forced to remain inside, the sweltering heat of the hall flushed cheeks more so than sexual appetite. Orlaith dragged Áed across the room towards Rónán and pushed him down beside his friend. She sat opposite, next to Achall. 'Get us all a drink,' she said to the girl.

Achall looked at her with disgust. 'Get your own drink.'

'I'll go,' Áed said. He had an idea what Orlaith may say in front of Rónán if Achall had wandered away.

'I'll come with you,' Rónán said, clearly relieved of the break from his future wife. At the wine barrels, he said, 'She likes you.'

'Orlaith?' Áed shrugged. 'I think she likes everybody. I am just a friend to her.'

'I assumed as much.'

'What is that supposed to mean?'

Rónán placed a hand on Áed's shoulder, his thumb grazing his throat, and said, 'Never mind.' He took his cup and returned to the girls.

When Áed returned to the others, smiling, Orlaith wrapped her arms around his neck and rested her head on his shoulder. 'I should find a man to hold me,' she whispered, but she made no motion to leave. Then she looked at Achall. 'Have you been made a woman yet?'

'Excuse me?'

Orlaith pointed at Rónán. 'Did he make you sing like the morning birds?'

Rónán choked and Achall's cheeks reddened. 'That is not your concern.'

'I didn't think so,' Orlaith said.

Achall stood. 'Come, Rónán. We're leaving.'

'I wouldn't have touched her either,' Orlaith said to Rónán.

Trying not to laugh, Rónán said, 'No, thanks. I'm fine right here,' and Achall stormed away.

'By the visions of Danu, she's an angry little *bitseach*, isn't she?'

They laughed, and Rónán said, 'You shouldn't have upset her.'

'But she makes it so much fun.'

'She does,' Rónán admitted.

Soon, Orlaith went to find the comfort of a pair of arms that would respond to her, and Rónán went in search of his bride-to-be. Áed, woolly-headed but not yet drunk, went out into the rain and walked to the smithy.

On his way, a drunk voice called to him from the darkness between two stores.

'Who's there?'

Dillon staggered towards him, an empty wineskin flapping in one fist. 'Hey, sword boy. Where are you going?'

'Go to bed, Dillon, you're drunk.'

'Don't be scared, boy, now that you don't have Rónán and his arrows to protect you.'

'I'm not scared. Just leave me alone.'

Dillon reached out for him, an awkward, swirling grasp, and Áed sidestepped him. He grabbed Dillon's arm, yanked it behind his back, and forced him to his knees in the mud.

'I'll kill you,' Dillon said through gritted teeth.

With his free hand, Áed withdrew his dagger and flashed it before Dillon's face, pressing the cool blade against his neck.

'Not tonight, Dillon. Not any night. I'm not a child anymore. You don't scare me; not even back then. You were just bigger and uglier. But think about this: how easy it was for me to get you on your knees and pull a blade on you.' He twisted harder on his arm, forcing a cry from the older boy. 'You're pathetic. You ever look at me the wrong way and I'll gut you in front of everybody. Hell, Oisín might even hold you down while I do it.' He pressed just a little tighter with the blade—not enough to draw blood, but enough that Dillon would feel its sting. 'We don't have to be friends, Dillon. But we can't be enemies. We'll be at war soon. Focus on that and you won't end up ripe for slaughter at the hands of the real enemy.'

He leaned closer to Dillon's ear, making sure the tone of his voice was violent but quiet, threatening.

'Stay out of my way and I'll stay out of yours. Deal?'

Dillon said nothing.

'Do we have a deal?'

'Fine. Just keep away from me.'

'Deal,' Áed said. He let go of Dillon, who fell face down in the mud.

Áed walked away. He had forgotten where he was going and headed up to the steps in the rampart wall. He knew Dillon would not follow. With over six hundred boys at Ailigh, their paths would likely seldom cross. At least for now.

On the wall, he sheathed his dagger and loosened his fingers; he had been gripping it tightly the whole time. He flexed his shoulders and looked out into the darkness. The lough was a black stain on the ground far below. Turning to the east, a flicker of orange caught his attention but, in the darkness, it took him a second to find it again. Then there was another flicker, closer, and another.

The signal fires were burning. The east was calling for help.

In the rain, Áed slipped down the wooden steps, dragging his arse behind him, and he stumbled to his feet. He ran, bumped into Dillon who had finally found his legs and was walking in the darkness.

'Fuck off,' Dillon said, but Áed ignored him, ran on.

He threw open the door of the hall. 'The fires!' he shouted. 'The fires are burning.'

But no one heard him. The raucous festivities were loud and there was laughing and dancing and drinking and cheering.

He fought his way through the throng, looking for Oisín.

'Áed?' Rónán stopped him. 'What's wrong?'

Áed pushed on, knocking into revellers, unapologetic. When he found Oisín sitting alone with a cup held in both his hands, his head bowed as if in sleep, Áed gripped his shoulders, shook him.

'The fires,' he said. 'The signal fires are burning.'

Oisín hauled himself onto his feet.

'This is it,' he shouted. 'The war has come.'

Chapter 14

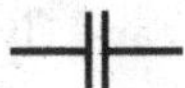

Airic heard the commotion and had time to pick up his sword and come out of his smithy before a stranger confronted him. The man, bearded and tattooed, came upon him quickly, a spear pulled back and ready for his charge, but Airic weaved and swung with his sword, cutting the man's arm off and slicing into his torso in one swift move. As the man fell, Airic plunged his sword into his chest, withdrew it with an arc of dark blood, and ran towards his home.

Doirean would be preparing evening meal and little Bec would be—he swung at another foreigner, taking the man in the throat, and carried on. Bec was somewhere in the woods, climbing trees and weaving leaves together as a crown; he hoped she had the good sense to remain quiet and undiscovered.

A quick assessment: these men were similar in appearance to those he had fought some years ago, the advanced skirmishes of an invading force that had initiated Ó Mordha's call to form a standing army of their boys. Áed would be fifteen years old now, maybe sixteen. Airic was not a man to consider the finer details of life, preferring to work his days with metals, but he was always keen of news from Ailigh when it came. And the news was good—their boys trained and worked hard for a noble cause. Áed, they had been told, was adept with the sword, a master of technique. Perhaps, Airic thought, if this was the start of a full-scale invasion, he would get to see his boy work the blade on the battlefield, perhaps fight alongside him as he had never had the chance to do with his own father.

As he ran to his home, his eyes scanned the sept. Tattooed men surrounded them, spears flying, swords clashing with local men. Many of the buildings on the outskirts were on fire.

A gruff man, almost a foot taller than he, naked from the waist up, charged him, a spear in one hand, a sword in the other, and Airic jumped back from his lunge, thrust out with his sword, and they clashed, hard metal against metal, a hot spark stinging his cheek. Black smoke broiled around them. This was not the invader's prior technique of a gentle raid-and-relinquish. These men were not testing the strengths of Éirinn's men, they were pushing hard. This assault was meant to be felt, although why it took them so many years to return, he could not say.

He swung, ducked, swung again.

They had assumed that the threat had passed, that the conflicts of those years gone by had been nothing more than an incompetent raid that amounted to nothing. Local chieftains had started to wonder what advantage the Ó Mordha had in retaining their boys instead of returning them to work the fields. The pressures of daily life had been felt in their absence.

But should the invaders get north of here, Airic was thankful for the warriors that had been training for so long. Ordinarily, he would have trained Áed with the sword himself. But a formal training network such as Ó Mordha's was a necessary evil that now became all too apparent.

The huge man growled a word in an unfamiliar accent. 'Die.'

Airic refused. He twisted, gripped his sword with both hands, and swung hard in a wide arc. Although he could not hack through the man's thick neck, he did cut deep enough so that the man fell to his knees and sullied the reeds with his foreign blood.

He cut through three more men before reaching the entrance of his home, but inside, he was too late. Doirean was being held by two massive men, whose tattoos were all of similar design but varying patterns. Her face was already swelling with angry welts.

Airic raised his sword in rage but another foreigner jabbed it from his hand and knocked him to the ground. He was set upon by three men, beaten and kicked while Doirean cried violently.

One of the foreigners pulled on Airic's hair, raising his bloodied face from the ground to stare at him. He pointed at Doirean. 'Husband's wife?' he snarled. The foul stench of his breath choked Airic.

The man raised his tunic and lowered his trousers. He urinated on Airic's head, then turned to Doirean.

'No!' Airic screamed.

The man took her against the wall as her two captors held her tight. He stared back at Airic all the while, turning once to lick Doirean's face with a blotched tongue as he continued to thrust against her.

Doirean locked eyes with her husband. She had stopped screaming, stopped struggling. She knew the end of it, he could tell, and he wept for her, struggled against his own assailants, trying to get up, screaming as hard as he could.

Doirean shook her head discreetly, mouthed a word to Airic that he could not understand in his blind rage.

When Doirean leaned her face in close to her rapist, he moved to listen to her whispers, and she bit hard on his ear, tearing it between her teeth.

The man jumped back, drew a dagger, and plunged it into her chest.

Airic roared. His vision clouded and he struggled hard, pulling an arm free of its grip, twisted, punched, kicked, and reached for his sword on the ground. He was kicked in the ribs, but his fingers found their prize and he swung with it, tearing at one man's thigh, knocking him back and awarding Airic with some slight purchase to manoeuvre. He swung repeatedly, cutting at his assailants. They fell around him and he forced his way forward as the other men, those who had been holding his wife, released her limp body and pulled at their swords.

There was blood in Airic's eyes—his, theirs, he did not know—but he pushed on, barrelling into the men and cutting limbs. His wife's rapist was holding his bloodied ear with one hand, swinging with the pathetic little dagger in his other. With the other men dead, Airic drove into him, knocking him to the ground with his shoulder, and he stood over him. He raised his sword, plunged it down between the man's legs, piercing through his still exposed genitals, and he twisted the blade. The big man screamed the way, perhaps, he had wanted Doirean to scream. His blood soaked the ground around Airic's boots. Airic sucked the blade back out of his body and thrust it again, down into the centre of the man's chest. He twisted it, coming to his knees for extra force.

It was then that he felt a searing pain penetrate his torso. Looking down, the sharp point of a spear had gone clean through his stomach. He had the energy to turn on his knees, felt the spear-shaft shifting inside his body, and faced a foreigner who stabbed him with a shortsword.

Airic fell beside the crumpled body of his wife, his eyes open, forever staring at the history of a happiness lost.

In the forest beyond the sept's walls, Bec hid among the dense leaves of a tree, high in its boughs, and could smell smoke and blood. She had not had time to react when the big men came and cut their way through their homes. She had thought to run to her mother's side, but the men were everywhere. They were inked in tattoos across their torsos, arms, backs and faces. Their beards, long and thick and bushy, were not in the style of local men.

From the heights of her hiding place, she watched with silent tears as her people were culled. She cried into her hands and yelped when she heard a voice from below calling her name. Looking down through the leaves, she saw Odhran, a shortsword in his right hand, his bag of runestones in his left. His cloak was spattered in blood and he was treading lightly as he stepped through the underbrush. His whispers carried up to her. 'Bec? Are you there?'

'Odhran,' she called.

He looked up.

'Who are they?' she asked.

'I can't—I don't believe it,' he said. 'Are you safe?'

She cried. 'I hid. I should have helped, but I hid like a child.'

'Stay safe,' he said. 'Stay in the trees; when they are gone, travel east. Warn the other tribes before it's too late. How far can you go in the trees without coming to the ground?'

'My parents?' she asked.

'How far can you travel in the trees?' he said.

She looked, saw nothing but leaves. 'Far,' she said. 'At least to the clearing. Who are they?'

'Fir Bolg,' he said.

'Impossible. Our ancestors killed them all. Dagda, Nuada, the Morrígan. Everyone knows the ancient stories.'

'Some of them escaped, it is said.'

He fell to the ground then, a spear pinning him down. Bec covered her mouth for fear of screaming when one of the huge men came and stood over Odhran. He looked up into the branches.

'Girl, come down,' he growled. He pulled his spear from Odhran's back and raised it to her. 'Girl, come down.'

Terrified, she remained where she was until he punched the tree bole with his fist and she felt the vibrations through the branch under her feet.

She descended.

The man dragged her into the centre of the sept. Dead bodies were heaped in piles and she dared not look at them lest she see her parents. Her hands were tied and she was lined up with other girls and women, each of them crying for the loss of their husbands and fathers. She did not see her mother among them.

They were kept there under watch until all the bodies had been brought from their homes and stacked together for burning. Bec closed her eyes against the images and, when she did, she saw the face of Odhran, her one faithful friend, the only person to listen to her when she spoke, listening to her sentiment as much as to her words. She watched in her mind, repeatedly, as he fell to the ground—swift, silent save for the dull thud of his body as it touched the earth. She wept.

Soon, one of the men stepped forward and took off his round helmet of buffed bronze. He walked the length of women, inspecting them, tugging their skin, their hair, checking their hands and feet. Some of them he asked questions, some more of them he pulled out of the line and passed them to his men.

He stood before Bec, pulled hard on her hair, lifted her chin and touched her neck, felt the thickness of her fingers and then her hips. 'Can you cook? Sew?'

She spat at him and he wiped his face, laughing. He pulled her from the line and pointed to a foreigner. The lad was younger than most, twenty-two or twenty-three winters old, she thought, although it was hard to tell through the blood and soot that covered his face. He gripped her upper arm, thumbed his chest. 'Urasid,' he said. 'What is your name?'

She did not speak until he slapped her face and made her talk.

'Bec,' he said, trying the name out. 'You are mine now, Bec.'

He dragged her away by the arm.

That night, all the girls were raped by their new owners and then tied tightly to their men, a short length of chain between their wrists so that they could not run, their other arm strapped down to their waists.

Bec had stopped crying shortly after Urasid had first penetrated her and caused her unbearable pain. He had muffled her screams with his hand. She stared at his chest for the duration, counting the rings of ink that circled there.

Her sleep, when it finally came, camped as they were in a clearing, the smell of burning flesh still ripe in her nostrils, was fitful. She heard her mother calling to her and as she came down from a tree to greet her, her mother's face was covered in dark swirls of ink. In her dream, she knew the truth.

'Go to the Otherworld, mother,' she said. 'Go and be free.'

Chapter 15

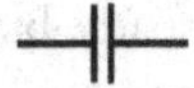

They came for her in the night.

Grainne woke to the sounds of shuffling in her room and in the dim starlight that shone through the small window high up in the wall she saw the outline of three tall figures. They lifted her from her bed and carried her out into the night. She screamed, but no one came.

'Where are you taking me? Put me down.'

She struggled against them, but they were strong. They carried her by the armpits into the woods, her feet never touching the ground. She could not see their faces; they were wearing hoods that hid their identities.

'Put me down.'

They came to a hut among the trees and she recognised it at once. She stopped struggling.

'What are the rules?' she asked. 'What must I discover about myself this time?'

The men opened the door and carried her inside. When they were gone and the door was closed, she was plunged into absolute darkness. She could not remember how many years it had been since Cáer had visited her and touched her chin with godly fingers in this very room. The isolation hut itself had been the beginning of her journey; it had set her on this path of discovery. Inside its walls, she had learned the truth of herself—the sunlight in darkest night—although she still did not understand its meaning. Would the hut now be the end of her? Would Cáer come and revoke her wisdom?

Grainne knelt on the reeds that covered the floor and lowered her head against the heady blackness. 'My most revered lady, Cáer,' she said. 'Come to me and tell me what it is that you must. I am starved of light and yours is the only brightness I know.'

There came no response. The darkness ate at the words as she spoke them.

She lay prostrate on the ground and could smell the dried soil, the lifeless reeds. With her arms outstretched, she incanted the words of a druid's prayer, one that made her feel safe when she was alone. She scratched a mark in the ground with her fingernail, a rune of protection, and repeated the prayer.

She was no longer a child; she had stopped being a child when Cáer had spoken to her all those years ago. Perhaps not yet an adult, she was a druid, and that was all that mattered. She had devoted her life to the ways of these people, become one of them. There was not as much mysticism in the way the people had considered, the way the druids had let the people believe it. There was simply a knowing, an understanding of the ways of the universe, of the passing of time, of the tides that leave but must always return. She had studied, and she had learned, and knowledge had been gifted upon her. She knew the way of things simply because she did—that was the light in her darkness. Cáer had given to her the truths of the earth and in return she would spend her life in that service. That she found herself now in this blackened room was as much a part of who she was as it is of who she will become.

Grainne was a druid. She could say this with certainty. Not an acolyte, nor a trainee. She entered this building for the second time as a young woman in the flourishing years of her life. She would leave it as a druid.

She stood, found the wall and walked its length. She laughed. Her stride had lengthened since her last visit to the isolation hut, and her confidence had grown.

The stones smelled the same and she smiled.

When she slept, the white-haired boy came to her. He held the hand of Cáer and the woman smiled at Grainne. She wore a blue dress whose sleeves came to her wrists and whose hem touched the cool ground. She had a golden thread weaved through her long black hair and her white skin was the colour of the boy's hair.

Cáer pointed behind Grainne, who turned to see. The fires were rushing towards them, as in each of her previous dreams. But as the flames came upon them, each lick became a spear and Grainne shrank from their force. When she stood again, Cáer and the boy were unharmed and all about them were the bodies of dead men and the acrid smell of fresh-spilled blood. The flames had gone.

Tears came to the boy's eyes and they left tracks on his pale cheeks. Cáer let go of his hand and wrapped her arm around him.

A war comes, Cáer said without speaking. *And a reunion of souls.*

'War is always coming,' Grainne found herself saying.

'Men thought dead have now arisen,' the boy spoke, his voice soft and melodic. He pointed and Grainne looked. In the distance, too far to see clearly, a warrior carried the body of a fallen man. Their solitude was vast in its completeness.

'One can stop it,' Cáer said.

'Me?' Grainne asked.

The boy shook his head. 'One other,' Cáer spoke for him.

Grainne looked back at the man in the distance. She could sense the keening of his voice though she could not hear any words. When she looked back, the boy was on the ground, dead, a spear through his tiny chest.

'Who is he?' Grainne asked of Cáer.

'My father.'

She looked again and the boy was not a boy but a man, his long white hair stained red with blood, his impressive beard equally dyed.

'What can we do?'

'It is already done.'

A multitude of birds darkened the sky and coloured the air with their cries. When Grainne turned, Cáer was standing beside her.

'The end of man,' Cáer said, 'will not be sallow. It will be dark.'

A strong wind stirred their hair and their dresses and all the dead men that had littered the ground stood and marched as one into the west. The ground itself was wet with blood. Only one body lay there still—Ethal Anbuail, Cáer's father. He was no longer impaled and he was spotless of blood, a ceremonial shield resting upon his torso, a crown of gold at his head. His white hair shone like the sun.

The birds in the sky followed the march of the dead and the wind died to a whisper.

They were alone.

Cáer took Grainne's hand and she could feel the warmth of the goddess' fingers upon her skin.

'How can this course be prevented?' Grainne asked.

'It cannot.'

'Is there nothing I can do?'

'You will witness the end, as I have done. Many will die. Await the reunion. You will see.'

'What will I see?'

Cáer raised Grainne's hand and kissed the back of it. At once, she became a swan, her black hair now a stain of feathers along the back of her graceful neck. She spread her massive wings and took to the air. The flap of wind that came back to Grainne smelled of golden samphire and of salty seas.

When she woke, she was not in the hut. The trees around her were tall and full. On the ground, a blanket had been draped over her. She sat up and saw the archdruid sitting on a fallen tree.

'You took me from the isolation hut?'

The old man shook his head and smiled, his eyes disappearing in folds of creased skin. 'We opened the door and you were not there.' He gestured the woods around them. 'We found you here this morning but you would not wake.'

'How did I get here?' She stood and wrapped the blanket around her shoulders. She could still smell the yellow flowers though none were present.

'I was hoping you would know,' he said. He smiled again. 'Some tribes who are without a resident druid will arrive at dawn. You will choose one.'

'For what reason?'

'You will become their carer.'

'I am graduating?'

He laughed. 'You have graduated.'

'But I am a girl.'

'Young, yes. But no more a girl than I am.' He stood, walked away from her with the use of a staff. 'Your chosen tribe will have you after the ceremony.'

Her ceremony of passing was a joyous affair. They slaughtered a cow to Cáer and, she insisted, to her father Ethal Anbuail. She told no one of her dream.

That evening, they sang and danced in her honour, but she could not shake the feeling of doom that she had succumbed to. While they washed her and perfumed her hair, the sadness in her heart swelled so that her chest ached. As they drew her gown over her head and draped her ceremonial cloaks around her shoulders, a tear itched her cheek and she brushed it away so that no one would see.

They stood her on a dais and they bowed to her. The archdruid came forward and offered to her a staff, cut and carved from an alder tree by his own hand. She took it, studied its length, and then stood it at her side. The archdruid bowed and she returned the gesture.

She gave him a purple flower and he ate it. The archdruid offered her one and she did likewise. Then he wrapped a thong around her left wrist and said, 'It is done.' That he now echoed Cáer's words in her dream, Grainne was all too aware.

The assembled druids cheered for her and they passed around a cup of wine that they each sipped from. And in the pit of her stomach, she felt a blackness gnawing at her in urgency. She was on a path of destiny that, now, she could not change. Not even if she willed it.

In the morning, the chieftains of four tribes came before her and pleaded their case for her service, enticing her with property and status. These tribes had possessed, at one time, their own resident druid, but with the dearth of acolytes, many tribes had lacked the guidance of the learned men.

The first chieftain, a man called Iollan, came to her with his many sons and offered her the choice of them as a husband. She questioned him of his tribe's allegiance to the gods, and then she dismissed him.

The second, Proinsias, could offer her nothing but gratitude for her service. She thanked him and awaited the third chieftain.

When he came before her and bowed theatrically, she could see the sweat that glistened in his thinning hair. 'My most respected lady,' he said. 'I am but a simple man, but I offer to you my—'

She stopped him. Although at once she was sickened by his appearance, she was drawn to his presence. 'You can offer me nothing that I do not already possess,' she said. 'I, however, can offer to you the ways of the earth that you must surely be lacking.'

She had cut him, but his smile was tight. 'You are the wisdom of all wisdoms.'

'I have chosen,' Grainne said.

The archdruid leaned in to her and said, 'There is another chieftain awaiting an audience with you.'

'I do not need to see him.' Grainne stood, came to the chieftain before her. 'There is something within you that calls to me. You will have my service.'

He bowed to her again. 'I am Donal, son of Ultan. I welcome you to my tribe with open arms and we will feast in your honour for seven nights.'

She could not say why—perhaps Cáer spoke to her again, perhaps Ethel Anbuail pointed the way—but this portly man who reeked of wood smoke was the answer to a question she had not known to ask.

If, upon her arrival at his sept, there were golden samphire flowers lining their gardens, she would quite possibly cry with joy.

Chapter 16

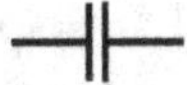

When dawn broke, the fires were still visible atop the distant mountains in the east. Overking Déaglán assembled his men and boys and spoke briefly of honour and of the afterlife of warriors. They would stride into battle and many would die. But for the sake of their lands, for the sake of their peoples, they would fight with valour and with pride. He stirred them with his words every bit as much as Oisín had done previously. He walked among them, becoming one of them, standing in their lines and telling them that no man was lesser than another, that they were all legends in the making. He recited his lineage back to Mordha the Terrible himself, and they cheered him.

He stood before Áed and winked at him. 'Now I get to see how well your sword works when a man's neck is in front of it.'

Without fear, Áed said, 'He may have a neck when you are finished, but he will not have a head.'

Déaglán laughed. 'No man will have a head when we are done, am I right, boys?'

He returned to his position at the front and surveyed his people. 'You have trained well, all of you. Even if you die, you are not marching to your death; we march to victory and, in doing so, the dead will rise in the Otherworld and eat well at the table of the gods.'

He stepped in the back of his carbad, raised his sword, and shouted, 'To battle!'

By nightfall, as the sun crept lower on the horizon and the burning fires brightened the corners on the mountaintops, as the colours of the world were leeched from it, Áed's body was still awash with the tingle of anticipation. He was not thinking about dying. Nor was he thinking about how many heads he would cleave. His thoughts were on the minutia of ordinary life—that a man must have cattle to be considered of worth; that no blade of grass would ever look the same as another; that the sound of the wind in the treetops was like that of the voices of his gods. This night started just as any other: with the lowering of the sun and the blanketing stars caressing their earth. The following night it would do the same, and the night after. Millennia from now, the stars would still shine and their bodies, dead now or dead in years to come, would be burned and forgotten, feeding the flowers that would grow from their ashes. The ashes of their ancestors went into the earth and sprang up as flowers and grass, and those grasses were eaten by the cattle that were slaughtered and fed to men. It could be said, therefore, that a part of their ancestors, of Mordha the Terrible and of the Dagda, resided in each of them. And when marching into battle, they did not go alone, but they carried with them, inside them, all of the great warriors and legends who came before.

These were his thoughts when Rónán nudged him from his musings and, in the thickness of night, his eyes sparkled with stars in them. Áed told him his thoughts, about the ashes of their peoples, and Rónán said, 'That would be a great battle speech. Remember it for when you are king.'

Achall chuffed to herself like a child and pulled her cloak tighter around her shoulders. 'I'm tired,' she said. 'When will we stop?'

That morning, all the girls were sent home with orders to tell their tribesmen of the war, to say that every able body should march east to assist them.

Achall, she had told them, had family in the east, a cousin married into a tribe some years before. She requested to walk east with her future husband, at least as far as her relations where she would remain until the battle was won. Oisín, in his good graces, agreed, but he had pulled Rónán aside and said, 'If we meet our enemy before reaching her tribesmen, or if we should find them wounded or worse, you must either give her a sword and quickly show her how to use it or kill her yourself before she gets in the way.'

Her baggage was tied to a pack horse along with rations of cured meats and carefully wrapped breads. The boys each carried one small sack over their shoulder with a spare tunic and leather boots. They marched with their shields on arms and their swords in scabbards at their hips. Rónán and a company of about seventy other boys had their bows slung over their backs and a quiver of his finest arrows. They would hunt the woods at dawn and dusk each day when they could and replenish the food that would be eaten, and for their work they would be awarded an extra morsel of whatever animal they caught.

With the men in Déaglán's employ, and those who quickly joined them that morning at the foot of Ailigh, ready and eager to fight, their marching company now swelled to almost one thousand. It was not a whole army, but when they joined the frontline they would become one arm of it, a unified nation against a marauding force.

When they made camp they were still on the buzz of pre-battle and sleep was not easy to come for many. Achall breathed steadily at Rónán's side while he and Áed, who had found a patch of ground beside them to sleep on, stared at one another and talked quietly. So as not to disturb her, Rónán had shuffled closer to Áed, their faces close, their voices low. They attempted to retain the normalcy of their nights at Ailigh, talking about their day, making up stories of their heroism, but under the canopy of leaves among the trees, they could not dismiss the war that was at hand.

'Are you scared?' Áed asked.

Rónán shook his head then changed his mind and nodded. 'A little. Are you?'

'I know what we are doing, what has to be done. But it doesn't make me want to do it any more than shitting in my own stew.'

'We trained for this,' Rónán said. 'But we are boys among men. We may not even see the war; it could be over before we get there.'

'We aren't boys any more, Rónán. This Samhain I will be sixteen. The enemy won't pat us on the heads and seek out an older man to slaughter. We will see the battle, I can guarantee it.'

'Maybe our fears are a good thing,' Rónán said. 'Brave men must fear death as much as weak men, but brave men act regardless.'

'Do you feel brave?' Áed asked.

'I will on the battlefield,' Rónán said, 'with you at my side.'

They fell asleep that way, facing each other, Achall forgotten for the moment.

In the morning they broke camp and started east again after a hurried breakfast of oats. At times Achall sat on the floor of a carbad, at times she walked alongside her future husband, and still other times she lagged behind in a sullen and solitary trudge.

Later that evening, when they reached the first settlement they had encountered since leaving Ailigh, they were told the men and boys of the tribe had already gone east in support of the war, but the women would feed and shelter them for the night to strengthen their spirits for the coming days. Many of the boys at the back of the company could not even see the small houses of the sept from their distance, but to be fair, Déaglán suggested they all draw lots to see who would sleep in a bed and who would have to draw up straw around himself in a field for the night. Achall was automatically awarded a warm room and she was led away by an elderly woman who told her they would sing songs until she fell asleep.

Áed and Rónán were grateful to be housed together and they shared a small bed next to a young girl whose blond hair reached the small of her back and hung loose around her face. She asked for their names and their ages and informed them that she was five winters old. She clung to a wooden figure in her bed as she slept with a thumb in her mouth.

'Look at her, boys,' the woman of the house had said to them. 'She is what you are fighting for; she and every other little child that would be lost without their homes. Forget about me,' she said. 'Forget about all the women and the men too old to fight. You aren't fighting for us—you are fighting for the children's future, for without them, there is no future.' She took to her own bed after stoking the hearth and was quick to sleep.

Áed lay on his side, willing himself to sleep. He traced the gentle movement of shadows on the wall from the low-burning fire. His thoughts raced from one notion to another—did his father know the enemy had returned at last? Was Grainne still training to be a druid or had she returned to her mother's side? He had to think for a while to remember little Bec's real name. They had called her Bec for so long that the name Maebh sounded wrong in his mind.

If the rumour was true, that the invaders were the Fir Bolg returned, he did not know from where they came. The old stories spoke of them as being at turns monsters, at other turns giants of unnatural strength. But if they were stronger than ordinary man, or if they were monsters of hideous proportions, how then did Áed's ancestors—the Dagda and Nuada and the Morrígan—slay them and drive them away?

When the Tuatha Dé Danann arrived on the shores, they fought a land of prior settlers, the tales said—the Fir Bolg. They requested half of the land to live on, but the Fir Bolg's king, Eochaid, refused. The two sides battled at Mag Tuired and the Fir Bolg were slaughtered.

As the shadows on the wall dulled and steadied, Áed closed his eyes. His thoughts were not allowing him to sleep and they had a long day of travels ahead of them. As he willed his breathing to slow and he concentrated on the darkness within his own mind, he felt Rónán shifting in the bed and move closer to him. Rónán's arm came around his waist and held him.

He dared not breathe for a long moment. He clenched his eyes so that they would not open.

When Rónán made no further move and Áed had finished debating whether he should lie there in peace or speak, he whispered, 'Are you awake?'

'I'm trying not to be,' Rónán said, his voice barely carrying to Áed's ear. 'I can sense how tense you are.'

'Sorry,' Áed said. He turned in the bed to face Rónán, who did not remove his arm from Áed's side.

In the soft glow of the fire, Rónán's wheat-coloured hair shone bright as gold.

They looked at each other, unmoving.

At last, Rónán said, 'Why do you shiver?'

'Because I'm afraid.'

'Of war?'

'No.'

'Then why?'

Áed did not speak.

'You think too much about things that are beyond your control,' Rónán said.

'I know.'

'You think war is not about you but about the people. You would be selfish to think your sword means anything to anyone. You care about others.'

'Is that wrong?'

'It is right. You have the mind of a king.' He paused, then said, 'And the face of a god.'

Rónán shuffled slightly forward, tightening his arm around Áed's waist. And he kissed him.

Áed did not close his eyes; he did not have time, for the kiss was brief.

When again Rónán looked at him, Áed opened his mouth to

speak but Rónán shook his head.

Áed said, 'Achall—'

'Hush.'

'But she—'

'Hush.'

'Okay.'

They kissed again, longer this time, deeper. Áed's whole body tingled as his blood seared within him. He did not want to say another word. Could not.

When their kissing stopped, his lips prickling, Rónán held him tighter and whispered in his ear, 'Can you sleep now?'

'Probably not.'

'But we should try.'

'We should.'

'Turn around,' Rónán said. 'I will hold you until we are both asleep.'

'Tomorrow, we—'

'We can talk. Find some time away from Achall.'

At the mention of her name, Áed turned back to the wall, allowed Rónán to hold him tight. He would kill her if he thought he could.

He smiled. Orlaith would not believe him if he had the chance to tell her. He laughed.

'Why do you laugh?'

'Hush,' Áed said. 'Sleep.'

In the morning, Áed woke and turned. The young girl was asleep in their bed, lying between him and Rónán. She had risen from her own bed some time in the night and had crawled in beside them. Her kind mother, who had offered them a bed for the night without a thought, was cooking breakfast at the fire.

When he sat up and scratched his head, she smiled at him, nodded at her daughter. 'She tried to wake you both some time ago but you would not budge. You sleep like the dead. Eventually, she fell asleep again herself. I had not the heart to wake you.'

He got out of bed, stepping gingerly over the girl and Rónán.

'Some of your men are awake already but many of you sleep still. The sun has only just risen. I expect you'll be leaving very soon. You will eat breakfast first.'

He looked back at the bed, at his friend and the young girl. 'I should wake him.'

'Leave them,' the woman said. 'Where you're going, there won't be much sleep. Let him enjoy it while he can.'

He nodded agreement. 'You've been very hospitable to us. Thank you.'

'It is my duty,' the woman said.

Áed came outside into the morning sunlight and walked barefoot into the square. It was late summer, not too far from Samhain and the ground had already leeched some of the warmth of the sun. Oisín sat on a log-bench and sharpened his sword.

'Boy,' he called. Áed walked to him, yawning. 'Do you re-member your promise?'

'Promise?'

'When Rónán's father left us for the Otherworld and your promise to be my best warrior.'

'I remember.'

'Good.' He stroked the length of his sword again with his stone. 'Sit by me for a while. We should talk.' When Áed sat on the ground before him and crossed his legs, Oisín said, 'For eight years you boys have trained under my guidance. Would I not be a man to see all that happens within my walls?'

Áed felt a lump in his throat. 'I'm not sure—'

Oisín ran the stone along the edge of his blade. 'Dillon has hated you since the day you both arrived. And you have hated him equally. Is that going to be a problem for my army?'

Awash with relief that this conversation had not been about other things, Áed said, 'No, sir. We've had something of a heated conversation. We are on the same side in battle, if not in life.'

Oisín nodded. 'I would hate to have to slit your throats and deny our enemy the pleasure.'

Áed cleared his throat. 'Will we win?'

'The war? Of course. It may not be easy, but it will be adventurous. We have the advantage. If I was holding a pig and you tried to take it from me, who would win?'

Áed thought a moment. 'Is the pig alive?'

Oisín laughed. 'You always ask the right questions, boy. You have a head for strategy. Perhaps I'll invite you into Déaglán's tent for our next meeting.' He paused. 'No, the pig is dead.'

'Then you would win,' Áed said. 'Not just because you are bigger and stronger, but because you already have a grip on it. You just have to swat me away before I get a hold of it.' He paused. 'The same as with our lands; keep the foreigners away and we win.'

'You see?' Oisín said. 'A head for strategy. If we keep the foreigners out, we've already won.' He stood, sheathed his sword and waited for Áed to stand also.

Áed said, 'But the foreigners are already here.'

'Not all of them. Just a finger's worth. It's not enough to grip

our lands. We will cut off the finger and keep our lands to ourselves. And you,' he said, prodding Áed's forehead, 'you will be
my man. You will be the one to end this, yes?'

Áed puffed his chest in pride. 'Yes.'

'Now go and wake that fool you call a friend. We have places
to be.'

Chapter 17

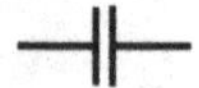

A torrential rain washed the hillside into a river of mud as Bec, chained together with seventeen others, forced their way to the top. The moon, if it could be seen behind the sodden, black clouds, would be full and luminous. Odhran had told her of the moon's cycle, how it cries itself to death and then rebirths to become whole again, in perpetual rotation.

Bec wiped her cheek of tears and rain with her sleeve as she trudged ankle-deep in the mud. She was sore and exhausted and her tears were for herself, not the loss of her dear parents. Her captors whipped the girls when they slowed or fell, but even they with their heavy leather boots were finding slight purchase among the slick grasses as they fought their way upwards to the top of the hill.

Although it had been dark most of the day from the storm, evening had now fallen and, although the winds would be stronger on higher ground and they would be exposed to the roaring elements, they would camp there for the night with the protection that its vantage point would offer them. Tribes make settlements on hilltops with clear visibility all around, and these foreigners with their girl-slaves banded together much like a tribe. They had camped on high ground last night, and did the same the night before. They were travelling north-east, as far as Bec could tell from the direction and movement of the moon. They were marching somewhere specific—of that she was certain. These wild men were not looking to make homes. Any one of the septs they had already pillaged would have sufficed for the thirty-strong party of men. Thirty men and their slaves could settle, stake their land-claims, fight off competition, and form an established tribe within a few years. But they burned every home they came to, killed the men and the elderly, and took the girls. What purpose she would serve was not yet made known to her.

They had marched for the last three days since the men raid-ed her home, an incessant pace that had Bec and her chain-gang companions tripping over their own feet. The foreigners had stopped only once to slaughter an entire sept and burn its build-ings. Bec and the other girls were kept under guard in a copse of trees nearby and could not see but heard the violence. She could smell the sickening stink of burning flesh and wondered how many mothers, how many fathers and children would die at the hands of their aggressors. The rough, helmeted men re-turned soon after with three more girls to add to their chain. In their yawning, coarse dialects, they joked and laughed among each other as though their raids were a sport.

Their language was not too dissimilar to Bec's, but their ac-cents were strong, making most of their words incomprehen-sible. When they were not close to her, she mouthed prayers for her fallen family, for Odhran and for their chieftain, whose body she had not seen piled among the dead, but she recognised his staff that was now being carried by the apparent leader of these men.

When the foreigners were near her, she shrank to minimise her appearance. She was, after all, still a girl, a child. Although she was of mothering age, their laws stated she was not yet of an age to be married. She was to remain a virgin until her eventual handfasting to whomever her parents chose for her. That she had been defiled in such a barbarous way meant, as the law sees it, the foreigner, Urasid, was now her husband, albeit in a soldier's fashion. When he was done with her, which would surely happen, he would dispose of her. When that time came, she wished that he would kill her fast.

Now, as they approached the top of the hill, lashed with rain and fierce winds, the girls huddled together while the men set camp. They lit a fire from dry branches that they had carried with them, sheltering its flames from the rains with a makeshift siding made of lacquered timber. It may at one time have been a shield, its markings faded through use, but it served well in protecting the fire.

Tents were erected and, as some of the girls were forced to warm meats over the fire and prepare food, Urasid removed his slave-wife's cuffs and dragged her into one of the empty coverings. He pinned her to the ground and mauled her neck with his tongue as he fumbled on top of her. She stared at his sword in the corner of the tent, too far to reach, a dream beyond scope. One day, she vowed, she would murder him with his own blade, darkening the earth with his black blood.

Urasid entered her and scratched her cheek with his stubble as he scratched her spirit deep inside. She had learned not to fight against him. When she tried, he back-handed her face and choked her throat. She was a tool for release, nothing more. As he bucked on top of her, grunting in her ear, his hot and aggressive breath burning her skin, she stared at his discarded blade and willed her tears to turn to blood, to wash her face of her sorrows.

Her hair was matted, rain-damp and thick with knots. That it fell over her face was a blessing, for she could no longer see his eyes as they glared at her in ferocious lust. He grunted, his hips rocking harder, and then he stopped, panting, and lay motionless on top of her.

When he withdrew and stood, his trousers still around his knees, he kicked her in the ribs. 'Cover yourself. You are pale and sickly. A whore of whores.'

She knew the name, knew what it meant. And she knew that she was exactly that now, reduced to nothing but a piece of warm flesh for his gratification when he desired it. She lashed out to whip his feet from under him but the chain with which he had pinned her to the ground was too short.

He laughed, crouched and gripped her throat. 'Are you still hungry?'

She could see that he was hard again.

'Get off me.'

She struggled now as he took her a second time, clawing desperately at his face, bucking her knees to try to shake him off. He pinned her tight and her angered spirit made him laugh. He finished quickly and then slapped her cheek as hard as he dared. There was a ringing in her ear that equalled the howl of the winds outside the tent.

'Still more?' he asked.

She turned her head from him, clenched her eyes.

'For my mother,' she said, 'one day I will gut you from throat to heel.'

He slapped her again.

When he put her back outside in the rain with the other girls, clustered together for warmth and shelter beside a thick bush, she knelt in the mud and cursed him. He was twice her size, more than twice her age. But she would best him. She would cut off his penis and beat him with it.

'They killed everyone,' one of the new girls sobbed. 'My whole family. Everyone is dead.'

Bec took her in her arms as much as her chains would allow. 'Not everyone,' she said. 'We are still alive.'

The girl wailed. 'We are more dead than the others. Everyone else was burned or stabbed—a quick death. We get to die, night after night.'

'They cannot kill us,' Bec soothed. 'We have breath, and as long as we do, we are alive. When they take you, think of the sun. Think of the warmth it gives you. For your family—for my family—we cannot die. I won't allow it. We will be free again. They will come for us and we will stand over these foreigners as they cry in death.'

'Who will come for us?' the girl asked. 'Anyone who could is already dead.'

'There are warriors, armies. And if they do not come, we will be our own warriors. I promise you, I will set us all free.'

She held the girl until her sobbing had ceased. By the morning, the skin at her wrist was torn and bloodied from her futile attempts at trying to pry free of the iron cuff that bound her.

With the passing of the storm, the morning sun warmed her dirt-streaked face and dried her clothes. She stood and combed the knots from her hair with her fingers. She needed to bathe but these men did not seem to know of such a practice. They came from their tents, pissed in the grass, ate rations, fed the girls some meagre amount, and then broke camp to continue travelling.

Every step was calculated so as not to upset the chain of girls before and after her. They were cuffed together at the wrists and ankles and one misstep would cause a reaction that brought them all to their knees. When that happened, the men would whip them back to their feet or drag them by the hair.

Often, she caught Urasid leering at her. She could not tell if he was plotting her death or savouring her appearance. But so long as they marched, she was safe from his advances. And if they marched, they were going somewhere. They were not ambling through the countryside on a trade mission. If they could avoid as many tribes along the way as possible, she would be happy. When they reached their destination, whether it was on her own shores or another, more people meant less observation, and a better chance at escape.

She began to scheme her release. When they stopped at the next settlement, most of the men would be too busy burning and killing. If she could convince the other girls that it was their best chance, they could overpower the remaining guards, free themselves from their chains and flee into the forests. No man fighting a war would have the patience or inclination to search every treetop for his missing slave.

She shook her head; she could not kid herself. They were girls, weak and hungry. Even eighteen of them would have a tough time against three of four grown men with swords and axes.

This was her life, a north-easterly march away from the memory of her people. Away from her mother. Towards a fate that would kill her regardless of her pleas to Odhran's gods.

She would die. But when she did, she would take Urasid with her. Him and all his people.

Chapter 18

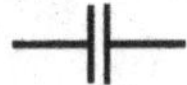

They had left the welcoming fires of the sept behind two days ago and Áed and Rónán had not yet had the opportunity to talk. Or to kiss again. Áed replayed those kisses in his mind on a continual loop, remembering the hot breath, the soft lips. Every step they took southeast did not take him from his prize. Rónán marched close to him as they travelled across open grasslands, reached out and touched his shoulder once as they crouched under the low-hanging boughs in a copse of trees, shielding themselves from a torrential downpour of rain that took them by surprise that morning. But always Achall was by his side, her thick, blonde hair a constant reminder of her close connection to Rónán, not yet family but already analogous to the wife she would become.

As the company crested a hill, the long grasses sweeping low in the wind and already browning at the end of summer, they heard the galloping of hooves from the south. When they looked, they saw over forty men riding horseback towards them. Áed's people used horses to pull carbads, but few would mount a beast to ride on its back. The sight bore the qualities of a nightmare come to haunt them.

'Foreigners,' someone called. At once the air was thick with the sound of swords being drawn from sheaths. Rónán had already cocked his bow and let loose an arrow, his hand swiftly returning to his quiver for another. His first shot hit true, one of the foreigners dropping from his horse with the arrow shaft protruding from his chest.

'Formations,' Oisín shouted. Shields were raised and their weapons recoiled.

Rónán pushed Achall behind him, stood beside Áed and drew his sword. The foreigners were too close for bow-work now.

Áed smiled. Any fear or worry was pushed from his mind as the foreigners bore down on them. 'Ready?'

'I'll kill more than you,' Rónán responded, and he braced for impact from the horses.

One of the foreigners swung low with his axe and Áed blocked it with his shield, the force reverberating through his whole body. He stepped aside as the horse bore on him and he sliced his sword round and up. It took the foreigner's arm off and sent it soaring over his head. The man dropped from his horse and Áed lunged at him, shield down on his face, sword plunging into his chest. The blood that splashed his cheeks felt cold as it hit him.

He stood and turned, searching for another quarry. But there were none.

Oisín surveyed the carnage and laughed. He turned to Déaglán and said, suddenly sombre, 'What ill spirit sends forty men into battle against a company of a thousand?' He looked around again; most of the men and boys had not even been close to the action.

'They were likely scouts,' Déaglán said.

'Forty scouts seem excessive,' Oisín said. 'Besides, scouts

would have laid in wait until we passed, or retreated to their company with the news of our march.'

'This far inland,' Áed said, 'they were either lost from their people or they were an advanced party hoping for smaller raids and little gains. If they move in smaller packs they'll be less likely to be spotted.'

Oisín flattened his lips in something that closely resembled a smile. Pointing at Áed, he said to Déaglán, 'This one is your newest advisor.'

'A swordsmith and a thinker,' Déaglán said. 'Should I just hand him my crown now?'

They laughed as Áed blushed.

Oisín wiped his sword on the body of a fallen foreigner. He had lost none of his own men. 'Stack the bodies downwind. We'll burn them and move on. Keep alert for more of the wily bastards; your first skirmish was a success, but I have a feeling the gods won't be so kind to us next time.'

With his own sword cleaned and the bodies long since burned, Áed fell into step beside Rónán and Achall. The girl looked worried but said nothing, her eyes downcast, her hair covering her face. She walked as close to Rónán as she could.

'Horses,' Áed said.

Rónán nodded. 'Do you think that's normal practice for them, riding on their backs?'

Áed shrugged. 'You can't steer and fight at the same time.'

There was nothing in Rónán's voice that indicated any desire to be alone, to talk. Áed worried their snatched moment of passion two nights before had been a dream, but no dream could feel so comforting and so intensely terrifying all at once.

Áed's body was no longer sore and weak from their march

southeast as they intended to skirt the shores of Lough Neagh. His legs grew accustomed to their incessant footfall, but still his mind was tired of a horizon that never for a second came any closer, tired of the harsh winds that flayed across the tall grasses, tired of the song of the bush-crickets in the evenings and the snores of his comrades. He longed for a time when he could close his eyes and not have the need to keep his sword at hand. But this was his life now, as reflective as he could be after only one minor scuffle, not even a battle, hardly even a skirmish. He was a soldier now, a protector of the people. Despite Rónán's words in bed two nights ago, it was entirely Áed's responsibility to protect everyone. If a man does not protect his friends and neighbours, is he even a man at all? Each man should be responsible for all that he sees and when all people are protecting their neighbours, no man is ever alone.

He knew the boys around him would have his back in battle. When they fought, it would be as one unit, one fist. But what of the woman and her daughter who had so graciously offered them a bed when she was under no tribal obligation to do so? That she willingly gave up a mattress for them, and shared her food, put the responsibility for her life squarely in Áed's hands. He would fight not for himself, not for his king, but for her— for her and all the women and children who remained at home when their husbands and fathers took up arms and left their sides.

When the sun set, Áed slept close to Rónán but could not get beside him, for Achall clung to him like morning dew. He closed his eyes and slept in fitful bursts, the clear image of this morning's kill floating sickeningly close. He marvelled at how intimate the killing had been and thought about the man's family in whichever land he had originated from. No doubt he had left a wife behind, or a sister, or a mother. Or a lover. Perhaps he had said to them that he would return. Or perhaps he had said his final farewells in the knowledge that he would never again grace their own shores. When Áed left his mother as he first ventured to Ailigh, a boy with only eight years under his tunic, had she known there was a possibility that she would never see him again? Had he? He thought about that. Training for war at Grianán Ailigh had seemed like a wonderous adventure eight years ago. But he had been certain that he would return home in a few months, a year at most. He would train, learn the sword, and then return to his family and assume a role at his father's side in the smithy. Eventually, a call would come for battle and he would venture east, kill where he could, and once again return home.

As it was, he could scarcely recall his mother's voice let alone her face. If he returned now, she would likely not even recognise him.

In the morning, he stepped away from their camp to bathe in a nearby burn. Sitting on the rocky bed, his modesty was only marginally covered by the slow-flowing water. He used silt from the river to scrub his flesh until he was pink. A few other boys were dotted in either direction, performing a similar ritual. Áed leaned back to soak his hair in the water and he closed his eyes, letting his arms drift to his sides. When he heard Rónán, he sat up and smiled.

'Are you displaying yourself to the birds or to the gods?'

'Both, if they'll have me.'

Rónán stripped and knelt on the bank, cupping his hands in the water and bringing it to his lips. Before drinking, he said,

'You haven't pissed in this, have you?'

'No, but I can't promise the boys upstream haven't.'

Rónán shrugged and drank, and Áed returned to cleaning himself. He could not look at his friend without wanting to touch him and his body was responding to those thoughts so that he had to turn away and splash water in his face.

'Where's Achall?' Áed asked without turning back.

'Asleep.' He touched the skin of his stomach. 'I still have the imprint of her arm on me, she gripped so tight in the night.' He came and sat in the water, splashing it in his armpits. 'Scrub my back?' he said and turned.

Áed gingerly rubbed Rónán's back with a fistful of silt. The muscles were tense underneath.

'Remember—' Áed began, then stopped.

He felt Rónán breathe heavy, his back arching. 'I will never forget.'

Quietly, Áed said, 'I'd like to do it again.'

'Me too.'

'Not now. Not here.'

'No.'

'Then where? When?'

Rónán turned to him, his eyes scanning up and down the river. 'After breakfast. We'll find somewhere.' And then he leaned in and brushed his lips gently across Áed's. He stood, swiped excess water from his chest and arms, and stood on the bank to dry himself.

But they did not get the chance to find a secluded moment after breakfast; Oisín gave the order to move out even before some of the men had time to eat.

They had marched not more than half a day before they were

ambushed. The foreigners leapt from the trees around them
and killed some twenty men before the boys could muster some
semblance of a wall of protection around their king and fight
back. Achall thrust a small dagger in front of her but had not
the wherewithal to use it, and Rónán pushed his way in front of
her with his shield raised and sword swinging.

Áed took note of their position. The foreigners had surrounded them and set upon them with such ferociousness that
Ailigh's warriors were hemmed together with little room to
manoeuvre. They were boxed in and cramped. Unless they
could cut through and spread out, they would have no hope of
success.

The foreigners wore leather on their chests and legs, but
Áed's blade cut at the arms and heads of any olive-skinned man
before him. When his second kill dropped at his feet, he was
no longer thinking rational thoughts. In a rage of violence, he
swung, jabbed, cut. He ducked and blocked an axe that flew at
him and he rolled to his feet, pushing forward with his shield,
knocking several invaders over and continuing without stop-
ping for the kill—others behind him would have the honour.
He cut a path through the men and sucked a lungful of air, span
on his heels and took the head of a foreign man with a double
swish of his sword. On this side of the fray, he had more room
for wider strokes, although he was still limited by the press of
trees around him, and he was not the only man to have broken through the ranks. The ambush had been calculated and
well-considered, but Ailigh had more men.

He looked for Rónán but could not see him.

He tried to wipe thick blood from his face with the shoulder
of his shield arm, but he had little time. A foreign man threw

an axe at him and then leapt towards him in a follow-through. Although he avoided the axe, the man tumbled into him with such force that it winded him. They fell to the underbrush and rolled together. Áed had dropped his sword and the straps of his shield were cutting his arm. Twisting, he brought the edge of the shield up hard in the man's face and blinded him with pain. He smashed again until the man fell off him and he rolled on top, smashed his shield into the foreigner's face one more time—he could not hear but felt the crunch of bone—and he found his sword and stood in time to pierce another adversary in the gut. The man's eyes widened and the growl in his throat ceased.

Áed moved. He had long since learned that a standing target was a dead target. He cut down another two men before noticing another in a tree, axe at the ready to swing.

'Look up!' he cried. 'Men in the trees!'

He raised his shield for protection, sighted, and he leapt forward, throwing his sword into the boughs. The man dropped from the tree and Áed retrieved his blade. It would only be luck that drove every thrown sword into the flesh of a foreigner, but as he scanned the neighbouring trees, he saw that Ailigh's boys were already firing spears.

The trees made for good cover, he realised. First one wave of men dropped and surrounded them, a second batch remaining among the leaves and picking off their enemies with unseen fire.

He jumped as an axe almost took his foot, and he turned, turned, swinging with precision at the men who remained on the ground. He kept low, his feet agitating, always moving, and when there were no more foreigners in front of him, he span, sought out another.

But it was over. The sound of clanging metal resounded in his ears but Ailigh's boys had stopped fighting. There was no one left to kill.

Someone gave a cheer.

'You three,' Oisín said, 'go that way. You boys, double back. Spread out; make sure no one got away from us.'

'Losses?' Déaglán asked.

'I'll count, but thirty. Maybe forty.'

'We'll bury our own and burn the rest,' Déaglán said. He wiped his blade clean, pointed it at Áed, and said, 'When this is over, you can make me another sword. I want one for each hand.'

Áed looked around. Rónán came towards him, sucking gulps of air, his face, hair and tunic red with blood.

'Are you injured?'

'Scraped,' Rónán said, indicating a shallow wound on his upper arm, 'but nothing that can't be fixed. You?'

Áed checked himself for wounds. He, too, was covered in blood. 'I can't tell. I don't think so. Achall?'

'Alive,' Rónán said. She appeared behind him, almost unblemished from foreigner's blood save for a small splash across her sleeve.

'I killed one,' she said. 'I'm not sure how, but I killed one dead.'

Later, away from the carnage, away from the trees, when they had set camp and had eaten, Oisín called for Áed and brought him to Déaglán's tent. The overking and his righthand men were the only ones in tents while the mass of boys and men outside would sleep under the stars.

Outside the flap of the tent, Oisín put a hand on Áed's shoulder. 'Speak when spoken to. You have a head on you, boy, but you're not an advisor. You can learn.'

'Why me?' Áed breathed, his voice low.

'Because I've seen you on the field. You're quick—quick with your thoughts as well as your sword. Just don't piss me off.'

They entered.

Inside, three men sat on stools in a semicircle, Déaglán among them. There were two more stools and Oisín indicated that Áed should occupy one.

'How many did you kill?' Déaglán asked when Áed took his seat and clasped his fingers together in his lap.

'I—' Áed thought about it. 'I'm not sure.'

'Good,' Déaglán said. 'A man who knows precisely how many enemies he has killed on the field is not performing his job well; if he has time to count, he has time to kill another.'

Áed lowered his eyes and smiled meekly.

'You were one of the first to break ranks,' Déaglán continued. His words were accusatory but were not without mirth.

'If we didn't get outside their mass, we would have lost a lot more men than we did.' He lowered his eyes again in acquiescence.

'That is why you are sitting here now. Oisín informs me you have a mind for tactics. You proved that out there today. Tell me, if you were to go to sleep now and then wake up and it was this morning all over again, what would you do differently?'

'Differently?'

'The ambush hasn't happened yet. You don't know that it's going to. But you wake and we march. Do you do anything different this time around?'

Without thinking, Áed said, 'I'd send scouts ahead of us. A rotation of men, with one coming back regularly to report, another man going out in his place.'

'We had scouts out,' Déaglán said.

Oisín said, 'But they weren't reporting back.'

'No, they weren't.' Déaglán gave this some consideration, then said, 'We have night-watch, we have scouts—however poorly they performed today. I know these lands; I grew up in them, travelled them extensively. We know these grasslands better than our enemy and yet they were still able to get a drop on us. They use tactics we hadn't considered. Sitting on the tops of horses and hiding in trees like brave cowards.' He nodded, as if to himself. 'Tomorrow we will send five scouts, and a further five behind them. A forerunner will report back to the aft who will report back to us. And as the boy says, we will send a fresh man forward each time.'

'My lord,' Áed said, his voice low, timid.

'Speak,' Oisín said.

Áed looked at Oisín, then at Déaglán. 'We're going south-east. Yet we're ignoring the northern coast. If we skirt around the shores—'

'The fighting is in the east,' Déaglán said. 'We've had no reports of battles in the north and skirting the farthest reaches will slow or tracks. We will go around the underside of the lough and come up from beneath.'

Áed nodded, though he was not satisfied. He was worried for his family in the west.

At length, Déaglán said, 'Oisín, send a small convoy north. They can re-join us in the east.' He stood. 'Leave me now. Get some rest. Tomorrow we will no doubt fight some more.'

Outside the tent, Oisín once again took Áed's shoulder. 'Walk with me,' he said.

The sun had all but disappeared and the bush-crickets were heralding their demanding pleas. The sound of singing came to them from some nearby men. Áed and Oisín picked their way around the perimeter.

'Do not presume that you know more than King Déaglán. Or myself. When I call you to the tent in future, you will speak when spoken to, or you will not speak at all, am I clear?'

Áed nodded, but for clarity in the fading light, he said, 'I understand.'

'These people—your people—will always need a good smith. But when you are not forging and you are not fighting, you will be my apprentice.'

'Apprentice?'

'Maybe one day, if you survive long enough,' Oisín said, 'you can replace me in serving the overking and leading this rabble of boys you call friends.'

Áed smiled. 'Not friends,' he said. 'Family.'

Chapter 19

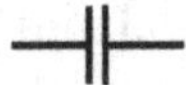

Bec draped Urasid's tunic over a low-hanging branch to dry after she had scrubbed it with a flat-stone on the bank of the burn. Her wrists were locked together with two feet of heavy chain between them so that she could perform menial tasks when he required it of her. Her ankles were chained likewise. She was allowed to bathe in the mornings and evenings, but had to do so with her chains on, and she was always under watch from one of the men. Her womanhood was only just beginning to reveal itself on her body and she felt sickened every time Urasid took her as his woman, or every time one of these foreigners would look at her with a leering, vacant stare. Often, she would bathe with her dress on. She was thankful, at least, that when Urasid did take her, he did so without an audience. She could stand his slaps and the stench of his breath and the pain inside her when he lay on top, but for someone else to witness it would be intolerable. And although he was a mean-spirited bastard, and brutal with his fists, he was not as old as the other men, men who could be her grandfather, men who raped these girls without embarrassment of their shrivelled dicks and greying pubes.

With half a chance, she would gladly separate every single

man from his most prized organ and watch them bleed to death.

This was what she had become. Two weeks ago, she was an innocent, active child. Now her eyes were darkened and clouded with despair, her mind awash with murderous thoughts. Every footstep, every movement was no longer her own. Urasid would command and Bec would comply and say thank you when he threw her some food and she would smile and curse him without speaking, curse him to every single god whose name she could recall.

Their lives had fallen into a pattern. Her enslavers would march them for half a day, camp for two days, march another day, and burn any sept they came across. The killing and burning would slow them down a day more. They would drink their sweet wines as the sun dropped low and they would stand and watch the homes burn, swaying their bodies in a flamelike dance, unfazed by the stink of death that surrounded them. And then any new girl that was forced to join them would be unceremoniously raped and beaten and told of her place and then beaten some more.

They were still marching north-east. Bec was adamant that they were walking to somewhere specific but she had never ventured far from her sept before and did not know the locations of other tribes or their holy places. She was certain that they were nowhere near the druids where her sister was, or Grianán Ailigh where her brother trained. But every couple of days brought another sept to be plundered and they still weren't nearing the end of their journey.

They had been joined a few days ago by more foreigners who met them warmly and slapped each other's backs and talked of how many girls they had and who owned each of them.

The girls were appraised and the men were lauded for their accomplishments.

That first night of their arrival, a fight broke out between two of the men, a newcomer and one of her original captors. They were arguing, it seemed, over one of the girls, a redhead just a year or two older than Bec, whose body under her loose garments was already full and womanly. The fight turned from fists to blades and the other men did not intervene. The newcomer's face was unrecognisable, bloodied and swollen, when they carried his body away from camp. If this would become a nightly ritual for these foreigners, Bec and the girls would be free of them within two months.

Every night, under the shelter of darkness, Bec scraped at the iron cuffs on her wrists with a stone. She made minute scratches here and there, but she knew she could never wear them away even with a thousand years to do so. Spitting on her wrists, although it soothed her grazes, was not enough to slip her hands free. And even if she could get free, kill Urasid, maybe kill a second man, she would be recaptured, beaten and raped, or murdered. It never crossed her mind to flee; if she managed to escape her manacles, she would stand and fight, for all the aggravation of a bumble bee that she might cause. But although she would not eradicate her lands of these outsiders singlehandedly, she would gladly die after stinging just one.

The following day, they approached yet another community and, chained to the trees as they were, Bec had a view of the carnage that unfolded among the homes. The elderly druid was brought out and slaughtered in front of his people. The foreigners allowed his guts to spill onto the grass before him, even as he gurgled and begged for his life. With the able-bodied men off at war, what defences did these women and children have? The boys and the girls who were deemed too young, were killed in front of their mothers whose sobbed heartache darkened the afternoon. The remaining girls were rounded up and chained, and the older women were slaughtered.

The rest of the day saw Bec and the other girls clearing out the homes of food and tools, stockpiling them in carts to take with them when they left. One of the girls from the sept clung to Bec's side, begging her to find her doll, before she was pulled away by the hair, cuffed to a tree and punched. In the girl's home, searching for food, Bec found a small, wooden figure with thread-hair and a yellow dress. She hid it under her skirt and made her way back to the carts with some bread and cured meats. When she was sent back to the trees to be chained with the others, she discreetly pushed the doll into the girl's hands and told her to keep it hidden. The girl was younger than she, too young to be forced for sex, too young to understand the consequences of what she was now a part of. Her naturally wide eyes were now squinting in tears and would remain so until her innocence was taken from her and she locked her childhood away in the darkness of a mind that would soon break.

While the men drank and sang their songs and watched the village burn, the girls huddled under the nearby trees and cooed at the new girls that they would be fine, all would be well. Someone hummed a mother's song and, those that could, joined in with the quiet melody.

Later, when the sun was down, the men came to take what was theirs. Urasid gripped Bec's arm and hauled her away into the trees. As she was dragged, she saw one of the older men touching the young girl's cheek and grinning at her.

With her wrists still bound but her ankles free, Urasid bore on her, holding her chain with one fist, clenching her jaw with his other as he thrust at her. He was drunk, the smell of sweet wine and bile on his breath. The stench of death on the air had become so frequent, so normal, that she barely recognised it anymore, but she would never grow accustomed to his breath.

During his actions, Urasid lost his erection and he slapped her as though it were her fault. He fumbled for a few moments, cursing her—or himself—in words she did not understand, before forcing himself back upon her and burying his face in her hair.

Bec did not cry, or scream, or moan in agony. From now until the day she died, she knew, she would forever remain immune to pain. If nothing else, Urasid had given her that much.

She heard the soft, welcoming hoot of an owl somewhere in the distance, calling out to her as though he knew her, and she closed her eyes. *Do not watch me, owl. Do not watch what is become of me.*

In time, his thrusting quickened and then, with a final forceful shove, he convulsed on top of her and lay there, motionless, breathing hard against her cheek, whispering words in a foreign dialect, harsh words whose meaning was conveyed only in the guttural draw from his throat.

He did not move and she allowed him to crush down on her, hoping that his weight would crack her bones and squeeze the life from her bruised flesh. When she realised he was asleep, she laid there still, until at last she pulled her wrist-chain free of his loosened grip, lowered her arms and pushed her dress down as best she could. His sticky flaccidness grazed the back of her hand and she retched. But still she lay there, under him.

Even the owl had grown silent.

She began to count, and when she reached a high enough number that she could not recall which number came next, she struggled out from under him, rolling him off her legs as gently as she could without waking him. Had it not been for the wealth of wine, he would already be awake and on top of her again. As it was, he curled one arm around his face and continued to sleep on the ground.

The knife-belt from his waist was left beside a tree, taken off before he had mounted her. She took the knife, hefted it in her hands, and looked at him.

Then she turned and crept away.

Although her wrists were still bound, she had enough freedom to climb a tree and shuffle from one bough to another, back towards the burning village. Several of the girls had been returned to their station and chained together to await morning, their captors having had their fill of them for the evening. Bec looked for the young girl with the doll and could not see her there.

With cat-like stealth, she moved from tree to tree, seeking out those men who were still rutting with their girls. In one hand she held Urasid's knife and with her other, she gripped her chains to stop them from rattling.

When she found the young girl, huddled at the base of a tree, curled up and crying quietly, Bec looked for the old man. He sat on the ground, propped against the opposite tree, his head drooped back and his eyes closed. She watched the rise and fall of his chest, timed his breathing, and waited until she was certain he was asleep.

Bec dropped lightly from the tree and clamped her hand over

the young girl's mouth to stop her from screaming.

'Hush. It's me. It's okay.'

The girl's eyes widened, then narrowed. She nodded her head to indicate she wouldn't scream.

Bec released her and stood. She looked at the old man. 'Did he touch you?' she asked. 'Did he hurt you?'

The girl shook her head. Whispering, she said, 'He sat and drank and stared at me. Then he fell asleep.'

'Good,' Bec breathed. She hefted the knife in her fist, adjusted her grip on it. 'Look away. Close your eyes.'

The girl scrambled to turn.

Bec stepped closer to the old man, picking her feet over brambles, and she crouched. She raised the knife, holding its point a breath's distance from his neck, and she paused. She inhaled, clamped her lips shut, and pushed outwards and upwards with the blade.

It penetrated his skin, plunged into his neck at a rising angle, and stopped about two inches in, stuck on something inside him.

The old man opened his eyes and his mouth. She could see the blade's tip protruding from his tongue. He tried to struggle against her, but she dropped a knee into his groin and pushed again on the blade.

It shoved a further two inches in, sewing his jaw shut as the knife went through the roof of his mouth.

He stopped fighting against her and lay motionless. When she turned, the girl was staring at her in terror.

'I told you not to look. Don't tell anyone. Promise?'

The girl nodded.

It took all her effort to remove the blade from the old man's

head. When finally it sucked free, she wiped it on his trousers to clean the blood and darkness from it. She took the girl
back to the others and sat her on the ground beside them, stop-
ping once to hide behind a tree when one of the men stumbled
drunkenly by. She told them all to be quiet and then she scrambled back up into the trees.

When she returned to Urasid, he was still asleep. She slipped
down to the ground, sheathed his blade and put his belt back
where she had found it, and then she lay down beside him, trying not to breath hard, trying to stifle the nervous laughter that
was building up inside her.

She raised her arms and let his fingers encircle the chain.
And he grunted.

Chapter 20

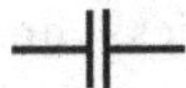

Ailigh's boys had spent another day marching southward around the shores of the lough, slowed by the hilly countryside and the maze of densely-populated forests that choked the mid-regions of the province. At times, under the impenetrable awning of ash and alder leaves, it felt like an everlasting midnight, coupled with the soughing of the wind through the upper branches that brought a nightmare quality to their journey, their skin washed green and dark with otherworldly shades. In clearings and hilltops they paused to be warmed by the sun and to eat, and in those quiet moments when the crying wind no longer accosted their senses, Áed would sit with Rónán in hushed silence, neither saying what was on his mind, both understanding their desire for a touch, a kiss, a tender embrace. If Achall had grown suspicious, she did not say it. Áed could not be certain if their moments together had changed since their younger days; if they looked at each other differently now, or spoke softer or longer together.

It was later that afternoon, during a routine ration inspection, when several of the boys had proceeded south and north on brief hunting expeditions, that Áed had found a moment alone with Rónán. They did not speak a word, and in the darkness beneath the cover of trees, they sought each other out by touch and senses rather than by spoken direction. When Rónán's lips came and rested upon Áed's, Áed shivered in anticipation, his hands reaching out and cupping Rónán's face. Rónán pressed him against a tree, their lips locked, and through the fabric of their tunics, their arousal was evident.

With halting insecurities, unsure of themselves, they stripped and lay on the rough ground together, their bodies wet with perspiration, conjoining in an awkward embrace that caused more pain than pleasure. When they were spent, panting and laughing, they lay there as their bodies cooled, Rónán's fingers entwined in Áed's, his head resting on his damp chest. He traced the wispy trail of dark hair below Áed's navel, and he yawned, kissing the sweat-moistened hollow at his breastbone.

The hoarse cry of a pheasant echoed from their left, some distance away, and Rónán said, 'I've worked up an appetite, but I don't want to move.'

'You can eat the moss beneath my head,' Áed said. 'Then cut me open and drink me so that I will always be inside you.'

'That isn't funny.'

'It wasn't meant to be.'

The pheasant croaked its coarse, grating call again and Rónán lifted his head. 'We should kill it and return to the others before we are missed.'

'Achall will be looking for you, no doubt.'

Rónán knelt, looked away. 'When we are alone together, never say her name to me. She is not a part of this.' He gripped Áed's flaccidness. 'When I see this, I do not want to be thinking about her. Or about anything. Anything but how sweet you taste to me.' He leaned down, kissed Áed with vigour, and then he stood. 'Come, I have a pheasant to catch.'

Áed's muscles were tense, but he forced himself up and dressed even as Rónán was disappearing into the forest with his bow.

Much later, after they had eaten and cut half a day's slow progress around the southern edge of the lough and through the impenetrable countryside, leaving a wake of broken vegetation behind them, a call came out from the front of the company. A multitude of smoke columns were spotted in the east, rising into the evening sky, darkening the twilight horizon into a swirling fog of violent cloud.

'A sacked village?' someone asked.

'A camp,' came the reply.

'One of ours or one of theirs?'

Oisín ordered several scouts to advance and report back, and when they had returned, he was told that the camp was the frontline of the war, their own tribal armies nearest them. The men of the Ó Fuinseog.

'The small bands of the foreigners that we have stumbled upon so far,' Déaglán said, 'had not been front-lining or advancing, but must have infiltrated the west by means of other ports.'

When they reached the Ó Fuinseog camp, a thousand men cheered their arrival. They were not the first to join them and the clear definition of camps between tribes was evident in the placement of their tents and latrines. These men were working together to defeat a common foe, but they still retained their tribal identities as separate from each other.

Achall was pleased to spot several other women—as were the boys—and she immediately joined them in conversation.

At the front, Déaglán, Oisín, Áed and the advisors advanced to the Ó Fuinseog tent and entered for discussions.

Before entering, Oisín said, 'They will host us well and we will be free to speak inside the tent, but remember you are my apprentice, not a seasoned advisor. If you have considerations, you bring them to me first.'

They were greeted warmly by King Fergal, tribal ruler of the Ó Fuinseog, and he embraced Déaglán in a bear hug that lifted him off his feet. Fergal was almost as broad as he was tall, his arms scarred from fresh war and his cheeks ruddy and full.

'Déaglán, you brute of an animal,' he said with a laugh. 'Am I to concede to your laws immediately or are we to fight first?'

'No sooner would you touch your sword than I'd be throwing your severed head into the enemy's camp to sup from,' Déaglán laughed.

'Sit, sit. We should drink to your arrival. With you here, we will defeat these bastards before yule and I can return to my wives.'

'If I know your women well, they are likely glad of your absence.'

'Which is why I long to return to them so that they do not grow bored without me.'

They sat, and Fergal told them of their days so far. They had been camped here for three weeks and they had lost almost as many men as the foreigners, and the line of contention between armies was moving back and forward every day. They were holding strong, but with Déaglán's help they would surely make ready advances.

As was customary, each side observed a ceasefire from the moment the sun touched the distant horizon until daybreak, so that first one army and then the other could retrieve their dead, worship their deities, and recover from the losses of the day before. Litters were dragged back from the battlefield and bodies were burned with ceremony so that their valiant journey into the Otherworld would be met with the cheering and jubilation of their ancestors. Druids were on hand for the rituals that a layman could not comprehend.

In the morning, they would fight strong, but for now, Déaglán and his company were free to drink and eat and enjoy the meagre comforts of a nation united by foreign blight.

When they returned to their allocated area, Ailigh's boys had already made camp and lit fires for warmth and for cooking. A bright moon lit the sea of tents and sleeping areas and songs were being sung by visiting bards that told sorrowful tales of battles along the north and east coasts. By their words, Áed learned of the sacking of many coastal tribes, and it was with a heavy heart that he ate charred fruit from their campfire and sat in silence.

When Rónán found him and sat with him, Áed told him of Fergal's campaign so far. 'He is convinced that with our help we can win this quickly.'

'We will,' Rónán said. 'We swell their ranks by a thousand —half of what was already here.'

Áed sighed. 'Don't you think we are just little boys playing war with our father's swords? It was different back there. We outnumbered the foreigners we came across ten to one. But here, this is the frontline. This is where we win or lose by our actions, not our might.'

'You didn't make me feel like a little boy this morning,' Rónán whispered. 'Besides, we have trained for this. This moment—this is what we have longed for. This is why we left our tribes and our families half a lifetime ago. This is what will make us legends in the eyes of all who come after us.'

'If I am still alive at the setting of sun tomorrow, only then will I start to feel less like a child and more like a warrior.'

Rónán glanced around. 'Let me play with your sword tonight and I'll make you feel like a warrior.'

Áed laughed. He finished eating his fruit and together they walked off in search of seclusion. They passed Achall, who spoke to Rónán briefly before returning to her conversations with the other young women. That she could now enjoy the company of girls meant that Áed and Rónán could have longer moments alone.

With the morning sun came a call to arms. Áed, Rónán and everyone else who had gathered, assembled on the field for the promise of blood. Spears and javelin were brought forward among the ranks, and Rónán took his place among the archers. At the sound of the horns, a volley of spears and arrows from either side blackened the cloudless sky. When they were at their height, the men of both armies made their battle sounds and ran to meet each other in the field.

Pushed back by older, more experienced warriors, Áed crouched and raised his shield as the foreigners' javelin came down on them. Then he ran hard, his sword aloft. As he entered the bout, he took a deep breath, cried aloud, and barrelled into a foreign man. As they went down, he rolled over his head, sprang to his feet, stabbed another man, and then brought the edge of his shield down on the fallen warrior's neck. He turned to find his next kill.

When the sun was at its highest point in the sky and among

them they cast no shadows, a horn sounded and a lone rider from the enemy's ranks rode out into the field on the back of a horse as the armies returned to their sides. He dismounted at the mid-point in the valley and spurred his horse back towards his people.

'Who among you can defeat me?' he called out.

Someone close to Áed said to him, 'He comes out each day for single combat and each day we lose a man to that giant.'

Áed watched as one broad-shouldered, redheaded native strode out onto the field, ripped off his tunic, and said, 'I'll kill the bastard whore-son.' He charged alone towards his quarry with sword and shield, cheered on by his compatriots.

'What is he doing?' Áed asked. 'He'll be killed.'

'Every army needs a champion,' the man next to him said.

The fight lasted some time as each of the champions parried and riposted with equal measure. At a moment when it seemed that the foreigner had bested his foe, he was knocked off his feet and jabbed at. Once, the foreigner hit out so hard with his shield that the homegrown champion was thrown backwards and his sword was sent form his hand into the grasses. As the olive-skinned aggressor bore down on him, the native flipped a dagger and slashed at his arm, wounding him but not badly.

From his position in the line, Áed could hear the grunting of the two men as they fought for dominance.

The duel lasted some time until, wounded, bleeding, and ragged, the foreigner made a last attempt to sever his opponent's head from his shoulders and succeeded. A cheer erupted from his fellow army and a horn sounded from the far side of the field. The successful champion retreated to his side and two men were sent out from Ó Fuinseog's army to retrieve their fallen friend before the distance fighting would resume.

A week later, tired from the incessant fighting, it was proving increasingly difficult to find a man willing to take on the foreigner's challenge, although every day someone would step up and die in his attempts.

One evening, hidden among the nearby trees, after they had made love twice and were now lying naked in each other's arms on the damp ground, Áed said, 'The champion fights take too long. We should stay out there and fight them to reclaim our lands.'

'Just promise me,' Rónán said, 'that you won't champion yourself against that monster of a man.'

'I cannot promise that. He's too big for me, of course, but I strengthen every day. At this rate, we will still be fighting this field come Imbolc or the Imbolc after that. One day I will be big enough to overcome him.'

'But until then, keep rank.'

Áed brushed his fingers through Rónán's damp, blond hair. 'I will.' He turned into an embrace and, after kissing him, said, 'I've been studying him. He moves fast and agile, but he favours his left. He delays minutely before riposting an overhand blow, as though he had not been expecting it or if he isn't entirely sure how to defend against it. He succeeds, of course, but an overhand swipe with a shield-blast to the abdomen would surely best him. Knock him down, sever his head, and then carry it proudly among his ranks so that everyone can smell his blood before I gut them all.'

Rónán rolled on top of him, his body firm, muscles taut, his member already straining with hardness again. 'Tell me again how you'll gut them all singlehandedly.' He leaned down and flicked his tongue along Áed's jaw. He slid a hand under Áed's buttocks and squeeze gently. 'Tell me how hard you can be on the battlefield. Is it as hard as this?' He moved Áed's hand so that he was touching him.

Áed grinned and kissed him. 'You're insatiable.'

'He is never so insatiable with his bride,' Achall's voice said.

The boys clambered away from one another and covered themselves. Achall and one of the other girls were standing some feet away and it was unclear if they had been sneaking up or if the boys were so enamoured of the moment that they simply had not heard them approach. Flushed and angry, Achall turned and stormed away, leaving the two naked boys and her female companion to stare at one another with unease.

Rónán stood, dressed, and then crouched down to Áed to kiss him, indicating that this cruel interruption would not spell the end of their lovemaking, and then he ran after the girl that had been chosen to be his wife.

The other young woman stared at Áed with open joy at his misfortune until he said, 'You can leave now, I'd like to get dressed.'

Áed found a quiet spot away from his kinsfolk but close enough to a fire that he could remain warm in the dying light. It was foolish of them to have even attempted intimacy during such times. And with Rónán promised to another, too.

Rónán was not just a gratifying release due to a lack of female companions; Áed had no such interest in that. And, he was certain, Rónán must surely feel the same. Had he just wanted sex, he had a woman to request it from.

And yet he was betrothed. And they were in the middle of a war. And Achall had looked so absolutely confounded when she had come across them in such an intimate embrace.

Áed buried his face in his hands and wept.

The sun had long since disappeared when Rónán found him. 'She wishes to speak with you.'

'Me?' Áed's eyes widened in terror. 'But I don't know what to say to her.'

'Trust me, you need to speak to her.' He clasped Áed's hand, helped him to stand. 'She's—I can't describe it. Just come, speak with her.'

When they approached her, sitting near a fire with a gaggle of girls fussing around her, she looked at Áed and said, 'I will be married and I will have a child. There is nothing you can do to stop that from happening.'

She shooed her girls away so that only the three of them re-mained. She looked from one to the other, standing side by side as they were, and for a long time there were no words.

Then she stood. 'I have known about this for a long time.'

'But we—'

'Or I suspected, at least. Now I know the truth of it.' In the red glow from the fire, she looked much older than her fourteen years. The boys, however, felt no longer sixteen and instead were more like the eight-year olds they had been when they first met. 'This customary practice of unwed boys will continue whether I ask it to stop or not,' she continued. 'I may be young, but I am no fool. That said, I have conditions.'

Áed was unsure how he was supposed to feel in that mo-ment. Was she truly giving them her blessing for their actions?

'Rónán and I will be married without a handfasting,' Achall said. 'On the yule. With Overking Déaglán's consent, we will use any of the druids who are willing to perform the rituals.

And I will be with child by Imbolc.' Rónán was about to pro-
test when she cut him off. 'Your dick won't work for the likes
of me, I am sure. So, I will take to the bed of another man. Of
multiple men if I must. The child will be known as Rónán's
offspring and raised as such, as an heir to the house of my uncle
who desires this union.' She looked at Rónán. 'You will rise
through the ranks of this forsaken people and your son will rule
nations one day. And once we are wed, you will act according-
ly. You will adore me and devote your time to me. I need no
bride-price from you, only your unwavering commitment to
our union. And on the nights when you are not spitting in each
other's mouths, you will sleep on the floor beneath my bed
like the dog that you are. On those occasions when I allow you
your freedom to rut with this—this *boy*—you will do so far
away from here where no one will see you. And then you will
bathe before returning to my floor so that I will not be forced
to smell him on you. Do I make myself clear?'

'Yes,' Rónán said, all too quickly.

She looked at Áed. He was still processing the words she had
spoken. 'Do you understand me, wretch?'

At last he nodded.

Achall sat back down by the fire. Quietly, she said, 'Get out
of my sight lest I change my mind.'

Chapter 21

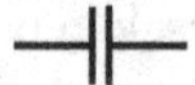

Grainne tended to her small garden patch of herbs and cultivated flowers. She was still adjusting to life away from the archdruid's watchful gaze, but on the morning that she left, he had assured her that she would be visited regularly. She might very well be qualified and presiding over a tribe of her own, but she still had much to learn.

Village life was not as she remembered it. Before travelling north to train with the druids, her existence had been so small. She had known the names of everybody in her sept, had been able to extract dyes from plants only with her mother's assistance, and she had journeyed no more than a tribe's distance for market and only once when her mother had permitted it. Now, she had spoken with the gods and she was a chieftain's principal counsellor; she knew which herb would cure a man and which would kill him—and all before she had seen out fifteen winters. If anybody in Donal's tribe had any misgivings about her fledgling abilities as a child-druid, they kept them to themselves. By law, she was a woman, unmarried as she was, and as a druid, she would be respected and obeyed without question. She had already meted out fines for some minor infractions since her arrival.

Donal, although a sycophantic chieftain with delusions of majesty and a proclivity towards young women, had been nothing but supportive of her since they met. In the two months since she took up residency in his tribe, he had entertained her for dinner almost every evening, calling upon one child or another to sing or dance for her delight. She had smiled and laughed and applauded every time, but the festivities where dulling her senses and she needed respite. She had devised a system of accepting his nightly invitations three evenings in a row, then begging his forgiveness on the fourth night for a headache, or a poultice that was urgent, or some legal matter that needed immediate consideration and could not possibly wait.

This morning, Faolán's shadow darkened her garden and when she looked up from nursing a rather young angelica herb, he said, 'Father has sent for some gut medicine.'

Faolán's presence disturbed her greatly, the way his lips thinned when he smiled, the way his eyes never quite looked her directly in the face, as though he had dark thoughts he'd just as well not reveal. He would sit too close to her at dinner and she could spot the flaring of his nostrils every time she moved around him. But he was Donal's first-born son and the pride of his tribe.

'Is he suffering greatly?' she asked him.

Faolán rubbed his own stomach in illustration. 'Probably too much wine.'

Grainne's smile was perfunctory. She disappeared inside, glad of the cool shadows within and glad that she was away from the young man's stares. She retrieved a small wooden vial and returned to the sunlight. 'A little drop of this in some water and he'll feel well in no time.'

Faolán sniffed the vial. 'What's in it?'

'An ancient combination of plant extract and herbs.'

'Smells like pig shit.'

'And it tastes as bad, too, but it works.'

She dismissed him by returning to her gardening, but he did not leave. His shadow still blocked half of her plant patch and she could hear him breathing.

Without looking up, she said, 'Is there anything else I can help you with?'

'I was just thinking,' he said, 'about my mother's desire for grandchildren.'

'Do you desire a child of your own?'

'No, but I do desire the act of making one.'

When she looked at him, he was smiling that thin-lipped sneer that made her stomach tense. 'I'm sure your father has a lucky woman already picked for your marriage bed.'

'You could bless my bed before I use it with another.'

Grainne dusted soil from her hands and stood. 'That's not quite how a blessing works. Besides, if we slaughtered a lamb in your marriage bed as a gift to the gods, would you not fear that your community might think you had done some other things with that lamb in your bed—things that are unspeakable?'

His smile became a grimace and he waved her comments away. 'Better get this to father before he screams for murder. Will you be at dinner this evening?'

She turned back to her plants. Lying was easier when you didn't have to look a man in the face. 'I have some urgent legal matters to consider before morning. But if I have the time, I will.'

In the afternoon, the neighbouring tribe's druid visited with news of an invasion on northern and western shores. 'And how are your bird's-foot blooms coming along?'

'Are we in any danger?' Grainne asked. The druid, Máire, had brushed so easily over the news that surely it could not pose any immediate threat. 'I should speak with Donal about this.'

'We're too far south. The men of the northern tribes will stop the infraction, of course. The bird's-foot?'

Grainne pointed to the small wash of pale pink flowers that had been potted in earthenware so that it could be easily moved as the sun travelled across the sky. 'It's not doing very well. I don't think it likes our rich soil.'

'If you tend it well, it will reap you many benefits. Another year or two of growth and you should be able to use it in your remedies.'

'I do appreciate the gift,' Grainne said. 'Since I completed my training and came south, everybody has been so welcoming and giving.'

'No one gives without expectation of return,' Máire said. 'Myself included. One day I may call on you for a favour.'

'I will happily oblige.'

'As for everyone else, they will continue to bring you gifts until you've been established a year and a day. After that, they will expect you to look upon them favourably when they come before you in a property dispute or some such.'

They chatted briefly about Grainne's recent dispute resolution and Máire agreed with her rulings. When she left, Grainne sought out Donal in the chieftain's hall where he spent his afternoons.

'I'm told of an invasion in the north,' she said.

'I have heard of it,' Donal told her. 'If they cut through the northern tribes and make it this far south, there will be less of them to slaughter.'

'Are you concerned?'

'Our northern tribes will send word if they need our help. Come, join me for a drink of wine.'

'I have matters to——'

He slapped his hand on his table, the first sign that his ingratiating demeanour was in fact a façade. 'Wine!' he shouted over his shoulder, and his youngest son came into the room with a pitcher whose contents sloshed as he ran.

Grainne nodded her thanks when the boy handed her a cup and she turned back to Donal. 'Your gut medicine is working, I trust.'

'Why do you always stand?' he asked. 'Sit, sit.' This was not the first sip of wine to pass his lips this afternoon, she thought. 'Tell me, do *you* think we should be concerned about the invaders?'

She thought about it for some minutes. 'If they are confined to the north and east, I am sure we won't come to any harm. If it is small raiding parties, they may likely never venture this far south. If, on the other hand, it is a massive invasion, do you have a plan for such times? For aiding our northern brothers?'

She had not heard Donal's first wife enter the hall. Muirgel cleared her throat directly behind Grainne and said, 'There are two plans.' She walked around the table, kissed her husband's cheek, and sat at his left. 'If we outnumber the foreigners, we will slaughter them and be victors. If they outnumber us two to one, we will still slaughter every wretched one of them.'

'And if they come as an army and outnumber us ten to one?'

'Then we will negotiate our freedom on their terms. Give

a man what he wants and he is less likely to kill you in your sleep.'

'Don't we have the might to reach northward and aid our countrymen?' Grainne asked.

'It may be too late to send our men north,' Donal said. 'And if we did, there would be nobody left to defend our tribe lands.'

He put an end to the matter and spoke of dinner. Grainne was unable to dissuade him on this occasion and she spent the evening nursing the same cup of wine, eating meats and fruits, and listening to one of Donal's children singing in pitched tones about the ancient kings and their conquests.

As she lay on her mattress that night, listening to the sounds of the wind and the distant river that fed in from the coast, she wished for Cáer's presence to visit her dreams. She had not seen the goddess or her father, Ethal Anbuail, since leaving the north. She prayed that the sun would rise in the morning and that Donal would continue to treat her well. When she slept, it was in sporadic flashes, and she dreamt about war, about invasions, and about a multitude of death. Her sleep was so disturbed that she rose before dawn and set to work in her garden. The sun had already been and gone that day when she finally stopped for a rest.

On the late-summer morning when the foreigners did come to Dáirine, they rode up the river in a host of currach, each hide-skin boat holding ten men. There must have been sixty currach approaching them as Donal, Muirgel and Grainne stood on the sand surrounded by platters of fresh fruit and cured meats. In the distance, at the mouth of the river, three massive warships had been docked for two days.

Before they were even in earshot, Donal waved his arms in

the air and shouted a greeting. An arrow landed at his feet, but he was convinced it was not meant to harm him. 'Only a warning shot,' he said.

'They may not even speak our language,' Grainne said.

In the four weeks since she had first learned from Máire of the foreigner's invasion, she had spoken with Donal and Muirgel often in a bid to thrash out a solid plan of action. He refused to send his men north to aid their neighbour tribes, and he was adamant that their own defences would suffice. 'We will negotiate with them,' he had told her.

'We have no assurances that they will listen to negotiations,' Grainne said. But he was hopeful and she bowed to her chieftain's judgement, just as she bowed to him this morning before they walked down the sands to the river's edge. She wore her ceremonial robes, its stitched runes woven with golden thread, and she touched the rune of protection over her breast as the first currach ran ashore.

Donal kneeled in the damp sand, and as the colossal foreigners approached with their weapons drawn, he lay prostrate on the ground and begged his wife and his druid to do likewise. Muirgel complied but, although she took a knee, Grainne did not lower herself further.

'We offer you a kindness,' Donal said, keeping his face out of the sand. 'We wish to negotiate terms.'

The men stopped before them. 'The terms are: I take your head,' one of them said. His accent was thick, undeniably foreign, but his words were clear enough.

'Wait,' Donal begged. 'I can get you what you want. We can help you. You will be better with a man who knows these shores. We have women, plenty of women. Or men if you prefer. And knowledge. I have much knowledge that can help you.'

When the foreigners did not reply, did not move, Donal pushed himself up onto his knees again. He raised a warding hand of supplication and smiled as best he could.

One of the foreigners, whose long, dark hair extended almost to the midpoint of his back, whose skin was patterned with dyes and his beard clipped short, came and stood before Grainne. 'Druid?'

She refused to look at him.

He took her chin in his hand and stared at her. When he undid the string at his leather vest, she saw a rune of protection dyed onto his chest. 'Druid?' he asked again.

She nodded. 'You?' As an acolyte, she had studied the art of warfare, had trained in some simple combat techniques, but hers was a quiet art that required peace of mind, and no soldier had peace before his death.

'My brother,' he said. He reached for Grainne's hand and helped her to stand. To Donal and Muirgel he said, 'Get up. Tell me this knowledge that you have to help me.'

Struggling to get on his feet, Donal took a moment and then said, 'We will gladly be of service, so long as we have your word that you will not harm us. I can get you power. Power over the north, and from there, power over all of Éirinn. My surrogate son is in the north. He shall be promoted to overking and he will do always your bidding. You have my word of it.'

'I can take the king-seat myself,' the man said.

'But they have an army up there.'

The man laughed, pointed back to the mouth of the river. 'You can see I have not come with just my mother. I can take the king-seat alone.'

'You will need someone that our tribesmen will obey. What good is conquering a land if you kill all its people? My surrogate son will be a good king under your direction and his people will listen to him. All will bow to your words.'

The foreigner considered this for a moment. 'I enjoy the killing. Killing is good fun. But whores and servants—perhaps this is better, no?'

'Much better,' Donal agreed. 'We can prepare a feast for you and your men.'

'I will sit and eat with your people before I decide if I should kill you all. My name is Eorid. Your druid will sit at my left when we eat and she will give thanks to her gods that it was I who landed on these shores and not another of my countrymen. We are a bloodthirsty nation seeking vengeance, and I can easily gut you as look at you. You have until sundown to prepare. My men will set camp on these shores.'

As they hurried away, Grainne said, 'You threw yourself at him like a worm.'

'I have protected my people, as is my obligation as their chieftain. Would you rather I had let them all be slain?'

'This plan of yours will bear no good fruit. Whomever your surrogate son is, this boy of king-power, I will pray to Cáer for him.'

Chapter 22

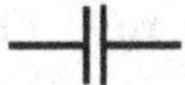

Áed ran a bundle of spears to the frontline, threw one with force at the opposing army, and felt no satisfaction when it struck a mark, pinning the foreigner to the ground. He ran out into the fight without a cry. He had not felt satisfaction in any of his kills since Achall's declaration. Nor could he stand too close to Rónán for fear of what might happen between them. For more than a week, he worked the battlefield, dedicated much of his free time to apprenticing under Oisín, and spent the remainder of his hours in the makeshift smithy, mending the swords of their fallen warriors. When he had occasion to speak to Rónán, he did so curtly and without sensitivity. At night, he lay on his back and watched the stars, unable to keep his eyes open but unwilling to close them. He could not remember feeling so alone in all his life.

As the days turned into weeks, he took out his anxieties on the foreign army. He charged out into the field to go hand-to-hand with the enemy, and he cut them down as though they were sheaves of straw. Every day, they gained the field and then lost it again as each opposing side made ground, fought with fierce desperation, shifted forward, and were pushed back again. The sky remained dark with a rain of javelin in lash after lash of resilience, and the ground was boggy with blood on both sides. The churned patch of grass in the middle of the field where the champions fought was growing daily.

In the king's tent, Áed sat beside Oisín and tried as best he could to remain silent while the men spoke of battle plans, of diminishing numbers of their warriors, of the perpetual growth of the foreigners' army. They could not continue like this, throwing spears at the sky and losing as many men on the field as they killed.

As they spoke, a messenger entered the tent, panting from the exertion of running. 'My king.' He dropped to a knee and bowed his head.

'What news, man?' Fergal asked.

'News from the outlying tribes, my king. Many have been sacked.'

'In the east, yes. That much is evident.'

'My lord, forgive me. News comes from the north and the west. The invaders come ashore from all directions. They kill and they burn without pause. Many coastal tribes are already laid to waste.'

'And inland?' Áed asked. As soon as he spoke, he lowered his eyes; he had spoken out of turn.

The messenger nodded. 'Inland, too. These bastards travel far and fast.'

Fergal stood, towering over the messenger, and reached a hand out to him. 'You have run far. Come, sit. Fetch this man a drink. Do you know the tribes?'

'I have memorised them all, my lord,' he said and, as he sat on a small stool, he began to recite the names of the tribes that had fallen.

When Áed heard the name of his own sept, he leapt to his feet. 'Are you sure?'

'Fallen,' the messenger confirmed. 'Like the others.'

'All dead? Every single person?'

'Dead or captured. No one knows for certain. The villages blacken the sky with the smoke from their burning corpses.'

Oisín stood and put a hand on Áed's shoulder. 'Take a seat, Áed.'

'I need to—'

'You need to take a seat. You can grieve soon. But now, we have a war to win.'

Áed sat. There were no tears to fall. If these foreign bastards had slaughtered his family, he would see to the deaths of each of them. Singlehandedly, if he had to.

'My apologies, King Fergal. My apprentice is but a child, and grief is harder on the young.'

Fergal looked at Áed, then Oisín. 'At forty-something years, if I had just learned that these foreign whores murdered my parents, I would be inconsolable. He has every right to want to attend to his personal needs. Do you wish to leave, boy?'

Áed swelled his chest and raised his head to look directly at the king. 'No. I want to fight.'

Fergal nodded. He asked the messenger to continue and after a time, the man came to the end of his list.

'There may be others since then, but that is all I know.'

'Forgive me, my lord,' Áed said. 'May I ask your messenger—what of the druids in the north? My sister resides there in training.'

'I have no word of them,' the messenger said. 'The gods will defend them.'

'Thank you,' Fergal said. 'You may eat and return to your post.' When the messenger was gone, Fergal sat and said, 'In the morning, we will begin again. Another day of blood. And we're running low on champions.'

King Déaglán said, 'We're running low on everything. Champions, spears, food. How much longer can we keep this up?'

'I'll go.' Áed was on his feet again although he was not sure how that had happened. Since learning that his sister may still be alive while the rest of his family had surely suffered, a heat had warmed his chest. He would do everything in his power to stave off the foreigners and protect Grainne, protect what was left of his family, of his tribe, of his life. Oisín was right—he could grieve later. And he would; in bed, alone, not in front of these others.

When nobody responded to him, he said again, 'I'll go.'

'Fight the champion?' Déaglán asked.

'I'll kill him, too.'

'Sit down,' Oisín said.

'I'll fight him, and I'll win.' Áed turned to Déaglán. 'I've been studying him. I know his moves, his weaknesses. I'm good. I can do this.'

'You have a gift for making swords, I'll grant you, but you have little experience.'

'I have trained under Oisín's command for eight years. And I have fought these fields for weeks now, or months even. I'm the best swordsman you've got. Who else out there can say they are trained fighters? Our armies are made up of farmers and smiths.'

Déaglán gripped the hilt of his sword. 'Oisín, control your

boy.'

'Áed, outside. Now.'

'I speak the truth.'

'Boy—'

'I am not a child. I can defeat him. If we cut off their champion, we have a chance at slaughtering them all.'

'Outside. Now.'

'My king,' Áed said, kneeling to Déaglán. 'Allow me this honour. For my family.'

Oisín took him by the neck of the tunic and turfed him outside the tent where he fell in the dirt. When the tent flap slipped closed behind them, Oisín said, 'You need to cool off, boy. You just lost your family, so I can forgive your insolence in there. But open your mouth once more this evening and I will smash it closed forever.'

Áed made no attempt to speak.

'You're the best man I have. I know it as well as you do—as you promised me you would be. That is why I cannot have you walking out to your death in hand-to-hand combat with a giant. On the field is where I need you the most. You fight well, but you are foolhardy. You are not invincible. I see you every day, itching to feel their blood on your hands. We whittle at them daily, but it is not enough for you. You expect too much, too soon. You have sat on the advisors' counsel every night since we arrived. You know our plans. You have helped shape them. To walk out there on your own would be asking the gods to strike you down. And what use would you be with a sword in your gut? What use would you be to your people?'

'I have no people.'

'Who am I if I am not your people? And Déaglán? And

Rónán? When you came to us as a child, you swore an oath. What is your name?'

'You know it.'

'Say it.'

'I am Áed Branath, son of Airic.'

'Ó Mordha,' Oisín said. 'What is your name?'

'Áed Branath, son of—'

Oisín backhanded his cheek. 'You gave an oath. What is your name?'

'Ó Mordha,' Áed said. 'But if I am Ó Mordha, you will let me fight.'

'You are fighting, Áed. You just need to remember what you are fighting for.' He turned and entered the tent, giving Áed no indication that he should follow.

Áed sought out a wineskin and sat near a dying fire, its warm embers casting flickering shadows of spirits in its halo. He was alone.

'Father,' he said, and he drank. 'Mother.' He drank again. 'Bec.' Again, he drank from the skin. Grainne was alive; she had to be. Without her, he had nothing left. He pulled his knees up, watching ash dance above the fire.

When Rónán found him and asked if he could sit a while, Áed made no response and so he took the ground beside him. Áed passed him the wineskin.

'We haven't spoken in days,' Rónán said. 'Are you well?'

Áed took the skin back and drank deeply from it.

'Achall is asleep,' Rónán continued. 'She has been quiet as well, since that night. It's like no one wants to speak to me anymore.'

'You are not the most important thing in everyone's lives,'

Áed said.

'What is your problem? Achall gave us permission to—'

'My family is dead.'

Rónán had no words. A sound came from his throat, but if it was an apology Áed did not hear it.

'A messenger came. The foreigners breached western and northern ports. We fight them in the east, but there are more behind us.'

'Then we double our resolve to fight back. Send half our army westward to meet them.'

'If we divide our army now, we lose.'

'What other option do we have?'

'I will champion myself tomorrow.'

'No,' Rónán cried. He knelt, tried to take Áed's hand. 'You cannot.'

'You sound like Oisín.'

'You'd never listen to Oisín. Will you listen to me?'

'Why should I? You have a bride. A family. What am I but a stain on the grass to be forgotten by morning.'

'You are what I have,' Rónán said. 'You are what I want. Look at me. You are my friend.'

'And lover?'

'Yes, and lover.'

'It means nothing. I am a fuck, then you go to bed with your bride.'

'I won't marry her.'

'You have to marry her. You *should*.'

'I won't let you champion yourself.'

Áed pushed him away. 'Stop me if you think you can.'

'Áed. Please.'

But he walked away, leaving Rónán in the dirt by the fire.

In the morning, when the sun broke over the eastern horizon and the far side of the valley flashed with glinting metals from their foreign assailants, Áed took his place on the frontline and hefted a spear. Without looking, he knew Rónán would be two hundred yards to his right, where he always was at dawn, bow in hand, quiver of arrows angled at his hip. He was one of seventy men who were adept at the bow. In the days since they arrived, Áed was sure the small outfit of archers had killed more foreigners than all the sword-wielding warriors combined.

Behind them, Achall and the other girls would be carrying vessels of water back from the river's edge, washing clothes and boiling vegetables. If Áed wasn't to champion himself, perhaps Achall should do it. She would either talk the foreign beast to death with her sternness, or he'd kill her.

They fought throughout the morning, Áed's sword a blur, slashing heads and arms, cutting low at ankles and knees, his shield both blocking blows and making them.

In the midday sun, the giant foreigner rode into the valley.

At once, Áed felt Rónán's presence beside him. 'Don't do this.'

'It is my right.'

'I won't lose you.'

'I'll come back, dragging his body behind me.'

'Áed, please. Don't do this. I know you are grieving, but I am your family, too. Stay, for me.'

'Bring a wineskin,' Áed said. 'I'll want a drink when I'm done.'

The foreigner had stopped in the middle of the field. 'Who among you can defeat me?' he shouted. 'Send out your best and

I will return him to you in pieces.'

'I will challenge you,' Áed called.

'No,' Oisín commanded from his post by the kings.

But Áed was already striding out into the field. He carried with him a spear, his sword and shield, and a dagger at his hip. His face was stained from a morning at war. As he approached the foreigner's champion, the man threw his head back and laughed.

'They send a child against me? Are the men of your people too busy in their dresses?'

'I am Áed Branath, son of Airic, member of the Ó Mordha tribesmen. What is your name so that I may tell my people who it is that I have killed?' He stopped before the giant who towered almost two heads taller than him.

'I am Gal Surid, son of no one, father of all.' He hefted his longsword. A leather shirt was stretched taut across his chest and he wore leather trousers, and a cap of blackened leather covered his head. His shield was oval and without decoration, but his forehead and cheeks and his chin were decorated with dye. 'When you lie dying at my feet,' Surid said, 'I will piss on you to quench your thirst before you enter your spirit world.'

'Are we talking or are we fighting?' Áed asked, assuming a solid stance and raising his sword. He had dug the spear into the ground at his side.

'Lay down your arms and I will make this quick. There is little sport in felling children.'

'I lay down with your mother last night. She made it quick, too.'

Gal Surid lashed out, as Áed had predicted. He easily side-stepped and jabbed with his sword, but Surid was swift on his feet and he blocked with his shield.

Surid said, 'You have a tongue on you for one so young. Did your father not teach you respect?'

Áed smiled. 'I will show your people respect by waiting one day after I murder you before killing them all.' He swung high, a feint, and pushed out with his shield, knocking Surid back on his feet. Surid countered and parried and the clash of swords rang out across the valley.

The giant jabbed back and Áed ducked, rolled to the side, and sprang back to his feet in time to block another crack. As on the training field at Ailigh, the sword had become an extension of his arm. He saw Surid's movements before they were made and he was able to swipe and counter them. Despite Surid's impressive size, they were matched well at combat.

When they were both sweating under the mid-afternoon sun and no blood had yet been spilled, Gal Surid said, 'I am rapt of your skills. You fight like a man.'

'Or perhaps you fight like a boy.'

Again, Surid thrust out with his longsword. Áed brought up his shield arm to take the blow, and from underneath, he flicked his own sword, cutting through the leather at Surid's side. Blood came, but the wound was not deep.

'You tickle me,' Surid said.

'You talk too much, old man.' He whipped his shield arm sideways so that the shield lay flat, and he jabbed forward, hitting Surid in the stomach. Knocked back, Surid nonetheless swiped his sword out and nicked Áed's shoulder. He felt the blood soak the sleeve of his tunic.

They bashed shields together and struck blow after blow of sword against sword, but neither got close enough to make another cut.

Áed had no knowledge of how long they had been fighting, but the sun was now behind him and the army at either side of the valley had grown quiet. 'Do I tire you, old man? You are talking less.'

Surid simply laughed and span a full turn on his heels, swinging his sword wide. As he turned around to face Áed again, his sword-arm swinging aft, Áed crouched, readied himself, and rose fast so that his shoulder hit Surid's forearm, knocking the sword from his hand. Surid tried to bash him with his shield but he had been standing at an awkward angle and they both tumbled to the dirt. Áed flipped over him and rolled to a stop on his stomach. He was quick to his feet, but as he lunged, Gal Surid whipped his body around and swiped him with his feet. Surid rolled over onto him and punched his face. Punched again. Again.

Áed reached around the dirt at his side. In his fall, the sword and flown from his hand and his shield-arm, shield still attached, was trapped under his own weight and that of Surid who sat on him.

Surid gripped Áed's head, brought it up and bashed it back to the ground.

Áed's hand sought out through the grass, fingers digging into the hardened clay. He whipped up, throwing clotted dirt in Surid's face, and then he struggled underneath him, throwing the man off balance. Áed brought his knee up into Surid's crotch, lifted himself so that he could get his arm out from under him, and swung with the shield against Surid's face.

With one eye swollen and closed, Áed staggered to his knees, then his feet, and looked for his sword. Surid came up behind him, barrelled into him and they both went down again, but Áed rolled away so as not to be pinned by the giant a second time. He skidded in the dirt and knocked his spear out of the ground. As it tumbled, he grabbed at its shaft, flipped onto his back, and raised the spear as Surid came at him again, his sword back in his hands but his shield discarded.

Surid saw the spear tip in time and swung his sword, cutting the spear head from the shaft, but he was too late to stop himself from falling. As he came down, Áed braced the half-shaft against his side and held it steady. Surid fell on it and the sharpened, jagged point pierced his leather shirt and sank into his stomach.

On his knees, Surid gripped the shaft. It had not gone right through him but had lodged in his gut. He struggled to pull it out but there was already blood on the ground before him.

Áed found his feet and staggered a backward step, wiping his own blood from his face. He turned, found his sword, and dived for it as Surid tried to stand, the wooden shaft still penetrating his stomach.

'I am invincible,' Gal Surid laughed. It sounded like a cough.

Áed came before him with his sword. 'No one is invincible but the gods. And they are not on your side, my friend.' He drew back the sword and plunged it into Surid's stomach beside the spear. As he withdrew the blade, Surid came to his knees. Áed raised it, took a breath, and swung. Sharpened to the finest edge, the blade took Surid's neck and tore through it. The head did not fly far as Áed would have expected. It remained where it was, shifted only slightly to the side, and then it fell to the ground. It did not even roll, but lay there, its open eyes vacant and still.

Áed had not noticed how dark the day had become until he kicked out at Gal Surid's still-kneeling body and watched it fall, shadows gathering around them. He dropped his sword and un-hooked his shield. He stood up on Surid's chest, hitched his tunic, and let a stream of urine splash on the man's detached head. 'Who's pissing on who?' he asked.

He did not hear the cheers of his people and did not remember being carried out of the valley on their shoulders. Later, lying on a mattress in the druid's tent, his wounds tended to and patched, a salve-soaked cloth strapped over his blackened eye, Oisín came to him and sat a while beside him.

'I am certain I have called you foolhardy before, but I did not think you were also a fool.'

'Is he dead? I cannot recall.'

'You pissed on his severed head. You can safely say he is most definitely dead.'

'He would have done the same to me, given the chance. Let me rest now; we will kill them all tomorrow.'

Oisín stood. 'Many men are lined up outside to greet you and wish you well.'

'I would see none of them tonight. Allow me to rest.'

'Just one of them,' Oisín said. 'I will send the others away.'

He had left just seconds before the tent flap drew back and Rónán entered.

'You live, still.'

Áed touched his chest where his heart was beating. 'I think so. Why have you come?'

'You defeated the beast. I wanted to see you.'

'Because I defeated the beast?'

'No.' Rónán sat beside the mattress. 'I came because you are my friend.'

'Rónán, I—I said things I am ashamed of.'

'Do not speak of it. You were grieving your family.'

'If they lived, I would not have faced Gal Surid. Another man may have defeated him in my stead.'

'No other man could do so.' Rónán came to the bed and lay next to him. 'Does it hurt?'

'A little.'

'Here?' he asked, touching Áed's purpled cheek.

'No.'

'Here?' He touched his throat, a patch of downy stubble just forming under his chin.

Áed felt the fingers there when he swallowed. 'No.'

Rónán lay his hand on Áed's chest and felt the quickened beat of his heart. 'And here?'

'A little,' Áed said.

'Can I make it better?'

'Only you can,' Áed said, and he closed his uncovered eye as Rónán's face came down to him and they kissed.

Chapter 23

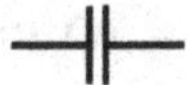

The funeral for the old man was an abrupt affair. Bec watched from the chain of girls as their foreign captors stacked tree branches in a pyre and laid his body on top. They had argued about who had killed him for a full day until they openly admitted that he had been an aggressive bastard in his days and their lives would be less luckless without him. That they had not considered Bec or any of the other girls surprised her. But that the little girl who had been the old man's companion that evening was unsuspected was of immense value. She was too small to fight back, let alone drive a dagger through a man's skull. Perhaps Bec could use her as cover a second time.

They had been delayed in migrating north-east by these events and they had camped outside the burned village for a further three days, eating, drinking, sleeping with their girls, and sparring with each other. Bec had not seen a warrior in action. When her father had gone to war she had been incredibly young and she was still young when he returned. If her brother, who was training somewhere in the north, fought like these brutes did, they may stand a chance at driving the foreigners from their lands. But she could not imagine any of her peoples being so ruthless and cruel as these uncivilized thugs. In all her short life, the tribes surrounding her own had been polite and grateful for trade, aiding each other when needed, and marrying among themselves to maintain peace and prosperity. There was always a kind word at markets and haggling was generally done in good spirits. These foreign monsters appeared to lack any such civilities, preferring instead to beat their way through life; that they were even here, on someone else's shores, trying to take it from them, was testament to their rotten ways.

Bec did not have another opportunity to slice the throat of a foreign pig during those days outside the sacked village. She watched the old man's body burn on the edge of the field from her position with the girls, and each one smiled at her and thanked her without speaking. Each one among them knew that she was a saviour born to protect them. In those nights, they lay with their men knowing that, soon, the one called Little Bec would come in the night like a spirit and end another life.

She had hoped to teach them all that they could be free if only they stood together against their despots, but she was never given the chance.

On the morning that the men were packing up to leave, Urasid took Bec aside, into one of the charred homes, and he willed that she lay down for him in the dirt that he did not have to take her by force this time. She complied, stripping herself of her clothes and laying on the ash-blackened floor for him. 'You have my blessing,' she said. She would submit to his every command in the hope that her willingness might give her a certain freedom to slaughter them all.

As he raised her hips and lay on her, he buried his face in her hair as he normally would. 'What is this smell?' he asked.

'Wild orchids. If I crush them in water it makes a scent for my hair when I bathe.'

He finished quickly and he stood. Looking down at her nakedness, he said, 'We will wed in two nights' time. And then you will bear me a child.'

She did not tell him that she was yet a child herself, because that child had been left behind with the death of her parents. Now she was just a body, nothing but flesh; her soul had escaped and left this husk behind. She nodded. 'Say it and it will be so.' The words came as a whisper and she cleared her throat to repeat them.

Two nights later, outside another burning sept, a foreign man spoke words in a language she did not comprehend, and he took her hand and Urasid's hand and laid them together on a branch from an alder tree and bound them with cloth. The man mixed berries in a wooden bowl, dipped his finger into the red mixture, and then painted a symbol on Urasid's cheeks and then on Bec's. As was the foreigners' custom, the newlyweds stripped naked and travelled three times around a bonfire to invoke the spirits of both virility and fertility. Idols with extended appendages were set around the fire and all the gathered men and the girls in chains turned their backs so that the new couple could join together in venery by the warmth of the fire and in the presence of their gods. Those who had gathered sang loudly and clapped their hands and stamped their feet to mask the sounds of lovemaking. And even though some of the girls cried, there was an air of cheerfulness among them all.

When the nuptials were complete and Urasid was certain that his wife would be with child by morning, even the girls were awarded some wine and fermented waters. Chained side by side as they were, the girls danced around Bec and sang blessings to their own gods that she would be treated well as a bride and that the kisses of the god Óengus be always upon her head. The little girl whose name was Ciara gave Bec her wooden doll as a wedding gift and hugged her tightly, whispering that she should kill her husband this very night.

Bec came to her knees and held the girl. 'I will not. Urasid may be a beast but he is the best of these.' Then she winked. 'Stay calm, little one. We will all be happy yet.'

In the light of the fire, Bec asked for more wine that she might toast her husband's good graces. All men were to drink, she insisted, stating it was her people's custom that no wine be left undrunk. It was a fine custom, someone said, and they drank long into the night.

Urasid led his young wife to a tent that had been erected for them and he struggled to get undressed.

'Unchain my wrists, husband, that I should help you. I am your willing wife.'

Drunk, he reverted to his own dialect, but he unchained her and stood still while she removed his tunic and his trousers. When they had finished laying together, she rested a hand on his cheek and stroked his temple. 'Sleep now, husband. Sleep.'

He grumbled something unintelligible, and in time he began to snore.

Bec waited. Outside, she could hear the revelry of the foreigners. She was sure many of them had gone among the trees to rut with their girls, but many more remained by the fire to drink and sing. When all the noises of drunkenness had subsided and she waited another while for certainty, she rose, finally unchained, and dressed. She took Urasid's dagger and crept from the tent.

She circled the outskirts of the firelight, keeping to the shadows, and found a group of men asleep on the ground. There were too many of them. If one made a sound as she killed him, the others would wake. She kept moving, her small feet an advantage among the fallen leaves and the twigs. Summer was almost over and soon the skies would darken and the days would grow colder.

Bec entered the forest, her eyes adjusting to the dimness, and she inched from one tree to the next in search of a quarry. One of the foreigners faced a tree, urinating against its base. That he would die with his dick in his hand gave her much pleasure. The man swayed, unsteady, and Bec slowed her breathing. She adjusted the grip on the hilt of her dagger and leapt on his back. She drew the blade across his throat and she gagged his mouth with her free hand to muffle his sounds. With Bec still on his back, he dropped to his knees in the puddle of his own piss, and then he lurched forward, hitting his face against the tree.

Bec bounded back from him and hid behind a neighbouring tree until she was certain he was dead and that nobody had heard his muted cries. She pressed her lips together because she could not be confident that the bubbling emotion in her throat was not laughter instead of screams. In time, convinced that no one was coming, she came to his body and kicked him. Then she moved on.

She was forced to abandon a second kill because the man was not nearly as drunk as he had first appeared. He had been sleeping but awoke to the sounds of her feet scraping through the underbrush, and so she waited for him to roll over again before she moved on to find another. The night was dark, but dawn would not be long in coming.

Moments later, she came upon two of the men lying head to toe among the trees. One still clutched a wine jug, its contents long since spilled and soaked into the earth. She knelt at the head of one, readied her blade, and made to cut his throat when his eyes opened. She sliced him before he could reach for her, but his companion awoke and sat up.

The man was quick to his feet, if not a little unsteady, and he fumbled for his longsword but it was not in his belt. Bec, suddenly terrified, pounced at him and knocked him backward. She had dropped her blade in the process and so, kneeling on his chest as he lay on the ground, she gripped his thick neck and squeezed. But she was not strong enough and he flicked her from him like a fly from a horse's tail. She rolled away and he came at her, and she leapt to her feet, jumped for a low branch, and kicked out at his face.

He grabbed her leg, pulled, and she fell to the ground. As he dragged her from the trees out into the clearing, she gripped a tree root and yanked her ankle free from his grip. He turned and threw himself upon her.

Bec swung her legs and her arms around his body and refused to let go. She could smell the fermented waters on his breath as she bit his cheek. He stood, her small body still clinging to him, and he fell against a tree. She gripped the back of his hair and smacked his temple against the biting bark. He let go but she hugged to him still, her legs tightening around his waist, her arms now around his neck, her teeth cutting into his ear. His screams would surely waken the entire camp.

When he went to his knees, she hopped from him, found her blade in the moss, and thrust it through his eye just as he had opened his mouth to cry for help.

His body went limp. Bec jumped for a tree branch and pulled herself into the tree. She moved away as fast as she could.

When she dropped down into a small clearing, she circled back to her tent in the hope that Urasid was too drunk to have woken. Peering through the flap, she saw him on their bed and she entered at once. In the candlelight, she noticed her dress was covered in blood and she could feel it sticky around her mouth where she had bit him. She undressed, washed her face with water from the cleansing bowl, and slipped into bed beside her husband.

Some men came moments behind her to wake them, and it took a great deal of prodding to rouse Urasid. News that three of their comrades had been killed by another man meant that they would tear the camp apart to find their murderer.

Their deaths had been Bec's wedding gift to the girls.

Chapter 24

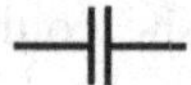

Áed walked back off the battlefield, the victor. Although it took him four days to recuperate after championing himself against Gal Surid—and in those days they lost four new champions to the foreign army—he was well rested and prepared to walk back out into the valley on his own with nothing but his sword and shield, a dagger, and a spear. He did not wait for the foreigners to send a man out; when the sun was directly above the valley, the armies retreated to their sides, and he strode out with pride. 'Who will die at my hands today?' became his regular cry.

Gal Surid had been his largest foe. Since facing the almighty beast, the foreigners' champions grew less fearsome, less competent. On occasion, he was matched well for long hours on the field, sparring as near-equals, but none came close to Surid's impressive stature.

Áed had never again urinated on the corpse of his fallen rival, but the boys from Ailigh, and the other companies from their army, spoke of it often. A visiting bard, who had not witnessed the combat himself, sang about an hour-long stream that splashed the fallen warrior's face and washed the valley like a river. In the shaven-headed man's rendition, Áed the

Executioner then kicked the warrior's head back into the middle of the invading army and they wept in fear. All legends, he later told Áed, are borne in truth and embellished in wine; he had not invented the exaggerations himself but had heard them from a couple of soldiers over a jug of wine by the fire on the evening the bard had arrived in camp.

Áed allowed the embellishments to stand. If the song made its way to the foreigners and struck fear in them, let them quake each time he walked out onto the field. If the enemy is afraid, you are at an advantage.

When he wasn't slaughtering foreign men, he spent his evenings cleaning and sharpening his blades, conferencing with Oisín and the kings on strategic rewards, or in the arms of Rónán. That they had wasted so much time before falling into a mutual embrace saddened him.

'We have the rest of our lives,' Rónán told him. He took Áed's hands and kissed their palms. 'And all our lives are in your grip.'

'I see you when I fight. In my head. I see you telling me to hit harder, hit faster.'

'I do not take my eyes from you when you walk out there,' Rónán replied. 'I hold my breath until you come back.'

Their usual meeting place was on the banks of the river that wound around a distant copse of trees. True to their promise to Achall, they would not couple in the camp. As the nights grew darker and the yule was fast approaching, they brought deer skins with them for warmth and they made love under the whisper of the spirits among the trees. Áed grieved often for his parents, and Rónán would hold him tight until at last Áed would sigh and look at him and whisper that he loved him.

'When I am not in your arms, I am a warrior. When I am in them, I am nothing more than a piece of your heart. I wish to stay here forever, to grow old in your arms and die in their embrace.'

They made love again before wrapping themselves in their deer furs. The sky was slate with clouds and not a star could be seen.

'The yule comes,' Áed said.

'I am trying not to think of it.'

'Has she found a druid willing to perform the rituals?'

'Many,' Rónán said. 'A battlefield wedding will be good for morale, I am told.'

'I know I should respect her on your wedding night, but not to be with you for that time will feel like an eternity.'

Rónán nudged his ribs. 'We will make up for the lost time the following night.'

'We still have to make up for the eight years I have known you and not taken you,' Áed laughed, and he kissed him and they made love on the chill ground again.

By agreement, both armies put down their weapons to observe their respective yule celebrations. Fires burned bright on both sides of the valley, but no one ventured from one camp to the other; they were enemies still, after all. For twelve nights the battlefield remained empty save for the occasional hare darting this way and that among the frost-white grass.

On the seventh night, the evening after the sun's weakest moment, when it was returning to new life once more, Rónán and Achall faced an army of ruddy-cheeked warriors and proclaimed their wedding commitment. He would provide for her—property and comforts—and she would provide children for him, as was the way of it. The druid bound them together, and then they danced for their gathered friends to demonstrate their obligation to each other and to signal a fruitful start to their days of union. Flowers were strewn in the bride's path and gifts were granted them that they may prosper in affluence.

The celebrations continued most of the night and as the dawn's light brightened the horizon, dousing the foreigners' fires in morning brilliance, Rónán and Achall entered their tent and did not come out again until the sun was behind them and the music of the evening bards drifted gaily across the plain. He would later tell Áed that he and his new wife had spoken not one word to each other while they were in the tent, they had not touched, of course, and she had barely looked at him at all. She had thrown herself on the bed, turned away from him, and waited for a suitable length of time to pass that suggested they had been busy engaging in newlywed acts of lovemaking before venturing back outside.

Unprepared for confrontation, Áed had not anticipated turning around from a table of meats to find Achall standing behind him. When he saw her, he dropped his fistful of mutton on the ground and was too afraid to stoop to retrieve it.

Achall folded her arms. 'The mighty warrior faces death every day in single combat, championing himself for his king, but he fears a girl?'

He blinked, could think of nothing to say.

'Despite my hatred of you, I appreciate your efforts on the field. You keep the future safe for my child.' She touched her stomach as though perhaps she was already pregnant. Was she teasing him in pretending that Rónán had already—and willingly—sown a child within her? He knew it was not the case.

'I gave a promise to Oisín to be his best warrior. I am only doing what I said.'

'Either way,' Achall said, 'that I don't kill you with my own fingers is my thanks for your continued favour on the battle-field. I would not see you die at anyone else's hands.'

They stared at each other for a moment.

Then Achall continued, 'My husband has made me prom-ise that I will not humiliate our army's champion by declaring you the boil of my marriage. You should pray that you remain Déaglán's champion. When you are through, I will ensure your name is never again associated with courage and strength. The bards will forget Áed the Executioner and your memory will be as the underbelly of a snake.'

She left him, and Áed walked into the night, forgetting his fallen food, forgetting about meeting Rónán on the deep-sloped bank of the river's bend. He went out into the valley between the armies and lay down on the frozen ground, staring up at the silhouette of the Giant's Ring on the distant hills. Nobody came after him, and no foreigner approached him. He watched the roiling clouds that threatened snow and he welcomed it, though none came. The frost-coated grasses would have to cool his blood on their own.

Five months they had faced the enemy on this field. Five months they had shifted forward and back, gaining and losing ground. He was weary, but he knew that if he was to truly fall asleep, deep into a dreamless void, he may never wake. He could not count the men he had killed in his champion's frenzy, day after day, a new face, a new name that he always asked but never remembered. Gal Surid, his first, was the only foreigner whose name meant anything to him. It meant change. It meant longing. It meant retribution.

He sat up, his tunic peeling away from the frozen earth, and he wondered how long he could remain champion—until the end of his days, if Achall's threat was to be believed. Soon, he was convinced, a foreign man would come before him and spill his blood in such a fury that his decimated body would be unrecognisable.

There is no life after being a king's champion. Either a man lives a long and undefeated life, always the champion, or he is lost to battle, nothing more than a recollection in song. A man does not retire from such a life. He does not return to his homelands and raise cattle or work the smithy. He does not hang up his sword, never to consider its uses again. Where he travels, he is always a champion, and always there is someone willing to challenge him for his title. For his very life.

Áed walked the edge of the battlefield until he came to the river, and he followed it upstream into the darkness. When he came across Rónán, he was asleep under furs. Waking him, Áed said, 'I am late.'

'I know.' Rónán raised the furs and beckoned Áed under them. They curled up together, both too tired for lovemaking, and the heat of Rónán's body warmed him.

'When the yule is over, I will kill them all.'

'You are already killing them, one by one.'

'I will destroy them. I make you that promise.' He turned to face his swain and ran his hand across Rónán's broad chest. 'How old are we? I cannot even recall.'

'Ancient.'

'I feel it. But we have changed, haven't we? Taller, yes. Broader in the chest and longer in the leg. But that's not what I mean. What happened to our childhood games?'

'We still wrestle,' Rónán said, pinching Áed's hip.

'We would lie at night and talk until we fell asleep. We would disappear from Ailigh without anyone's knowledge, carrying skins of wine, and we wouldn't return until we were thoroughly drunk. Why must we grow up? When a boy grows up to become a man, he becomes something different, something unexpected. As children, you punched me and we became friends. As adults, if you punch me it will finish me.'

'You are my champion,' Rónán said.

'I do not want to be. I will protect you always, but I am so very tired, I fear that one day I will slip. I am not yours; not in the way I wish to be. I cannot blame your wife, but I do blame your chieftain. And if she is with child by Imbolc as she predicts, I cannot bear to share you with them both—it is all my will just to share you with one.'

'The child will not be mine. I cannot love it. It will be a bastard and it will grow to know that I hate it.'

'Do not say that. The child will be raised as yours and should be treated as such.' He shifted his weight and put an arm behind Rónán's neck. 'Will we always be friends?'

'We are more than friends.'

'But in time, when we are too old to be lovers, too old to wake early and sit side by side as we watch the days sicken into nights, will we still be friends?'

'Always,' Rónán said.

Áed smiled and folded himself further under the furs. 'Wake me when the yule is over.'

Four nights later, on the final evening of the yule celebrations, Áed gathered with Oisín, Déaglán, Fergal and the advisors, and they discussed the coming days on the field.

'We cannot continue this way,' Áed said. 'We gain a foot and we lose a leg almost daily. Our army is already split with a second wave of foreigners behind us. They mean to box us in and they have succeeded.' He drew lines in the dirt with his sword point. 'They fight us here and here. And were it not for the river, they would fight us from the south, too.'

'What do you propose, Executioner?' Fergal asked.

'Their greatest numbers are before us in the east. What lies beyond them? What are they trying so desperately to protect from us?'

'The main port in the north east,' one of the advisors said, taking his own sword and drawing a circle in the dirt. 'Knockdhu. We can only assume they took the stronghold in their early campaign.'

'Can we storm it?'

'It is a walled hillfort on a cliff's edge. Reclaiming it would not be easy.'

'But not impossible,' Oisín said. 'We have the numbers with us if we can keep them alive.'

Áed took his sword again and drew a line through the foreigners. 'Then we cut a path through them, killing as many as we can in the process. If we get to the stronghold, we can cut off their supply of fresh warriors in the north.' He made another mark behind their current position. 'We leave a contingent of men here to fend against the smaller western advance, and we send runners to the other tribal armies. They should be protecting their ports if they aren't already. Once we cut them off from all sides, we can better deal with those who are already ashore.'

'Any man who does not have a sword of his own,' Déaglán said, 'needs to be granted one immediately. We cut for the north in the morning.'

Chapter 25

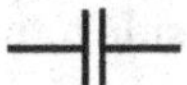

Grainne had entered the stilled darkness of her home and cast the bones. They were not being kind. She cast them a second time and studied their patterns. Her teachers would have told her that interpretations were not always easy to find, but she saw the meaning of the bones at once. She was surrounded by death.

She called upon Cáer to guide her, but she received no response. She swept the floor and knelt, putting her fingertip on the ground, and she closed her eyes. The rune that she drew was not of her doing; she had allowed the gods to channel through her, let her finger be guided by their motions. When she opened her eyes and looked, she wept—the gods had drawn a burning tree by her own hand, the end of all she would hold dear.

There was no escape. The foreigners had taken over Donal's sept and, she was convinced, their entire peaceful island. Her parents, her brother and sister, they were either dead or captive. The druids in the north—perhaps they would survive this rash of death; Eorid himself had displayed a certain trust in Grainne when he took to their shores. He did not, at least, kill her instantly. She could not bear to think of a time without the archdruid. His presence in her life had changed her, as it had for all the druids who studied under him. What child would follow the druid's path if the archdruid was not the one to show them? She thought of Odhran. He had appeared so young, so carefree, the happiest druid she had ever met. If he, too, was gone, then all courage was lost to the world.

At Donal's feast, the foreigners gathered in his great hall, the local tribesmen forced outside, and Eorid took Donal's seat, much to Muirgel's vexation. Grainne was called upon to sit at Eorid's left and when a platter of meats was placed before him, he said, 'You will taste the food before me. If it is poisoned, the gods will punish your chieftain by taking his druid from him. And then I will slaughter everyone in your tribe.'

'I assure you, my lord—' Donal said from his position further down the table, but Eorid slammed the flat of his hand on the table for silence.

'She will eat first, or I will skin you alive and feast on your carcass.'

Grainne drank some water to moisten her desiccated mouth and chewed some meat. Her thoughts were everywhere, and she could not even identify the food she was tasting. Her furtive glances at Donal, at Muirgel, even at Faolán, were going unnoticed. She needed to get them alone, to plan an escape. To seek out an army to rescue their tribesmen. But perhaps Donal had been right to negotiate with the foreigners; there had been no deaths in the sept since their arrival. If this was the new regime, the new way of things, were they not better served on the side of might? She would not think of it. An escape plan must be considered.

Eorid was looking at her, she realised. When she had tasted the food and not died of poisoning, he laughed and palmed her back with a forceful but gregarious hand. 'We have trust, you and me, yes?' he asked.

She indicated the rune at his chest. 'Our gods offer us both protection.' She refused to show him the terror that was behind her eyes, that gnawed like a wolf at the lining of her stomach.

When Eorid had eaten enough, he told everyone to leave except his chief advisor, a broad-shouldered man only slightly less intimidating than his master, and he requested Donal, his chief-wife, and his druid to remain.

'This plan of yours. You have a son?'

'Many fine sons, my lord,' Donal said. 'But one surrogate son who is in line for the kingship in the north, or very soon will be. My niece has already travelled to him to be wed. He is a fine man. With him on the king-seat, you will rule behind him and the people will trust you both.'

'What distance is this king-seat from here?'

'Six nights,' Donal said. 'No more. I can ensure safe passage through the tribal lands of my people, so long as you can guarantee passage for us with your men and through any outposts you will no doubt have established on our isle.'

'My people have already taken your northern shores in the east. Where is this king-seat? My men may already have taken it from you.'

'It is in the west. Well-fortified. I offer no disrespect when I assure my lord that it would be a hard seat to conquer from the outside alone. Together, we can walk through the gate and bend them to our will.'

Eorid laughed. 'It is *our* will, now, is it? Very good.'

Muirgel cleared her throat.

'Your woman wishes to speak for you?'

Donal glared at his wife. She ignored him and spoke. 'The whole of Éirinn will know of your arrival on our vast shores. If the seat of Ailigh knows it, they will have already advanced east to contest your arrival. They are a trained army, after all.'

'My wife, though she speaks out of turn in your presence, my lord, makes a valid argument. My surrogate son and his king—if he is not yet king himself—will have travelled to war with your army.'

'Then the seat will be empty for me.'

'My lord, you will still have an army at your back, seat or no seat.'

Eorid turned to Grainne. 'Druid, what would you advise?'

Grainne considered her words with prudency before speaking. Giving Eorid the king-seat would force her to declare an allegiance to his rule. But marching him into battle against her own people could have any number of outcomes. She remembered the warning from the bones. 'I have heard of the seat at Grianán Ailigh, but I am not aware of its defences. I trust my chieftain to know more of these things. I live for peace. If you truly intend to keep my chieftain's son alive and allow him to rule under your watch, stealing his seat is not wise. But neither is meeting him on the battlefield. A truce must be called for discussions. You are a man of faith, I can tell. Your gods may not have the names of my gods, but any god should be able to judge fairly in the matter. Will you allow me the evening to deliberate on it? I will have you an answer by first light.'

'Agreed,' Eorid said all too readily. 'Pray to your gods and, in the morning, we will advance north, either to the king-seat or to meet your army on the field.'

Grainne twisted the hem of her cloak in her hands as she

waited outside the chieftain's hall for Donal. Foreigners stood around looking less like guests than the usurpers that they were. As the evening sun dropped behind the distant hills, Muirgel stepped out of the hall and pulled a fur around her shoulders.

'Your husband?' Grainne asked.

'Asleep. He has given our bed to the foreigner and he kicks in his dreams like a dog on the floor.'

Grainne took her arm, walked her around the squat building so that they were away from earshot of the invaders. 'Do we have a plan, or do you propose to go through with this madness?'

'The plan is to lead these men north and take them away from our people,' Muirgel whispered.

'But what of the north? The king-seat.'

'What of it? These men are big and powerful. If we have them on our side, we can prosper under their rule.'

'If we lead them north, they will just stamp us out like insects under their boots. You cannot believe this is the best course of action.'

'What would you have me do? Tell my husband to kill the foreign leader? Let his men murder us all in revenge? The gods have given us an opportunity. My husband knows what he is doing.'

'You don't speak for the gods,' Grainne snapped. 'I have trained to interpret their messages and all signs point to death.'

Muirgel rose up as tall as she could stand. 'Know your place, child. A druid does not speak the will of the gods. She speaks the will of her chieftain as though the gods had uttered it themselves. You would do well to remember that we gave you a home, and under my husband's guidance you may retain it.

Cross me and your next godly sacrifice will be your own virgin body.' She stabbed a finger at Grainne's chest. 'In the morning, you will tell the foreigner to go north onto the battlefield. He will not take the seat at Ailigh until we have Rónán under our charge and ready to sit as king at Donal's bidding.'

Grainne watched as Muirgel strode away from her. This was Donal's ploy. He did not care about pleasing the foreigners so long as his surrogate son took the king-seat. That Donal an tSaoir Ó Dáirine hosted lofty ideas of himself was undoubted, but that he was so boneheaded as to consider this an effective countermeasure to foreign invasion was absurd.

She retired to her home and, having given Eorid her word, she consulted the bones, cast the runes, and prayed with fervour to every god whose name came to mind, chiefly Cáer and her father, Ethal Anbuail. She wrapped strips of fabric around her face to shield her eyes from all light, and she lay prostrate on the floor, her arms and legs extended, calling upon her gods and her ancestors for help.

'One can stop it,' Cáer had told her in a dream. Not her, but someone else can stop it. What happens cannot be revoked. 'It is already done,' Cáer had said. Whatever happened was going to happen regardless. Grainne removed the wraps from her face and lay on her mattress. The words she spoke in the morning to Eorid would be the correct words, the appropriate words. Weighing the pros and cons of decisions made no difference now. The fate of them all was sealed. When she speaks to Eorid, the decision will have already been made by the gods.

Chapter 26

Although she was a wife, she was still a slave. Urasid would not let her forget that. From the chain of girls, she watched for three days as the men argued about who had killed their people. Another two were murdered in the process—not by her hand—and at length the foreigners decided to forget the matter and move on. They were here to fight, after all, and not to squabble like mindless women.

It took them only two more days to reach their destination. Meeting up with other groups of foreign warriors, they now equalled one thousand men, and they took to warring with a huge army of natives who had been busy battling an assault from the east.

Never close enough to see the battlefield itself, Bec heard whispered rumours running among the men that the natives had a weapon so powerful as to be immortal. He was called the Executioner, but her captors called him Rockside. They say if you stabbed him in the chest your blade would crumble, for he had a stone heart. Legend had it he was eight feet tall and almost as wide, though no one this far back from the field could verify it. Whoever he was, he was singlehandedly tearing through the invaders and had been untouchable. In her own small way, Bec thought, she had helped Rockside by killing a small number of them herself. If she got to meet him, she would tell him as much and hoped that he would rescue her from her subjugation. She would join him on the battlefield and fight alongside him.

If these people ever made it back to their homeland with stories of this war, mothers would terrify their children with threats that Rockside and his female companion would snatch them in the night if they were naughty.

In the evenings, when the fighting stopped with the fading of day, Bec was taken into a tent and Urasid would lie with her until he was satiated. Every night, she looked for an opportunity to free herself from his grip and murder another foreigner, but every night since her previous killings, Urasid had been vigilant in chaining her up. And every morning for the past three, she became sick and vomited where she was chained. She assumed it was from the water that had not been cleansed by a druid or boiled before drinking. By afternoon, when the fighting was at its peak, the sickness would pass and she would set about her tasks of washing Urasid's clothes and caring for the wounded men. She called him husband because it was less sickening than forming her lips around the syllables of a hated name, and he slapped her when she was not quick to come to his side or his food bowl was not full enough, and he beat her when she vomited in the morning before he took to the field.

Two months into their campaign and her sickness had not passed. She stood behind their tent and vomited. Although her wrists and ankles were chained, she was free to move around the immediate vicinity of their camp to complete her daily tasks. Surrounded by one thousand foreigners, there was no chance of escape. When one of those foreigners approached her, wounded in the shoulder from an arrow that he now carried in his fist, she turned away from him to continue retching.

'I hear your people scream loudest during sex,' he said.

She looked at him. 'If you touch me, I am not the one who will be screaming. I am Urasid's bride. Go find another sorry slave to rut with.'

'You say your husband's name like I should be impressed. Or that I should even know him.'

He reached for her and she gripped his wrist. 'Come near me again and I will take that arrow from you and pierce your dick with it. I may be small, but I am not helpless.'

The man raised his other hand, the one holding the arrow, and made to plunge it into her face.

Bec ducked, kept hold of his wrist, and twisted. She swung onto his back, the chain that bound her wrists taut against his throat, and she pulled it tight. He struggled, swinging at her with his arms, but her grip was tight. She choked him until he fell to his knees, and she choked him further until he was wheezing. When she let go, he dropped to the ground, his eyes turning up in his head.

Bec knelt over him. 'No. Wake up.' She slapped his face, rousing him. 'Stay with me, I'm not finished.'

She reached down and took the arrow. Then, as she had promised him, she raised it high and drove it into his crotch. When he screamed, she was grabbed from behind. She struggled against two sets of strong hands that held her firm, but it was too late for her victim; he bled to death almost instantly.

She spat on him before they could carry her away.

She was chained inside her own tent, bound to a stake in the ground that she could not move, and was left alone until nightfall when Urasid returned. He came in with the two men who had captured her and, without a word, he smacked her in the face so that her vision clouded.

'A wife does not kill warriors.'

'He would have raped me.'

'A husband would punish him. Not the wife.' In his anger, his accent became stronger. 'A slave-wife does not kill a man.' He hit her again.

She refused to cry, but when she vomited and clutched her stomach, he raised a hand to strike her a third time. She looked at him, bile on her lips and chin, and said, 'Kill me, then. End this misery.'

Urasid kicked her leg, grabbed her by the hair, and pulled her up to the extent that her chains would allow. He punched her face. 'No time for death. Time to learn your place.'

She dangled like an empty sack in his hands as he punched her with repeated force. Each blow stung her as a sword, but still she would not cry for him. If he wanted her to beg, she would not. One more punch and she could die. One more. Or the next.

One of the other men grabbed Urasid's shoulder. 'She's pregnant,' he said.

Urasid's next punch did not materialise, his fist close to her face but not connecting.

'No,' Bec laughed, her face red with blood. 'Hit me again. You must.'

Urasid threw her to the ground. 'She is not with child.'

The man pointed at the beginnings of a swell in her stomach. 'I have seven children at home. I know a pregnancy when I see one.'

Urasid came to his knees and shook her. 'Is it true?'

Without thought, she touched her stomach. 'I cannot be.'

'Ask around,' the man said. 'Anyone with his own children will know the look of it. She must be three or four months gone already. She is skin and bone but fat in the belly. You will be a father of a filthy slave child.'

'Get out,' Urasid commanded. The men left them alone.

He turned to Bec again and slapped her bruised face. 'Is it a boy?' When she laughed, he punched her again and she lost consciousness.

Later that night, she awoke, unable to see clearly from the swelling in her face. She sat up and felt a metal collar around her neck. With her fingers, she followed the chain it was attached to and found the other end chained to Urasid's wrist. Wherever he goes now, she would have to follow.

She held her stomach. She was not sure if she was truly pregnant, being nothing more than a child herself, but she was grateful that the bruising on her face, neck, arms and legs did not extend to her belly. If she was pregnant, the child would be hers; never Urasid's. He would lay no claim over it. She would train the child to fight, and it would grow to become a warrior greater even than Rockside with his heart of stone.

Her husband yanked her chain everywhere he walked, except to the battlefield. During the day, when he was fighting, she was chained to an iron latch that had been buried so deep into the ground even Rockside wouldn't have been able to shift it. She sat on the cold early-winter ground, unable to move, unable to bathe, unable to eat. When he visited her for sex in the afternoon he dragged her by the collar into their tent, made grunting noises for a few moments, and then returned her to the latch in the field. He would throw bread at the edge of her reach and watch her scrabble for it, then kick it towards her when the sport became tiring. Other men spat at her and her husband did not discourage it. She had murdered a comrade—perhaps others, too—and the only reason she lived was because of the child.

At night, he chained her up in the tent and she slept on the floor. And in the morning, he took her right back to the latch and left her there.

By the time of the yule ceasefire, when the foreigners had lit their fires and sang to their gods, Bec's belly was swollen and her small breasts were beginning to gain weight. She was thirteen years old, and now her young body was preparing itself to give birth. She had been of mothering age when she was nine—she knew that because of the bleed cycle that her mother had promised her was the greatest blessing—but she had never considered giving birth so young. It would be spring when the baby was born, if indeed she carried it to full term. Chained in the cold for endless days, the frozen ground beneath her would surely freeze the child in her stomach. She was grateful for the lull in war during the yule celebrations, for it meant that Urasid was free in the days to walk her around or bring her inside their tent away from the blistering winds that now swept the valleys. He had stopped laying with her because of the child, but she often caught him lusting after her when he thought she wasn't looking. No doubt he was bedding another woman until her child had been ripped from her body and he could pounce on her once more.

On the twelfth day of yule, when the sun was waking from its long slumber and beginning to climb the ladder of clouds, the foreign men in her camp were readying themselves for to-morrow's renewal of warfare. Javelins were cut and shaped from trees, bronze heads wrapped around their tips into four points for maximum damage, and swords were sharpened.

The following morning, marking the end of yule, a horn was sounded and the men marched out onto the field with their gleaming weapons.

Bec sat on the cold ground and closed her eyes against the fine mist of rain that had started to fall when she woke.

Chapter 27

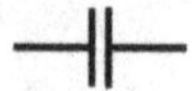

When all the men and boys of Éirinn assembled on the field, organised by company, by tribe, and by aptitude with a sword or a bow or a spear, Oisín nodded at Áed. 'This is your plan. Get out there and rouse them.'

'I do not know what to say.'

'You will.'

Áed hitched his sword belt, adjusted his tunic, and walked onto the field. Turning to face a multitude of men, his smile was shy. The plan had not been to just cut a swath through the foreigners and push beyond them—there were too many of the trespassers for that. When he had first mentioned the plan to force their way towards Knockdhu and cut off the coast from further intrusion, he spent the remainder of the evening contemplating a strategy. He sat with Oisín, Déaglán and Fergal Ó Fuinseog and they thrashed out a plan of attack. A delegation would remain on the field to fend off the rear assault, while a third of the men would split in two, drawing the foreign army to each extreme of the horizon, and Áed would lead the remaining men through the middle of the field, taking out as many as they could on their way.

Getting through their ranks was only half the battle. Once

they had succeeded in dividing the foreigners and cutting a path through their lines, a new delegation of men would close the gap and fight back on themselves to slow the foreign army down.

In principle, his plan had been a sound one, but looking at the faces of his people this morning, the winter sun brightening the Giant's Ring on the distant hills, he was not sure it could work. If the foreigner's slaughtered his men, it was all for nought.

'You all know the plan,' he said, then cleared his throat and repeated himself, louder. 'We are two thousand men; they are four. But what we lack in bodies, we make up for in strength, in might. I've seen you fight. I've seen how brave you are. We are not a people to easily give in. Ó Mordha boys, I've been with you for half of my life or more.' He sought out Rónán among the men and continued, 'I trust you.' He looked at his old rival, Dillon. 'I trust you all.' Dillon tipped his head in acknowledgement.

Áed turned to the others. 'I have fought alongside every one of you these last months. And I would die for all of you. We charge out into that field not with blind faith that we will be spared, but with the knowledge that some of us may not make it through. I am at peace with that—if I die, at least I died defending my tribe, my country. If I die, I will do so with a foreigner's guts in my clenched fist. This is our land. These are our fields, our hills, our ancestors' sacred dwelling places. I am not about to let some bastard take it from us. Are you with me?'

The army cheered.

'Are you with me?' he shouted, and they cheered louder. 'Do it with pride,' he bellowed. 'Do it with bravery. But most of all, do it with a fucking sword through the head of every foreign bastard who dares to come before us.' He raised his sword and the assembled men erupted in howls of insults at the foreigners. 'Oisín,' he said, walking back to his place, 'on your order.'

Oisín slapped him on the back. 'Not bad, young man. You'll get better in time, but that wasn't bad for a first rousing speech.' He looked at his trumpeter and nodded. The man raised his bronze carnyx, the open horn side carved into the gaping jaws of a wild boar, and blew hard and long.

Áed looked at Rónán, who was too far away to talk to, and they nodded at each other. If they survived, that nod was an acknowledgement that they would see each other on the far side of the field. If not, it said all the words it needed to.

To the sound of the horn that echoed across the frozen grasslands, two thousand warriors took to the field at a run. Their cries flooded a path before them as they crossed the barren space. Across from them, the foreign army beat drums as they, too, entered the divide.

From the back of his carbad, standing tall above the crouching driver, Áed gave a call and a third of his army, those men at either end of the company, split off to flank the field. Seeing this, a number of the foreigners broke their ranks to fan out in defence, just as he had predicted.

As he steadied his stance and gripped a spear, Áed watched the oncoming men, all of them clad in leather, their round shields already raised, swords or javelin in hands as they tramped down the field towards them. When he judged the distance to be close enough, he made another call and he watched as Rónán and his fellow archers cocked their arrows and let fly without breaking their stride. The sky turned black with their hail. A second wave of arrows quickly followed, just as the foreigners slung their javelins in the air.

Shields were raised, and everyone crouched against the onslaught. Then they were back on their feet and continuing forward. Áed saw Rónán and his men shoulder their bows and draw their swords.

Closer they ran, to the thump of twelve thousand feet on icy grounds, to the drumming of the foreign beaters, to the cries of charging men.

In an instant, the armies clashed. The driver managed to control his horse as he circled. Áed threw his spear and raised his sword. The spear slammed the shield of a foreign man but did not injure him. Áed dismounted, swung his sword, cleaved a head, and jumped back onto the carbad. The din of sword against sword ran a tingle down his spine.

Áed pushed off again, into an oncoming enemy, and as he did so, his driver was pinned to the carbad's floor by a javelin. He died before he could even scream. On foot, Áed hacked his way through the men, tasting bitter blood as he swung, blocked, ducked and jabbed. He did not realise he was screaming until his mouth ran dry.

He stumbled over a fallen body, righted himself and cut the raised sword-arm from an assailant. One of the foreign men, recognising him as Rockside, the Executioner, hesitated and was too late to block Áed's violent blow. The man's body fell without his head.

As he was reaching the top of the valley, a devastation of bodies in his wake, he did not see a huge foreigner step from his left and swing at him. The man's sword cut into Áed's shield and destroyed it, but it was wedged, and Áed span, pulling the shield back and yanking the sword from the foreigner's hand. He kicked out, knocking the giant backward, and he plunged his sword through the man's chest and twisted.

Áed dropped his shield and double-handed his blade. He wiped his face of blood with his upper arm and cut through another man. As the foreigner fell, he thrust out with his sword and caught Áed in the thigh. The blow was weak, hardly deep, but it affected his balance and he stumbled.

Another man bore down on him and, just as Áed raised his shield-arm and realised he was without one, the man fell at his feet, an arrow in the back of his head.

Áed stood, looked, and saw Rónán nod to him before turning and firing another arrow elsewhere.

Áed laughed. They were near the top of the field, the foreign army thinned out. He jabbed and parried with another foe, dropping the body at his feet, before taking a glance behind him. The once green field was now red, a chaos of bodies littering the ground in all directions. At the far end, back where they had started, the delegation that remained behind were fighting off the eastern attack with success. If Áed and his men could cut off the field's exit and slow down the invaders, Déaglán and Oisín could make it to Knockdhu by tomorrow.

When he passed the tail of the invading army, he turned to fight back and block their retreat. Nearby, he saw Oisín cutting through men like they were sacks of grain, and Déaglán was swinging his sword—the sword that Áed had gifted him—as though he were possessed of all the gods at once.

As was the plan, Áed and the others who reached the top of the field turned and held their ground. Until their army had crossed, they would remain where they were.

Coming up the middle of the field, a convoy of three over-sized carbads carried the women of their camp, each one holding a shield above her head as she crouched beside her neighbour to make a roof of protection. Assuming their survival, they carried rations with them that would see their people right for a day or two.

On the periphery of his vision, Áed saw Oisín take a dive, then come up screaming and slashing. Déaglán could not be seen. Determined to hold his place, Áed ripped out at a foreigner and kept an eye on Oisín who scrabbled on the ground. He was dragging someone towards the hilltop—Déaglán.

Áed swiped another man out of his way, ran to Oisín's aid and they hauled their wounded king clear of the fighting.

'Go,' Oisín said. 'I'll protect him.'

When their army was through the fog of blood, Oisín called to him.

'Let's go. We can make it to Knockdhu. Leave your men to form a wall.'

'How bad is he?'

Déaglán coughed blood. 'I still have all my limbs.' The hole that gaped in his stomach was raw and angry.

'We can't move him,' Áed said.

'We have to. Come.'

They picked him up and Áed searched for Rónán. 'I'm behind you,' he shouted. 'Get moving.'

Áed could no longer look behind him. He could not be sure how many men lay wounded without anyone to carry them, or how many men had already perished in the fight.

As they came down the far side of the hill, ploughing into the remains of the foreigners' camp, those olive-skinned men that were on guard were quickly slaughtered. This was not a time for hostages.

Áed and Oisín laid their king down on a discarded blanket of wool, and King Fergal came to their side. He dropped to his knees.

'Déaglán, you fool. There isn't a woman in all of Éirinn who could get that stain out of your tunic.'

'Fuck you,' Déaglán coughed. With a weakness that Áed could feel emanating from the king's lithe body, he motioned for Oisín to draw near. 'How many did we lose?'

'More than I wish,' Oisín said.

'Less than those foreign bastards?'

Oisín laughed. 'Less by far.'

'Good.' He coughed again, blood spattering his chin. 'We fought well.' He looked at Áed with closing eyes. 'Your sword did me well, boy. Put it in the pit with my ashes.'

Áed knelt beside him. 'We will get a healer. You'll be fighting again in no time.'

Déaglán shook his head. 'Oisín is your king now. As my tanist, it is his right.' The old man took Oisín's hand and then Áed's hand, and he pressed them together. To Oisín, he said, 'This boy is a good study. The Executioner. It is your will to choose, but he should be your tanist. Let him look out for you the way you have looked out for me.'

'Déaglán, we have no time to—'

'Hush. There is no time to argue. Here, take these,' Déaglán said, unhooking the gold discs at his breast and, with weak and trembling fingers, pinned them to Oisín's tunic. 'Raise me, that I might be the first to kiss you.'

With Áed's help, they raised Déaglán onto his elbows and he

leaned in to kiss the discs at Oisín's breast.

'We are at war,' Déaglán said. 'Your ceremony will have to wait. May all the gods protect you, my king.' He lay back down on the blanket and closed his eyes. They thought he was dead until he began to sing in a soft, wispy voice, the song of his forefathers, the song of the Ó Mordha.

But after a few lines, he stopped. And his jaw went slack.

Oisín and Áed stood.

'My king,' Áed said. He leaned in and kissed the discs at Oisín's breast.

They clasped arms. Oisín said, 'Honour his words as my tanist and one day the world will be kissing your breast instead of mine.'

When Rónán approached, Áed gripped him in a tight hug. 'We made it.'

'Not all of us,' Rónán said, looking down at his former king. 'We must hurry. The foreigners have realised our plan and are doubling back on us. Our men have formed a wall across the field, but they cannot hold it forever.'

'My lord?' Áed asked of Oisín.

'Piece together a litter.' He picked up Déaglán's sword. 'We will carry him with us until we can build a pyre for him. King Fergal—you had Déaglán's allegiance since you first took power of your tribe. You have mine also, if I have yours.'

Fergal clapped Oisín on the shoulder. 'There is no better bastard I'd march with that is still alive.'

'Executioner,' Oisín said. 'Rally the men. We head for Knockdhu at once.'

Chapter 28

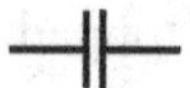

Grainne studied the omens before they set off. They were not favourable. A dark and threatening sky was on the verge of unleashing a deluge of icy rain and the birds were silent. The bones from her pouch were giving inconsistent outcomes and the winds were blowing south, against them.

A wagon was hitched for Eorid and he expected Grainne to ride with him. His open hand was not an invitation but a command. She drew her hood up and sat beside him. Although nobody had yet been chained or cuffed, it was plain that Donal's people were prisoners. They were under constant guard, surrounded, and if any man made a break for freedom, he could be felled in an instant. Eorid had made a king's promise not to murder anyone unnecessarily but stressed that any wrong doing would be punished swiftly. He was trusting in Donal and the Dáirine tribesmen to honour their agreement.

That morning, Grainne had made a sacrifice to appease her gods; they would know that Donal was leading a foreign army towards power in their lands and she asked forgiveness for her part in the matter. Had lambing season begun, she would have sacrificed every newborn in the land.

Donal was unusually quiet this morning, sitting beside

Muirgel and another of his wives on the wagon behind Eorid's, Faolán and his other sons walking demurely behind.

'You do not trust him.'

'Who?' Grainne asked, refusing to look at Eorid.

'Your chieftain says a lot of things when it is to save his skin, am I right?'

'He says a lot of things to save his people,' Grainne said. She looked over her shoulder again at her plump leader. 'It is honourable.'

'There is no honour in slavery. My people know this.'

'You'd have him put a knife in your back?'

Eorid laughed. 'He would not live to get so close.'

Grainne wrapped her cloak tighter around her body as a fine mist of rain began. 'Why are you here?'

'I trust your chieftain less than you do, but either way I intend to take the king-seat in the north.'

'I meant why have you come this way from your own lands? What brings you here—there are plenty of peoples between here and whatever wretched world you come from.'

Eorid lowered his head under a branch as the sept gave way to a copse of trees and the flattened earth that served as a road became rocky. 'We have travelled many, many nights to come here. To exact revenge.'

'Revenge upon whom?'

'Upon your forefathers and your gods.'

'What could our gods possibly do to your people so far away?'

Eorid watched his men marching in front of them, their spears swinging in time as they walked. He had not given an order when they set off, but they marched in perfect alignment all the same. 'Many centuries ago—almost a thousand years—my ancestors came from a land called Hellas. They were slaves there, but in time they made boats and they fled in three directions. When they came here, they found green and tempting pastures on which to build their settlements, and no other peoples to disturb them; it was theirs for the taking. Five brothers divided it among themselves for their kin and for nine kings they lived in perfect peace.

'But then your gods came with their warriors and sought a great battle for the hills. In the time of my ancestor-king, Eochaid mac Eirc, no rains fell to blight them, and harvests were plentiful. But your gods left him thirsty in the war and when they hid all sources of water from him, they waited until he was near death from the dryness of his lips and they killed him in Beltra. They tore his limbs from his body and they carried them to all the corners of the land so that my people could see how cruel they were, that they would not rest until we were eradicated from their sight. We were defeated. Those of us who were not slaughtered fled the lands in our ships and vowed that one day we would return.'

Grainne was silent for a moment. Then she said, 'The first battle of Mag Tuired. This is legend for us. Many bards still sing of it when they have little better to lament about.'

'Then you know why we have come.'

'I understand that every tale has two side—three, if you include the fiction and embellishments that always accompany a bard's words—but your account of this battle between your people and mine differs greatly from my acquaintance with the story. As I remember it from my teachings with the druids, our king, Nuada, brought his people to these shores and peaceably asked to share the land with your ancestors. There is a song—I cannot recall it exactly—that recounts the war that ensued. Eochaid refused my forefathers' request to share the land and the battle lasted four days. A champion of yours struck Nuada and sliced off his hand. The first battle of Mag Tuired was our creation story, how we came to these lands and thrived.'

'Then we shall have a second battle of Mag Tuired and this time my people will win.'

'There has already been a second battle. It was against the Fomorians, a race of people far worse than the woes you bring with you.'

'When I have won this battle, I will strike out and find these Fomorians and I will defeat them also.'

'You are missing my point,' Grainne said.

'I understand your point, my druid friend, but I cannot agree with it. As you so rightly said, every story has two sides. You have your beliefs, I have mine; beliefs that have been held dear for a millennium. Listening to you narrate a false account of my ancestors makes the anger within me swell even more. I have promised not to kill you, but I make no promise not to cut out your tongue of lies. When we break for food and to rest the horses, you will read the omens and you will tell me, honestly, that we are marching in the right direction.'

When they stopped, Eorid's people kept their distance from her. Perhaps, she considered, the mysticism to which her own tribesmen elevated her was the same in all countries.

As Eorid had directed, she read the omens. They were still not favourable, but they were travelling in the correct direction. The smell of the earth's decay was carried on the wind, and the rain—if she stared at the middle distance—was tinted with blood. She told Eorid this and he was satisfied with her work. He did not have the same fear of her as his people did, perhaps because his brother, as he had told her, was also a druid. Every morsel of food he ate was first tasted by her. 'If your cooks wish me harm,' he said, 'they will harm you first.'

She retreated to a tent to be alone. In the failing light, Eorid announced that they would camp for the night and march at dawn. Grainne lit a tallow candle and buried a bronze bracelet in the ground as an offering to the goddess Bríg, daughter of the Dagda, bringer of healing. She spoke some words, asking Bríg to heal their land and all those who reside on it, foreign and native. If an agreement can be reached between both sides, there need not be any more deaths.

She closed her eyes to sleep and when she opened them again, she was standing in a vast field of bright heather. A white swan with a black streak on its head lay on the ground before her, its neck broken, its chest carved open and bloody, its eyes open and staring at her.

Grainne fell to her knees and cradled the bird's head. 'My gracious lady Cáer. What has befallen you?'

She wept, and when her tears touched the lifeless swan, its wings fluttered, its chest closed, and its neck straightened. In a blink, the swan was gone and Cáer lay in its place, clinging to Grainne's arms.

'Your faith is admirable.'

'What prophecy is this?' Grainne asked.

'You journey into death and I cannot stop it. You, my sweetest child, will be witness to an event that rips at my heart.'

'Then I shall not go. Tell me how to avoid this.'

'You cannot. It is done. One other will end these bloody

days. Until then, your journey is set.'

'If I am to die, I will face it.'

'If you are to die, I would take you upon my wing and carry you away,' Cáer said. 'The deaths you will face are not your own. The time of kings is upon you. The outcome has been forecast. We are all but pieces in a game of fidhcheall, moving where we are destined to go. There will be no winner, for we will all lose in this game.' Cáer hugged tighter to Grainne. 'Close your eyes and hold me, child, for I will not see you again in this life.'

When she woke, a cold dawn encroached on her tent and she made to bathe and pack her things. Donal, his wife and Faolán were eating with their usurper-king and the sight of them made her wish not to eat another meal again.

In the days that followed, they encountered the devastations of war on their journey north. Townships were burned, and bodies were unceremoniously stacked in tall piles of rotting flesh. That Eorid was travelling with them without slaughtering them all was a wonder. She was convinced his endgame would not be so friendly.

The sight of a bloody battle stretched out before them for miles in either direction when at last they stood under the shadow of the Giant's Ring that crowned the hills above them. A massacre of this magnitude would have taken many days to accomplish. Everywhere, fallen warriors of both sides lay indistinguishable from one another, covered in blood as they were, many with their heads or arms shorn off.

'This battle ended badly for each of us,' Faolán said, 'but the war isn't over. Our people wouldn't leave their dead on the field. They would be given honourable send-offs.'

Eorid scanned the field. 'Your people came from that direction. The Hellas warriors came from there and they met for months of battle.' He pointed towards a darkly stained patch of frozen grass. 'Champions fought there for many weeks.'

'From the mess,' Donal said, 'it looks like we had a champion far greater than yours, my lord.'

'That will be revised when I meet him.' He turned, surveying all that could be seen. 'The battle went this way. The coast is'—he looked around—'in the same direction. Your warriors mean to take your beaches from us.' He laughed. 'I only hope that not all have been slaughtered by the time we arrive. Come, let us join the fray. It has been a long time since I killed a man.'

Chapter 29

⊣⊢

Knockdhu rose on the heights of a hill ahead of them. Three defensive banks, topped with spiked palisades, protected the fort on its western side, wrapping north and south to a sheer cliff-drop on the east. Its imposing defence structures and altitude made it almost impenetrable, but the foreigners had succeeded in overthrowing its occupants. Home-fires burned within its huts, columns of silver smoke rising to a grey sky. In the mist-shrouded bay beyond, a wealth of warships jostled on the choppy waves.

Several hectares to the south, with clear visibility in all directions, Oisín, Áed and Fergal stood on a hilltop ahead of their army and watched as foreign men entered and exited Knockdhu at will, its entranceway thrown open as if the need for defence was negligible. On its outer perimeter to the west, at the bottom of the hill, a delegation of foreign men—perhaps three hundred in all—had made camp. How many more were inside, they could not tell.

Shielding his eyes from a sharp wind, Oisín said, 'The minute they close the entranceway, we'll never get up the banks, over the walls and inside. Not alive, anyway.'

'They're certainly not going to roll over and let us scratch

283

their bellies,' Fergal said. 'It's a march to death if we try.'

'Executioner, you're my new favourite tactician. Short of falling on them from the sky, how do we get in?'

Áed surveyed the area before them. 'The eastern drop— could we climb it?'

Fergal said, 'I've spat over that drop many times. The cliff-side is rocky, but we'd never get up unspotted either from the fort above of from the ships in the bay.'

'And the fences—do they butt up against the fall at either end?'

'On the inner bank, yes. What are you thinking?'

The plan was a simple one, but it meant they would have to split their army in four, something Áed had hoped they could avoid. 'We send a small company around to the north, and another to the south-eastern edge. A third will get behind the cliff and they'll share eyes on the clifftop as well as the bay behind them. How far is the shore from the fort?'

'About three hundred rods, at a guess,' Oisín said. 'If it weren't so foggy out there, you'd see Albanach on the horizon, if it hasn't already been plundered into the sea.'

'Too far for spears or arrows, then. They'd only have to fear fire from the fort itself. The rest of the men,' Áed said, 'will attack from the west, straight towards the walls, drawing as much fire as they can. It'll have to be big enough for the foreigners to assume that's our full force. Just before dawn, the north and south components will sneak along the cliff's edge, round the fence at either side, and attack from within. Most of them will be asleep; if we're quick and quiet we can slaughter half of the bastards before the fore-fighters even know we've penetrated from behind. The western assault will have to time their attack precisely or we'll lose the advantage.'

'And the men who go beyond the drop?' Fergal asked. 'What use are they on a cliff face they won't be able to scale?'

'They'll remain hidden until we're inside, then they can skirt around and join us. They'll be a lookout. If there's a chance we're spotted on our approach from the north and south, they'll draw fire. With any luck, in the dark, some of those blind bastards will fall over the edge without our help.'

Oisín laughed and slapped him on the back. 'We'll keep flames to a minimum,' he said. 'We're not here to sack the fort but to reclaim it.'

Áed nodded. 'Look at all those homes inside—a hundred or more, for sure. Five or six men to a hut and we can house most of our army, even if they do have to sleep on top of each other.'

'May the gods look favourably on those who have already fallen,' Fergal said. He turned and walked back down the hill.

He was right. Since breaking through enemy lines two days ago, they had lost several hundred men from the foreigners that followed them. 'If we can get in,' Áed said to Oisín, 'we won't lose any more men. We can end this.'

They waited until nightfall before advancing. Fires lit the inner wall where guards were stationed, but the companies skirted wide to avoid detection. Although Rónán should have run east to flank the cliff with the rest of his archers, Áed asked for him to accompany his delegation to the north face. 'I'll need your strong arm once we're inside,' he said. They had moved away from the others and embraced. Achall had remained behind with a small contingent of men who guarded the women, but they were still being discreet in honour of their word to her. 'Once we've taken the fort, we'll have private homes. I long to lie in your arms again.'

'Sadly,' Rónán said, 'situations of war seem to trump love. I've hardly seen you in weeks. Had I not heard people talking about the Executioner, I could have assumed you had died in battle.'

'But I'm the Executioner. I don't die; others do.'

'Keep it that way,' Rónán said, and he kissed him before they returned to their men.

With the moon deep in the western sky, and low, scudding clouds making the cliff's edge almost invisible, Áed and his men began their crouched climb. To the south, Oisín would be leading twenty men, and Fergal was on the west with the remainder of their warriors, ready to assault as soon as the boys were near the top.

Hearing the sudden clamour from the field below, Áed knew it was time to act. He motioned for his men and they made a dash for the fence line. Fergal had been correct—the fence butted the cliff's edge and getting around it would be tricky without falling. Áed gripped the outermost post, glanced around the wall, and saw foreign men running towards the front, javelins in hand. The distraction was working. He only hoped Oisín was at the far fence, so they could enter together.

Áed Swung a leg and twisted so that the other leg followed, and he backed up against the inner side of the fence. He had no time to look down. He quickly pushed away and slid in behind the nearest hut, drawing his sword as he moved. He heard Rónán and the others coming behind him. Inside the first hut, he beheaded two men before they could rise. He cut a mark on the entrance as he left, an indication that it had been cleared, and he ducked low, running to the next hut.

He had miscalculated how many men would be asleep. The uproar from outside the walls was enough to wake the dead and many of the foreigners were leaving their huts and running to the inner bank. He paused beside a doorway and cut through a man as he came out. Across the way, he saw Rónán stepping out of a hut, carrying a severed head. Rónán threw it at an oncoming foreigner and then pierced him through.

They had cleared less than a quarter of the northern section when a call went out and those protecting the walls now turned towards them. He was thankful, at least, that many of them were still sleep-fogged.

Archers on the inner wall were lighting arrows to send into the field, burning men regardless of whose army they fought for. In the dark, there was no telling who was native and who was not.

Áed fought his way to the wall alongside Rónán. Without shields, they cut and jabbed with a sword in one hand and a dagger in the other, using blades and pommels both, leaving a trail of guts behind them.

At the wall, they wrestled for possession of a bow, and as Áed defended him, Rónán began picking off enemy warriors around him. No sooner had he let loose an arrow than another was cocked and ready.

On the southern side, Oisín cut down three men with one swing. Over the din, Áed could hear him singing.

The Executioner and the forty men who infiltrated the fort had slaughtered almost three hundred men as the sun's rays broke the dawn. In the coordinated attack, he had lost only four of his men, and each death stung him with copious salt. Outside, the battle for the field waged on, and as the sky brightened, Rónán and several others took up bows and fired into the fray. Oisín advised against going out to join them and Áed saw the logic in it. They should now concentrate on the eastern cliff, building a new defensive wall against further intrusion from the enemy; those who had remained in their warships would likely be on their way.

By midday, the fighting was over, and the fort was theirs. They secured the entranceway and began to build a rear wall by scrapping several huts for reuse. With a contingent remaining outside, the dead were burned and, inside, the foreign bodies were thrown over the cliff to join the natives who had already succumbed when the foreigners had first arrived. Of the men under Oisín and Fergal's command who had made it to Knockdhu, less than six hundred had survived. They claimed their homes and rested; although they had repossessed the promontory, they knew they would be under imminent attack.

As the day gave way to dusk, Áed sought out Rónán's home. At the entrance, he called out and was invited in. Achall crouched by the fire, tending the preparations of a grouse. She looked up when he entered, but quickly returned to her chores.

'Can we talk?' Áed asked of Rónán.

Achall stood, wiped her hands, and said, 'I am thankful to you for securing us a new home. I will stay with the girls for this night and return in the morning.'

'I do not wish to drive you from your home,' Áed said.

With an absence of mind, she rubbed her stomach in slow circles. 'I cannot forget the pains you have gone to in aiding the war. You may have the night and tomorrow he is mine again.' She left, and in the stillness that followed, the boys stared at each other for a long moment before speaking.

Rónán lay on the bed and opened his arms. 'I need to hold you.' When Áed was secured within his embrace, he said, 'Every night I dream of you, your eyes as bright as the sun, your hair like flames.'

'What do I do in these dreams?'

'You stare at me. Nothing more. Just as you did when you entered a moment ago. Do you think it means something?'

'I do not have the insights of a druid,' Áed said, 'but perhaps it means I am always here to keep you safe. To watch over you.'

'When we were boys, it was I who watched over you.'

'I remember.' Áed turned to face Rónán. 'But there is nothing more important to me than your life; not even my own. I would rather die than lose you.'

'If you die, I would follow you into the Otherworld. I have no life without you.' He pressed his forehead against Áed's and Áed smiled.

'You smell like memories,' Áed said.

'It has been too long since we lay together.'

Áed turned again, nestled in between Rónán's arms, his back to Rónán's stomach, and he stared at the flames from the hearth. The spit and crackle of the twigs in the fire, and the intake of Rónán's shallow breathing, was all that kept them from absolute silence. When they made love, it was slow, their energies already spent on the field, and they lay as one until the dawn.

When Áed woke, his face buried in the nook of Rónán's neck, he stretched with torpidity, and turned to face Achall standing over them. He sat up at once, and Rónán followed. The dawn's light cast her as a silhouette before them.

But she was smiling. 'I am with child,' she said, touching her

belly. 'I confirmed it this morning, although I have suspected
for weeks.'

They stared at her.

She blinked at them.

'You should congratulate me,' she said. 'And also congratulate Rónán, who will be proud to be a father.'

Chapter 30

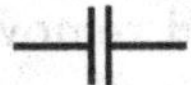

It was a surprise when the native army tore east through the line of foreigners. To Bec, chained in a tent with only a limited view of the field, it appeared that every man from her captor's army was now pushing forward into the quarrel. She laughed and felt the baby kick. With the yule over, she counted that she was five or six months into her term.

Urasid and his men fell back when their leader was killed, and they took their possessions and their slaves, and swept south around the main body of the battle. Bec's dress had grown too tight around her swollen stomach that she now wore one of Urasid's long tunics. She thought they were fleeing until she realised that their circular curve had taken them back onto a northern pass. They travelled with caution, a slow and deliberate stalking of a foe that now outnumbered them. For two nights they walked through mud and moss and they now stood on a hill in view of a large promontory fort that overlooked the coastline. They watched as dawn drew near and their enemy took the fort with force.

'Rockside does this,' Bec said, then called him by the name her own people supposedly used. 'The Executioner.'

Urasid back-handed her cheek, drawing blood. But she spat

and laughed. He released a length of the chain that was collared to her neck and he whipped it across her back. When she fell, he kicked her leg.

Bec drew herself into a ball to protect her unborn child. 'If I do not kill you myself, I will watch you die at the hands of Rockside,' she said when he leaned down to her. 'He will drain the life from your body and remove your head from your pathetic shoulders.'

Urasid gripped her hair, pulled her head back and wrapped his fingers around her throat. 'Enough. Child or not, I will cut you open and dance on your guts.'

'Shut it,' a man called. 'We wait until dark and then we must skirt around to the ships in the bay. If they are unmanned, we will take one.'

'And go where?' Urasid asked. He yanked on Bec's chain to draw her onto her knees. 'You seek to flee?'

'We are three hundred men, and half again of slaves. Would you rather walk up that hill and ask Rockside for his favour?'

'We are not the only ones left, Garrid,' Urasid said. 'We will hold this hill until more arrive and we will fight for as long as it takes. We will take the fort and I will personally slice this Rockside from throat to ball-sack.'

Garrid squared up against him. 'Who put you in charge? You left your clan master behind.'

'He died on the field like you would have done if you'd the balls to stand out there.'

'Enough squabbling,' another man said. 'Set camp. We'll re-evaluate at dawn.'

They camped on the leeward side of the hill, away from the imposing fort and the harsh winds. Bec was left to herself, away from the other slave girls, the *cumal* that would keep the men company during the wintry nights ahead. Urasid had not touched her sexually in weeks and she was grateful for the relief. Since her belly had begun to swell, he looked upon her with less frequency, and when he was near her he maintained a tight grip on her chain. He would order her to walk ahead of him, and then he would pull on the chain to rope her back in. Three times in the last week he had called her mutt or dog.

With her dress too small for her, he liked to keep her naked except when they marched.

On the ground of her tent, she scratched the bare skin of her arms and legs with sharply bitten fingernails until the scratches became sores. With a jagged nail she traced one of Odhran's runes into the flesh of her belly until it scarred. At all costs, she aimed to protect the child.

She could not recall the last time she had bathed. The sun had been warm, so it must have been many months ago. She was caked in the grimy dirt of war and her hair was matted and knotted around her face. Had she been handed a fine bronze mirror, the face staring back at her would not have been her own.

She curled up on the ground in a useless attempt at sleep. In recent months, when it came to her, it brought only darkness, a void, and for weeks she pinched her arms to remain awake. On the frontline, she had listened to Urasid's snores in endless nights and then listened to the sounds of war in the day. Alone, this sudden and consuming emptiness tore screams from her soul, erupting from her lips in dry, cracked splinters, her lips as chewed and dry as her voice, droplets of blood seeping from the broken corners of her mouth.

She could not remember the last time she had cried. She had been sad and angry in equal measure, but to be tearful was no longer a part of her identity. Many nights she lay on the ground and tried, bringing up thoughts of the hardships she had suffered, thoughts of her mother and father, of Odhran in his druid's robes, but her eyes remained dry. Thoughts of her unborn child only made stones of resolve form within her, and thoughts of her death only made her smile in welcoming relief.

She turned her back on the entrance of her tent and could feel the chill airs blister her. Naked and without a fire, the only warmth she felt was from the child within her.

She twirled her fingers in the dirt, making patterns that reflected the mess of her mind. If Urasid would treat her like a dog, she would become one. She growled, low and guttural, from deep in her throat. He would be asleep, she imagined, in his own tent, away from her. Or he would be rutting with another girl, sowing his seed for an army of his own. She clawed the ground and growled louder, baring her teeth. The litter inside her would be hers alone.

When the tent flap opened, she turned, rolling to her knees, and she barked.

Garrid stood there, the man who had confronted Urasid on the hill. In the semi-darkness, she recognised his posture and his scent.

She barked again, rolled on the ground at the length of her chain.

'I've an itch you can scratch, girl,' he said, 'if you're careful with those claws.'

She turned on her back and exposed herself, panting.

'I'd have you on your knees so I can't see the beast that grows inside you.' He unstrapped his sword and lay it out of her reach. Judging the length of her chain, he circled around behind her. 'Good girl,' he said. 'Be still.'

She nuzzled towards his feet, but he was out of her staked circle. When he gingerly ventured a step forward, she licked his toe and he recoiled.

'Animal,' he spat.

She yapped.

He was far from repulsed; she could see the tenting in his tunic.

'You want to fuck like a dog?' he asked. 'You want to play that game?'

Bec got to her knees and shook herself. She could imagine wet fur splashing him.

Garrid sprung towards her, landed on her back, and hitched his tunic up. She backed onto him so that he could enjoy himself for a moment. Then she growled again. He slapped the back of her head, and when his arm was outstretched, she reached back for it and pulled, twisted her body in the opposite direction so that she fell one way and he the other.

She was quickly on top of him. She had managed to pull him towards the stake that secured her to the ground, and with the chain slack, she wrapped it around his neck and pulled tight.

Garrid's face reddened and he tried to cough. His hands punched out at her and struck her breasts. She choked him, barking in his face. As his eyes bulged, she drew her tongue along his stubbled cheek.

When his body went limp, she continued to choke him with the chain. At length, she released him, unwrapped the chain from his neck, and climbed off him. She looked at him and spat on his face. 'If you're going to lie with a dog, expect to get bitten.'

Bec crawled to the farthest reach of her chain, away from him, and she licked her palms that had ached against the chain links as she had strangled him. When Urasid finds her in the morning, perhaps he will kill her at last. Or perhaps he would reward her for killing his enemy.

She lay her head on her hands and stared out into the wet night. She had lost count how many foreigners she had now killed. Maybe, she hoped, it was as many as Rockside.

Tonight, when the blackness came with sleep, at least it brought a soothing void.

Chapter 31

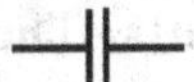

Áed left Rónán and Achall to talk about their child and, with Oisín's help, he oversaw the dismantling of several *brú* huts, rebuilding them into smaller ones, turning ninety homes into one hundred and twelve. The girls stitched old tunics into mattresses and stuffed them with heather and moss that had lined the rear of the croft along the inner palisade wall. With construction of the new cliff-wall complete, Knockdhu was once again impregnable.

He looked out to the west. Among the ferns and secreted in uncountable valleys, he knew the foreigners were assembling. That morning, when the fort was fully secured, Rónán and his archers ventured out towards the eastern coast with a view to setting fire to the nearest warships, thereby cutting off the bay from further intrusion. If they could protect the shoreline, they could turn their full attention towards the foreigners who were entrenched among them. Messengers had already been dispatched for coastal tribes north and south, who should then carry the news to the next tribe and the next. If they could not build an impassable wall around the country, they could at least bridge between them a wall of fighting men. Cutting the land off from invaders inevitably meant killing all foreign trade, too, but in the short term, until their homes were safe from harm, it would be unavoidable.

For three weeks they held the hillside, fending off their attackers with volleys of spears and arrows from the walls, ensuring none could get close enough to breach their defences.

In one of the workshop huts, Áed found clay moulds for swords, spearheads and butts. There was a lack of iron, but a store of chalcocite from which, if he had the time, he could leach copper from the ore, though the war would not wait for his metalwork. With further investigation, he discovered several bronze ingots that he could hammer down for use. He employed some of the boys from Ailigh, the ones he trusted most, to help him when Oisín called for a tacticians' counsel that morning. On his way to the great hall on the southern pass of their confinement, a familiar face stopped him with a hand on his shoulder.

'Dillon,' Áed said. 'Glad to see you're still alive. I haven't seen you in so long I forgot you were even here.'

'I've been busy on the walls, fighting off an army of whores and asses. My kills are uncountable. Listen,' Dillon said, squeezing his fingers on Áed's shoulder just enough to create pressure, 'all that stuff I put you through when we were young? You're the Executioner now. Oisín's tanist.'

'I may be next in line to the king-seat, but you'll have a long wait to see it. King Oisín's one tough bastard.'

'I never expected you'd amount to anything. What I'm saying is, I'm sorry. We were children, you know?'

Áed smiled. 'I appreciate it. We were nothing more than agitated boys, restricted to a stone wall and two fields. What else were we going to do but fight? And that beating I gave you—seems like so many years ago. Let's forget it all, okay?'

'I let you give me that beating,' Dillon said. 'But yes, it's over now. And we'll win the war, for sure. We'll go back to Ailigh when this is done, and you can learn to be king and I'll raise my child.'

'Child?' Áed asked, but he already knew the answer.

'Your lover doesn't make house with his wife, is what I hear. She came to me for a bedding.'

Áed took a step away from him. 'The child is Rónán's and will be raised as his.'

'It's my little bastard child and when I tell Oisín and the boys, Achall will have Rónán put to trial and killed—he desires you more than he does his own wife. She has a right to his death when he favours another. I can't kill you myself, you're a hero, adored by everyone. But watching you lose your lover will hurt you more than any blade.'

Áed pulled Dillon into a tight embrace with his left arm. In his right hand, he had already drawn his dagger. He felt the blade penetrate Dillon's upper abdomen and the blood wash over his fingers. With his left hand on the back of Dillon's head and his lips close to his ear, he said, 'I have suffered the loss of my family and many of the boys I grew up with, and each death killed me just a little. Your death revives me. Your death brings me life. As it seeps from your chest, it enters mine and fills me with song. I am Áed the Executioner. And I can win this war without your jealousies.'

He withdrew the blade and gripped Dillon's face so that he could look upon his killer. 'You will not be a martyr. You will not be remembered. My spirit is unbroken and when I dump you over the wall to join the other dead, you will be nothing more than a speck in the histories of men. You are nothing to me, do you understand? You are nothing.'

Dillon's eyes were already dull and drooping. A line of blood traced the corners of his mouth. Áed looked around. From their position between two huts, they had been unseen. He dragged the body behind his workshop and hid it beneath a pile of discarded metal debris. If Achall had intended on continuing to see the ungrateful bastard, she was out of luck. She could find a new man to rut with.

He wiped his blade, washed his hands and changed his tunic before seeking out Oisín in the great hall. He did not feel guilt over Dillon's death; in matters of love, death is an inevitability. Rónán and Achall's secret must be kept if she wishes the child to be raised as a king. Perhaps it was not as she had planned, Áed becoming Oisín's tanist instead of Rónán, but in the distant future, when Áed eventually ascended to the king-seat, Rónán would of course become his own tanist. Achall's need to be at the top of the hierarchy was manifest in how she carried herself, how she spoke to others, and how she bowed to nobody. Her own desire or her uncle's, Rónán's chieftain-father, Áed was not sure, but in all certainty, she would carry out her plan without fault. If Áed had not killed Dillon, Achall would have done so beyond doubt.

In the great hall, large enough to house thirty men for sleep but currently only containing four for their tactical meeting, Áed bowed his submission to his new king and apologised for being late. 'I found some bronze and several moulds. We can replenish our spearheads, and there should be enough for a few basic swords that, once hardened, will last a day or two of fighting but not much more.'

'If we can hold the walls,' Oisín said, 'we might not need the extra swords. Spears and arrows, those will be our main line of defence.'

Áed took a seat. 'Rónán has already set to fletching. If those chickens that were in the yard when we arrived belonged to the foreigners, it will be even more fitting when their feathers flight their path into their chests.'

'Speaking of chickens,' Oisín said to Fergal, 'what's the food situation?'

'We filled a store with the foreigners' food and whatever we managed to bring with us. We have enough to last us two more weeks, three if we cut back.'

'Then we have two weeks to win this bastard war. Have the druids made sacrifice yet?'

'What druids?' Fergal said. 'Only one made it off the front-line when she came through the field in the women's wagon, and she lost her life outside before we retook this hold.'

'We're without guidance from the gods,' the fourth man said.

'We'll be our own guidance,' Áed replied. 'No one knows how to make sacrifice like a druid; we'll just have to trust that the gods are still watching over us. When we get through this, we can sacrifice seven times a hundred calves to each of them.'

The man bowed his deference.

'Áed's right,' Oisín said. 'The gods are on our side or we're doomed. There's nothing we can do about it now.' He poured drinks from a jug and handed them to the others. He drank his own to sate a thirst, and then poured another. 'How are the walls?'

'Refortified and holding,' Áed said. 'Ditches have been dug

deeper than they were, and the cliff-wall is in place. The palisades are under constant guard and the log posts are too thick to be burned readily by a torched arrow. Short of pulling the fences down, there's no way in but for the single entranceway on the south, and I'm not about to let anyone pull my walls down.'

Fergal said, 'They won't hurl their spears at us for long. In the last three weeks, they must have depleted their resources. They'll come for the walls and they'll come hard.'

'We'll fight back harder,' Oisín said.

'The boys we left behind in Ailigh,' Áed said, 'should hopefully be able to hold the hill. If every coastal province does the same, all we have to do is kill the remaining bastards that are hemmed in and reclaim our land.'

Fergal laughed. 'You make it sound easy, Executioner. Oisín, I can see why you picked this one.'

'Although he is young, he is my greatest warrior. He has the instinct of a true god. When they sing about him,' Oisín said, 'I'll make sure they give you a mention.'

Fergal bowed low. 'The ladies will love me for it.'

A commotion stirred outside their hut and when they went to investigate, they saw Rónán and his men coming towards them, bows in hand.

'What's happening?' Oisín asked.

'Some foreigners approach from the south. Looks like they mean to talk.'

They hurried to the walls to look out as archers fanned along the palisade. Four horses, one of them carrying two passengers, trotted across the field and when they were within shouting distance, their riders dismounted.

'Defectors?' someone asked.

'Fat chance,' another archer said.

Áed, Rónán and Oisín jostled for a vantage point, and Rónán cocked an arrow.

'Parlay!' one of the foreign men shouted. 'Send out your king that we may talk.'

Of the party that arrived outside their walls, their speaker, their evident leader, was by far the tallest. With him were two other foreigners in their leather armour, shields and spears held lightly in their hands, as well as a naked and obviously pregnant slave girl on the end of a chain, a plump man with a gold torc at his neck, and a druid who wore the robes of a local order.

Oisín called back to them. 'You can talk from there, stranger.'

'I would see the face of the man I wish to make an accord with,' the foreign leader shouted.

'You don't believe they mean to make a deal,' Áed said. 'You step outside, alone, and they'll gut you as soon as look at you.'

'I don't know,' Rónán said, his voice low, soft. He had already lowered his bow. 'That's Donal.'

'Who?' Oisín asked.

'The fat one. My chieftain. And my father.'

Chapter 32

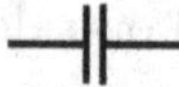

'Parlay!' Eorid shouted. 'Send out your king that we may talk.' He had arrived with his army the morning before, cresting a hill of naked heather with the druid, Grainne, at his side. 'This is where the last vestiges of your people reside? You may be offering many passage rites through the tunnels of death if they do not abide by your chieftain's proposal.'

'You wish them to reject you, don't you?' Grainne asked. 'You don't want a king to rule in your place, you want to kill us all.'

'There are some of your people I could have a fondness for, my dear druid lady. But, yes, I came here to fight and conquer.'

'And if they accept your offer?'

'I will be true to my word. In your story of my history, one version rumours that we were given a province to thrive in. This was not true, of course, but should the king kneel to me and accept me as his ruler, I will gift to him and his people a small section of this lush island. I will not be a heartless ruler. They can live out their days in servitude to me and you will become my personal confidante.'

Grainne looked at the fort over thirty rods away and, even at this distance, she could make out a hive of activity beyond its walls and the fighting foreigners below it. 'Your army may outnumber those men ten to one, but if they do not accept your terms—and I anticipate that they won't—they will fight hard and you will lose many men.'

Eorid laughed. 'If they wish to fight, I will relish it. Come, druid.'

They turned and marched down the westward slope, Donal, his wife and son following among a guard of armed warriors who would not let them near their leader. Among the trees in the valley, they were halted from further travel by a group of leather-clad men with javelin and crossbows.

'Name your clan,' Eorid said. 'I am Eorid of Clan Ysithac, son of Secorid.'

One of the men came forward and bowed. He touched his left shoulder with his right fist in salute. 'Clans Hir, Gathi and Beris. We camp beyond the trees, my lord, and we fight the enemy daily.'

'How long have you accosted their walls?'

'Three weeks, my Lord King. We will starve them out if we cannot burn them out.'

'How are your provisions?'

The man bowed. 'We run low on food, but we send hunters out each day. And we are surrounded by tall trees; the gods have given us sturdy wood for spears and catapults.'

It was a short march through the copse of trees into an open valley. Eorid entered the camp and, recognising either his face or his posture as a leader, those in the camp took a knee.

'Who leads you?' Eorid asked.

A man stepped forward and saluted him. 'We are many clans together, lord. Too many leaders are among us, but we will all bow to your word. I am Urasid.'

They went to confide in a tent. Asked to wait outside, but without guard, Grainne looked around the camp of foreign warriors. The men ranged in age from mere children to those who sported locks of greying hair tied back in plaits. Despite their swarthy complexion and their dark eyes, they could have been members of a local tribe, displaced by a war they had no part in. Overall, they looked shabby and tired, shadows of ghosts clawing at the faces. She imagined the men inside Knockdhu looked the same. War has a way of breaking the soul like no other toil does.

'Lady,' one of the boys called to her. He was no older than Grainne. 'How are the omens?'

She went to him and crouched before him as he sat on the frozen grass. 'What is your name, child?'

He shrank from her. Druids should never be so familiar. 'I am Sharid, son of Sharid.'

'Named for your father,' she said. 'That is a good omen.' She put a hand on his shoulder. 'The war is almost over.' She did not know who would win—the omens would not tell her that— but she knew it would not last much longer. 'Your father—is he with you?'

Sharid lowered his eyes and made an unusual sign with his fingers. 'Dead.'

Grainne took the pouch from her belt and dumped the bones on the grass to look at their patterns. 'Did he receive the rites?'

'No druid was with us when he died,' the boy said. 'I burned his remains and buried them with his sword.'

The bones did not speak to her, but she studied them and then smiled. 'Your father has passed into the Otherworld successfully. He is at rest.'

An older man nearby, who had overheard their conversation, asked, 'What of my brother, Connthid? He died also.'

She looked at him. He was too old for the childish need for peace, but she picked up the bones and cast them again. 'He, too,' she said. 'Him and many others made it safely into the calm seas of the spirit world.'

The man smiled and nodded. 'If I die in the coming days, will you give me the rites? I am never as lucky as my brother; I would get lost on the way.'

Grainne stood and put her bones away. 'I am not of your people—you can tell by my appearance—but I walk beside Eorid. He trusts me, and you must also.' Louder, so that all those nearby could hear, she said, 'Those of you who perish, though I sincerely wish for a peaceful end to this incomprehensible madness, I will guide you all into the Otherworld. None among you will wander the spirit lands without a direction. Whatever your belief systems, I believe that your afterlife and mine are one. Call your gods by whichever name you choose, they are one and the same. You have sun gods and moon gods, and gods of brave warriors, just as we do.'

'If they are the same gods,' someone said, 'then no war could ever be won. If we worship and make sacrifice, our gods will look favourably on us. If the enemy does likewise, why would the gods favour one side over the other?'

Grainne considered this. She sat, so as to be on the same level as the men around her. 'Gods do not win wars,' she said. 'People do. If both sides of a war worship their gods equally, the victor is not decided by how many calves he has sacrificed, but by how hard he thrusts his sword. The gods grant you the strength to fight; it is on you to prove your worth.'

After a moment of measured silence, the men appeared to accept this as truth, although Grainne was unsure if it was accurate. She wished it to be the case; if her gods were their gods, one side still had to win. Looking around her at their open faces, their tanned skin making their brown eyes seem deeper, she again wished for a peaceful resolution. If Donal's son was king already, she prayed to Cáer to appeal to his instincts of preservation. These foreign men who now surrounded her and asked for a reading of their omens may appear friendly when not wielding a sword or javelin but, on the field, they would be ruthless. A war is fought between strangers and won by the enemy, for both sides are the enemy of life.

When Eorid came out of the tent, he called for his men to assemble. The other clan leaders did likewise and Donal, who was still under guard, asked to be heard.

Eorid approached him. 'Your son. If he is inside the fort, he will take a knee or he will die.'

'He will kneel to you,' Donal said, 'so long as I am with you when you request it. I can get us in the gate and you can assume command.'

'I do not like you,' Eorid told him. 'If your son refuses my terms, I will cut your throat in front of him. I trust you can ride a horse?'

'I have never done so, my lord, but I have watched your men. If I can get on one, I can ride it.'

'We will rest for a night and eat. Then we will go to your son and I will make him kneel.'

The following dawn, as Eorid mounted his horse and held a hand out for Grainne to climb on behind him, Urasid and another of the clan leaders came before them. 'We will accompany you. If they attack, our men will launch an assault against them.'

Urasid took to his horse and he was handed a chain, on the end of which was a naked, pregnant, feral girl, younger than Grainne. She was muddy, filthy, crouching on all fours, and panting like a dog. Her matted hair covered her eyes. She leaned in under the shadow of Urasid's horse and barked once.

'You bring your pregnant slave to a parlay meeting?' Eorid asked.

'She kills my men when I turn my back on her. She is vicious; she may be useful when we face the enemy.'

Eorid nodded and clicked, turning his horse towards the treeline.

Passing out across the open valley below the fort, Grainne got a closer look at the structure. Three wooden palisades stretched in an arc from one side to the other, with a cliff behind. The only way in without bloodshed would be the single entranceway, and with an invite from the king.

When they were close enough to the outer wall to shout, but just outside the range of arrows, they dismounted and Eorid called for a parlay.

Someone beyond the wall shouted, 'You can talk from there, stranger.'

Grainne gripped the bag of bones at her hip. A storm was coming in beyond the burnt ships on the shore. The omens were speaking at last, but they were not sympathetic.

Chapter 33

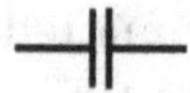

Thick, bruised clouds were amassing on the east. Outside the walls, the foreign leaders stopped short of firing range and called to them. In the field beyond, their army stood at the ready.

When Rónán recognised his chieftain, Áed thought he was going to jump from the wall and run to him with sword in hand, but the boy did not move.

'What do you mean, it's your father?' Oisín asked.

'A surrogate, after the death of my own father.'

'I understand that, but what's he doing here?'

Behind them, Fergal pushed his way along the palisade and stood among them. His sword was drawn. 'We go out and we fight.'

'No,' Oisín said. 'If we go out to fight, we will die.'

'But we'll take those bastards with us, right?'

Áed studied the formations outside. The leaders were too far from their army to be protected, and they would not bring a druid, a local chieftain, and a pregnant *cumal* into battle. 'They mean to talk,' he said. 'Their army is battle-ready, but they are relaxed enough not to be anticipating a fight. Their leader has dug his spear in the ground. It's close enough for him to reach quickly, but if he reaches for it before you go out there, he breaks his word and the war begins. Rónán—he's too far for a normal archer to reach.'

'I'm not a normal archer. I can put one in his eye and one in his chest before he knows it. My king, if you go out there, I'm coming with you. If my surrogate father is out there, he'll want a word with me. Where's Achall? We should bring her. One wrong move from Donal or the foreigner and I'll cut her in half in front of him.'

'She's your wife, is she not?' Fergal asked.

'And she's his niece—which do you think is more important to him?'

Fergal turned to one of the nearby warriors. 'Fetch his wife. Now, boy.'

'Oisín,' Áed said. 'He's going to ask for your surrender. As your advisor, I'm counselling against it. We took this fort with forty men and we've held it for weeks. We can take on his army with the five or six hundred warriors we have. You've seen them fight. You know what we can achieve.'

Oisín clapped him on the back. 'I have no intention of surrendering. Let's go see what they have to say.'

Áed directed archers to the outer walls and instructed them not to fire unless they had to. He stationed two lookouts at the rear wall, anticipating a cliff-face attack while they were distracted, and then they opened the gate and walked outside.

The five of them walked in a solid line, Rónán's hand gripping Achall's upper arm, his other on the hilt of his sword. She touched her belly and recoiled when she saw the pregnant slave girl squatting on all fours.

'I am Eorid of Clan Ysithac. Which of you is king?'

'I am,' Oisín said. They stopped out of sword's reach.

Donal raised his arms as if to embrace his niece. 'My dear girl, how have you been?'

'She is pregnant,' Rónán answered for her.

'A happy blessing.'

'This is your boy?' Eorid asked. He looked at Rónán with disgust. 'I was told you might be king, but I see this is not the case. No matter.' He turned back to Oisín. 'Drink with me in honour of our parlay and then we can discuss terms.'

One of his companions, a brutish foreigner with a facial scar interrupting the line of his stubble, held out a wineskin.

Áed watched them closely. The slave girl was crouched and flicking the dirt with her fingers, her tongue licking at her chapped and cracked lips. If she ever had a mind, it was gone now. Eorid, their leader, was tall, taller even than Oisín, but he was standing in something of a casual manner, as much as he could do under threat of attack. The foreign man who held the slave's chain was tense, tugging on it when she tried to wan-der. The other foreigner was of little consequence; he could take him down with one swing. The druid intrigued him. Her hood shadowed her face and only one spill of hair came from its corner. Her robes were adorned with gold-threaded runes, some of which he recognised—strength, like the one he wore around his neck since birth; protection; growth—and others were a mystery to him.

She must have caught him staring at her while Oisín and Eorid were sharing a drink, for she raised a finger to her lips for silence, and she pulled back her hood enough for him to see her features.

Older, yes; thinner in the face—but the druid was Grainne,

his sister. He wanted to explode with happiness that she was alive, but she covered her head again and remained where she was. He knew to remain silent.

'What are you doing with this foreign scum?' Rónán asked Donal.

'We will get to that,' Eorid said, 'when your king and I discuss terms.'

Oisín handed the wineskin back and said, 'There will be no terms. You and your army will get back on your ships and leave, or you will die. All along our shores, men are blocking entry for your kind. You are surrounded across the entire land.'

'Surrender or die, he is telling me,' Eorid said to Donal. They shared a brief laugh. 'How many men do you have behind those walls? Two hundred? Maybe three? I'm sure the army behind me hasn't gone unnoticed. And that is just a few of my men. We outnumber you. If you do not agree to my terms'— here he paused for emphasis—'not a man among you will live to see the dawn.'

The black clouds had come in off the shore and a chill fell around them. The rain had not yet begun, but they could smell it in the air.

'My terms are simple,' Eorid said. 'You will be unharmed, and I will let you govern your people. In turn, you will bow to me. As your gracious overking, I will gift to you a province of your choosing. You may live there with your wives and your farmers, and your children will know that I am great and generous. These lands will be mine, even the fields that you plough and the grasses from which you make your beds. When I ask something of you, you will give it to me. When I take something from you, you will know that I do it because I own you. And you will be grateful for the life I let you keep and the food I let you grow. Refuse, and you will die. These are my terms.'

Oisín breathed deep before replying. Áed tightened his fist on the hilt of his sword and he could see that Fergal did likewise. Rónán eased Achall behind him so that she was protected from any fallout.

'You have made your terms clear. In countering these, I will tell you this—'

'You misunderstand me,' Eorid said. 'There are to be no counter terms. You will accept my gracious offer, or you will die.'

'With respect to your parlay, I refuse. And before the day is done, you will be fucked by every sword I can get my hands on if you attempt to take our walls.'

Eorid smiled. Then he whistled, short and sharp. They did not hear the arrow as it approached. It struck Oisín in the chest and he was thrust backwards with the force of it, his entire body folding against the wind. When he landed, he did not move.

Áed screamed and drew his sword, but the foreigners had already pointed their spears. He could only kill one before dying himself.

The slave girl barked and yapped and hopped on her feet, clapping her hands.

'Shut that little bitch up,' Donal said. The foreigner who held her tugged on her chain.

Eorid clapped his hands for silence. 'That was unfortunate, but you understand it is my right to rule these lands. So, with your king dead, who replaces him? Who is king now?'

'I am king,' Fergal said.

'You replace this man?'

'I hold power in a southern province.'

'The south is already taken,' Eorid said. 'You have lost your king-seat. Stand down or you will suffer the same fate as him.'

The slave girl's barking grew more intense, interspersed with guttural growls.

'Who replaces this northern king?' Eorid asked.

'I do.' Áed sheathed his sword and faced the foreigner. If an arrow was coming for him, he would take it.

'No,' Rónán breathed.

'At last. What is your name?'

The incessant yapping continued as the pregnant girl turned in circles on the end of her chain.

'I am Áed Branath, son of Airic, of the Ó Mordha tribe. I am the Executioner.'

The slave fell quiet and looked at him for the first time. When she spoke, her voice was like dry dirt. 'Executioner.'

Grainne took a small step forward but did not make any other move.

'Executioner,' the slave said again. 'Áed.'

'You have heard of my deeds,' Áed said to her. 'When we win this war, I will free you.'

'Áed.' The slave came to her feet, standing upright for the first time since they had arrived outside the gates of Knockdhu. Beneath the dirt and grime on her skin, it was hard to tell how old she was. She was small in every way, except for the stomach that was full of child.

'Control your slave,' Eorid said.

Her captor tugged on her chain but she lashed out at him and turned back to Áed.

'Áed, I am Maebh. I am Bec.'

'Bec?' He looked at her, then at Grainne. Grainne lowered her hood and stared at the girl in shock.

'I am your sister,' Bec said.

Her foreign captor pulled on her chain and threw her off balance. She fell to the ground.

'I am your sister.'

The man held a dagger blade to her throat while she writhed beneath his hold. When Áed drew his sword again, the foreigner said, 'I will kill her.'

Áed held a hand up for peace. He looked at Eorid. 'I am Áed the Executioner, and I challenge you—fight me. I have killed your champions. There is no man among your army that I cannot beat. These are my terms. Face me and fight.'

'I have heard the rumours, Executioner. You will be a fine rival. Your challenge is accepted.'

'Wait,' Achall said.

Rónán tightened his grip on her arm. 'What are you doing?'

Achall said, 'Rónán is your son, Uncle. If you side with this foreign man, we stand with you. He should champion himself for this leader and fight in his stead. Is this not a recognised practice?'

'No,' Áed said.

'I would never,' Rónán said.

'You are my son. You carry the weight and responsibility of my clan. Offer yourself as King Eorid's champion. I command it.'

'Never.' Rónán pushed Achall out of his way and drew his sword. 'I would kill you quicker than betray my people. You are a cur for siding against us.'

'You are duty-bound as my son,' Donal said.

'You gave up the right to call yourself a father and a chieftain when you stood beside this whore-son.'

Bec still struggled on the ground beneath her captor. Grainne looked panic-stricken and unable to move.

'Fight me,' Áed said to Eorid. 'King against king. This is no time for champions. You have already accepted my challenge— or are you not an honourable man?'

The clouds moved slowly over them, but they had not yet broken open.

'Fight me,' Áed said again.

Eorid extracted his spear from the ground and drew his sword. With his free hand, Áed withdrew his dagger.

'Áed, don't,' Rónán said.

'It is already done,' Áed replied. And Grainne began to cry in silence.

Those people who accompanied them stepped back to allow the two warriors room to fight. Bec was dragged out of the way by her captor and she snapped and snarled at him.

'I admire your resolve, Executioner,' Eorid said as they began to circle each other. 'I will not toy with you; I am offering you a kindness. This shall be quick.'

Áed swung his sword by his side to feel the weight of it. It had only been a day since he used it, but already it was feeling foreign in his hand. A warrior who is not fighting is just a man. 'The first champion of your army that I faced,' he said, 'I cut off his head and pissed on him. He said he would kill me quickly, too. I guess in your land that means something different.'

Áed levelled his breathing and found his fighting stance.

The sword was becoming a part of him again, an extension of his arm. He twisted and drove the blade down against his foe. Eorid backed out of its path and thrust the spear forward, but Áed blocked it with his forearm. He kicked out and Eorid jumped clear of him.

A second thrust with the spear, and Áed swiped at it with his sword, cutting it in two. The spearhead clattered to the frozen ground.

They parried, blow against blow, sword against sword.

Áed was blind to all else; his rival moved before him as though he was the only thing in existence. He was yet to determine the man's weaknesses, but once he did he would attack with force. They sparred and danced and thrust. Eorid raised a knee and jacked out his foot, connecting with Áed's hip. Áed stumbled backwards and dropped his dagger. He gripped his sword with both hands.

Calling out in rage, he turned, swung high, and brought the blade down. Eorid sidestepped him and as he twisted, he drew his blade across Áed's stomach.

It was not deep, but it stung. Blood discoloured his tunic. Someone shouted his name, but he could not be certain who.

Following Eorid's movement, Áed planted a foot in the back of the man's knee and cut downward with his sword, tearing a chunk of flesh from his left arm.

Eorid rolled and came back to his feet. 'I will take your hand off for that,' he said. 'Just as my ancestors did to your ancient king.'

Áed came for him, his sword held over his shoulder for an arcing swing. Eorid leapt, kicking him in the wounded stomach, and then he fell out of the way as Áed went down.

Áed rolled, but the muscles in his abdomen ached. He got to his knees, dug his sword in the ground for leverage, and struggled back to his feet. Eorid came at him again. Áed blocked the blow and stepped back, but he could feel the reverberations of the sword stinging through his arms.

He crouched low, and as he turned, the tip of the sword drawing a line in the dirt, he swung, shifting his weight as he did so. Eorid was already mid-attack. The sword hit Eorid's forearm, tearing into the flesh, and cut off his hand. It fell to the ground, fingers unfurling around the hilt of the sword it still held. Eorid screamed and came to his knees, gripping his arm as dark blood spilled from the ragged and torn stump.

Áed dropped to his own knees from the pain in his stomach, and he shook his head to clear the fog. He tried to rise. 'You were right,' he said, 'about someone losing a hand.'

Eorid had picked up his sword with his left hand and descended on him, blade first, mouth agape in a guttural wail. His sword drove through Áed's stomach as they fell together. They tumbled in the grass. For a moment, Áed blinked. He could not focus. He blinked again. On his back, he looked down at his stomach. There was no pain anymore. There was only blackness.

Rónán screamed.

Bec shouted her brother's name.

Grainne fell to her knees.

Eorid backed away and his men surrounded him to create a wall of tight defence. Clutching his arm above his shoulder to stem the bleeding, the man was ashen-faced and beaded with sweat.

The slave's captor pulled on her chain, but she broke free

and started running towards her brother. The man caught up with her, gripped her hair, heaved her back, and raised his knife.

She turned on him, pulling on her chain, and kicked at him. 'No more,' she said. She ducked his swing and wrapped the chain around his leg, tearing him off his feet. She leapt on him, her stomach allowing only for short movements, and she clawed at his face. She spat on him.

Urasid punched her cheek, tried to turn, but her weight was too heavy for him. His fingers sought through the grasses for his knife as Bec found her chain and cracked the links against his head.

Urasid touched his blade, gripped it, and swung. It penetrated Bec's throat and her screams were cut from her.

Struggling, she reached for the knife in her neck as Urasid laughed beneath her. With weak fingers, she tore it from her throat and drove it into his chest. As she fell forward, her body pushed the blade deeper. And her blood spilled over her captor's face. She could not speak, but as her life left her, she was smiling.

A short distance from her, Áed's torn body bled on the grass. Rónán ran to his side and picked up his head. He called his name. Called again.

Grainne staggered to her feet and went to Bec. She grabbed under her arms and pulled. 'Help me,' she shouted. She looked over her shoulder to Áed. 'We have to get them inside. Now.'

Eorid retreated with his guards.

'What do you mean?' Rónán asked.

'Help me!'

Fergal came to her, picked up Bec's legs. Rónán pushed his

arms under Áed's heavy body and picked him up.

And they ran for the gate as a hail of arrows came over their heads from behind the walls and towards the army on the outside.

Chapter 34

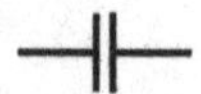

They came through the gate, Achall hurrying behind them, and it was sealed shut in their wake. Outside, the foreign army marched into position. Arrows showered from either side as the clouds finally succumbed to their heaviness. Fat droplets of rain smacked the cold, hard ground.

'Is he dead?' someone asked. Rónán hurried passed him and shouldered open the door of the great hall. Fergal and Grainne came in after him with the pregnant slave.

'Druid, save him,' Rónán ordered.

They placed the girl's lifeless body on a table. Grainne touched Bec's stomach, pressed her sides. 'We can still save the baby,' she said.

'Save Áed, he's the king,' Rónán said. He lay him down on another table and cradled his head. 'The girl is dead,' he said. 'You need to save Áed.'

Grainne rolled up the sleeves of her robes and wiped tears from her eyes. She looked around. 'I need water and blankets. Quickly. And a bed. They cannot lie on tables.' Fergal ran to fetch them.

She went to Áed's side and felt his forehead. 'Brother,' she said.

Rónán looked at her. 'You, too? Is his whole damn family here? Do something.'

Grainne felt behind Áed's left ear and pushed a finger into his right armpit. She pressed hard with both hands at once, sending a jolt of pressure through him. Áed's eyes snapped open and he sucked for air. His arms shot up and Rónán tried to hold them down, to keep him still. Grainne looked over the wounds in his stomach. They were large, bleeding in plentiful waves. She tore strips from the hem of her robe and packed the wounds.

'Áed,' Grainne said, and she leaned down to kiss his face, washing him in her tears.

He hugged her. 'Grainne. What of Bec?'

'She's here. She's—'

'Where's Rónán?'

'I'm here. Are you okay?' Rónán took his hand, squeezed it, and Áed reached his free hand up to touch his face.

When Achall ran into the room, Rónán turned on her.

'Get out! Traitor.'

'I was trying to protect him,' she said. 'If you had championed yourself, we could have resolved this. I knew the foreign man would kill him.'

'He didn't kill him. Get out of here. Go.'

'Rónán,' Áed said, his voice low, wispy. As Achall stormed out of the hall, Rónán turned to Áed. 'It is done,' Áed said. 'Leave her.'

'It is already done,' Grainne said, quoting not only Cáer but also Áed when he stood before Eorid on the field. 'Áed, are you in pain?'

'I—no. I feel very little.'

Fergal returned with a bowl of water and some blankets.

Grainne said, 'Bec is gone, brother.' She wiped her face again. 'But her child; I know I can save it.'

'You need to save your brother,' Rónán said.

Grainne ignored him. 'You are overking now, brother. I am at your disposal. Command it and let me save the child.'

'He's dying.'

'I'm fine.'

'Command it.'

'Do it,' Áed said.

Grainne left his side and went to Bec.

'Rónán, listen to me.' Rónán gripped his hand again. 'Do you know that I love you? Trust me. Trust me now more than ever.'

Grainne washed the mud from Bec's belly and wiped the area dry. 'What have they done to you, my poor sister?' The blood was already drying around her neck but with the effort of moving her inside, her wound gaped, and fresh blood soaked her ears and her matted hair.

'She is not full term,' Grainne said. 'The child will be weak. Small, like her mother.'

'What can I do to help?' Fergal asked.

'I need a clean blade. And a prayer.'

'You have done this before?'

'Never,' she said. She touched Bec's stomach, felt where the baby was. If she waited any longer, it would die. She took the blade that Fergal handed her and positioned its point against Bec's flesh. She closed her eyes and made a prayer to Cáer for guidance. The rain on the thatched roof was her only answer.

She cut, pushing the short blade into the wall of skin below the child. She arced the knife inward towards the navel and then, extracting it a little, leaving only the tip inside the skin, she drew the blade upwards and over the belly. Fluids made her fingers slick. She dropped the knife and pried the skin open. She could see the soft outline of the child, still inside its sac. Grainne reached in and pulled the tiny child free. She tore the sac and cut the umbilical cord with the knife, tying the end in a knot. Then she pushed her finger into the child's mouth, held the baby up by the ankles, and smacked her rear.

There was nothing.

'A blanket,' Grainne said. Fergal handed her one.

She wrapped the child and rubbed her vigorously, wiping fluids from her face.

Áed tried to sit up and Rónán helped him.

Fergal clasped his hands together.

Grainne rubbed with both hands. She had no brooklime. She had no herbs. She had nothing with her that could help to revive the child.

'Light a fire,' she said. 'We need warmth.'

Áed struggled to touch his neck. 'Here,' he said. He unfastened the stone that he wore, with its rune of strength, and held it out to Rónán. 'Give her this.'

But it was unnecessary. Under Grainne's forceful rubbing, the child squirmed, opened and closed its mouth.

Grainne breathed. 'She lives.' She kept rubbing, with less power now, to keep the child warm. She came to Áed's side and her brother took the child in his arms.

He smiled. 'I am an uncle. I loved your mother very much. I will love you just the same.' He kissed the top of her head and then he took the stone and tied the thong around her neck. 'It gave me strength when I was born. Now I give it to you.'

Grainne took the child back and kissed her brother. 'We should call her Bec, in honour of her mother.'

'It is a well-deserved name. She is tiny.'

Grainne brought the little one to the fire that Fergal was preparing in the central hearth and the stoic king took her and kept her warm in his arms as the flames fanned.

Áed groaned as fresh blood escaped his wounds. When Grainne came to him again, she inspected the fabric that bound him.

'Will you help him now?' Rónán asked.

Áed reached for Rónán's hand. 'How bad is it?'

'I cannot lie,' Grainne said. 'The wounds are deep. Without my herbs and medicines, there is little I can do.'

'Seal the wounds. Close him up,' Rónán said.

'If I close the skin, the blood will continue to drain inside him.'

Weak, depleted of energy, Áed lay back on the table and closed his eyes. 'You must do something for me.'

'Anything,' Rónán said.

'Carry me to the doorway. I want to see the world.'

A man entered the hall, carrying a cot-bed. 'What else can I bring?'

'Nettles,' Grainne said. 'As many nettles as you can find. And dock leaves. Eyebright if you can find any.'

'I don't know what that is,' the man said.

'It's a white flower with a yellow centre. The underside will be purple.'

The man hurried away.

'It is winter,' Áed said. 'What flowers do you expect to

bloom here?'

'I'm trying to save you,' Grainne said.

'Help me to the doorway. I think the rain has stopped.'

Together, they carried him to the cot-bed and he stared through the door. Outside, his warriors were running to and from the wall. There were shouts and screams. But the morning sun was burning through the clouds.

'What is happening out there?' Áed asked.

'We fight,' Rónán told him. 'It's what we trained for. We fight, and we will win.'

Rónán knelt beside him and Áed touched his face. 'I am dying,' he said. 'There is nothing my sister can do for me.'

'No. I won't allow you to die.'

Áed smiled, a weak and tired movement. 'I am your king. You must do as I say.'

'Áed, please.'

'Listen to me, Rónán. I make you my tanist. You will take the king-seat when I go.'

'No.'

'I am bleeding. And I cannot feel the pain. That is not a good thing. If I cannot feel it, it means I am already gone.'

'The druid will help you.'

'Grainne,' Áed said. She came to him and knelt at his other side. 'How long do I have without your flowers and herbs?'

She touched his chest, careful not to move the wraps at his stomach. 'The blood will drain from you slowly. The wounds are crusting, but it will not stop them from seeping. I am sorry, brother, but you will not see it through the night.'

He held her face and kissed her. 'You have trained as a druid. Tell me, sister; there is one thing I long to know. How do I get to Tír na nÓg? When my spirit leaves me, where should it go?'

Grainne smiled through her tears. She leaned in and whispered to him the secrets of the dead and the location of the Otherworld.

When she finished, he lay back down and smiled. 'West,' he said. 'Father was right.' He turned to Rónán, touched his chest. 'I cannot die at length.' He reached down and took Rónán's dagger, the one he had forged for him, and he pressed it into his hands.

'No,' Rónán said. 'I cannot.'

'Promise me you will look after the child.'

Rónán looked at Fergal who still held the baby.

'That one, yes,' Áed said. 'But also Achall's child. Forget its father, he is gone. Achall is your wife. When it is born, raise the child as your own. Teach him to be like you.'

'I will teach him to be like you,' Rónán said.

Áed smiled again. 'They will sing about us,' he said. 'You told me that many years ago.'

'They already sing about you, Executioner.'

'And they will sing of you, too,' he said. 'You will win this war, and you will do it as king.'

Tears came to Rónán's eyes. 'I cannot kill the one man in this world that I love.'

'It is because you love me that you must.' He turned to Grainne. 'It is so good to see you again, sister. You will be Rónán's advisor. Protect him and he will protect you; he is your brother now. I have loved no one like I love him.'

Grainne smiled, took his hand and kissed him. 'I will honour your wishes. You have the blessings of Cáer upon you. I did not know it, but she was watching over you. She will lead you to where you want to go.' She took Rónán's hand also. 'I have seen you—both of you—in my dreams. The Lady Cáer revealed you to me. You,' she said to Rónán, 'carried my brother in your arms, just as you did so here. And you,' she said, smiling down at Áed, 'you have turned the tides of war. With your deeds, you strengthen your army's resolve. They will win. I am sure of it.' She kissed them both, and then she went to Fergal and held the child.

'Áed, you ask too much of me,' Rónán said.

'You cannot let me suffer until death draws to me in the night. What honour is there in dying this way? Bleeding slowly into the Otherworld is not a warrior's death. Take the blade. Send me to my peaceful rest. Become the king that I know you are destined to be.'

Rónán leaned down and kissed him with thirst, then pressed his forehead to Áed's. 'You have been the light in my otherwise blackened life. I do not wish to lose you. I have no purpose without you at my side.'

'Even in death I will remain beside you. You will hear me whisper to you in the darkness and you will know that I am there.' He took the dagger and gave it to Rónán once more.

In tears, Rónán said, 'I love you.'

'I love you, too.'

Rónán's hand shook, and he used his other hand to steady it. The clouds had dispersed and the day was brightening.

'I love you,' Rónán said again.

Áed smiled and closed his eyes. 'I remember the field in which I first saw you,' he said. 'And with the gods as my witness, let no man condemn you for your actions. I forgive you.' He took Rónán's arm and held the blade closer to his neck.

Outside, dogs were barking. 'Be at peace, my love. My king.'

Rónán cried. 'I cannot.'

Áed raised a hand and brushed Rónán's hair from his face. He kissed his closed eyelids. His words were soft, distant. 'Send me into peace.'

Rónán sobbed. 'It will end me.'

'It is your beginning,' Áed whispered. 'You have the strength. Send me into peace that I may rest.'

'Áed—'

'Hush,' Áed soothed. 'Give me the warrior's death.'

By the fire, Grainne held the child close to her face and sobbed tears into its blanket. Fergal rubbed her back and held them both.

'I love you,' Rónán said. He kissed Áed's cheek, the corner of his nose and his lips, dampening his face with tears. His vision clouded and his throat was tight and raw. And then he pushed the knife forward. He closed his eyes and he pressed his lips to Áed's forehead, sobbing into his hair.

When Áed's hand fell from the bed and his fingers touched the ground, Rónán picked it up and he lay down beside him, wrapping Áed's arms around him. He hugged him tight and kissed his cheek, and he lay there, rocking, embracing, remembering.

Grainne came to them, knelt at their side, and held Áed's hand to her face, washing his fingers in tears. She touched Rónán's shoulder, and she knew Cáer would be standing nearby, ready to greet her brother as he rose a warrior into her arms.

Chapter 35

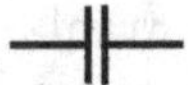

They built a pyre in the centre of their walled enclosure as the sun was setting. Oisín's body was brought in from the field and his gold discs were pinned to Rónán's chest. Fergal was the first to kiss them, honouring Rónán's authority as overking. Oisín was wrapped in a shroud and his body was placed on the pyre beside Áed and Bec. They did not have seven days to mourn their losses.

Outside, the fighting had ceased for the night. Arrows no longer rained on them, and any fires had been put out. Almost a third of their huts were destroyed, but the palisade walls held firm. The clouds had passed and, in the east, stars were beginning to appear.

Rónán held a lit torch in his hand and he stared ahead at the pyre. Beside him, Grainne, with the baby in her hands, touched his shoulder and eased his tormented soul. She had been weeping for the loss of her siblings.

One of the warriors among them sang the song of Áed the Executioner, and Rónán breathed deep, stepped forward, and lit the pyre. Others were joining in the song. Grainne cradled the baby and rocked her to sleep, making soothing sounds next to her pale temple. When the flames took hold, the men cheered in honour of their fallen kings and the child cried.

'Will he make it?' Rónán asked Grainne. 'Will he make it to the Otherworld?'

She nodded. 'Good men always do.'

The flames burned through the night and Rónán stayed, his gaze lost in the fire. He sat on the cold ground with a jug of wine, said, '*Sláinte*,' and he drank. With everyone else gone to sleep except the guards who watched the night, Rónán was left to watch over his friend, his love.

When the sun returned in the morning, bringing with it a warmer day, signalling the close of winter, Rónán dug three pits and buried the ashes of his kings and the slave girl. In each, he placed a bowl of food, their swords, and a prayer.

He returned to the great hall and donned his sword belt and his dagger. It was still tarnished with Áed's blood and he kept it that way. When he walked back out into the morning, Achall came to him.

'You did not come to bed,' she said. 'Are you well?' Seeing the sword at his side, she said, 'You do not mean to go out there alone, do you?'

'I am your king. I will do as I choose.'

'And I am your wife, despite what you choose. I am with child. If you go out there this baby will be fatherless.'

'I made a promise,' Rónán said. 'I will protect the child. And this is how I intend to do so.'

'Then let me come with you. I can speak to my uncle, get us safe passage back to Ailigh. Or back home. We can go home now, you and I.' She touched her stomach, though she had not even begun to swell. 'Just the three of us.'

Rónán gripped her arm and brought her inside the hall. He

took the chain that had been cut from Bec's neck and he tied his wife to a post. 'I am protecting you,' he said. 'I will not have you following me outside or I cannot guarantee your safety. That child may not be mine, but I will raise him as if I had bedded you myself. This is the promise I made to a man whose deeds were far greater than any you could ever comprehend. This is the promise I made, to protect you and raise our child. Let me do what I must. Allow me to honour my friend.'

He walked outside, crossed the compound, and threw open the gate. As he walked down into the valley below, he shouted, 'Bring me your king. We will end this.'

A foreign warrior approached him, but Rónán cut through his head with his blade and walked on. 'I challenge you to fight me.'

Eorid came to the valley and stood with Donal, Faolán, and several of his foreign warriors, his arm swaddled in blood-blackened cloths and a tourniquet above his bicep. The breeze around him was tainted with the smell of seared flesh. 'Have your side not lost enough men already? Surrender and kneel to me.'

'My people do not kneel to foreigners,' Rónán said.

'I assume you are king now?' Eorid asked. He looked at Donal. 'You must be proud.'

'A challenge,' Rónán said, still advancing.

'Very well, then,' Eorid said. 'We shall play together for a few moments before I kill you like I have done the rest of your kings.'

'Look at you,' Rónán said. 'A great king with an army at his back, fearless even with only one hand. Am I to expect an arrow from your men like you did to Oisín? You stand there in your leathers, protecting your skin when it is your words that you choose to cut with. I need no such armour. My people need no such protection.' He loosened his sword belt and drew his tunic over his head. 'I am naked of armour,' he said, throwing the garment on the ground at his feet. 'Yet I will still beat you. Look upon me before we fight, because it is the last sight you will see.' He tightened his belt and drew his sword. 'Fight me,' he goaded. 'I will kill every one of you. You have no more time to flee. I will not grant you passage out of here to return to your own lands. This is your end. This is how you will be remembered: dead at my naked hand, you in all your armour. Dead and then forgotten.'

Eorid waved off his men and he approached the field. He drew his sword with his left hand. 'You speak well. Do you fight as good?'

'Come and find out.'

They clashed swords and the sound rang through the empty field. At the gate of Knockdhu, his men spilled out to watch, and on the far hill, Eorid's army stood at the ready.

Rónán thought of Áed, of the swiftness with which he moved on the field, and he drew on all his training. He was no longer an archer or a fletcher's son. Now he was a warrior. Now he was becoming Áed, fighting as he fought, moving as he moved. His feet were planted firm on the ground and he blurred in motion, swinging, cutting, jabbing.

Eorid was quick, but he favoured his right side, compensating for fighting with his weaker hand. This had long been Áed's lesson—find the weakness and exploit it.

Rónán arced his sword low, aiming for the legs, but Eorid blocked and jumped aside. The reverberation made his skin tingle.

Eorid twisted, swung, and Rónán weaved.

On Eorid's downstroke, Rónán kicked out at his knee, feint-ed left, and then swung an overhead arc. Eorid's leg gave out, but he fell back and rolled aside, screaming as his bloodied stump crushed against the cold ground.

Rónán lunged for him. Missed.

Eorid jumped and Rónán followed. He barrelled into the taller man and knocked him back. With Eorid off balance, he kicked again and then swung.

The sharpened edge of his blade cleaved through Eorid's tattooed neck. Rónán swiped the sword free, tearing through flesh, and the foreigner fell to the ground.

He ran. He did not stop to think. Moving up the hill, for-eign warriors were coming towards him, spears already flying towards him. He weaved through each of them and charged towards Donal. His chieftain-father shrank away from him, stumbling backwards, his arms raised.

'You killed my father,' Rónán said. 'I have known it all along.' He did not wait for a response, for a plea of mercy or denial. He drove the sword through Donal's chest, kicked the body out of the way, and dived into a foreign man, blade first. The man fought back hard, and in his rage, Rónán did not feel the cut to his arm. He punched the man in the face, gripped the back of his head, and plunged his blade through his chest.

As he got back to his feet, he was gripped from behind and spun around.

'I'll gut you, you little whore-son,' Faolán said.

Donal's eldest son smacked Rónán in the face with his fist and pushed him back. He fell, but as Faolán came for him, he kicked both his feet out, winding the taller man, and he rolled to his knees. He swung wide with his sword and it sliced through Faolán's face.

Outside Knockdhu's walls, his men were stripping off their clothes and running into battle, war cries on their mouths, spears and swords raised. They had seen how he intimidated his foes, and every man among them charged into battle, naked as a newborn. It would be passed down for years to come, stories and songs of the naked warriors who defeated their enemy with no protection but the skin they were given from the gods.

Rónán turned, fought off another of the foreigners. He was looking for Muirgel, Donal's wife, the true ruler of her tribe, whispering into Donal's ear from the moment they were wed. He made no decision that had not come from his first wife.

He could not see her. She was hiding or had fled in disgrace.

Rónán screamed in the face of an enemy and cut him through. In the bright morning sunlight, the grass was turning red and the field was littered with the dead from both sides. His men were fighting well; if Áed's death would bring them anything, it would be victory.

He ploughed through the foreign army, cutting his way beyond it, and entered the foreigners' camp. He tore at their tents until he found Muirgel huddled on the ground. He went to her. 'Get up, woman.'

'Don't kill me,' she begged.

Rónán stooped and pulled on her hair to make her sit. He held the point of his sword to her throat. 'Why did you have my father killed?'

'Please don't kill me.'

'Tell me why you had him killed.'

'I did not,' she cried. 'Your father died in an accident.'

'It was no accident,' Rónán said. He recalled the first time he heard of it, pulling back into his sept with Áed at his side, the news of his father's death weighing heavy on his shoulders. His father had died under a wagon that collapsed on him. 'No man crawls under a propped wagon without help.'

'It was an accident,' she repeated.

Rónán dug the point of his sword at the raw flesh of her neck. 'What happened?'

'He was fixing—' Her snivels made her face buckle and she clenched her eyes.

'I want the truth,' Rónán demanded, and he pressed a little harder with the sword, gripping the hair at the back of her head.

'Okay,' she cried. 'Okay. Faolán had taken a girl as his own. Against her will. Your father came to us with his concerns.'

'And?'

'Faolán went after him. It was not your father's business. The girl was no relation of his. If he had left it alone, he would be alive.'

'And the wagon?' Rónán asked.

'Donal's idea. I swear it. They had arranged it between them before I even knew it. They placed your father under a wagon and—and they dropped it on him. He was already dead. I swear it, I knew nothing until it was over.'

Rónán released his grip on her and she fell back to the ground. He towered over her, pointed his sword in her face.

Muirgel closed her eyes and cried. 'I swear it,' she repeated. 'I swear it.'

'I have had my vengeance. Your husband and your son are dead at my hand. Go,' he said. 'Flee home to your tribesmen and tell them that I am king of the northern lands. Tell them that if they wish to join me, they are welcome. And tell them to elect a new chieftain. You will live alone for the rest of your days. I have taken from you what you took from me—everything I held dear in my childhood. But I will be a father now. And every generation that succeeds me will know your name and they will know what your family has done to mine. If I see you again, I will tear you apart.' He swished the blade across her cheek and cut her. 'When you touch your face in future, you will remember this.'

He left the tent. The fighting had spilled into the camp. He could see his men, naked and wailing, cutting through the enemy with a renewed vigour. He killed another foreign warrior and climbed back to the top of the hill. Below him, on the grasses outside Knockdhu, the number of dead was uncountable.

The enemy had lost their leaders. They were fighting hard, but they had little direction. Rónán grinned and strode back into battle.

As he came down the hill towards the field, a spear shanked his feet from under him and he tumbled. A foreign man dived on him and pierced his side with a short blade. They continued to roll together and stopped when they hit a beheaded body. Rónán thrust a knee into the man's groin and kicked him backwards. The knife was still in his side. When he got to his feet, the man was already up. The foreigner kicked out, smacking the knife's handle so that it gouged a piece of Rónán's flesh.

Rónán stumbled back, tripped over the dead body, and the air escaped his lungs when he landed. The man dived for him again, but Rónán peeled the blade from his side, rolled, screaming, and jumped. His knee connected with the man's face, and as he came down on him, he thrust the knife into his neck.

He stood, still screaming, his blood staining his hip and thigh. The enemy was thinning out.

The fighting continued throughout the day and into the night. At the setting of the sun, when the fighting would usually cease and the dead were cleared from the field, Rónán called to his men to fight on, to fight harder. Torches were lit and used as weapons as well as for light.

Rónán ploughed through the now-muddy field, limping but fighting with a fury that strengthened his resolve and his arm. In honour of his friend, he would kill them all. In honour of his love, he would win.

And by morning, the fighting was done.

Chapter 36

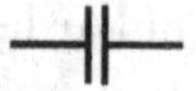

When they returned to Ailigh, it had been ransacked, but they rebuilt it. They repurposed the outer wall that they had built some years before as a perimeter wall around the training fields, handing down each post in a production line of warriors. Of the one thousand men and boys who left Ailigh last year for war, only two hundred returned. The battles had decimated their numbers, and the gods would be busy naming each of the fallen for years to come.

Rónán, overking of the Ó Mordha tribesmen, keeper of the north, worked alongside his men to bring Ailigh back from the decayed ruin that it had become in their absence. He opened the doors of his inner quarters every morning, and he insisted that no man ever call him the name they had bestowed on him after the war was won. Anyone could enter his rooms at will when the doors were open, so long as they entered with a smile. In the days that followed, he kept a watchful gaze over his people as Ailigh was rebuilt, and then he sent everybody home to their families, to their parents. For some, it had been more than a lifetime since they slept in their own beds. For many, he knew, they would be going home to a ruined sept, their families killed or burned. To those, he said, he would offer what he could to help remake their homes. He could not return their fallen families to them, but he would do what he must. These boys—men now, each of them grown as much as he—were his family, his brothers. And in the memory of the fallen, each brother among them was given a name of their dead, and each person now bore two names so that they could keep their deceased friends with them always.

Rónán Áed Ó Mordha walked through the empty huts and around the perimeter walls daily, ensuring that each remained strong, sturdy. Runners were dispatched from around the coastal tribes and each reported that their war was over. Rónán asked each runner for the number of their dead, and when he had heard from all of them, he wept. Where before, only a year ago, these fields and these huts had been filled with boys, with laughter and with song, now the fields looked bigger, despite his growth. His hair had lengthened and his body had filled. His father would not recognise him if he was alive to see him.

When his men began to return to Ailigh, he welcomed them with pride and with love. 'Brother,' he greeted each of them as they came to him. They kissed the gold discs at his breast and swore their fealty.

When the summer came and Ailigh was once again as strong as it had been, Rónán sent runners to the local tribes, those that had survived the war, and announced that he was reopening their stronghold as a training ground for warriors. Boys and men, regardless of age, could come and learn the ways of fighting, and together they would unite against any threat from abroad or from within.

On the shore below, he erected a stone monument to Áed's memory, and he carved the image of a sword in the face of it.

Every morning and every night, he would come to it and he would bow in its presence. And he would swim in the lough within sight of it, and then climb atop it and sit in the sun.

Local chieftains came to him with their problems, because they had heard that he possessed the wisest druid in the land, one who spoke directly with the gods and could interpret any sign given to her with immediate accuracy.

True to their word, Rónán and Grainne remained by each other's side, keeping a protective watch on the other. She had come with him to Ailigh after the war and assumed her role as advisor to the overking. She slept in the rooms next to his, with little Bec in a cradle beside her bed. The child would cry when thunder rattled the skies, but otherwise she was a pleasant and affable girl who laughed every time Rónán picked her up and gurgled in his ear.

In time, when Achall's stomach had swollen, Grainne coaxed her through the birthing process with a tenderness that Rónán was yet to allow himself towards his wife. He had waited outside the hut and listened to the sounds of her screams and the gentle words of encouragement from Grainne, and when it was over, he was brought inside and was presented with his child, a son.

Grainne knew the truth about the child, that Rónán was not the father, but she kept the secret out of respect for her brother. The real father, a boy named Dillon, had been found under a mess of wood within the bounds of Knockdhu, dead by some unknown hand. Rónán had been pleased when he discovered the truth of him, and Achall had confided to him that she, too, was content to learn of the boy's death.

'Your boy is healthy,' Grainne told him. Achall, who lay on

the bed, blinking sweat from her eyes, smiled in exhausted silence.

Rónán took the boy in his arms and smelled the top of his head. He would never forget that fresh smell.

'You do not need to name him yet,' Grainne said. 'There will be a ceremony, of course.'

'Áed,' Rónán said. 'I shall call him Áed. He will be my fiercest warrior.'

Grainne nodded. 'I suspected as much,' she said.

Now, some months later, the child lay in a crib beside him while Rónán conducted business with a chieftain from the neighbouring tribe. He took immense pride in presenting young Áed to any man who would look upon him, and they all called out the similarities between father and son. 'A fine-looking boy, my lord. A warrior in the making, just like his da,' they would say. 'He has your nose,' they would say. 'A good, strong nose.'

He could almost forget that he was not the real father.

Achall, for her part, confined herself to the kitchens. That her husband did not love her, she knew. But that he adored his son was evident in the way he picked him up and held him nightly. She kept busy with the cauldrons, cooking vast quantities of food for the hundreds of men and boys who now filled the huts and fields of Ailigh. She did not take another man to her bed. The guilt of her actions filled her with sorrow, even though she was grateful for the miracle of life that had sprung from her body. If Rónán wanted a second child, she would insist that he give it to her himself.

When Rónán's business was concluded, he picked up his child and carried him out into the fields. For a time, he watched the boys training under the supervision of their elders, the boys who had grown up in Ailigh and fought alongside Rónán and Áed last year. He called out to a few of the boys, words of encouragement, and then he walked down towards the shoreline. He bowed to the stone marker and touched the imprint on its side.

Along the way, sitting in the sand, Grainne was bent over and studying something on the ground before her.

Rónán walked to her and sat Áed down on a blanket beside little Bec, who gurgled delight at him. He ruffled her hair. Today, she was one year old.

He turned to Grainne. 'What do you study?' he asked.

'I have cast the bones,' she said. 'The omens are good.'

'You will join me for the celebrations tonight?'

She looked up at him and smiled. 'Áed may have been more your brother than mine in those years of his life that I was away, but you would not be able to stop me from attending. Come, sit with me.'

'You are not cold?'

The winter was almost over again. The sun was not at its warmest, but it heated the sandy track enough to make it comfortable.

'You miss him,' she said.

'Every day,' he told her.

'I could see that he loved you.'

'Do the gods speak of him with you?'

'They do not speak to me of anything these last months.'

'Do you think that is a bad sign?' he asked her. 'Is their silence an omen?'

She looked at the bones again, then picked them up and put

them away. 'I think it is a good sign. Lady Cáer and her father, Ethal Anbuail, spoke to me when times were bad. But now we are at peace.' She looked at him, touched his cheek. 'Are you at peace?'

'I am,' he said. 'And you?'

'Everything around us is in balance,' she said. 'I am at peace.'

Rónán stood and reached down to help her up. 'Come, let us celebrate the day of our brother. I can almost hear him singing to us the song of the Executioner.'

Grainne laughed. 'And your song, also. He would love that one.'

'Please don't say it. Do not say what they called me,' he begged.

'Why not?' she laughed. 'You will always be the bare-arsed warrior to me.'

He laughed along with her, and then they picked up their children and returned to Ailigh. The feast had begun.

9 781916 383838